Angela Huth has written three collections of short stories, and eight novels – *Nowhere Girl, Virginia Fly is Drowning, Sun Child, South of the Lights, Wanting, Invitation to the Married Life, Land Girls* and *Wives of the Fishermen*. She also writes plays for radio, television and stage, and is a well-known freelance journalist, critic and broadcaster. She is married to a don, lives in Oxford and has two daughters.

Land Girls was released as a major feature film in 1998.

ANGELA HUTH

Land Girls

An *Abacus* Book

First published in Great Britain by Sinclair-Stevenson 1994
This edition published by Abacus 1995
Reprinted 1995 (eight times), 1996, 1997 (twice), 1998

The author and publishers are grateful for permission to
reproduce words from songs as follows:

'They Can't Black Out the Moon' (Strauss, Miller & Dale)
reproduced by permission of EMI Music Publishing Ltd,
London WC2H 0EA

'We'll Meet Again' (Parker & Charles) reproduced by permission
of Dash Music Co Ltd, 8/9 Frith Street, London W1V 5TZ

Every effort has been made to trace holders of copyrights. Any
inadvertent omissions of acknowledgement or permission can be
rectified in future editions.

A CIP catalogue record for this book
is available from the British Library.

ISBN 0 349 10993 1

Typeset by M Rules
Printed in England by Clays Ltd, St Ives plc

Abacus
A Division of
Little, Brown and Company (UK)
Brettenham House
Lancaster Place
London WC2E 7EN

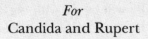

For
Candida and Rupert

'If a man will begin with certainties,
he shall end in doubts;
but if he will be content to begin with doubts,
he shall end in certainties.'

Francis Bacon, 1605

Prologue

Agatha saw Prue creep along the crossbeam of the barn, arms stiffly outstretched, awkward, determined, brave. Her thin white legs were lit by a torch held far below. Her thick regulation socks and heavy brown shoes were cast somewhere into the hay.

Agatha saw Prue pause, flutter, not daring to look down. Her left foot wavered, suddenly unsure where to land. The toes panicked. She was nearly at the end, where a ladder waited. But she could not make it.

Agatha saw Prue fall into the darkness, heard her scream. No one in the house could have heard, because at that moment a siren began to wail. Its mournful voice and the ragged shriek coiled into a terrible sound that, even now, some fifty years later, Agatha still heard.

With an effort she withdrew from the picture of that night, and returned to her place at a prim restaurant table in a London hotel.

Agatha was the first to arrive, as always. Stella could never be on time. Prue was unpredictable.

She pulled off a slither of black kid glove and let her finger run over the whiteness of tablecloth that radiated before her. She hoped the nearby waiter, officiously observant, would not present her with the enormous menu poised in his hand nor make enquiries as to her desire for a drink. She did not want anything, except a few moments

1

to gather herself before the others arrived. It had been a long journey from Tiverton, and her grandson Joshua had driven through the London traffic too fast for her liking. She felt a little ungrounded. Cities always filled her with unease. She was glad she had refused her daughter's invitation to stay the night, and had decided to return on the five o'clock train. Her husband would be at the station to drive her home. He would have lit the fire and put the pie in the oven as instructed. In old age, she relished the safety of their quiet evenings together. There were few occasions for which she would sacrifice one of them for a night in London. She came up rarely, now, though nothing but real disaster would keep her from the annual meetings with her oldest friends.

When she looked up she saw that the waiter had turned his back. He had probably decided an old lady, peacefully waiting, was not worth approaching. Quite right. Agatha knew the usefulness of her stern look, and she was glad she had employed it. The professor had married her, he always said, because she was so alarming. He had wanted to know whether, over the years, he would grow less alarmed by her. Had he? She didn't know. It was not a question she could ever ask.

Outside the window, the trees of Hyde Park were more thickly gold than the trees in Devon. Their own beech had only just begun to turn. She remembered that frivolous park trees were always far ahead in their maturing. This she had observed so many times while waiting for the others. It was a wonder the amazement remained. And the trees, of course, were the reason they had chosen this place originally. As ex-land girls, all of them, they wanted to be able to see the sky while they were eating. They had had their first reunion lunch in this very dining-room just after the war, a few months before Prue's wedding. Terrible food – corned beef and boiled potatoes – but none of them had minded. Some years later they had experienced their first avocado

2

together – a table in the corner, if Agatha remembered rightly. It had been exciting, that first slipping of silver spoons into the creamy green flesh of an unknown fruit. That was the year, Agatha recalled, when the lunch had started more easily than usual – all laughing over their reactions to the avocado. They had felt none of the initial awkwardness that overcame them on re-meeting after a gap of a year or more. They lived so far apart, their lives had taken such different directions – it was difficult, sometimes, to know where to begin.

Agatha's fingers, calmer now, slid up the thin silver flute of the flower vase. It held a single pallid rose and a wisp of fern. She tried to work out how many times the three of them had contemplated each other's metamorphosis over similar, scant little flower arrangements. But what did it matter, how many times? It was a tradition that would go on till one of them died. Then, would the remaining two . . .? When one of them died, would the remaining two consider it loyal or disloyal to continue the lunches?

Agatha looked up. She saw Prue in double image – young and high on the beam but, more sharply, a tiny figure dwarfed by the great door of the dining-room, alert little head pecking round the tables in search of her friend. Agatha waved her glove. Prue smiled, pursed her bow lips. She hurried over with such speed that waiters, poised to offer their assistance, saw any help would be redundant and stepped back with secret smiles. They were used, Agatha supposed, to eccentric old ladies.

When Prue reached the table, Agatha stood up. They bent towards each other, making a triangle over the rose. They kissed. Prue smelt of the exotic, musky scent she had always worn: Stella and Agatha had never been able to approve. She was dressed in green, as usual, to match her eyes. A velvet beret slumped fashionably over one side of her forehead, half hiding the white fringe. In the past the fringe had been very long – a cause of constant complaint – and blonde. From under it she would flutter those down-turned eyes at any man who came into the farmyard, in imitation of the glamorous film stars whose lives she found so fascinating. The eyes were still an extra-ordinary green. It was hard to imagine that Prue, the youngest of them, must be nearly seventy. Whereas she, Ag . . .

'You look just the same, Ag. How are you?'

'In pretty good spirits.'

They sat down, both fiddled with their stiff napkins, veered their eyes from each other lest further scrutiny reveal changes they had no wish to see.

'Sorry I've kept you waiting. Manchester train's not usually late. Still, I've beaten Stella.'

'I had a postcard from her only last week saying she'd be catching the eight fifteen from York.'

'So did I.'

'Did she mention her health?'

'Only to say there'd been another attack of bronchitis.'

'She wrote the same to both of us, then.'

'She always does.'

'She always had such an innate sense of fairness, dear Stella.'

'So fair, yes.'

'That time – that harvest time.'

'That harvest! I often think of that.'

They paused. Agatha was fingering the damask cloth again, while Prue ran a pink nail up the stem of her wine-glass. A nearby waiter, seeing his chance, was upon them in a trice.

'And would the ladies care for an aperitif?'

Agatha put on her fiercest face. She didn't care for the way waiters addressed people these days.

'You'll be having your usual White Lady, Prue?'

'Why not?' Prue twinkled.

'And I'll have a Kir Royale.' Then, in a voice so low the

waiter was denied the private information, she added: 'Something Joshua introduced me to last Christmas.'

'Joshua!' Prue, who had no grandchildren, clapped her hands. Agatha had always admired her enthusiastic interest in other people's relations. 'He must be thirty?'

'Almost,' said Agatha.

But she was not thinking about Joshua. She was thinking about her husband: at this moment he would be sitting with his cheese sandwich by the Aga, preoccupied by the future of his Friesians. Alone, without her there to deflect his thoughts, he would be worrying once more about whether they would have to sell up the farm. Agatha dreaded his decision. They did not want to move, after forty years.

'*So?*' said Prue, when the waiter had gone off with the order.

'So,' said Agatha.

The very thought of having to distil her news made her curiously tired. The friends had not met for eighteen months, though they had kept in touch with occasional letters and cards. In that time nothing exciting had happened to Agatha: probably nothing very much exciting had happened to the other two, either. But having made the effort to travel so far to see one another, each felt it incumbent upon her to do her best to entertain. What usually happened was that they found themselves racing through contemporary news with perfunctory speed. However much they intended to convey to the others the nature of their present lives, what really fired them was their past. To reminisce was so much easier – the jokes that never dulled, the intriguing speculation about what might have happened, the realisation of what the hard years of the war had taught them. Prue and Stella and Agatha never ceased to marvel at the powerful warmth that still emanated from a shared experience of so many years ago. They would leave their meetings reinvigorated:

5

newly grateful that something that had bound them in the past could remain so benevolently alive, untouched by the vicissitudes of the intervening years.

Agatha and Prue glanced at each other with a feathery shyness that would soon be dissipated by their cocktails. They had a mutual need of their friend to enliven this reunion. Stella, who was always the best one at breaking the ice. Stella, who used to say she could not imagine living without being in love – it would be a wasted day, a day not loving someone, she used to say. Stella, who, as Agatha had recognised the moment she met her, was blessed with the kind of exuberance for daily life that could accommodate other people's awkwardness. Agatha had learned so much from Stella.

'She'll be here any minute, I expect,' she said, a little desperate, longing for her drink, and longing even more for the train journey home when she could dwell on all that was about to be said.

'Of course she will. Dear Stella,' said Prue, also a little desperate, and flashing her green eyes in what Agatha recognised as a familiar, hopeful fashion towards the door.

One

On an evening in early October, 1941, John Lawrence drove the three land girls home from the station.

It was unusually cold for the time of year. There had been a hard frost that morning which had not melted all day. Frozen puddles spat at the wheels of his cumbersome old Wolseley. He could hear the angry hiss and crackle as the ice splintered. The noise reminded him of those small fireworks that he had waved round in his hand, on bonfire night, to please Joe when he was a child. He kept his eyes on the road.

There were two girls in the back, one by his side. Faith had told him their names several times, but he remembered none of them. At the station, he hadn't liked to ask. He had shaken hands, introduced himself, and picked up their suitcases before they could protest. They looked a nice enough lot, far as he could tell. The district commissioner had guaranteed she would send some good ones.

But good or not, Mr Lawrence was unhappy about the arrangement. He knew nothing about girls, didn't much like what he'd heard. He and Faith had married at eighteen, two months before the 1914 war was declared. Faith had managed on her own, somehow, for the four years he was away. She had never complained, in her wonderful letters, about the cold and meagre cottage, the poverty, the giving birth to Joe alone by a small fire. When Mr

Lawrence came back alive, unwounded, she said they must never part again. They never had: they never would. She was the only woman in his life. He could not imagine another one. He was glad they had no daughters.

It had taken him some time to be persuaded about this land girl business. But his two farmhands had been called up within weeks of the outbreak of the new war, and it was clear he and Joe could not physically cope with the farm on their own. They worked a sixteen-hour day and still things were left undone. Why not try this Land Army plan, Faith had said, as one who read every word of the newspaper on the days someone brought one to the house, and knew all about the scheme. If it didn't work, she said, they could think again. With an acute shortage of men in the whole neighbourhood, Mr Lawrence was forced to agree there was no alternative. He had conceded with reluctance.

Now, here they were, the three of them, in his car. Very quiet, not a word between them. Mr Lawrence sniffed. The pungent smell of wet collie, which had eaten its way into the fabric of the car years ago, was pierced by a new, high-pitched feminine smell, the kind of thing Faith would call exotic. Disgusting, in his opinion. Already an invasion into his car, where he liked to be alone with his dogs and their rightful smell. He rubbed his nose in protest. The girl beside him stiffened. He could see from the corner of his eye that she had turned her head to look out of the side window. Slowing down, he took this opportunity to glance at other parts of her: prim little gloved hands folded on her lap, skirt made of a pinkish fuzzy stuff. Her legs were crossed, just one knee visible. The small, square plane of knee bone strained against the bronzish fibre of a stocking. As Mr Lawrence looked, fascinated, a streak of light broke through the grey cloud, flared through the windscreen. For an infinitesimal moment the knee bone dazzled like a jewel. Mr Lawrence withdrew his eyes. Rayon stockings! That was it. Faith only had one pair, for church. Well, this young lady would soon learn there was little time or place for rayon stockings on the farm. Already he could not like her. She'd be all over the house with her blessed stockings, hanging them up in the bathroom to dry if he wasn't careful – he could see it all. Total invasion.

'And what's your name?' he asked.

'Stella.'

Stella! Christ. He might have known she'd have a fancy name. He determined not to ask the others. The names would come to him in time. If he gave them time, that was.

He adjusted the mirror, glanced at the passengers in the back seat. Two blurred little faces, spotted and clouded by the imperfections of the glass. One of them had a long pale fringe that covered most of her strange-looking cat's eyes, greenish as far as Mr Lawrence could tell. She wore more lipstick than Clara Bow. Obviously saw herself as a film star: he'd enjoy seeing her scrape the shit off a cow's backside, he would. The thought made him smile. The other one struck him as more schoolmistressy, prim. Dark bobbed hair, pale skin, nothing on her lips. What a trio, he thought. With them in the house . . . still, he'd give them a chance. He was a fair man. He could be wrong.

'Just half a mile to go, now,' he said. He felt a general shifting in the car. 'This is where my land starts, on the left. You'll be working the fields up here.'

A turning of heads. A swing of blonde curls reflected in the freckled mirror. Curious widening of green eyes. He wondered how they saw his neatly trimmed hedges – a master hedger himself, they would never believe how many man hours the job took him, and what satisfaction it gave him. He wondered how they saw his nicely harvested fields, the yellowing woods on the rising distant land. Did it seem wild to them? Alarming? Faith had said none of them was a country girl. Somewhere as remote as Hallows Farm would seem very strange.

He swung the huge steering wheel. The Wolseley

lurched through an open gate, throwing the dark girl up against the fair one. Slight nervous giggles. Apologies. He slowed down through the farmyard, came to a halt near the house. When he had switched off the engine, he returned his hands to the steering wheel. It crossed his mind that he should attempt a smile and say, *Well, here we are, girls*, in a voice of welcome. But he decided against it. He was not a man accustomed to stating the obvious, and lack of histrionic talent meant he could not disguise the foreboding he felt. On the other hand, he had no wish to be unfriendly, and the girls must be puzzled by his long silence.

'This is it,' he said at last. 'I'll hand you over to my wife, Faith.'

God, how he longed to hand them over.

The girls clambered out of the car. Mr Lawrence saw them scanning the ground, each one silently planning her route through seams of mud that had spilt through the frost. While he unloaded their cases from the boot, he watched them skitter from patch to patch of hard, silvered gravel, protecting their fine little shoes from the spewing mud. The tallest one, the dark one, seemed to be the most skilful on her feet. The pink skirt was hesitant, delicate; the film star teetered and giggled and almost fell. They looked like an unrehearsed chorus line, Mr Lawrence thought: bright banners of colour – pink, green, pale blue, so odd against the dour stone façade of the house. They reminded him of flowers.

One of Faith's neurotic birds came squawking round the corner.

'Look! Have you ever seen such a small chicken?' squealed the film star in a broad northern accent.

The tall dark girl bent down over the bird, as if to stroke its frantic head. 'I think you'll find it's a bantam,' she said.

Faith appeared in the doorway of the porch. Her eyes met her husband's, then sped from pink to green to blue, uncritical.

'I'm so glad you're here,' she said. 'You must be ravenous and tired. Come in, come in.'

Mr Lawrence watched the coloured banners march
through the dark doorway to begin their invasion.

The girls followed Mrs Lawrence into the kitchen. Prue
was last in the line, silently smarting at the snub by the
snooty dark girl. How was she supposed to know a bloody
bantam from a hen? There had been no instruction on the
subject of poultry at the training course, and the only birds
she saw in Manchester were hanging upside down and
naked at the butcher's.

The kitchen was large, dim, steamy, billowing with a
warm mushy smell of cooking, a smell Prue could not quite
place. The pale flagstone floor was worn into dimples in
front of the enamel sink. On the huge spaces of the dun-
coloured walls, scarred with flaking paint, the only
decoration was a calendar, dated 1914. Its faded picture
was of a young soldier kissing a girl in front of a pretty cottage. *Farewell* was the caption, in copperplate of ghostly
sepia. Prue felt her eyes scorch with tears. She longed for
the small box of a kitchen at home, the shining white walls
and smell of Jeyes Fluid, and the shelf of brightly coloured
biscuit tins her mother had collected from seaside towns.
This place was so horribly old-fashioned, gloomy, dingy.
And the two collies lying on a rag rug in front of the stove
looked dangerous. Prue hated dogs. She turned to look
out of the window so that the others should not see her
tears. But the view was smeared with condensation. All she
could see was the indistinct hulk of a barn or outbuilding,
and the slash of darkening sky.

The characteristics of a hard-working farm kitchen that
so distressed Prue left Stella unmoved. In her dreamy state,
having left Philip only twenty-four hours ago (Philip whom
she loved with her whole being, Philip for whom she trembled and sighed and longed with a pain like hot wire that

11

strangled her gizzards – the simile had come to her in the train), she was indifferent to all external things. She knew that in automatic response to her disciplined childhood, and the four weeks' training course she had enjoyed, a sense of duty would ensure she worked efficiently. She would not let her mother down, and would willingly do whatever was required. On the other hand, she would not be *there*. Her soul would be with Philip as he boarded ship at Plymouth, so *meltingly beautiful* in his uniform that the very thought of that stiff collar cutting into his neck filled her with glorious weakness. And in the impatient weeks waiting for his first letter her mind would feed on the memories she had of him, rerunning the pictures over and over again. She would never tire of them. The best, of course, was Philip at her birthday party, removing his jacket, despite her father's disapproving look. It was too hot to waltz in comfort, he had said. That waltz! Their skill at dancing had been hampered by their mutual need to be joined at the hip bones. Exactly the same height, they had found the need increased – breast bones, chins, a scraping of cheeks, a clash of racing hearts becoming clamped together. By the time the music had slowed they weren't dancing at all, merely rocking gently, oblivious to everything but their extraordinary desire.

'Jellies are now served in the dining-room,' her mother had shrieked, 'and there's plenty more fruit cup.'

Stella and Philip had not wanted jellies: they'd wanted each other. They'd slid from the room and raced upstairs towards the old nursery. It housed a large and comfortable sofa, useful to Stella on several passionate occasions in the past. She had shut the door behind them. Blackout was nailed to the window frames, the darkness unchipped by any glimmer of light. Stella had taken Philip's hand and guided him past the rocking horse, giving it a wide berth: one of her suitors had bruised his leg so badly that kisses had been interrupted by howls of passion-quelling pain.

They reached the sofa. Blindness added to the excitement. She had felt him sit next to her and wondered impatiently why he was fiddling with his sleeve.

'What are you doing?'

'Taking out my cufflinks.'

'Why are you taking out your cufflinks?'

'I want to roll up my sleeves.'

'Why do you want to roll up your sleeves?'

'I always roll up my sleeves, that's why.'

'Rather as if you were getting down to *gardening*, or something?' Stella giggled.

'That sort of thing.' It didn't sound as if he was smiling.

Philip had pushed her back on to the sofa. As his mouth splodged down on to hers (in the blackness she suddenly forgot what it looked like, but tasted sausage roll and beer) she felt him expertly flick up the skirt of the sophisticated dress that old Mrs Martin had made from a *Vogue* pattern. As Philip's finger had run up the back of her leg, following the line of her stocking seam till he reached the stocking top, Stella realised Mrs Martin was the only person she actually *knew* who had been killed by a bomb. The finger continued its journey over the small bumps of suspender – not to object to a man's acquaintance with her suspenders was surely a sign of real love, she thought – and by the time he had reached the leg of her knickers, all sympathy for Mrs Martin had fled. Stella had heard herself moaning, and felt herself squirming in a way which could have been embarrassing had she been visible, but in such utter darkness anything seemed permissible. Then, as Philip employed a second efficient finger to part the way, the warning siren had wailed through the room. They disentangled themselves, made their way back through the blackness, whispers lost in the siren's moan. The music had stopped. Shouts of instruction came from downstairs. Stella remembered feeling very cold.

If it hadn't been for the siren, what might they have done?

Crowded into the wine cellar with the other guests, Stella had watched Philip roll down his shirtsleeves and put back his cufflinks. He'd whispered to her that it had been a damn shame, the interruption.

'But my first shore leave, I promise . . .'

'Promise what?'

'You know what. We must be patient.'

Stella had felt the tremor of his impatient sigh. They'd held hot hands.

'How can we be patient?'

'We can't. But I love you. What a place to have to tell a girl.' He looked terribly sad. Stella took his other hand.

'Say it again and again and again so I believe it.'

'I love you.'

'Well, I love you too. Listen: that's the all clear.'

'That was quick. Thank God no bombs.'

The guests had shuffled back upstairs, but the party was clearly over. Philip had kissed Stella goodbye at the front door. Then he'd left her in such a deliquescent state of love that today's journey had brushed past her like ribbons. She'd had the sensation of not moving, though finding herself in trains, in cars, landscape flowing by her.

But she was standing still at last. Things had stopped rocking and swaying. Reality imposed itself more sharply. She could focus again, focus on the large expanse of scratched but clean blue oilcloth that covered the kitchen table, the four white mugs fit for a giant's kitchen, a mahogany-coloured teapot big enough to house several Mad Hatters, the matching jug filled with creamy milk that frothed like cow parsley.

Stella raised her eyes to her new employer's wife and wondered if Mrs Lawrence could see the state of her tangible love. Mrs Lawrence gave the slightest nod, and bent to wipe the immaculate oilcloth with a clump of grey rag. This small acknowledgement was enough for Stella. She was instantly drawn to the gaunt, bony woman with her cross-over apron, sinewy forearms, ugly hands, and grey hair rolled so high round the back of her neck the vulnerable hollows between the tendons were cruelly revealed. Stella liked her flint-head face, its slightly protruding jaw, sharp nose, wrinkled lids over dark brown eyes. She admired the beige flesh scored by years of hard physical labour. She looked down at her own unsullied hands, nails buffed to a luminescence that was apparent even in the dusk-grained light of the room. She felt a sense of guilt at her own easy life.

Mrs Lawrence was pouring thick noisy tea into the first mug.

'I must get you straight,' she was saying. 'Which of you is . . . ?' She glanced at Stella, who felt the honour of being chosen first to reveal herself.

'I'm Stella Sherwood.' The breathiness of her voice was a private message to Mrs Lawrence.

'And you?'

'Prue Lumley.'

'Prue. So you must be Agatha?'

'Yes, but please call me Ag. Everybody does. Nobody calls me Agatha.'

'I wouldn't think they would, would they?' said Prue, still smarting from the incident of the bantam.

Mrs Lawrence handed the girls the mugs of dark tea, told them to help themselves to bread and butter: she had arranged thick slices on a plate. Prue, suffering withdrawal symptoms on her first day for years without a chocolate biscuit, scanned the dresser. All she could see was a rusty old bread bin. She thought Mrs Lawrence was pretty odd, not offering them biscuits after their long journeys.

'When we eat this evening my husband will explain the plan of duties,' Mrs Lawrence said. 'We eat at six thirty. I'll take you upstairs, let you unpack, settle in.' She paused, gathered herself to break difficult news. 'I hope you don't mind all sharing a room. We only have two small spare rooms, so one of you would have had to board in the

15

village. I thought you'd rather be together . . . so I set to work on our attic, a lot of unused space. It's nothing very luxurious, but it's clean and comfortable. In the evening you're at liberty to sit in the front room with us, of course. We have the wireless on, and the wood fire. It can get quite snug in there.' She paused again, braced herself for another difficult announcement. 'All I would ask is that you don't try to engage my husband in conversation in the evening. He's exhausted after his day. He likes to listen to the news with his eyes shut . . . You could always bring down your darning, the light's better than in the attic.'

Darning? Stella and Ag looked from Prue's appalled face to one another.

Their mugs of tea finished – in Stella's case only half finished – the girls followed Mrs Lawrence. The stairs were covered in antique linoleum, and led to a single passage with walls of stained wood. Its old floorboards, spongy beneath their feet, hollowed as if they had been carved, were covered by a strip of carpet worn to its ribs of fibre. The passage led to a bathroom similar to Prue's in Manchester only in its small size. As she gazed at cracked tiles, the tail of rust from taps to plug in the bath, the scant mat on the linoleum floor, Prue was overwhelmed by the memory of fluffy pink bath towels and the crocheted hat which covered the lavatory paper at home. She felt tears rising again.

'We all have to share this,' said Mrs Lawrence, 'but it can be done. Two baths a week, evening if you don't mind, and easy on the water. Three inches, my husband says. Four if you cut it down to one a week. And please remember to clean the bath before you leave, and keep your towels upstairs. We'll be through by four forty-five, so you can fight to wash your faces after that.'

Four forty-five *a.m.*? In her astonishment, the comforting thought of the pinks of home faded from Prue's mind. Mrs Lawrence, sinewy arms folded under a flat chest, led them up a steeper, narrower staircase to the low door of the attic room.

It stretched the length of the house, a sloping roof on one side, with three dormer windows. The exposed beams had recently been limewashed: there were spots of white on the scrubbed floorboards and the few old rugs. Ag, with her observing eye, immediately appreciated how hard Mrs Lawrence must have worked to achieve such sparkling cleanness. As one who had spent five years in spartan boarding schools, it was all wonderfully familiar to her: the narrow iron bedsteads with their concave mattresses and cotton bedspreads – these, Ag guessed, must have begun their days as dustsheets. She took in the marble-topped washstand with its severe white china bowl and jug, the two battered chests of drawers, the lights with their pleated paper shades. Each bed had a wooden chair at its side – at school there was an inspection of these bedside chairs every night. If clothes were not folded neatly upon them, there would be a black mark. Ag wondered how neat her companions would be. The room did not dispirit her. She liked it already. By the time each one of them had arranged her things, stamped her own corner with ornaments and books, and arranged photographs, it would be very agreeable as dormitories go.

What Ag would miss, she knew, was privacy. In her three years at Cambridge, her greatest delight had been in retreating into the solitude of her small, bare, cold room. Here, there would be nowhere to be alone. That, for her, would mean great deprivation. Somehow she would have to find an hour a day on her own – a walk, perhaps. She did not know the West Country but she had read her Hardy and was eager to discover it. The east coast was home. The house in which she had been brought up was almost unprotected in a plain of flat fields. She liked it best when the fields were planted with cabbages: she liked the way they clicked and chinked as you walked through the sharp frills of their stiff, silver-purple leaves. She had never understood why painters did not find cabbages as beautiful as flowers. Ag glanced out of one of the small windows. She would miss the Norfolk skies, too, and the nearness of the sea. All the same, she saw the job as an adventure, a chance she had eagerly accepted. One day, should she survive the war, she would enjoy telling her grandchildren what it was like to be part of the Women's Land Army. 'That first evening I wished there had been a bookshelf,' she said to herself, as she took a pile of Penguins from her bag. Ag often found herself dictating her memoirs even as she led her life.

When Mrs Lawrence left the room, Prue picked up her case and dumped it on one of the two beds that stood side by side. The third bed was at the far end of the room, by a window.

'If you don't mind, you two, I'd rather be next to some-one,' she said.

'I don't mind where I am,' said Stella. Wherever she was, she would be alone with Philip, so to her it didn't mat-ter. In her state of all-consuming love there was no such thing as physical hardship, only the pain of waiting.

'Then I'll go over there, if that's all right.' Ag sounded relieved. The extra distance from the other two would be some small measure of privacy.

Prue was pleased by this decision, too: she was not a one to bear a grudge, but it would be some time before she would get over the bantam incident. Instinctively, she didn't fancy Agatha. Making a fool of her in public so soon: it was a mean thing to have done. She found herself sniff-ing again – stupid tears.

'This your first time away from home?' Stella asked.

Prue nodded. 'What about you?'

'Oh, I was sent away to a convent at twelve,' said Stella.

At her far end of the room, Ag, piling up her Penguin copies of Hardy, gave a small acknowledging smile.

'I never been ten miles from Manchester, myself, except for the training course.'

'You get used to it.'

'Hope so.'

Prue sat in the hammock-like dip of her bed, child's legs swinging above the ground, a photograph clutched to her chest. She was extraordinarily pretty – the beguiling looks that come from a timeless mould, recognised in any age. Nothing original, but the kind of simple juxtaposition of features that makes prettiness look so easy when it's before you – heart-shaped face, curling lips that are halfway to pouting in profile, slanting eyes, tousled ash hair. Yellow-green tears glittered in her eyes. One of them spilt on to her cheek and instantly lost its colour.

Stella put a hand on the girl's shoulder. 'Show me your photograph,' she said.

Prue held up a picture of the façade of a small shop. *Elsie's Bond Street Salon.*

'My mum's hairdressing shop,' she said. 'If it hadn't been for this bloody war I'd be almost under-manageress by now. I'd done eighteen months of my apprenticeship, shampooing and perming and that. I was just about to get on to tinting.' She giggled. 'Perhaps I can keep my hand in here. Be of service.' She smiled up at Stella. 'You've got nice hair. I've brought my scissors, my peroxide, my kirby grips.' She nodded towards Ag. 'I could give you a new style any time, too – you only have to ask.'

'Thanks,' said Ag.

'Blimey: who's the handsome fellow?' Prue indicated the photograph Stella was holding. She handed it over: a large Polyfoto portrait of Philip. It had been taken in a studio in Guildford only a week ago – Philip the sub-lieutenant, stern in his uniform, defiant hair cowed by Brylcreem, mouth a thin line of serious intent, though Stella herself could perceive the tiniest upturn at one corner which privately indicated the other side of him.

'Cor,' said Prue, after a moment's awed silence. 'He's quite something. You in love?'

'Totally, hopelessly, absolutely.' Stella laughed, pure happiness. 'I can't sleep for thinking of Philip, I can't eat for thinking of him, I've lost half a stone.'

'That's going quite far,' said Prue. 'I've never felt like that. Have you, Ag?'

'No,' said Ag. She was wondering if the others would mind if she arranged her books on the top of one of the chests.

'You're right lucky, then,' said Prue.

'I am.' Stella took the photograph back. 'But then what's the point of life if you're not in love? I always have to be in love. I can't imagine not being in love.'

'Has it always been Philip?'

'Good heavens, no!' Stella laughed again, a delighted cooing laugh that Prue envied. 'There've been lots of others, but Philip is the *real thing*.'

'Marriage, you mean? Wedding bells?'

Stella touched the outline of Philip's face. 'We haven't known each other long,' she said. 'But I think you know, somehow, when it's . . . I mean, I wouldn't be surprised, when the war's over . . .'

'Anyone mind if I put my photo on the chest of drawers?' asked Prue, standing up.

'Course not,' said Stella. 'I'll have Philip on my chair.'

'What about you, Ag?' Prue thought that if she tried hard enough she might eventually get the tall, snooty dark girl to loosen up.

'I'll put mine beside yours.' Ag took a small double leather frame over to the chest. On one side was a photograph of her mother, who had died when Ag was two, taken in the 1920s. On the other side was a recent snapshot she had taken with her own Box Brownie: Colonel Marlowe, her father, gentle solicitor, outside his office in King's Lynn.

'Now *she's* what I call a beauty,' said Prue, snatching up the frame as soon as Ag had put it down. 'Smashing, isn't she? Just like Vivien Leigh. Your mother, is it?' Ag nodded.

Prue returned the photograph to its place. 'Can't say you're much like her.'

Now their score was even, and Prue was full of regret. She wished she hadn't said that. It was worse than the bantam, more hurtful. She hoped she would be forgiven. But she could not tell what Ag, so dignified, was feeling. Ag quickly returned to her bed. She searched for something in her handbag.

Prue felt in urgent need of a cigarette. 'Anyone mind if I have a fag?' She took a packet of Woodbines and a box of matches from her pocket.

'Not at all,' said Ag, so lightly it seemed she had not noticed Prue's jibe.

'I don't mind anything,' said Stella.

Prue went over to Ag. 'Sorry I said that,' she said. 'I didn't mean it. You can't tell nothing from a photo. Don't know what got into me.'

'That's all right,' said Ag.

'But your mum *is* beautiful,' said Prue.

'Was,' said Ag. 'Hadn't we better be going down for high tea?' She looked at her watch. 'It's almost time.'

Prue moved over to the single armchair, sat on an arm, inhaled deeply. 'Just a quick drag,' she said. 'D'you suppose we're going to have to eat whatever that terrible smell was in the kitchen?'

'Rabbit and turnip,' said Ag. 'I'll take a very large bet.'

'Rabbit and turnip? Crikey, I'll never get that lot down my throat. And do you think Mr Lawrence'll find his tongue?'

'He was very nervous in the car,' said Ag.

'Huh! What did he think we were?'

'I wasn't nervous,' said Stella, 'I was just thinking of Philip.'

''Course you were.' Prue pecked fast at her cigarette. 'You were just thinking of Philip. As for Mrs Lawrence, she's a real old battleaxe.'

21

'I like her,' said Stella.

'So do I,' said Ag.

'That makes two of you, then,' said Prue. She swung her legs faster. 'It don't feel much like there's a war, here, do it?'

The dining-room had a patina of gloom. It smelt of darkly polished furniture. The central light, whose shade was fretted with the abstract wings of dead moths, feebly illuminated a bleakly laid table: fork, knife, pudding spoon, and napkin in a bakelite coloured ring at each place, glasses and a jug of water. In the centre of the table, island in a brackish lake, was a stand of lacy silver which held cut-glass pots of salt and pepper. A gleaming silver spine rose between the pots, its apex twisted into a small handle. This fragile object, the single shining thing in the sombre room, made Stella smile. She wondered when Mrs Lawrence had time to polish it. She imagined it was important to Mrs Lawrence to make the time.

Ag, standing by the table – none of them was sure what to do, whether they should sit down – straightened a table mat, a gravy-spotted scene of rustic Dorset a century ago. In the awkward silence that had netted them all, the grandfather clock ticked – muted, insistent, its fine brass hands stroking their imperceptible way round the brass sun of its face.

'Give me the creeps, grandfather clocks do,' said Prue. She moved over to the sideboard to study a photograph in a cheap leather frame. It was of a stern-looking young girl, her flat hair rolled up in the same way as Mrs Lawrence's. '*She* don't look like much of a laugher, do she?'

Mrs Lawrence came in with a pot of stew. It was rabbit. She was followed by her husband who carried a dish of mashed potatoes and roast turnips. The girls exchanged private looks. Prue, behind the Lawrences' backs, imitated someone being sick. But she took the piled plate Mrs Lawrence handed her.

'Where's Joe?' Mr Lawrence asked his wife, an

enormous plate of food in front of him. Mrs Lawrence, the last one to sit, had taken a tiny helping herself.

'Went to deliver that feedstuff to Robert. Said they might have something to eat at The Bells.'

Mr Lawrence sniffed.

There was a long silence, but for the subdued chink of knives and forks in thick gravy. Prue, despite herself, was eating hungrily. The ticking of the clock bored through her. She turned to Mr Lawrence, sitting next to her.

'Is that your daughter?' she asked, nodding towards the photograph.

'No,' he said.

Prue gave him fifteen ticks of the clock to tell her more. He kept his silence. She turned to his wife.

'Who is it, then?'

Mrs Lawrence wiped her mouth on her napkin. Already she had finished her food.

'That's Janet,' she said. 'Joe's fiancée.' She waited till Ag and Stella had both turned to look at the photograph with new interest, and returned to their food. 'They're to be married when the war is over. In the spring, we hope.'

'Depending on Mr Churchill,' said her husband.

'They know they may have a long wait. They seem quite resigned.'

Mrs Lawrence spoke tightly. Stella and Ag both hoped Prue would ask no more questions. Prue felt no such reticence. She turned again to the farmer.

'So Joe, your son, he's not been called up, then?'

'No, he hasn't, and he won't be. Asthmatic. Not a hope. Suffered all his life.'

'He's been very unfortunate, Joe,' said Mrs Lawrence.

'He would have liked to have joined the navy,' added her husband.

'He would have liked to have gone to Cambridge. He got a place, they thought very highly of him. But then the war . . . we couldn't spare him from the farm.'

'My – I have a friend in the navy,' said Stella.

'I went to Cambridge,' said Ag. 'He shouldn't miss it if possible. He could go once the war's over.'

'Perhaps,' said Mrs Lawrence.

They fell back into silence. The ticking clock dominated again. It wasn't until Mrs Lawrence had helped them all to large plates of apple pie and custard that her husband got down to business.

'You'll have heard about the place from the district commissioner, I dare say,' he began. 'Bit of this, bit of that, mixed farming. Up to now, we've done what we like best, though I hear there'll be orders any minute to turn the place mostly over to arable land. For the time being we've got a small herd of Friesians and a hundred or so sheep, though we're thinking of giving them up after the next lambing. Duties are pretty obvious. Faith, here, manages everything to do with the house – shopping, cooking, cleaning, laundry and so on. Land girls aren't supposed to help with domestic chores, but I dare say she wouldn't say no to the odd helping hand.' He watched his wife shake her head, cast down her tired eyes. 'She takes care of all the fruit – just a small orchard, we have, damsons, plums and apples. She does all the pruning, picking, boxing up, everything, don't you, Faith? Besides the jam and chutney – you'll not be short of good jam, here, will they, Faith?'

'They won't,' said Faith.

'Apart from all that, in a real emergency the wife helps us out with the milking, the lambing – she can turn her hand to anything, can Faith.'

He stopped for a moment, glanced at Prue. Once again glassy green tears danced in her eyes.

'I've never heard anything like it,' she said. 'Poor Mrs Lawrence.'

Mr Lawrence ignored her. His instinct had been right. He could see this film star bit of fluff wasn't going to be much use, women's tears at the very thought of an honest day's work.

'Everything else's up to Joe and me and you lot. You can all have a go at different things, see what you're best at. Five twenty a.m. there's tea on the kitchen table, five thirty it's down to milking. I'll sort you out, your various duties, in the morning. Anyone have any preferences?'

Prue volunteered at once. 'Well, I found on the course I loved tractors, Mr Lawrence. Don't suppose you'd ever believe it, but I could plough a pretty straight furrow, they said.'

'I'd find that hard, I must admit,' he replied, unable to resist a slight smile.

'I loved working with cows,' said Ag. She would be the one, perhaps, he would introduce to hedging. He could imagine her, slasher in hand – kind, studious face, thoughts hidden behind hooded eyes. He couldn't picture her, some-how, serious head bent into the muddy side of a cow.

'I'll remember that, then. And you?' He turned to Stella. The picture of her knee still flickered in his mind.

'I'm afraid I got to the course late because my father was ill, so I missed learning to milk. I'm just a general sort of all-rounder . . . I'll do anything.'

'That's good. Well, then, you start at dawn tomorrow. I warn you now, I'm a fairly easy man' – Ag saw his wife's mouth twitch almost imperceptibly – 'but one thing I can't stand is anyone late for anything, see? And another thing: there's to be no shirking. It's tough work, long hours, but it's the satisfaction of a job well done you'll get. The satis-faction of knowing you're doing your bit for your country in this damn war. Now –' he pushed back his chair, flushed from the exertion of so much speaking. 'I thought we should . . . celebrate your first night with a sip of the wife's home-made ginger wine. You'll never have tasted anything like it, I can tell you that.'

He strode over to the sideboard, opened a cupboard,

took out five wineglasses and put them on the table. Their glass, so pale a pink as to be almost an illusion, was engraved with butterflies that flew through swirling ribbons. It was a wonder their fine stems did not snap in Mr Lawrence's huge clumsy hands, thought Ag. They were the first beautiful objects she had seen in the house. She could not contain her response of pleasure.

'They're so pretty,' she said.

Mrs Lawrence blushed. She was confused by the least of compliments. 'My mother's,' she said. 'My mother liked to collect pretty things. We've not many left. We had to sell off gradually. Bad years.' She put her hand to her mouth, as if she had said too much. The merest gathering of shadows beneath her eyes – which almost smiled – indicated a feeling of modest pride as she watched her husband pour the thick golden wine. Filled, the blush of the glass deepened against the wine.

By now it was almost dark outside. No one put on the light. The room was warmer, furred with the merged smells of food and polish, and the faint note of musky scent that came from Prue. Mr Lawrence, his dutiful speeches over, was suddenly looser in his movements, sitting heavily back in his chair – the only one with arms – swinging a frail glass to his lips.

'A toast,' he said. 'To Mr Churchill.'

'To Mr Churchill,' the girls muttered, holding up their glasses.

The smoky light through the window joined the pink of glass and gold of wine. So now the glasses were the colour of misted plums, thought Ag, spurred by her usual private wonder at the antics of colour.

'And, of course, to you girls.'

'Thank you, Mr Lawrence,' giggled Prue. 'That's nice of you.'

Again the farmer could not resist a smile as he watched three white little hands tipping the glasses to their pretty

26

little mouths: tomorrow they'd be piling the dung heap, sweeping the yard, slapping grease on sore udders.

They all drank, Mrs Lawrence with tiny sips. The fiery wine burned their throats, their chests, their stomachs. It warmed their hands, and their heads spun with new ease and expectation.

The glasses were emptied, the cork put back with no invitations for more, the bottle returned to its cupboard. The girls helped Mrs Lawrence take the dishes through to the kitchen. Her husband stayed for a while in the empty room, made unfamiliar to him by the new presence of strangers. The wine still burned his lips, the ticking of the clock soothed. Perhaps he would get used to it, the full house. Might not be so bad after all. Even the film star looked as if she might shape up. In a moment, he would summon the energy to go out again. With Joe still not back, there was plenty to do before nightfall. He allowed himself a moment with his eyes shut, head thrown back. Behind the heartbeat of the clock he could hear laughter across the passage.

The kitchen was blurry from the steam of hot water from the sink. Mrs Lawrence's arms were deep in murky bubbles, from which she produced shining white plates. The girls fluttered round her, competing to snatch each plate from her first. They had tied dishcloths round their coloured skirts. In the near dark they fumbled through strange cupboards guessing where to put things. They bumped into each other. The ginger wine surprised them with its strength. It made them laugh.

As they were all tired, and eager to be alert on their first morning, they agreed on early bed. Mrs Lawrence warned them not to put on the light unless they pinned the blackout stuff across each window. None of them had the energy to do this: they undressed beside their beds, turning their backs to one another as they slipped nightdresses over their heads. Prue, the only one to have been denied these lessons at boarding school, copied the modest gestures of the other two. She had difficulty in seeing her face clearly in her hand mirror: it took her some time to wipe the mascara from her eyes and the lipstick from her mouth.

She watched, fascinated, as the other two brushed their hair with short, strong, dutiful strokes as if it was a ritual they had performed for many years. Ag's hair was dull and heavy. It needed thinning, shaping. Stella's could do with a restyle, too. When Prue knew them better, she would introduce them to her scissors, persuade them to allow her to make improvements. The plans in her mind diffused the small feelings of homesickness.

'Funny, me a hairdresser's daughter and never brushed my hair at night,' she said.

'Very odd, that,' agreed Stella.

Ag sat on the edge of her bed rolling up her stockings. She wore a flannel nightdress with a bodice of lace frills, and carpet slippers. So *grandmotherly*, thought Prue, slipping off her own pink velvet mules with their puffs of matching swansdown. And now the grandmother figure had laid the small neat bundle of stockings on her chair, beside a pile of books, and had turned to face Stella and Prue.

'I think I must tell you something,' she said quietly, folding her hands like a nun. There was a long pause. 'That is, my name isn't really Agatha.'

'Oh?' Prue was prepared to be surprised by any announcement this prim girl liked to make.

'No. It's much worse than that. It's Agapanthus.'

'*What*? Aga – what?' Prue doubled up with giggles. 'There's no such name.'

'Well, there is,' said Ag. 'It's both the name of a flower and the name of my grandfather's . . . boat.'

Prue studied her own incredulous face, with its mascara-streaked cheeks, in her hand mirror.

'Fishing boat, or what?'

Ag hesitated. 'More of a yacht, really,' she said at last.

28

'Just a small one. My father insisted I should be christened Agapanthus. He's a strange man in some ways. But he also agreed I'd have a bad time at school with a name like that. So we settled for Agatha – which isn't actually that much better, is it? Anyhow, in the end everyone called me Ag, so I never had to explain.'

She bowed her head. The warm confusion of the ginger wine was draining away. The compulsion to confess the matter of her name had come so powerfully upon her: now, having done it, she wondered why.

'I think that's *wonderful*,' said Stella. 'Agapanthus! You could be famous with a name like that.'

'Wouldn't be bad for a salon, to my mind,' said Prue. 'Have you ever told anyone before?'

'Just one friend at Cambridge. Desmond.'

'And here you are telling us the first night we meet? I'd say we're flattered, aren't we, Stella? Any trouble, and I'll be shouting it from the haystacks. "Agapanthus!" I'll shout!'

They all laughed.

Ag got into bed, sat with arms round raised knees. The feeling of the first night at a new school was overwhelming: on the one hand it was all so familiar, on the other there was the strangeness of being grown up in what felt like a child's world.

'I don't know what came over me. I just felt I had to tell you. Good night.'

At school, they always bade each other good night, no matter how sleepy. She lay down and in a practised way shuffled about until she found comfort in the unyielding mattress. In a moment she was asleep.

Prue, in her bed, tossed about in search of softness: she doubted she'd ever get used to a mattress like this. Still, the ginger wine had cheered her, and she had to admit there was something intriguing about Ag's confession. The tears her mother had warned her she would probably shed on her first night did not come. She, too, was quickly asleep.

Stella reached for Philip's photograph on her chair, as soon as she judged the others would not hear. Terribly awake, she kissed his face in the dark. She replaced it, but could not sleep. After a while – it was too dark to see her watch, and Ag's clock was too far away – she slipped out of bed and crept to the nearest window. There was a full moon. It shone hazily through dark clouds, fraying their edges. She looked down into the farmyard: looming black sides of barns and sheds, a huge pile of dung whose acrid smell just reached her. The night was so ominously quiet she feared bombs. Fighter planes often zoomed out of the deepest silence. What would they do in a raid? Mrs Lawrence had said nothing about a shelter . . .

Stella saw a man ride into the yard on a bicycle. He braked with a rather dashing little turn; had anyone been watching, she'd have thought he was showing off. He dismounted, pushed the bike into the barn. She could see he was tall, large. When he came out of the barn he paused, looked up at the moon, scratched his head. Now Stella could see he wore enormous muddy boots. Instead of moving towards the house, he turned back to the barn, leaned heavily against it, face to its wall. He protected his forehead with a bent arm, shoulders hunched. For a long while he did not move – two or three minutes, Stella thought it must have been.

She could be imagining it – he was a long way off – but his position struck her as one of despair. Eventually he moved, drew himself upright and took long mournful strides back the way he had come, towards the gate. Cold now, Stella returned to her bed. She picked up the photograph of Philip again, and clasped it in her arms. Under the bedclothes she kissed his icy glass face, and swore to love him till she died.

Two

W hen the wind was in the right direction, the church bells at Hinton Half Moon could be heard at Hallows Farm. The hamlet was no more than a straggle of stone cottages, one of which had been converted into a small sub-post office. It offered little in the way of provisions: Bird's custard, Horlicks, Bovril, a few pads of Basildon Bond, soggy from their long shelf-life. These basic provisions were sometimes enhanced by a few luxuries which appeared according to the mood of Mrs Tyler, who ran the shop. On a good day, she would be up early, baking, and set a few brown loaves on a sheet of greaseproof paper in the cloudy front window. The smell of baking would hail the neighbours at dawn. A queue of some half-dozen buyers would hurry to the door at eight thirty, official opening time. Mrs Tyler, a law unto herself, as she was so fond of saying, would wave a plump hand urging patience. Not until eight thirty-five, or even eight forty, would she at last turn the rusty key very slowly, and let the eager buyers in. There were never enough loaves. There was always an argument, disappointed voices. It was known that Mrs Tyler enjoyed these small dramas played out in her shop once or twice a week: it was her measure of power in an uneventful life.

From time to time, Mrs Tyler's annoying ways so incensed the other members of the community that they vowed to boycott her wares. But this plan never worked for more than a day or two. They needed stamps, their pensions, they needed to add a few shillings to their savings accounts. And once in the shop they would be tempted by a surprising cauliflower or cabbage, a punnet of tomatoes or Russet apples from the Tyler garden. These were put out, they knew, by way of a bait. The ploy succeeded. Despite their good intentions, the inhabitants of all the eleven cottages that made up Hinton Half Moon found themselves sneaking back into the post office, greed overcoming principle quite easily, to purchase Mrs Tyler's trap of the day.

Ratty Tyler, married to the post mistress for fifty-one years, was party to his wife's small triumphs, because she described them to him with untiring glee every evening. His reaction was neither to encourage nor to discourage. A dignified neutrality, he had discovered over the years, was the wisest attitude to adopt in matters concerning Edith. In the past, in the heat of youthful loyalty, he had found himself in many a scrape through lending her support. It was due to an unwise act on Edith's part that he had been forced to give up his thriving butcher's shop in Dorchester just before the last war. A question of slander, though the exact circumstances had long since evaporated in his mind. Total boycott of customers. Confusion. Shame. Ratty hated ever to remember it, though sometimes the whole horrible business came back to him when Edith was in a particularly tricky mood. He warned her that if she went too far they would be driven from Hinton Half Moon just as they had been from Dorchester. But Edith seemed not to understand the danger. She continued taking her risks.

When the Great War was over, the Tylers had found the cottage they still lived in today. Their first Sunday, Ratty signed up as a bell ringer, and it was in the cold vestry of the church that he met the young and energetic John Lawrence. In those days, the Lawrences, too, lived in a cottage in Hinton, but they owned a few acres of land on which they kept a small flock of sheep. The two men had a brief conversation in the churchyard. Ratty sensed Mr Lawrence's ambition: already he had his eye on Hallows Farm, occupied at the time by a senile old woman.

'And your line of country?' Mr Lawrence had asked.

'We've just moved here, sir. Casual labour's what I'm after. Any farming work, I'd be pleased.'

'We're beginners ourselves, but I could offer you a few hours a week.'

'Righto, sir.' The two men shook hands.

'John Lawrence.'

'Ratty Tyler.'

'Ratty?'

'Term of affection, sir, should you suppose otherwise. Adopted at the time of our engagement by my now wife.'

Ratty allowed himself the lie. The truth was that Edith had chosen the name for him as soon as they had been introduced. Reginald, his real name, she said at once, she could not abide. Ratty had been rather taken by her busy little head of blonde curls and her pretty ankles, and he feared his objection might have blasted the plan that was beginning to form in his mind. So Ratty he was from that day forth, though in the secrecy of his soul he often thought the name was more appropriate to Edith than to him.

It was plain from the start that he and Mr Lawrence understood one another. He began with three hours' labour a week, two shillings an hour. When the sheep did well and the flock increased, this was increased to a day and a half. By the time Mr Lawrence acquired Hallows Farm, Ratty was working every day, all hours. Within a few years, things became too much for the two of them: it was Ratty who suggested they should hire more hands. He found the two keen young lads himself – one from Hinton, one from a couple of miles west – and thereby earned himself the title of Farm Manager.

These days, although Ratty still thought of himself as Farm Manager, and Mr Lawrence would never do anything so inconsiderate as to suggest there was any change in the position, both men understood the title was now more honorary than practical. What with his arthritic hip and the bad pains that sometimes struck his eyes now, Ratty would only come up to the farm a couple of days a week. When the boys had been called up, he had reluctantly agreed that Mrs Lawrence's idea of land girls might be the solution.

Every working day of his life Ratty rose at four o'clock in the morning. He liked the silence of the dawn, the silence of the kitchen as he boiled water in the huge black kettle for tea, and ate a chunk of Edith's rich brown bread. Just before leaving he would take a mug up to the bedroom under the eaves, leave it on the table beside her. Sometimes he would pause for a moment to study the now white curls of his wife, and the creased face, cross even in sleep. Years ago, without disentangling herself from drowsiness, she would ask him for a kiss. He would oblige, and be rewarded with a sleepy smile. She had not smiled for years now, properly, Edith. Not with happiness. The only thing that brought a shine to her eyes was *triumph*. Scoring over the neighbours, her customers. Scoring over anyone she could find, not least Ratty himself. What was it, he sometimes wondered, that caused a carefree young girl to turn so quickly into a crusty old woman? Nothing Ratty could put his finger on: he did his best to please her. But marriage was a rum business, he had learned. At the time – foolish young lad – he had no idea what he was letting himself in for. But it had never occurred to him to desert his barren ship. He had made his promises to the Lord, and they would not be broken. Besides, if he tried hard enough, he sometimes thought, everything might miraculously change, and Mr and Mrs Ratty Tyler might become as happily married as Mr and Mrs John Lawrence.

Fortunately for Ratty, he was blessed with a compartmentalised mind. He was able to abandon the tribulations of his marriage as he shut the front door behind him. At four thirty precisely he hobbled into the lane that led to Hallows Farm, limping slightly, hands scrunched into the familiar caverns of his pockets, ears stinging cold beneath his cap.

For twenty years Ratty had been walking this lane, witnessing thousands of early mornings, each one so infinitesimally different that only a habitual observer could feel the daily shiftings that formed the master plan of each season. Since he had been forced by health and age into semi-retirement, and now only made the journey twice a week, the privacy of dawn was more precious than ever before to Ratty. He listened to his own footsteps on the road – no longer firm and brisk – and the scattered choir of birds. Sometimes a blackbird would soar into a solo, his song only to be muddied by a gang of jealous hedge sparrows. Sometimes an anxious mistlethrush would call to its mate, and be answered by a cheeky robin. There were few unseen birds Ratty could not identify by their song, and their sense of dawn competition made him smile.

He slashed the long grass of the verges with his stick and noted, as always, the neatness of Mr Lawrence's hedges. In the sky, a transparent moon was posed on a belly of night cloud. But the dark mass was beginning to break up where it touched the low hills. Streaks of yellow, pale as torchlight, illuminated the line of fine elms that protected Hallows Farm from northern winds. Over the gate that led into the meadow Ratty could see the Friesians, legless in a rising ground mist, intent on their last grass before milking. By the time he had walked the last half-mile the mist had all but evaporated, and the familiar outline of the old barn was black against the sky. A strand of smoke rose from the farmhouse chimney. In the old days, Ratty always arrived before Mrs Lawrence lit the kitchen fire. His current lateness troubled him. Although he knew Mr Lawrence would have understood, and urged him not to hurry, he took the precaution of disguising the precise time of his arrival. This morning, for instance, he would go straight to the barn to sort out some stacks of foodstuff. When Mr Lawrence dropped by some time between five thirty and six, he would have no idea when Ratty had started, and could be counted on not to ask.

This morning, too, Ratty had another reason for wanting to start off in the barn. The girls would be here this morning, and he wanted to get a look at them before they saw him. See what he was up against, as it were. Get their measure. He had never worked with women on the land, and could not imagine how it would be. But as a man who could be stimulated by very small changes, he was not against the idea – not as against it, in fact, as Mr Lawrence. Chances were they wouldn't be up to much – he couldn't see a girl on a tractor, himself. But in all fairness, he must give them the opportunity to prove their worth. And if they weren't up to the job, they'd be out. As he had agreed with Mr Lawrence, there'd be no mucking about with second chances. There was no time for mucking about with a war on.

Full of benevolent intent, Ratty reached the barn. His enthusiasm to tidy a pile of heavy sacks had waned. He could deal with them later. For the moment, he felt like a rest.

Ratty leaned up against the high bumper of the red Fordson tractor. Once a handsome scarlet, its paint was now chipped and dull. He fished for his pipe from an inner pocket, spent a long time lighting it. Its sour smoke joined the smells of the few remaining piles of last year's hay, rotting mangolds, tar, rope, rust. Up in the dusky beams, the dratted pigeons carried on with their incessant silly cooing. (Ratty's love of birds did not extend to indolent pigeons.) A cow screamed in Long Marsh: Betty, by the sound of her. He kept his eyes on the empty yard, looking forward to the entertainment of one of the girls getting down to sweeping. Confident his position would not be observed, he took a long draw on his pipe, began his patient wait. After a while he was conscious of a slight agitation in his heart. The feeling reminded him of something. Ratty struggled to remember. That was it: the long-ago event of his wedding. Standing at the altar, waiting for his bride, he had experienced exactly the same thunder of anticipation, excitement. And look where that had landed him . . .

At five fifteen, Stella, Ag and Prue presented themselves at the kitchen table. They stood stiffly in their new uniforms. Ag folded back the sleeves of her green pullover: its wool scratched her wrists. Stella was having trouble with the collar of her fawn shirt. Prue stamped her feet in their sturdy regulation shoes.

'Each one feels heavy as a bloody brick,' she complained. 'It's *these* I became a land girl for . . .' She stroked her corduroy breeches, gave a small wiggle of her narrow hips.

Prue was the only one who had taken the liberty of adding to the uniform – not against the rules unless deemed inappropriate. She had tied a pink chiffon scarf into a bow on top of her head. Although she wore no lipstick today, the mascara was thick as ever.

Mrs Lawrence poured mugs of her dark, hot tea, and passed a plate of thickly cut bread and butter. Her look at Prue made her silent opinion quite clear. Then her husband came in and spoke her thoughts for her.

'That thing on your head,' he said, 'won't stand much chance up against the side of a cow.'

Prue fluttered her eyes at him, defiant. 'I'll take that risk,' she said.

'Very well.'

Mr Lawrence found himself curiously moved by the sight of the three girls, eager to work for him, lined up in his kitchen so early in the morning.

'Besides,' said Prue, helping herself to a second slice of bread, 'I thought it was agreed I'd have a go on the tractor. I told you I was good at that.'

'This isn't a fairground, I'll have you know. You don't

"have a go" on things. You do a job of hard work. What's your name?'

'Prue. *Prudence.*' She raised her chin.

Mr Lawrence sniffed in distaste. 'And what's that *smell*, for Lord's sake?'

Prue, her cheeks two pink aureoles that matched the chiffon bow, was delighted he had noticed. '*Nuits de Paris,*' she smiled.

Her employer was silenced by the prettiness of Prue's cocky young face. 'This is a farm,' he said at last, his voice less rough than he had intended. 'I don't want my cowsheds smelling of the Moulin Rouge, thank you. You're a land girl, you understand, not a film star.'

Mrs Lawrence kept her eyes on her tea.

Prue smiled on, pleased Mr Lawrence should find something of a film star in her. 'Perhaps *Roman Days*'d be more up your street?'

'I want none of your fancy scents, just your mind on the milking, thank you, Prudence.'

Mr Lawrence was brusque now. He nodded towards Ag, not wanting to ask another one her name. 'You'll get going with the yard broom, and muck out the pigsty, young lady, and you, Stella –' he remembered her name all too well – 'will have to learn to milk before we can let you loose among the cows. Headquarters provided us with the wherewithal, didn't they, Faith?' His mouth twitched in a limited smile. He allowed himself a glance at Stella's knee. The jewel was now disguised by corduroy breeches, though its sharp edges were just visible. Again Mr Lawrence nodded towards Ag. 'You – you'll find Ratty Tyler out there somewhere. He'll show you the brooms, get you going. As for you, Lady Prudence, you'll take yourself over to the milking shed where my son Joe will sort you out in no time. Stella can come with me.'

Stella saw Mrs Lawrence's eyes raised to her husband's flushed face.

He went with the girls out into the cold early air of the yard. Stella followed him to the shed where she would receive her 'training', as he called it.

As she walked beside him, the squelch of their gumboots in step, the farmer felt an acute sense of betrayal.

He kept his eyes from Stella, and cursed the war.

Ag stood alone in the yard, hands in her pockets, wondering what to do. She could see no one who might be Ratty Tyler, and did not feel like shouting his name. Ratty? Mr Tyler? What was she supposed to call him? And who was he? Ag listened to the sharp clash of farmyard noises. She dreaded Mr Lawrence returning from the shed, to which he had gone with Stella, and finding her not at work.

A tall, large-boned man, hooded lids over very dark eyes, appeared from behind the barn. He carried a heavy spade, a pitchfork and a broom. Unsmiling, he approached Ag.

'Thought you might be wanting these,' he said.

'Thanks. I was looking for Mr Tyler.'

'Ratty appears when he appears. I'm Joe.'

'I'm Ag.'

Joe handed her the broom. He had had a hard five minutes in the barn trying to persuade Ratty to come out and show the girl what to do. But Ratty, in one of his most stubborn moods, insisted on staying hidden. He wanted to sum up the strangers unseen, he said. Take his time to get used to them. Joe was sympathetic. But in the end he took pity on the tall girl in the yard and agreed with Ratty to set her on her way.

'You want to sweep the yard absolutely clean, sluice down the drains with Dettol – buckets and water over there. Dung heap's round the corner. Pigsty's past the cowshed: only the one sow. Not good-tempered. Shouldn't get in her way. Plenty of clean straw in the barn. I'll be milking if you want anything.'

He strode away. Their eyes had never met.

Ag tested the weight of the broom, surprised at its heaviness. She must devise her own method, she thought, and began sweeping the corner farthest from the barn.

As there was no sign of Joe Lawrence in the milking shed, Prue took her chance to become acquainted with the cows. They were a herd of twenty Friesians. Each one, chained to her manger, had a name over the stall: Betty, Emma, Daisy, Floss, Rosie, Nancy – Prue wondered if she would ever be able to distinguish between them. She observed their muddy legs, but clean flanks and spotless udders. Looked as if someone else had done the washing down, thank goodness. That was the part of this job she could never fancy.

Prue came to an almost entirely black cow, Felicity. She had particularly intelligent and gentle eyes, surrounded by long blueish eyelashes. Prue wondered what they would look like with mascara, and smiled to herself. She glanced down at the swollen pink udder, with its obscene marbling of raised veins. She ran a finger the whole length of Felicity's spine, the wrong way, so that the cow's black hair was forced up over the bone.

'I like you,' she said aloud.

She raised her eyes above the animal's spine and found herself looking into the hooded eyes of the man she assumed was Joe. Cor! *He* was quite something . . . Her mind flicked through the handsome film stars she had dreamed of, but could come up with no one comparable. Anyway, she quickly decided, she'd be happy to sacrifice ploughing, and milk the whole herd morning and night if this Joe was to be her supervisor. His eyes shifted, expressionless, a bit *spooky*, to her hair, the bow. Funny how she'd been impervious to everybody else's opinion, but there was something about Joe's look that made her feel a bit foolish. The one thing she did not want was instant disapproval. That would start them off on the wrong foot.

'Why's she called Felicity, this one?' she asked at last,

head on one side, coquettish – a gesture she had learned from Veronica Lake.

'She was a happy calf. She's a happy cow.' Joe slapped Felicity on the rump. He seemed to have forgotten about the bow.

'Can I start on her?'

'No. We start at the other end with Jemima.'

Prue pouted. 'I'm Prue, by the way. Your father calls me *Prudence*.'

'I know. How's your milking?'

'Just the few weeks on the training course. I'm not bad.'

'Gather you're keen to get on the tractor.'

'I *said* that, just in case Mr Lawrence had any ideas about women not liking ploughing. I'm quite happy to milk.'

'Rather enjoy it myself. A lot of farms have gone over to machines. Isn't really worth it for a herd of our size, though Dad was talking about it before this bloody interruption.' They both listened to the noise of a small aircraft squealing overhead. Joe pointed to the far end of the shed. 'There are a couple I haven't washed down – Sylvia and Rose. Mop, bucket and towels through there. Rule here is that we change the water every two cows. Stool and milking bucket in the dairy. I'll show you how to put on the cooling machine when we've finished.'

'Don't worry. I *understand* about cooling machines,' said Prue. She managed to sound as if her understanding went far beyond mere technicalities.

'We should get going. I'm running late this morning, seeing to your friend.'

'I'll make a start.'

Prue blushed with annoyance: to think that Ag, asked merely to sweep the yard, had been the first to engage Joe's attention. She moved slowly down the concrete avenue that divided the two rows of cows' backsides, swinging her hips. Joe's eyes, she knew, were still on her. She picked up the mop and bucket with the calculated flourish

41

of a star performer, and began to swab Sylvia's bulging udder as if the job was a movement in a dance. When she had finished washing both cows, she sauntered back to where Joe was milking a restless creature called Mary.

'And where,' she asked, hand on one hip, provocative as she could manage in her given surroundings, 'might I find a cup for the fore milk?'

Joe released Mary's teats. He looked up at Prue, impassive. 'I don't believe we have one,' he said.

'Don't have one?' Prue's voice was mock amazed. 'We were taught it was *essential* –'

'Dare say you were. We don't do everything by the book, here. We just draw off the first few threads before starting with the bucket.' He turned back to his milking.

'On to the *floor*? Do you suppose,' said Prue, after a few moments of listening to the rhythmic swish of Mary's milk hitting the bucket, 'this is a matter I should bring up with your father? Or the district commissioner? Or –?'

'Bring it up with who you bloody like,' said Joe. Although his face was half-obscured by Mary's flank, Prue could see he was smiling.

In the dairy, she washed her hands with carbolic soap in the basin. She was aware of a small triumph, a feeling that some mutual challenge had been recognised. If nothing else, a teasing game could be played with Joe. That would give an edge to the boring old farm jobs – and who knows? One game leads to another . . .

Astride the small milking stool, head buried in Jemima's side, hands working expertly on the hard cold teats, Prue allowed herself the thrill of daydreams. Surprisingly, she was enjoying herself. She liked the peaceful noises – muted stamp of hooves, and chink of neck chains – that accompanied the treble notes as jets of milk sizzled against metal bucket. She was aware that the sweet, hay smell of cow breath obliterated her own *Nuits de Paris* – she would tell Mr Lawrence, at the right moment, he need have no fears.

The thought of the hugeness of Joe's boots made her feel at home, somehow – which was an odd thought considering this chilly milking parlour was as far away from her mother's front parlour as you could get. She found herself praying that milking would be her regular job, if Joe was to be her milking partner. But her mind was diverted from imagining the many possibilities of this partnership by the distant sound of rattling marbles. She stiffened.

'Miles away,' shouted Joe. 'Just practice, by the sound of it.'

Prue waited tensely for a few moments, fingers slack on the teats. She had forgotten the war. She stood up, easily lifted the bucket of foamy milk. It smelt faintly of cowslips. Beaten Joe to it, she saw with pleasure. It was tempting to point out to him what a quick milker she was. But Prue decided against this. She went to the dairy, sloshed the milk into the cooling machine and chose a bucket from the sterilising tank for the next cow. She had had her one small victory this morning. That was enough to begin with.

Stella, when she saw her 'cow', laughed out loud. It was a crude, ingenious device: a frame made of four legs, inward sloping, like the legs of a trestle table. From its top was slung a canvas bag roughly shaped like an udder and from which dangled four rubber teats the pink of gladioli. It reminded Stella of a pantomime cow.

'Oh Mr Lawrence,' she said, 'is this to be my apprenticeship?'

'Won't take long. You'll soon get used to it.'

Mr Lawrence gave her one of his curt smiles. He picked up a bucket of yesterday's milk and poured it into the bag. Then he squatted down on the stool drawn up to the ersatz udder, placed the bucket beneath the empty bag, and took a teat in the fingers of both hands.

He was no expert, and was aware of the ridiculous

picture he made. His fingers were curiously shaky. A feeble string of milk trickled from the teat.

'Easier on a real cow,' he said. 'Here, you have a go.'

Stella took his place, held the smooth pink teat.

'It's a rhythm you want to aim for,' he explained, when he had watched her for a while. 'Once you've got the rhythm, you're there, and the cow's happy. That's it, that's a girl.' The farmer moved proudly back from his pupil. She was bright, this one, as well as attractive. 'Fill the bucket a couple of times, and you can be on to the real thing tomorrow. All right?'

'Fine.'

Mr Lawrence allowed himself a few moments in silent appraisal. Funny girl. So formal in her speech, and yet so quick. He let his eyes rest on her back, the pretty hair tumbling forwards. Where it parted he could see a small patch of her neck, no bigger than a man's thumbprint. With all his being he wanted to touch it, just touch it for an infinitesimal moment, feel its warmth. As he stood there, fighting his appalling desire, his hands and knees began to shake. Dizziness confused his head. Stella's voice came from a long way off.

'Am I doing all right, d'you think?'

It was several moments – silence rasped by the silly sound of the squirting milk – before he dared answer.

'You're doing fine.'

He took a step towards her, watched his hand leave his side, stretch out to her innocent back: hover, quiver, withdraw.

Stella turned, smiling. She saw what she thought was a look of deep misgiving in Mr Lawrence's eyes. The shyness of the man! It must be dreadful, she thought, to find the peace of Hallows Farm suddenly disrupted by unskilled girls from other worlds. Sympathy engulfed her, but she could think of no appropriate words with which to convey her feelings.

'I'll be back in a while,' Mr Lawrence said. He waited till Stella returned to concentrate on the rubber teats, and quickly left the shed.

Alone, Stella sniffed the sour milk and manure smell of the shed. It was cold, damp. Her fingers on the teats were turning mauve. She determined to get her peculiar training over as fast as possible, and concentrated on the rhythmic massage of the ludicrous teats. At the same time she began to compose the funny letter she would write to Philip tonight: *my first day a land girl – with a rubber cow.* This prompted the thought of the post. Philip had promised to write immediately. She ached to hear from him. The two hours till breakfast, when she could ask about the delivery of letters, seemed an eternity. In some desolation, Stella looked down at the thin covering of milk on the bottom of the bucket.

Two hours later, shoulders and legs stiff from the awkward position (it would be much more comfortable with a real cow to lean against), Stella rose and stretched, her apprenticeship, she hoped, over. She had filled the bucket twice and felt like a qualified milker. Once she had got the hang of it – the rhythm, as Mr Lawrence had said – it had been quite easy. Behind the gentle splash-splash of the milk she had dreamed of Philip, going over in her mind every detail of the few occasions on which they had met. And when she swooped back to the present, she saw the humour of her situation – the adrenalin of being in love making bearable the milking of an imitation cow.

Now, she leaned over the bottom half of the shed door, looked out on to the yard. The Friesians were ambling towards the gate. They took turns to enjoy the distractions of familiar sights. Sometimes one would pause to give a bellow, puffing silver bells of breath into the sharp sunny air. Stella understood their lack of concentration, and smiled at the sight of Prue and Ag urging them on, with the occasional tentative whack of a stick. Prue's pink bow had lost some of its former buoyancy but still fluttered among her blonde curls like a small demented bird. She bounced and jiggled and enjoyed shouting bossily to the cows. In contrast, Ag walked with large dignified strides, never raising her voice. There was something both peaceful and wistful in her face. Stella felt drawn to this girl, wondered about her.

The last cow left the yard. At that moment two men came out of the barn. Stella assumed the tall one to be Joe, and recognised at once the shape of the man she had seen last night. His hand was on the shoulder of the much older man who wore thickly corrugated breeches and highly polished lace-up boots, the uniform of grooms before the last war. Joe seemed to be trying to persuade the old man of something, and was meeting resistance. On their way across the yard, Joe looked up and spotted Stella.

'Breakfast,' he shouted, but did not wait for her.

The idea of breakfast reminded Stella of her hunger. But reluctant to go into the kitchen alone, she made her way down the lane to meet the others returning from the meadow. They, too, declared their hunger. All three compared stiff joints and cold fingers, and hurried back to the farmhouse.

By the time they reached the kitchen the three men were already half-way through huge plates of bread, bacon, eggs, tomatoes and black pudding. Mrs Lawrence was shifting half a dozen more eggs in a pan at the stove. She wore the same faded cross-over pinafore as yesterday, which hid all but the matted brown wool of the sleeves of her jersey. There was something extraordinarily detached, but reassuring, in her back view, thought Ag. It was as if the outer woman was performing her chores, while an independent imagination also existed to power her through the mundane matters of daily life.

Mr Lawrence introduced Ratty to the girls, remembering all their names, having checked with his wife. Ratty, a man of economy in his acknowledgements, made his single nod in their direction extend to all three of them. In that brief moment of looking up, Ag observed his extraordinary eyes, grained with all the colours of a guinea fowl's breast. Here was a man who would provide much material for her diary, she felt, as she sat beside him, unafraid of his distinctive silence. Prue took her chance to sit next to Joe. Mr Lawrence observed her choice with a hard, flat look.

'Well, we got through that all right, I'd say, didn't we, Joe?' Prue turned to the others. 'I did twelve cows, Joe did the other eight. Just think, only a few more hours to go and we start all over again, don't we, Joe?'

Joe shook his head. 'Not me. Dad's on the afternoon milk.'

Prue's face fell. She accepted the plate of fried things from Mrs Lawrence and concentrated on eating.

Mr Lawrence, finishing first, seemed eager to be away. He outlined the chores for the rest of the morning. Ag was to help Mrs Lawrence with the henhouse, and try to patch up the tarpaulin roof. Prue was to sluice down the cowshed, sterilise the buckets, scour the dairy, and put the milk churns into the yard. 'Ready,' he added, 'for the cart. Think you'll manage to get them on to the cart, Prudence?'

Prue looked up from her eggs, alarmed, knowing what a churn full of milk must weigh. But she had no intention of looking feeble in Joe's eyes. 'Of course,' she said.

'I mean, you're at least a foot taller than a churn, aren't you?' Mr Lawrence's fragment of a smile indicated he was enjoying his joke.

Now he turned to his left, where Stella swabbed up egg yolk with a fat slice of bread. 'Know anything about horses?'

'A little.'

'Then you can come with me. We'll walk down to Long Meadow, give you an idea of the lie of the land.'

The three men rose, leaving their empty plates and mugs on the table. Mrs Lawrence sat down at last, with a boiled egg. Her cheeks were threadbare in the brightness, caverns of brown fatigue under both eyes. She cracked the egg briskly, looked round at the girls.

'You'll get used to it,' was all she said.

By the end of their first day, the land girls were exhausted. After four o'clock mugs of tea, they lay on their beds, trying to recover their energy for supper.

'If we're this fagged, what must poor Mrs Lawrence be?' asked Ag. 'Up before us, never a moment off her feet. And now cooking. Perhaps we should go down and help.'

'*Couldn't*,' sighed Prue. 'Twenty-four cows milked dry first day – ninety-six teats non-stop, you realise? That's me for day one. Finished.'

None of them moved, despite the guilty thought.

'We should be less stiff in a week or so,' said Ag, rubbing a painful shoulder, 'able to do more.'

'*More*?' giggled Prue. 'We're land girls, not slaves, I'll have you know.'

'I *liked* the day,' said Stella, sleepy. 'I liked the walk to get Noble, and then getting into a terrible muddle with the harness.'

'Mr Lawrence can't keep his eyes off you,' said Prue, after a while.

'What?'

'Haven't you noticed?'

'Don't be daft.'

Ag laughed. 'Your imagination, Prue,' she said, from her end of the room. 'I think Mr Lawrence is so giddied by our presence he doesn't know where to look. He's not used to women on the farm, or anywhere. But you can tell about him and Mrs Lawrence: soldered for life, I'd say. They don't have to speak, or even look. They're bound by the kind of wordless understanding that comes from years of happy marriage. My parents were like that, apparently.'

Prue sat up. She pulled the pink bow from her hair. 'Don't know about all that,' she said. 'My mum and dad love each other no end, but they don't half scream at each other night and day. Do you think we stay in these things for supper? I bloody *stink*. Cow, manure, Dettol – you name it, I reek of it. As for my nails . . .' She looked down at her hands. 'What are we going to do about our nails?'

'Give up,' said Stella, smiling.

'Not bloody likely. Land girl or not, I'm going to keep my nails, any road. Anyhow, what did you two think of him?'

'Who?' asked Ag.

'Joe, of course.'

'Seems nice enough. Shy.'

'*Nice enough*? Are you blind? Don't you recognise a real smasher when you see one? He's something, Joe, don't you realise, *quite out of the ordinary*? No easy fish, I reckon, but I'll take a bet. Joe Lawrence and I won't be too long before we make it.'

She looked from Stella to Ag, trying to read their reactions.

'There's Janet,' Ag said at last, 'isn't there?'

Prue giggled. 'Janet? Did you take a look at her photo? She's not what I'd call opposition.'

'But they're engaged,' said Stella.

'Long time till the spring.' Prue continued to study her nails. 'Anyhow, I'll keep you in touch with progress, if you're interested.'

'Immoral,' said Ag, half-smiling.

'Are you shocked?'

'Rather.'

'All's fair in love and war's my motto. And this *is* a war, remember? Don't know about you two, but I'm getting out of these stinking breeches. Green skirt, pink jersey, lashings of *Nuits de Paris*, whatever Mr Lawrence says, and Joe'll be beside himself, you'll see.'

While the other two laughed, Prue took a shocking-pink lipstick from a drawstring bag and concentrated on a seductive outline of her mouth. 'I've never gone for anyone so huge. What do you bet me?' She challenged Stella, the most likely to take on the bet. But Stella's mind had wandered far from Joe.

'The only bet I'm interested in,' she said, 'is whether or not I get a letter from Philip tomorrow. But *probably* he won't have time to write for ages.'

She wanted to begin the letter she had composed that morning. But tiredness overcame her good intentions.

By the time Prue had chosen the right pink from a row of nail polishes, and delivered her opinion about the hopelessness of men when it came to letter-writing, Stella was asleep. Ag, too, lay with her eyes shut and made no response. Pretty queer bunch, the three of them made, Prue couldn't help thinking, as she dabbed each nail with the brush of flamingo polish and wondered if her shell earrings, for supper, would be going too far.

Contrary to her predictions, the object of Prue's desire was far from beside himself at supper. He sat between his mother and Ag, silently eating chicken stew and mashed potatoes. He seemed not to notice the trouble Prue had taken with her appearance: spotted green bow in her hair, dazzling lipstick to match a crochet jersey, and smelling extravagantly of her Parisian scent. Mrs Lawrence, who as usual sat down at the table last, was the only one to react to all Prue's efforts. She sniffed, grimacing.

'Janet's coming, Sunday lunch, Joe,' she said. 'She rang while you were out.'

'Oh yes?'

'Janet,' Mrs Lawrence explained to the girls in general, 'manages to get here about once a month. It's a long journey. She's stationed in Surrey.'

'That's nice, her being able to get over at all,' said Prue.

'Nice for you, Joe.' A thousand calculations buzzed in her head. She gave Joe a smile he arranged not to see.

Mrs Lawrence's news failed to open a lively conversation. The aching girls became sleepier as they ate, only half listened to talk between Joe and Mr Lawrence about problems with the tractor. Supper over, they were invited into the sitting-room to listen to the news, but all volunteered to go to bed.

As the girls went upstairs – Mrs Lawrence insisted she needed no help with the washing-up – Prue observed Joe slip out of the front door. Where was he going? If her plan was to work, she must find out about his movements. The idea excited her enough to dispel her sleepiness. When the other two were in bed, their lights quickly out, she went to the window, stared moodily down at the farmyard. She saw Joe mount his bicycle by the barn and ride out through the gate. If his beloved Janet was three counties away, who was it he was going to see? Prue remained at the window, intrigued, until eventually she heard a distant church clock strike nine. Cold by now, she went to her bed, but could not sleep for the dancing of her plans.

On the stroke of nine from the same church clock, Ratty Tyler, sitting by the range in his small kitchen, knocked out his pipe and rose to make his wife a cup of tea. Edith was ensconced at the kitchen table, a dish of newly iced buns beside her, all ready to cause distress among early customers next morning. The dim light, over-protected by a dark tin shade, was pulled down as far as its iron pulley would go. Edith's hands, parsnip coloured in its murky beam, concentrated on the darning of a sock.

'So?' she said.

'So what?'

Ratty had been waiting for this all evening. He had observed the difficulty Edith had had, holding herself in, all through their soup and bread and cheese.

51

'What're they like?'

'What're who like?'

'You know what I'm saying, Ratty Tyler.'

'That I don't.'

Edith sighed, bit off a new length of grey wool with her dun teeth.

'The girls.'

'The land girls?'

'Of course the land girls. What other girls would I be asking about?'

Ratty gave her question some thought. 'Just girls, far as I could see,' he offered eventually. He put a cup of tea on the table. There were more questions to come, he could see that. He must play for time. Anything for time.

'Where's the sugar?'

'Same place it's always been for the last thirty years. Your mind must be elsewhere.'

It was elsewhere, all right. It was always elsewhere when he came home.

'I was thinking about Mrs L., so happens,' he said. 'Taking on the girls eases some problems, but makes a lot more work for her.'

'Pah!' spat Edith, disbelieving. 'Never known you trouble yourself about Mrs L. before. It's the girls you were thinking of, I've no doubt.' Her needle, newly charged with wool, dived swift as a kingfisher towards its prey of a hole in a brownish heel. 'You may as well tell me.'

Ratty placed the sugar bowl by the cup, returned to his chair. For peace, he thought, he may as well.

'There's the small one,' he said.

'Name?'

'Prudence, they call her.' He judged it not worth referring to her as Prue, as the others did. The implications of a nickname would be bound to set Edith's fears alight.

'Huh!' She was easily offended by mere names. Her indignation came as no surprise. 'What's she like?'

What was she like? Ratty asked himself. Prudence was the one with a face like the girls photographed in newspapers on the first day of spring. Small, but frightening. He wouldn't fancy time alone with her.

'As I said, not large. Nothing to write home about.'

Ratty had intended to say something more definite about her, to assure his wife that the girl, young enough to be their granddaughter, was no threat of any kind. But he feared that silent cogitation, striving for the right description, might itself inspire further suspicion. He need not have worried. For some reason Edith was not interested in the idea of Prue.

'And the others?'

'There's the medium one, the one I took to Hinton in the cart with the milk. Not much experience in harnessing up.'

No point in saying she'd been mighty quick to learn, that one. He'd shown her what to do his side of Noble: she copied quick as a flash on her side. And lovely manners. All polite remarks about the countryside, on their way to the village, and doing more than her fair share of unloading the churns. Nice face, too. He liked her.

'Name?'

'Stella.'

'Nothing like Cousin Stella?'

Ratty shook his head. Edith's Cousin Stella was the nearest to a witch he knew. No comparison with this girl. He smiled at the thought, knowing his wife, in her quick glance, would misunderstand his expression.

'You lay your hands on a Stella and it would be *incest*,' snapped Edith in the furious voice she used for her most illogical remarks.

'No fear of that.'

'And the last one?'

She was suspicious, here, Ratty could tell. *How* could she be suspicious? He cursed her instincts.

'The tall one. Agatha. Ag, they call her.'

'Much taller than you?'

'Good foot,' he said, permitting himself the exaggeration of an inch or so.

Edith contained a sigh of relief. 'You've never liked a tall girl.'

'No.'

Foxed her! Ag was the one he liked even more than Stella. He'd studied her for a long time from his unseen position in the barn. There was something about her kind, private face that had struck him. He had been intrigued by the way her short hair had blown apart while she was sweeping, so he had had glimpses of white scalp. Reminded him of watching a blackbird in a wind, feathers parting to show white skin of breast. If he'd met someone like Ag when he was a lad, Lord knows, he'd have done something about it.

'Blonde?'

'Dark.'

'You've never liked dark hair, neither.' Edith briefly touched her own white fuzz of thinning curls.

'I haven't, neither.'

He saw the tension in Edith's body slacken. She held the darned sock away from her, admiring the woven patch she had accomplished with such speed and skill. It would go unacknowledged by Ratty, like all the darns she had held up over the years. It wasn't that he lacked appreciation, but words to express it froze before he could utter them. Hence the constant disappointment he caused her.

'And what did they make of you?'

Ratty sucked on his empty pipe. Although he had anticipated this one, no firm answer had come to mind.

'We chattered nineteen to the dozen, all very friendly,' he heard himself say. Reflecting on this lie, he considered it permissible, after so much partial truth.

Edith sniffed. 'You be careful what you say.'

'You can trust me.'

'You were all sweet words when you were young.'

Ratty shifted. This was the nearest to a compliment Edith had paid him in three decades. It made him uneasy. He could never confront her with the truth: how she had killed the sweet words very early in their marriage by her laughter, her scoffing. It was she who caused his prison of silence when it came to women. The banners, with all the things he wanted to say written on them, still danced in his mind, sometimes, but their benefits went unknown, locked into wordless silence. No problems with Mr Lawrence, with Joe. On occasions he could even mutter a word or two to Mrs L. But three strange new girls all up at the farm in one day . . . to have spoken was quite beyond him.

'Time to turn on the news,' said Edith, picking another sock from the basket with the curious gentleness that she employed for inanimate things.

'So it is. I'll do it.'

Ratty felt his bones soften with relief as he got up – land girl conversation over for tonight. He hoped it wouldn't come up again for a while: give him time to gather his thoughts. Edith gave a small nod of her head, which was the nearest, these days, she ever got to a smile. She could never get the hang of the wireless, understand the tuning. Ratty twiddled the knob. His skill in finding the Home Service was one of the small ways in which he could oblige his wife with very little effort. Had she known the paucity of this effort, her appreciation might have been less keen. As it was, admiration for her husband's technical ability was conveyed in a small but regular sigh that Ratty had learned to recognise. The fierceness went out of her needle.

Three

L and girls were entitled to one and a half free days a week. Mrs Lawrence suggested that this first week they took Sunday off, even though they had only been working for two days. Unused to the physical activity, they would be needing the rest, she said. The girls conceded gratefully. They offered to make sandwiches and go off somewhere for a picnic lunch, keep out of the way. But Mrs Lawrence responded by asking them to stay to lunch with the family: Janet would be coming. She'd like them to meet Janet.

At five a.m. Prue, waking suddenly, remembered she had no need to get up. About to return luxuriously to sleep, a picture came to her mind of Joe alone in the cowshed. He would have to do all the milking himself today. When did *he* have any time off?

In a moment, Prue was out of bed, all sleepiness gone. She dressed quickly and quietly so as not to disturb the others, and chose a yellow satin bow for her hair. What a surprise she would give him. How pleased he would be – someone to share the work on a Sunday.

Creeping downstairs, Prue heard voices in the kitchen: Joe and his mother talking. She had no wish to dull the impact of her good deed by joining them for a mug of tea, so she crept towards the front door.

As she put out her hand to turn the key, she heard a sound like the slap of a hand on the kitchen table. And, distinctly, the shouting of angry words.

'You just take care, Joe!'

'Mind your own business, Ma.'

Prue's heartbeat quickened. Silly old interfering thing, Mrs Lawrence. His age, Joe could do what he bloody well liked. Quickly she opened the door.

In the cowshed the animals were chained in their stalls, restless as always before milking (how quickly she had come to learn their ways!), heads tossing, tails lashing, muted stamps of impatience. Prue fetched bucket and pail, began work on the first cow.

Joe arrived by the time the bucket was half full – she was an even faster milker by now. He must surely be aware of how quickly she'd learned. Prue felt his gaze upon her, from the doorway, but did not look up. She heard the slish and thud of his footsteps as he strode towards her. Still she made no acknowledgement of his presence, kept her head dug into Pauline's bony side. She knew her yellow bow was badly flattened, but resisted releasing one hand to puff it into life.

'What're you doing here? It's Sunday. It's meant to be your day off.'

Joe's voice was far from grateful. For a full minute Prue listened to the rhythmic hiss of the milk she was drawing from the cow's abundant udder, calculating her answer.

'I woke as usual. Thought you'd be glad of the help.'

'You did, did you?'

She could hear Joe moving away with surly tread. Why had her kind act so annoyed him? She felt the sickness of having made a bad decision. There was nothing she could do but carry on: she managed to avoid him each time she finished a cow and had to collect an empty bucket. The two hours went by in a frenzy of speculation. What had she done wrong? How could she put matters right? Usually, she could rely on the soundness of her instincts. This morning no answer came.

When Prue finished milking the last cow she stood up

and saw that Joe was no longer in the shed. Well, bugger him, she thought: he hasn't half taken advantage of my kind offer. Leaves me most of the work, then buggers off early to breakfast.

She stomped crossly up the aisle, swinging her last full bucket. Milk splashed on to the floor, mixing with streaks of chocolate-coloured water, paling it to a horrible khaki, that warlike colour Prue so hated. Bugger everything, she thought. I'm off back to bed.

Joe was standing by the cooling machine, arms folded, blank-faced, impervious to its insinuating whine. Steam, escaping from the sterilising machine, blurred the handsome vision. Prue, nose furiously in the air, inwardly quaked. She sensed there was to be some kind of showdown, and dreaded it.

Then through the steam she saw – she was almost positive she saw – a tremor of a smile break his lips, though his eyes were hard upon her.

'Little minx,' he said.

In her surprise, Prue lowered her bucket to the ground too hard. Wings of milk flew over its edges, curdling on the concrete: she didn't care. Nothing mattered now except that she should conceal her sense of triumph.

'And *careful*, for Pete's sake,' she heard him say.

He bent and picked up the bucket, threw the milk into the cooling machine with something of her own carelessness. He could blooming well deal with the sterilising, Prue thought, heart a mad scattering of beats as she hurried out without speaking, pretending to ignore all messages.

In the short march from the cowshed to the kitchen – smell of frying bacon quickening the early air of the yard – Prue reflected on her good fortune. She thanked her lucky stars she had made the right decision. Joe's earlier behaviour, she had somehow failed to understand, was merely a form of teasing. He was no longer a problem. Her path was clear, Janet or no Janet. It was now just a matter of *when* and *how*, and at what point she should tell the others how right she had been.

While Stella and Ag helped Mrs Lawrence in the kitchen, Prue spent an hour of luxurious contemplation in the empty attic room as she re-did her nails, chose combs for her hair instead of a ribbon, and finally decided to wear her red crêpe dress with its saucy sweetheart neckline.

Coming downstairs – heavy skirt of the dress flicking from side to side, not without impact – she found Joe and his father in the hall, both dressed in tweed suits. Mr Lawrence carried a prayer book. Christ, one Sunday it would probably be to her advantage to go to *church* with them, she thought – though she hoped it would not have to come to that. She'd never exactly seen eye to eye with the church, all those boring hymns. But she didn't half fancy Joe in his posh suit, despite the egg on his tie. She smiled. Mr Lawrence, with a look of faint distaste, hurried towards the kitchen. That left her and Joe alone in the hall. She carried on smiling.

'Been *praying*?' she asked eventually.

'None of your sauce,' said Joe. He swung past her up the stairs, banged the door of his room.

None of your sauce . . . Prue went over the words carefully. He'd said them with such lightness of tone, in a voice so mock serious as to be transparent in its meaning, that for the second time that morning Prue found herself triumphant. How she enjoyed the careful analysis of that short remark! What he meant was, he wouldn't mind a *lot* of sauce, but he would be grateful if she was careful. Well, she'd never been one to enjoy upsetting any apple carts. She'd play the game by his rules, if that's what he wanted. But there was no reason not to enjoy herself until the time came.

Prue slipped into the kitchen where Mr Lawrence was polishing his shoes. The three women were all hard at

59

work, stirring, tasting, moving in and out of clouds of steam that billowed over the stove.

'Can I do the gravy or anything?' Prue asked.

'It's all done.' Mrs Lawrence sniffed, distaste less well disguised than her husband's. She seemed to have some sixth sense, aware no doubt of everything that went on under her roof. Her disapproval would be terrifying to behold.

Prue left the room.

She found herself in the yard, leaping over patches of mud on to small islands of dry ground, trying not to ruin her scarlet Sunday shoes. On reaching the barn – she had grown to like the barn – she crossed her arms under her breasts, shivering. It was a cold, sunless morning. She leaned against the icy metal mudguard of the tractor, making sure she was hidden from the house. There was no time to ask herself why she was there, the tractor her only companion, because almost at once a small navy Austin Seven, beautifully polished, drew up to the front door. Rigid with curiosity, Prue watched a girl – probably about her own age – get out of the car, lock the door with a fussy gloved hand. She wore a grey coat. Her hair was rolled into a bun. She stood looking about, as if disappointed there was no sign of Joe to greet her. Then she moved to the door and rang the bell. Prue decided the girl's prim little step, in highly polished lace-up shoes, was proprietorial.

Joe opened the door. They exchanged a few words, moved back to stand by the car. Joe seemed to be admiring it. He put a hand on the gleaming bonnet. Janet patted his arm, tipped back her head. She seemed to be asking for a share of his admiration. Joe bent down and gave her forehead the merest brush of his lips. Janet took his arm. Together, they went into the house.

That's all I need to know, Prue said to herself. She skipped back across the yard so fast she splashed both the red shoes and her thinnest pair of silk stockings, but she didn't care.

*

Janet sat on the edge of an armchair at one side of the fireplace in the sitting-room. Joe sat in the chair opposite, while the hard little sofa was occupied by Stella and Ag. Ag looked about the olive and green furnishings, the cracked parchment of the standard lamp, the faded prints of York Minster. Joe fiddled with a minute glass of sherry, cast in silence. Janet, who had refused a drink of any kind, feet crossed on the floor, hands asleep on her lap, registered in her pose something between demure good manners and disapproval. She had a long face and a down-turned mouth set awkwardly in a protruding chin, giving her a look of stubborn melancholy. The surprising thing was that, when she ventured a smile, her down-turned eyes turned up, and the plainness of her face became almost appealing.

Stella, sensing the awkwardness, felt she should make some effort at conversation.

'What is your actual job in the WAAF?' she asked.

'Sparking plug tester.' Janet thought for a while, decided to go on, seeing the genuine interest in Stella's face. 'What I want to be, eventually, is a radiographer. But I don't suppose I'll ever make it.' She shrugged, looked at Joe. The thought of disputing this did not seem to occur to him.

'I'm sure you will,' said Stella, surprised by Joe's meanness. 'I can't imagine what it must be like, the job of testing sparking plugs.'

'No, well, it's not that interesting. And the working conditions aren't very nice. All day in a cold and draughty warehouse, oil everywhere . . .' She trailed off, eyes on the door.

Prue flounced in, a dishcloth tied over her skirt.

'You must be Janet,' she said. 'I'm Prue. 'Scuse my apron.'

She smiled wickedly, shook hands with Janet whose incredulous pale face bleached further. Prue unknotted

61

the dishcloth and shook herself free as seductively as a striptease artist. Joe drank his few drops of sherry in one gulp, not looking at her.

'I've come to tell you dinner's ready.'

Janet stood up, straightened her grey flannel skirt.

'Where've you come from?' asked Prue. 'In that wonderful car!'

'It belongs to my parents. From Surrey, near Guildford.'

The sharpness of her reply brought Prue's bobbing about to a stop. She looked at Janet with a new curiosity.

'Never been to Surrey, myself,' she said. 'Isn't that rather a long way to come for Sunday dinner?'

'It is, but if it's my only chance to see Joe, then I don't mind the miles.'

Janet tipped her head back again, giving Prue a defiant little smile which she then dragged round to reach Joe. Ag, from her corner of the room, admired the girl's show of spirit. Janet took Joe's arm, indicated they should be the first to leave the room.

Possessive little Surrey madam we have here, thought Prue, and winked at Stella and Ag.

'Have you ever been to *Surrey*?' she asked them.

'Shut up, Prue,' said Ag.

Janet sat between Joe and Mr Lawrence. Prue, taking Ag's advice, resisted sitting on Joe's other side and chose a place opposite him. Mrs Lawrence helped everyone to large plates of roast pork and vegetables.

'You'd never know there was a war on here,' said Stella, desperately trying to ease the silence.

'You would if you had to eat in my canteen,' said Janet. 'Last week they ran out of custard powder. We had to have cornflour sauce with the jam roll. As for the chocolate shape . . .'

'I love chocolate shape,' offered Prue, solemnly. 'Anything chocolate, for that matter.'

'I've never made a chocolate shape. And now I can't get

62

chocolate,' said Mrs Lawrence, to fill another silence. She glanced at Prue. 'So I doubt I ever shall.'

'And your mother, Janet, how's she getting on?' Mr Lawrence, struggling to do his bit, cast a glance at his son.

'She's doing fine, Mr Lawrence. A lot on her plate, what with the WVS and the knitting group she's organised.'

'You said, Joe, you'd bring down those piles of magazines from the attic for Janet's mother.' Mrs Lawrence looked sharply at her son.

'I did,' said Joe. 'I'll put them in the car for you.'

This was his first direct remark to his beloved fiancée, Prue noticed. Perhaps they made up in private for their public reserve.

'Mother will be pleased. Thank you, Mrs Lawrence.' Janet turned to Joe. 'Will we have time for a stroll before I have to start back? Father said he'd rather I was home before dark.'

Joe looked at his watch. 'Depends,' he said, 'on how quickly I can get through the milking.'

He didn't look at the girls, but Mrs Lawrence's eyes travelled from Stella, to Ag, to Prue.

'I'll do the milking!' Prue turned to Joe. 'You and Janet go for your walk.'

'We'll help,' offered Ag quickly.

' 'Course we will,' said Stella.

'Well,' said Joe. 'If you insist.'

'We do.' Prue giggled.

'That's very, very kind,' said Janet. 'Joe and I are very, very grateful. We get so little time.'

Prue giggled again. 'Shall I bring in the apple pie, Mrs Lawrence?'

This gave her the chance to rise slowly from her seat with a small flick of her skirt. Janet's eyes, she was pleased to observe, were riveted by her narrow hips, small waist and the rise of bosom above the sweetheart neckline.

Praise for the pudding did little to brighten the dismal

lunch. When it was finally over, Mr Lawrence was the first to get up, with the air of one about to make an announcement. He addressed the land girls.

'Faith and I make it our business to be off duty till teatime on Sundays,' he said quietly. 'It's the only time we get for a rest.'

Stella, glancing at Mrs Lawrence, saw that her face had turned a thunderous colour.

Joe, also embarrassed, patted Janet on the shoulder. 'Come along, then, Jan. Hope you've brought your boots.'

'We'll bring the cows in,' said Stella, urging the other two to hurry.

'Race you,' called Prue, brushing past Janet and Joe.

Ag was the last to leave the room. As soon as she was out of the door she heard a wail from Mrs Lawrence.

'John! How dare you!'

'Sorry, love. Sorry. I wanted them out of the way, didn't know how –'

Ag hurried after the others, wanting to hear no more.

Back in their breeches, the three girls strode down the lane towards Lower Pasture to fetch in the cows. Prue's previous high spirits had subsided.

'Lucky Janet,' she said.

'Oh, I don't know. She doesn't seem to be getting much response,' said Stella.

Ag swung her stick through the long grass of the verge. She turned to Prue.

'You were rotten,' she said.

'Rotten? Why rotten?'

'All that flirting. Crucifying Janet.'

Prue laughed.

'For Christ's sake, if she can't take another girl smiling at her man, she'll be in for a bad time. Where I come from, all's fair in love and – besides, Joe needs cheering up, any

64

road. He's made a sodding great mistake. He needs a bit of fun.'

'Whatever he needs, it's not your business,' said Ag.

'Lay off, posh face.' Prue struck the grass with her own stick, harder than Ag.

'Come off it, you two.' Stella moved between them.

Prue ignored her, turned an angry face to Ag.

'What you're saying, *Agapanthus*, is you fancy Joe yourself.'

The absurd accusation, so insulting, whipped the colour from Ag's face. Their eyes met in mutual hostility, but Ag kept her control.

'I'm not saying that, no. You can have no idea how wrong you are.'

Prue thrashed once more, but less viciously, at the grass. The silence that followed was broken by the pooping of a small horn.

They turned to see the Austin Seven coming up behind them. Joe was driving. Janet, smiling, sat beside him. As they went by, everyone waved. With the passing of the car the tension eased.

'He looks quite happy, actually,' said Ag.

'He likes cars, I dare say,' said Prue. 'New cars like that.'

'Well, good luck to them.' Stella's thoughts were more concerned with Philip and herself. She had had no word from him.

Prue looked at Ag, suddenly contrite.

'Sorry. Once I fancy a man, some devil gets into me.'

'You take care,' said Ag. 'Think of Janet.'

'I'm not one to upset apple carts, believe me.' Prue ruffled her curls, smiling again.

At the gate to the field all three girls paused for a moment, arms resting on the top bar, eyes on the herd of impatient cows. Ag thought that with any luck she could return to *Jude the Obscure* in just over two hours: so far, there had been little chance to read. Stella began to compose her next letter to Philip. Prue sighed.

'Wonder what they're up to,' she said. 'I can't imagine Joe would get very far with that grey skirt, can you?'

Mr Lawrence made sure that he was downstairs before the girls came in from the cowsheds. There were disadvantages, having your house full of strangers. But on the whole, judging by this week, the advantages outweighed them. Faith had been right about the land girls: they were shaping up pretty well. Faith was right about most things.

He cut thick slices of her home-made bread, hungry. But calm. The nervous energy, the buzz of anxiety that had been hounding him since the girls' arrival, had been dissipated by the hour of making love to his wife. As on all Sunday afternoons, he felt powerful. He alone was able to chase the rigidity from Faith's bones, soothe the tension, make her smile. The fascination of this regular unwinding of his wife never wore off, and the tea that followed, prepared by him, was the occasion he most looked forward to in the week. Newly bound together in a way that never became stale or mundane, Sunday afternoons revived John Lawrence's scattered energies, strengthened him for the days ahead.

Slowly, gravely, the farmer spread the bread with butter, put fruit cake on a plate, a spoon beside a jar of Faith's gooseberry jam. He wished the present silence could go on for hours, the girls never return, the war be over. But in a few moments they would be back, hungry. Nice of them to have done the milking, give Joe an hour or so with Janet. The girls, the girls . . . that Stella girl. As John stirred the tea, he found himself facing the truth – something that usually, in his busy days, he had no time to afford himself. But here it was confronting him, in all its starkness: he no longer felt unnerved by Stella. The curious, unwanted sensations she had aroused in him so unexpectedly, almost as soon as he met her, had abated. Further probing of the devil that had taunted him – and here the flow of milk from jug to cup wavered – found the exact nature of those feelings put into words: old man's lust. Disgusting, shaming, horrible. He was fifty-three, married a long time, never looked at anyone but Faith, had never had the opportunity to be tempted. Then an entrancing creature young enough to be his daughter arrives, and the unsettled feeling she causes him is like an illness he's unable to shake off.

Until now. Now, normal again, he could trust himself. What he would do to prove this would be to test himself. The test would be a simple one – nothing dangerous. On Monday, he would switch the girls' jobs around (good idea to make sure they could all do anything) and take Stella hedging with him. He'd enjoy teaching her the skill. At the end of the day he'd invite the others to help with a bonfire. By that means the ghost would be laid: he could never have cause for shame again.

Faith came in quietly, dark skin burnished in the deep afternoon light. She tied an apron over her Sunday skirt, stood straight and noble as she poured tea, the merest smile on her lips as she glanced at the thickness of butter on bread.

'Rationing, remember.'

'It's our own.'

'All the same.' Mrs Lawrence sat. 'I hid the last pot of damson jam. Do you want some before the girls come?'

Her small, innocent conspiracies were always a delight to her husband. He shook his head.

'Not today. They're good girls.'

'Not at all bad.'

Mrs Lawrence blushed for the second time that afternoon. Her husband read her thoughts.

'I've said I'm sorry. I'll say it again.'

'No need to go on.'

'What we could do is walk up to The Bells for a drink and a sandwich. Ratty'll be there.'

'Escaping Edith.' Faith laughed. 'He'd be so surprised to see us it might unnerve him altogether. It's been an alarming enough week for him anyway with the girls.'

'We wouldn't have to face them if we went to The Bells.'

'I don't mind facing them. Don't suppose Joe'd be very happy alone with the three of them, Prudence fluttering her eyelashes. Besides, you'd miss a rice pudding. And it's *Postscript*, remember. Can't see you missing Mr Priestley. We'll stay where we are.'

They heard the slam of a door, voices.

The girls burst in, socks and breeches muddy, bringing cold air with them. They had been for a long walk, got lost on the way back, had problems helping Prue over a stile. As they ate hungrily, laughing, easy, Mr Lawrence reckoned their minds had been far from Faith and himself, and felt relieved. This was the first meal, he observed, at which polite conversation had given way to real banter, merriment. Joe, who had slipped in just as the last of the bread and butter had been taken, seemed surprised by the laughter, the unusual liveliness. He sat by his mother, who cut him a vast slice of cake. He ignored Prue's surreptitious looks. Maybe he genuinely was not aware of them, but they did not go unobserved by Mr Lawrence, who for once was pleased to see his son's face as inscrutable as ever. He was a hard one to fathom, Joe. Always had been. Bit of fluff like Prudence would never get the measure of him, of that Mr Lawrence was sure. All the same, Janet's flat grey skirt and flat grey voice came to mind, and he felt uncomfortable. It didn't do to think too much about Janet. He slid his eyes to Stella: beautiful – despite mud on her cheeks, hair blown into tangles, total lack of make-up. She smiled at him, innocent. It did nothing to him. His resolve remained firm. Tomorrow he would teach her to lay a hedge.

That night, the girls joined the Lawrences by the wood fire in the sitting-room. Mrs Lawrence darned, Prudence repainted her nails, Ag half-concentrated on a crossword puzzle. Stella just sat, her mind on Philip. While they all listened to J. B. Priestley decrying the government's policy against ordering potatoes to be sold for a penny a pound,

Mr Lawrence gave Stella several glances, wondering at her preoccupation. Still he felt nothing but safety.

But at breakfast next morning the resolve wavered, then fled. The stirrings of disloyalty, an uncontrollable physical thing, assaulted him as he watched her sip her tea. He wondered at her distraction. She kept glancing at the window. When the postman arrived, she leapt up before Faith and took the bundle of letters from him through the window. Quickly she shuffled through them and snatched for one for herself. She slipped it into her back pocket with a look of such vivid joy Mr Lawrence knew he would have to change his plans. He could not hedge all day beside a girl in such rapture, and not be moved, tempted, agonised. She was all smiles again, now: pink cheeks, a portrait of high expectation. Happy the man who is loved by her, thought Mr Lawrence, and realised his wife's eyes were heavy upon him.

'I need someone to help with the last of the damsons,' she said.

'I'd be willing,' volunteered Stella at once.

'In that case, I'll take Agatha hedging with me,' said Mr Lawrence, 'and as for you, young Prudence, you can have your way at last. When the sheds are sluiced down, there's Upper Meadow to be ploughed. Joe'll explain the Fordson to you – she's a temperamental old thing, some days. He'll take you up there. Then you're on your own.'

'*Mr* Lawrence! I'll not let you down. You'll not see a straighter furrow,' Prue squealed. She put down her tea, flung excited arms round his neck. 'Thank you, thank you!'

Mr Lawrence awkwardly disentangled himself from her embrace, to laughter from the others. Even Joe was smiling.

'Calm down, child,' he said, 'and don't be surprised if the novelty wears thin after a couple of hours in the metal seat.'

'You wait,' she said. 'My *dedication* to the plough will

surprise the lot of you. Down in half a tick, Joe. Just do my lipstick. Never know who you might meet in a furrow . . .'

Faith explained that, as the last of the damsons were to be made into chutney and jam, there was no need to take great care in the picking. Picking plums for sale, the day before, Stella had chosen only perfect fruit.

She carried a large basket and a stepladder to the orchard, and made for the last unpicked tree, its branches weighed down by a heavy crop.

It was a fine, warm morning. The freak frosts of last week had not returned: Mr Lawrence said it had been the finest summer for many years. Its warmth overflowed into autumn, tempered with an almost imperceptible breeze.

Stella made firm the stepladder and climbed up, buried to the waist in branches and leaves. She liked fruit picking, had enjoyed stripping several trees of apples and plums, though she was still not half as fast or skilled as Mrs Lawrence, who had worked beside her the first few days.

In her last letter to Philip, Stella had tried to describe how she enjoyed the privacy of leaves, their green flickering with sun and shadow all about her, the whispery silence snapped by the breaking of a twig or the rhythmic thud of the new fruit dropping into the basket. Even as she wrote such things, she had been aware of her mistake. In their short acquaintance, Philip had never shown much interest in nature: most probably all he wanted to hear were declarations of undying devotion. She had included those, of course, at the end, but had wanted to convey what it felt like, this strange land girl life – one moment so funny, milking the rubber cow, another so hidden, among the fruit. She had written him three letters. By now, although her impatience for a reply was almost unbearable, she decided to prolong the agony. The reading of the letter would be a reward for filling the basket.

Stella picked faster than ever before, with agitated

70

fingers. Yellow freckles were beginning to splatter the leaves. Some of the fruit had burst upon the stem. From the gashes in the flesh, a kind of transparent gelatinous stuff had bubbled up and hardened, and sparkled fiercely as crystal. Stella threw these wounded fruit into the long grass under the tree. Sometimes she tried to polish a damson before eating it, but could not brush the blue haze from its skin. Damsons could not be made to shine like plums. Each fruit has its reasons, she supposed: fruits had as many different habits as roses. But she was too excited to dwell further on the nature of damsons, and as she was alone in the orchard she sang 'The Rose of Tralee' out loud in her clear voice. The letter burned in her pocket.

The basket was full. Stella wedged it between two branches. She could see no more damsons within reach. Her brown arms were warm, her job well done. She settled herself on the platform of the stepladder in an archway of branches, tore at the envelope of cheap paper that was standard issue for officers on HMS *Apollo*. There was a single sheet within. As Stella began reading, the leaf shadow jigged among the words, at first confusing.

My dear Stella,

    Thanks very much for your letters. Glad to hear you are enjoying life as a land girl so far, and get on with the other two.

    Here, it's the usual routine. We've been escorting Channel convoys all week, not very interesting, no trouble. I shall be glad when we go up to Liverpool, not that there's much change of scenery at sea.

    Last night I gave Number One a game of draughts in the Wardroom. His bark is worse than his bite. He's quite friendly, really.

    You keep asking me about leave and when we can meet. I go for a gunnery course at Portsmouth in a couple of weeks and will probably get a night off after that. Perhaps I could make a detour on my way back to Plymouth,

though with no car getting cross country would be difficult.
We'll probably have to wait for a boiler clean, when I'll get
five days. Then, if you could make it, we could manage
something. Forgive short note, I'm due for the mid-watch.
Somehow, I've managed never to be late so far. Miracle!
Careful of those cows. Will try to write again, soon.
Love, Philip.

Stella read the letter twice, incredulous. She crumpled up
the horrible paper, then quickly straightened it out again,
returned it to the envelope and put it back in her pocket.
There was nothing between those lines: nothing, nothing.
She lifted down the basket of damsons – oh, the stupid
hope that had speeded her picking! – struggled back down
the ladder, and set it on the ground. Then she sat in the
grass beside it, leaned back against the trunk of the tree.
She found tears of furious disappointment plundering her
cheeks. She bit her knuckles to silence her sobs. How could
he? How could a man who so recently had declared himself so passionately in love write such a hopeless, useless
letter, giving her no indication of how life was at sea, how
he felt, how he loved and missed her? Whereas she had
done so much describing, so much declaring.

When the worst of her sobs were over, a new thought
came. Perhaps it was merely that Philip didn't like writing
letters. There were, amazingly, such people. A dynamic
communicator of the flesh, perhaps he suffered from gross
disability when it came to expressing himself on paper.
Perhaps he had no notion of the pleasure of winging
thoughts to someone else, or indeed the pleasure such a
letter would give. That must be it, surely. No man was perfect, and the man she loved had just one small
imperfection: rotten at letters. There could be many worse
faults: she must consider herself lucky. Besides, once the
war was over, there would be no need to correspond. They
would be married almost at once.

Consoled by such thoughts, although they scarcely added up to a satisfactory solution, Stella got up at last, lifted the heavy basket of damsons. She dried her tears with the coarse wool of her sleeve, and turned to make her way back to the farm. Joe was coming towards her, not ten yards away. There was no escaping him.

With just a yard between them, he stopped. 'Anything wrong?'

Stella sniffed, managed a smile. 'Not really, thanks. Just overcome by my first letter from Philip.'

'Ah. He's, what . . .?'

'Sub-lieutenant. HMS *Apollo*. Escorting convoys across the Channel, that sort of thing. Nothing exciting. Hasn't seen any fighting yet.'

'Lucky.'

'Anyway . . .' Stella shrugged, prepared to move.

'It must be worrying. I mean, all the time.'

Stella nodded. 'The missing,' she said. 'The waiting for leave. The not knowing. Still, after the war we'll get married straight away. At least, I suppose we will.'

'Might not be too long a wait.'

'Hope not. *You* must know what it's like: you and Janet. Waiting.'

'I was on my way to see how Prue was getting on,' said Joe, as if he had not heard her. 'If there's a single wavy furrow, there'll be trouble.'

Stella found herself laughing.

Leaning against the gate, Joe watched Prue for some time before she saw him. The tractor was at the far end of the field, its snorting reduced to a distant stutter. The tiny figure of its driver, very upright, was bobbing up and down on the seat, so light she was bounced by every jolt. There was a speck of colour just visible on her head – a scarlet bow. In the air just behind her, a flotilla of gulls dipped and soared, while on the ground the dark earth was dragged into a

73

sluggish wave by the teeth of the ploughshare.

The tractor disappeared down a dip in the land, the noise of its engine now even fainter. A hundred yards to the hedge, Joe calculated, then it would have to turn. He waited to see it reappear over the slope.

But there was sudden, complete silence. After a few moments, Joe shifted his position. He made no move to enter the field. For some minutes, weight on the gate, he let his eyes follow a collection of clouds that chased, crashed, snapped off and went their newly ragged ways. At last a couple of snorts puckered the silence, then the rhythmic stutter began again, and the gulls reappeared.

Joe's eyes never left the tractor as it chuntered towards him across the long field: he saw the precise moment Prue noticed him, clutched harder at the steering wheel, deciding not to wave. She had managed almost a quarter of the field – not fast, but reasonably straight. When Prue was almost at the gate she stopped the tractor, but did not turn off the engine.

'How'm I doing?' she shouted.

Joe touched his forelock with a seriousness to match hers.

'Not bad. Not bad at all.'

'I've had trouble stalling.'

'Remembered to put in the paraffin?'

' 'Course.'

'And the sewing-machine oil?'

'What d'you take me for?'

'How about the plugs?'

'I checked them, idiot.'

'I'll look at her when you come in.' He made to open the gate.

'I'm not coming.' Prue began to pull at the heavy steering wheel, a dimpling of sweat on her nose and scarlet cheeks. 'So don't bother.'

'It's lunch-time, near as dammit.'

'I'm not eating a thing till I've finished this bloody field.'
Their eyes met.

'Very well,' shouted Joe. 'I'll tell Ma . . .'

The tractor was turning. She managed it with skill. For several moments longer, deep in thought, Joe watched the bobbing and leaping of her small bottom and the bow on her bouncing hair, then made his way to the barn.

'Trouble with hedges is they don't stand still,' Mr Lawrence explained to Ag as they walked the lane carrying their hooks, bill-hooks and slashers. 'They get in the hell of a mess if they're not cared for, sprawling out into the fields either side, clogging the ditches. Some people think hedging's a boring business, but I'm not one of them. In fact, there's no job on the farm I like better. You've got something to show for your work very quickly, besides a pile of firewood. There's a lot of satisfaction.'

Ag nodded in silence, wondering how skilled she would be at wielding the heavy tools.

They arrived at the destined thorn hedge, which divided a recently cut cornfield from a strip of mangolds. There were ditches, invisible under a mess of bramble and wayward shoots, both sides. Ag let her eyes trail the length of the hedge, which ended at the entrance to a small copse. She doubted her enthusiasm for trimming it into shape would match that of her employer, but gave a gallant smile.

'Don't despair,' said Mr Lawrence. 'You'll soon get the hang of it.'

He started to hack dead wood from the bottom, singling out new young shoots to judge their worthiness of being left to flower. The hedge, he explained, was a windbreak, so it should be left at a good height.

'I've been neglecting it, though, what with all the extra work,' he said. 'It takes time and a certain skill, that I will say, to lay a hedge decently, but it's a pleasing sort of task, to my mind. What you want to do is get a flexible stem, like this, weave it through other wood across a hole – something like darning – and make sure it's secure, won't pull out in a wind. Next spring, shoots will start to appear from every joint.' He turned to Ag for a moment, judged from her expression she understood. 'Best thing to do is you watch a while, then get into the ditch behind me and gather any stuff I throw down for a bonfire. When you're not dealing with my stuff you can start hacking away at the sides of the ditch: neaten it all up.'

Once Mr Lawrence had given his instructions he no longer seemed aware of Ag's presence, concentrating fully on the complicated geography of the thorn hedge. For a long time, Ag watched his deft gloved hands foraging in the leaves, weaving shoots, snapping off dead wood, hacking at stubborn joints with his slasher. She was glad he had not asked her to begin in front of him, and after a while began her own task of clearing the ditch. She stood on its muddy floor, a stream of brown water lying slackly around her boots. Slashing at the long grass and brambles was not hard and when, after twenty minutes, she paused to look back on the neat bank of her own making, she began to understand her employer's pleasure in the job.

After an hour, they paused for a few minutes' rest. The sun was high by now and they were hot. Mr Lawrence rolled up his sleeves. Ag, with aching back, sat a few feet from him on the ground. Mr Lawrence took a packet of Craven A from his pocket, offered her one, which she refused, and lit his own. They sat in easy silence, their eyes following the smoke.

'Finding it hard, this land girl business?' Mr Lawrence asked eventually.

'I ache a bit. We all do. But we're enjoying it.'

'Good, good. It's healthy work, anyway. As for the war . . . Terrible in London last night, they said on the radio this morning. Poor devils.'

'We're lucky here. Hardly aware of it.'

'Only danger is those German buggers dropping off their bombs on the way home. That happened not twenty miles from here just before you came. Flattened half a village, killed two.'

Ag's burning face was beginning to cool. The sweat on her back was drying. Mr Lawrence drew deeply on his cigarette. The smoke smelt pungent, good. A churring and a flapping of wings behind them broke the silence. A speckled bird flew into the sky, swerving towards the copse.

'Bugger me if it's not a mistlethrush, a storm cock. Haven't seen one for a week or so,' said Mr Lawrence. He gave a small smile. 'I used to know the Latin name.'

Ag paused. Then she said: '*turdus viscivorus*, isn't it?'

'That's right. That's it! Stone the crows – are you a scholar?'

Ag laughed. 'Far from it. But my father used to teach me about birds.'

'Know some of its other names?'

'I know shrite, and skite.'

'How about gawthrush?'

'Gawthrush, yes. And garthrush?'

'Then there's the more common jercock: Ratty talks of jercocks.'

'How about syecock?'

'I'd forgotten syecock.' Mr Lawrence stubbed out his cigarette. 'So you know your birds,' he said quietly. 'That's good. That's quite unusual, these days.' He smiled. 'Here's a bit of rum information for you: did you know there's a saying that a mistletoe berry won't germinate till it's passed through the body of a mistlethrush?'

'I've heard of that, yes. I think the idea came from the Roman writer Pliny.'

The expression on Mr Lawrence's face made Ag bite her lip.

'Did it, now? There's university education for you.' He stood up brusquely, took up his bill-hook. Ag feared she had offended him in some way. Perhaps the airing of such arcane knowledge sounded boastful. 'Joe got into Cambridge, you know,' Mr Lawrence said, back to her, surveying the hedge again. 'Rotten luck he wasn't able to go.'

Two hours later Ag had cleared several yards of ditch, and had made a large pile of undergrowth for burning. Her back ached horribly. Despite thick socks, her feet were cold in her Wellingtons from standing in the stream, and a blister seared her heel. Reluctant to say she had had enough for one morning, she remembered a promise to Mrs Lawrence.

'I said I'd bring in the eggs before lunch. Would it be all right –?'

'Off you go,' shouted Mr Lawrence, no pause in his slashing at a root. 'Thanks for the help. You've done pretty well.'

Ag hobbled back down the lane, coarse wool chafing her blister. She was hot, sweating, tired, hungry. The thought of a whole afternoon's hedging was daunting, though perhaps lunch would recharge her. Hedging and ditching were hard work, she thought, but she had enjoyed it. She had enjoyed her bird conversation with Mr Lawrence: funny man – sudden spurts of talk, then back to long, concentrated silences.

As soon as Ag reached the barn she sat on a pile of straw and began to pull at her boot. As she struggled, she wondered if there was any valid excuse for sending a postcard to Desmond. She knew instinctively, from the few brief conversations they had had, he would enjoy hearing about her life as a land girl. But what excuse would she have to write to him in the first place? He might not even remember her – despite her explanation about her odd name. He might have no recollection of their occasional meetings, which he believed were by chance. To write would perhaps embarrass, confuse, or, worse, warn him off an unwanted affection on Ag's part. So the answer to the question she asked herself was *no*: she should not write to him. Wait till it was time for a Christmas card.

Depressed by the solution she had known for days she would come to, Ag looked up to see Joe watching her.

'Can I help?' he asked. 'Looks as if you're having a bit of trouble.'

'Thanks.'

Ag lifted her leg. Joe pulled at the boot with both hands. It came off easily.

'You should put fresh chalk inside,' he said. 'We've got some in the house. Makes them much easier to get off and on.'

'Right. I will.'

'How did the hedging go?'

'I enjoyed it. I liked watching your father. His skill and speed are amazing. And I liked looking back to see the job I'd done on the few yards of ditch. Certain feeling of job satisfaction. I can agree with him there.'

'Looks as though Prue's experiencing some of that, too. She's managed a third of the field but refuses to stop till she's finished the lot. As a matter of fact, she's done rather well.'

They both smiled. Joe sat down opposite Ag. He watched her as she rolled off her thick wool sock, and the thin one beneath it. He watched her bending the leg so that she could look closely at the blister on her heel.

'It must be a funny contrast, this life, with Cambridge,' he said eventually.

Ag shrugged. She touched the soft swelling with a gentle finger.

'Well, that had come to an end anyway. I only half wanted to do a graduate course. I wasn't really sure what I wanted to do, in fact. Farm work gives me plenty of time to think.'

'I was due to go to Trinity,' said Joe.

'You still could, couldn't you? When all this is over.'

'Suppose I still could. Though I don't much fancy being a mature undergraduate.'

'Lots of others will be in the same position.'

'True. Meantime, the brain's rotting.'

'No!' Ag smiled.

'It is. When do I have time to read? It's a sixteen-hour day here. I listen to music on my gramophone when I'm in bed – five minutes later I'm asleep, book in hand.'

'I know what you mean.'

'So I might have to ask your help for some mental limbering up.'

'Fine! Sunday afternoons I could tutor you in the *Iliad*.' They both laughed. 'That is, if Janet wouldn't mind.'

'Janet's not here many Sundays.'

Joe got up and moved closer to Ag. He bent down, took her heel from her hand, gazed at the blister intently as a doctor preparing his opinion.

'Nasty. Ask Ma for something. Best cover it up.' He handed back her foot. 'You must have the smallest ankles in the world,' he said.

Ag laughed again, and put the socks back on.

'Sticks, my legs,' she said. 'I was dreadfully teased at school.' She made to get up. Joe put a hand under her elbow to help. 'Thanks. I promised your mother I'd collect the eggs from the barn . . .'

'I'll do that. You go on in, see to the blister.'

'Sure?'

'Sure.' Joe moved away. 'I'll be quicker than you. I know all their favourite places.'

'Thanks very much.'

'It'll cost you something.'

'My reflections on the *Iliad*? Really? Any time you like.'

Joe nodded. He cradled two brown eggs in his hand, that he had plucked from a hiding place. 'To begin with,' he said.

For the space of her hobbled journey back across the

farmyard, Ag thought about Joe. Was it disappointment about Cambridge that made him so gruff? Was it the punishment of asthma upon his youth and regret at his inability to join the war? Or was he by nature an unforthcoming and gloomy figure? And why – perhaps an unnecessary question – did Janet's presence on Sunday do nothing to cheer his spirits? For her own part, Ag would be delighted to find a kindred spirit with whom she could share ideas. She rather fancied herself bringing succour to the starved soul of Joe Lawrence. It was the sort of thing that would appeal to Desmond's humour. In fact, Desmond would hardly fail to be interested in the whole curious Lawrence family of Hallows Farm . . . If he responded to her Christmas card, she would write to him in the New Year. It would be an excitement she instantly imagined herself looking forward to.

Ag began to compose a description of the very gradual unbending of father and son, and of the strong and dignified figure of the woman who gently tended her blister, for whom, already, Ag felt considerable affection.

That afternoon, after milking with Stella, Joe walked down to the field where his father and Ag were still working on the hedge. He helped Ag drag the heavier stuff to the large pile of wood and bramble that would be burned before nightfall. None of them spoke. The quietness of the autumn afternoon was broken by the soft-edged sound of Mr Lawrence's slasher among thorn leaves: the snapping of small twigs, the drag of leafy branches over hard ground. Ag, proud of the length of her cleared ditch, could smell the pungency of her own sweat. She found herself working harder and faster than she had in the morning. Her blister no longer stung, her back no longer ached. The nearness of the earth affected her, as it did at home: the cloud of distant war was dissipated in the low light of the late sun, the long shadows thrown by the hedge, field, copse and men. *Oh, Desmond*, she thought.

At five, Mr Lawrence laid down his tools. 'Time for burning,' he said.

Joe took a box of matches from his pocket, bent down to light the base of the bonfire. In seconds it had caught, flames leaping high among the dry crackling stuff, their yellow matching a few high clouds in the sky.

They stood watching, Joe close to Ag, soon feeling the warmth. Ag had no idea how long the three of them remained there, unmoving: but suddenly she was aware of Mrs Lawrence and Stella at the gate. They carried a basket full of tin mugs, and a large thermos.

'Tea,' called Mrs Lawrence. 'We thought it might be welcome.'

Indeed, by now a thin sharp prickle of chill, intimation of a cold autumn ahead, had crept round Ag's body like a frame, while the centre of her being was still warm and sweating from her labours. She was glad of the hot, sweet tea, and of the flames on her face.

By the time Prue arrived the sun was low. Violet clouds were adrift among the yellow – gathering, consolidating, putting up an impenetrable defence against the last of the light.

Prue's entrance on the scene, catching the last webs of light, was impeccably timed. She prettily climbed the gate, scarlet bow bobbing on curls whose blonde rallied with a last shimmer.

'*Field's finished*, all! How about that?' She did not try to conceal her pride.

Mrs Lawrence handed her a mug of tea. 'Well done,' she said.

But Prue was looking for other praise. She cocked her head at Joe.

'You didn't think I could do it, did you?'

'I didn't have any opinion, as far as I remember.'

'Like to come and see my furrows? Straight as a die.'

'I will later.'

'It'll be dark in a minute. If you don't come now, it'll be too late.'

Joe slashed the fire. The confetti of ash made by his stick briefly arched before falling to the ground. The tiny red eyes went out as they touched the earth.

'Then I'll come in the morning,' he said.

'You mean beast, Joe Lawrence.' Prue stamped her foot. Ag saw she was near to tears.

'Will my opinion do, child?' Mr Lawrence asked with a smile.

'Suppose so. God, I'm hungry as a dog, aching all over, juddering from that bloody seat. My whole body's juddering still – do you realise?' Prue's petulance made everyone uneasy.

Again she looked at Joe. He concentrated on more bashing of the flames.

'Calm down,' said Mr Lawrence. 'We'll all come and see your handiwork. Joe can take back the tools.'

As Joe went to pick them up, Ag turned to tell him she had left hers some way along the ditch. As she did so, she saw Ratty leaning over the gate, his face flame-pale under a dark hat. She felt a moment's fear: the unexpected sight of him, the anguish in his face.

'Ratty!' she called. 'Come and have some tea.'

Mrs Lawrence, too, turned to the gate. But Ratty had already gone.

'He can smell a bonfire five miles off,' Mrs Lawrence said. 'He never misses one.'

'Come on, you lot. Please. My ploughing –'

Prue impatiently opened the gate. Mrs Lawrence gathered empty mugs into her basket. All but Joe followed Prue into the lane. He remained behind to quell the fire, knock out the last remaining flames, and to spread the embers to die in the cool of the evening that was now falling fast.

Four

Edith Tyler was the first to congratulate herself on making her war effort. In Hinton Half Moon she led the way, when the rallying call came, to hand in aluminium saucepans to make Spitfires. She left herself just a kettle, a frying pan and one small saucepan, and thrived on the difficulties that this heroic parsimony caused.

Generous, noble and honourable though Ratty was often forced to agree she had been, the culinary inconvenience they now had to put up with fired him with an irritation that often he could not control. Lack of kitchen implements became the most frequent reason for their quarrels. In Edith's relish of these rows Ratty was able to discern a malicious pleasure in taunting him that, he feared, might not cease even when the war was over. He increasingly suspected that victory would not be celebrated by Edith re-stocking with saucepans, and she would make some new excuse to keep the kitchen under-supplied.

On the evening of the bonfire, Ratty walked home with slow, reluctant step. He had set out, lured by the sweet smell of thorn smoke, to enjoy himself: he always enjoyed a bonfire. But he had arrived too late. By the time he reached the gate a tableau was in place round the flames. He felt that to enter would be to interrupt, to intrude. Nothing unusual about the sight of the boss and Mrs L., of course: it was the girls who had cast their spell. Unseen,

Ratty had gazed for a few moments on their fresh young faces, eyes full of the sort of wonder that never dulls when confronted by flames, and a million unspeakable regrets had gathered in his breast mysteriously as the swifts overhead were gathering in the sky. What were those regrets? Ratty had not liked to question himself too deeply: something to do with missed chances, unfulfilled love, wasted youth. The tall one with the short, dark hair – Ag – she was the one who had nearly been his undoing . . . the way she called to him asking him to join them – thoughtful, kind, such sweetness in her unformed face, lighted by the flames. He would almost call it holy.

Ratty had been tempted to hurry to her side, accept a mug of tea from Mrs L., join the magic circle. But even as he put a hand on the latch to open the gate, he knew he could go no further: he would be committing himself to too much enjoyment, a sensation Ratty had guarded himself against for years. He had learned from experience: on the occasions he had allowed himself unexpected moments of deep happiness, the return to reality, the barrenness of his life, had been too cruel.

So now he walked the lane, through a rising ground mist, with mixed feelings. On the one hand, he would have liked so much to have been part of the brief group, the fire a symbol of triumph at the end of a hard day's work. On the other, he knew that had he allowed himself to do this, the inevitable homecoming, and Edith's sneering, would have added further pain to his corroded heart.

Edith! Ratty saw her face in the evening sky, jaws working furiously in response to some imagined insult, unfairness or domestic difficulty. Was it his fault that she had turned so swiftly into one of life's enemies? When Ratty reached the cottage he paused for a moment on the front path, looking into the lighted window of the kitchen. Why hadn't the bloody woman put up the blackout? He had to tell her every day. They'd already been reprimanded by the warden a couple of times. Why couldn't she understand the necessity of any war effort, or cooperation, beyond saucepans for Spitfires? The selfish cow . . . Ratty could see her at the sink, peeling potatoes with the same defensive hunch as she darned, making the knife, like the needle, seem fierce as a dagger. And why weren't the bloody potatoes *on*, cooking? Ratty's hunger was a twisting fist in his stomach. He went in.

'No, your tea's not ready yet so there's no use looking like that,' was Edith's greeting. The smell of frying bacon increased Ratty's hunger. 'Potatoes not boiled yet,' she added triumphantly, 'then there's the carrots to do. I don't know how you expect me to get it all up together, just the single saucepan . . .'

'If we had just one more . . .' Ratty trailed off. He knew any such suggestion was a waste of breath.

'The command from the government was: give up your saucepans for Spitfires.'

'It wasn't a command,' Ratty sighed.

'Good as. Besides, if I bought another one I'd have to give *that* up, wouldn't I? Logic. Bare necessities are what we've got to put up with. Hardships of war. No point grumbling.'

'Is there a cup of tea while we're waiting?'

'*Tea*, Ratty Tyler? Don't you listen to a word I say? I told you last night: I said now there's rationing we've got to cut down to three cups a day. There's a war on.' She began to scrape carrots. 'We've got to do our bit. There'll be rewards. A week or so ago, when that Spitfire flew over, I left the shop to watch it. Noisy thing. Still, I thought, Spitfires are defending our country, and if it hadn't been for my own very small effort – just the six saucepans and cooking pots – that very Spitfire might not be there now. It might have been held up in the factory, waiting for a bit more aluminium to make the tip of the wing. For all I knew, my saucepans were a small part of the undercarriage

86

of the plane that was going over our house. That gave me a good feeling, I can tell you. That made me more determined than ever it's not our business to grumble if the carrots have to take their turn with the potatoes. Trouble is, you've got no vision. You can't see things like that.'

'I'll go and deal with the blackout,' said Ratty. '*My* war effort,' he muttered under his breath.

Later, sensing the vegetables were still far from ready, Ratty went to sit in the chilly front room to listen to ITMA on the wireless. But, distracted, he turned the sound down low, hardly listening. Instead, his eyes fell on the framed photograph of Edward – Edward Tyler, their only son, killed in action in the last war.

Stored in boxes in the attic were bundles of letters from Edward, written from the trenches, many of their envelopes mud-splattered. Strangely, neither mud nor ink had faded. Ratty knew most of these letters by heart. The descriptions of a soldier's life were so extraordinarily vivid that Ratty felt he had shared the experience of every sensation with his son: sometimes he used to think Edward would be a writer when the war was over. He had the talent, surely. Ratty never mentioned this to Edith: she would have scoffed at so unmanly a suggestion. She probably had no idea the letters still existed. Unsentimental woman. Ratty had found her screwing up Edward's letters as she read them. If it hadn't been for Ratty's secret hoarding, there would be no voice, no words from Edward left. Edith even threw away the official letter that came to announce Edward had been mentioned in despatches. Ratty would never forgive her for that. Her lack of pride in her own son's courage was proof of her paucity of imagination: she was unable to understand or picture the horror, the fear, the bravery of a life unknown to her. She had never been able to read a face, a heart, a soul.

And what a funny old war, this one, compared with the last one, thought Ratty. So much of it, to date, had been spent in suspense and anticipation since the Polish invasion. The Battle of Britain had meant a little excitement and anxiety for six weeks: the Blitz in London, for all its horrors, had little effect on the rest of the country. Raids on the south coast were rare. In rural areas what you were left with were the frustrations of wartime regulations: rationing and blackouts, shortages of farm workers and clock menders – Ratty's broken alarm clock caused him great sadness when he discovered every clock mender for twenty miles had been called up. Indeed, here in Dorset you could be forgiven for thinking the war did not exist. The only thing that never faded, through every waking hour of the day, and troubled the dreams at night, was the tension, the constant anticipation of unknown possibilities. If Edward had lived, Ratty would have enjoyed discussing the two wars, the philosophical aspects of the loathsome thrill of danger, the peculiar pulling together of people by a common cause.

Ah! Ratty would have enjoyed discussing that and a thousand other subjects that held no interest for his wife. If Edward had lived – wife and family nearby, maybe, grandchildren coming to their grandfather to learn the ways of the land – life might have been very different. As it was, all Ratty could do was to try to carry out his son's last wish. In a letter that Edward had not known would be his last, in which he had been full of his usual humour, optimism and hope, he had ended with the binding words *Take care of Mum till I come back, Dad* . . . Which meant, when Edward was blown up a week later, take care of Edith for ever.

'So there you are,' she scoffed, standing at the door, interrupting his reflections. 'One moment you're grumbling because the food's not ready, then when it's on the table you've vanished.'

Ratty got up. He was no longer hungry.

'What've the girls been up to?' Edith sniffed.

'The tall one was hedging with Mr L. That's all I know. There was a bonfire this evening.'

'Huh! Trust you not to miss a bonfire.'

'I didn't stay.'

'I should hope not. Standing round bonfires when there's work to be done.'

Ratty, tired, tried to deflect her mind from the girls. By now he had learned to his cost that they were a lethal subject.

'It's been uncannily quiet for a week or so, hasn't it?' he offered. 'I've got a feeling in my bones there's going to be a raid, soon. Something's going to happen.'

'If your bones are as full of silly feelings as your head, then there's nothing to fear,' said Edith. 'All gloom and doom as normal. I don't know what you're talking about.'

She handed him a plate of bacon rashers, boiled potatoes and carrots. She watched eagerly as he pushed his knife into the underdone vegetables, testing. Just as eagerly she waited for him to complain, her answer about Spitfires all ready to shout him down. But Ratty, no fight left in him this evening, had his own, small revenge.

'Very good,' he said.

At supper that night at Hallows Farm, Stella thought she detected a smell of thorn smoke that clung to them all, more powerful than the smell of rabbit stew and mashed swede. By now she was used to the dining-room, with its clumsy dark furniture and ugly light, and, during the day, often found herself looking forward to the suppers there, Mrs Lawrence's huge plates of food filling their hungry stomachs. There were still silences at meals, but they were easier. Sometimes a proper discussion flowered, and there was laughter. Mrs Lawrence would reminisce about her childhood on a farm in Devon; her husband would sometimes mention his concern for his brother Robert, who farmed in Yorkshire, and was suffering from terminal cancer; Prue would spend time between courses examining her hands, which she claimed were a dreadful red from the Lavalord that went into the bottle-washing water.

'Blow me down if I don't end up a *fright*, all this manual labour,' she would complain. 'Raw hands, filthy nails, weather-beaten skin, stinking of cow muck . . . Will there be a man in the world left to want me?'

This last question, with a slight cock of the head in Joe's direction, observed by Stella and Ag, was ignored by Joe who always made the minimum contribution to the meal.

Tonight, Mr Lawrence, after a day at his favourite occupation, and filled with the agreeable thought of further hedging tomorrow, was in rare good humour.

'Tomorrow,' he said, 'it's time to be rewarded for your first week's good work with an entirely new sort of job – the kind of job every land girl in the country most probably dreams of. Can you imagine what that might be, Prue?'

Prue, in a pink crochet jersey with tiny crystal beads sewn to its collar, blushed.

'Why you should pick on me for an idea, I can't think,' she smiled back. 'Still, if I had to say . . . I'd say a day on a tractor with a nice little shelter to protect me from the wind and rain, and a velvet padded seat.'

Mr Lawrence laughed. 'Out of luck, I'm afraid. No: tomorrow it's dagging, and checking for foot rot. Sheep.'

'It's *what*? And what?' Prue's expression of horror was comical.

The Lawrence family exchanged glances. Joe tried to suppress a smile.

'It's not one of the pleasantest jobs, and it doesn't have to happen that often, but everyone should know how to do it,' explained the farmer. 'You have to keep a check on the sheep's feet, pare the hoof if necessary. Don't worry: I'm an experienced instructor. Got young Joe down to the job at twelve or thirteen, didn't I, son?'

'And what's the other thing?' asked Prue.

'Dagging,' said Joe. 'I was doing that not long out of my cradle, wasn't I, Mother? Dad found me some special small shears.'

Joe, Stella could see, was beginning to enjoy himself.

'I think,' said Mrs Lawrence, handing round plates of steamed ginger pudding, 'you could explain that, John, when the time comes. I don't want people put off their food.'

There was a moment's silence, then Joe cast his eyes towards Prue. She met his glance at once.

'I can see you're dying to know,' he said. 'So here goes. Dagging, in a word, is cutting the dried shit off a sheep's backside.'

The shocked silence was quickly broken by the laying down of astonished spoons. Ag laughed, but was at once cut off by a whiplash look from Mrs Lawrence.

'Joe!'

'Sorry, Mother.'

Prue was smothering a giggle in her hands. 'Well, I tell you what, Joe, Mr Lawrence,' she said. 'Count me out. A girl has to draw a line somewhere, and if you think I'm going to cut shit off a sheep's bum you can think again. I'd rather . . .' she tried to think of some slightly less horrendous task – 'I'd rather *clean out the pig.*'

'You do what you're told, my girl,' snapped Mr Lawrence, his good humour suddenly gone. 'If you're so keen on cleaning out the pig, you can take that job over from Faith once you've finished the dagging.'

The girls had never known him so stern and darkly flushed. He picked up his spoon and plunged it into his pudding again. The others, all but Prue, followed his example. She looked down at her uneaten sponge, suddenly pale, and gasped.

'Oh my God! I've forgotten something.' She stood, addressed Joe. 'I've forgotten to put the sacking over the tractor engine.'

'Did you remember to drain the radiator?'

' 'Course I remembered to drain the radiator.'

'Then it's not that serious,' Joe said.

'Sit down, it can wait till we've finished eating.' Mr Lawrence's anger still simmered.

'I'll give you a hand.' Joe was less brusque than his father.

'I don't want a hand, thanks.'

Prue left the room at a run.

'Stupid girl,' said Mr Lawrence, and shouted through the door that there was a torch on the dresser.

The night was cool and hazy. A diluted moon cast greenish light over sauntering clouds, too feeble to light the farm-yard. Prue hurried across to the barn, the beam of the torch paddling like a single oar over the muddy ground and piles of dung.

Even in the darkness the security of the barn touched her: the smells of hay, chaff, sacking; the scurrying of mice in the straw, the purring of sleepy pigeons in the rafters. The tractor, in silhouette, was an enormous queenly hunk in this softly shining kingdom, old mudguards spread like proud but ailing skirts. Prue put a hand on the engine. The metal was icy cold, but not frozen. She found two or three sacks and covered it. She'd remembered everything else: how could she have forgotten this last, essential act?

Prue switched off her torch, moved towards a dim bank of stacked straw. She climbed until she was higher than the tractor, could look down on it and the farmyard beyond. In her hurry she had forgotten her coat. Although she had changed out of her working shirt and jersey for supper, she had kept on her breeches, thick socks and shoes. So only her arms were cold. But she didn't want to go back. Not just yet.

She clutched her arms under her breasts, rested her head on her corduroy knees. The feeling that prevailed was anger – anger with herself. The last thing she had wanted to do was make Mr Lawrence angry: her reaction to the dagging had been half in jest – surely he could have seen that? Of course she would have cleaned the blinking sheep's bum without a murmur when the time came – but a girl is entitled to make a protest, even if there is a war on. She wanted very hard to prove herself, guessing what farmers must think of hairdressers. But it wasn't easy. She'd spent ten hours ploughing that field, no stop for lunch or tea, furrows straight as a die – and what praise did she get? None. Not a word. Great reluctance on the part of the Lawrences even to come and look at her handiwork. Mr Lawrence had just stood by the gate, muttered 'Looks all right to me,' and had moved away when his wife had nodded, supposedly in agreement. They were cross with her, of course. Cross about Joe. And Janet. But if it hadn't been for Stella and Ag, almost too extravagant in their praise and amazement, Prue would have burst into tears. Just the tiniest bit of appreciation from the Lawrences was all she had wanted: the understanding of what it took for a girl used to doing permanent waves, in a warm and cosy salon full of chattering customers, suddenly to spend a whole day carving up acres of bitter earth, alone. At the thought of the salon, Prue began to cry.

She realised, in this first moment really to think since she had arrived, that she was homesick. She missed her mum: that funny, warm, bleached-haired, spoiling lady, buoyed by eternal optimism and nightly gin, never quite sunk by disillusion. She missed the local gossip, the northern jokes, the laughter, the intricate schemes for making do – her mum was a genius in that respect. Just before leaving home, Prue had been asked to a charity tea-dance in aid of the Home Guard: in a trice Mum had run up a beautiful dress made from left-over blackout stuff. She had stuck it with sequins and Christmas tree tinsel, swore it would look almost like ostrich feathers under the electric light. The next morning, when Prue presented the blackout dress ripped of its decorations (an impatient pair of RAF hands had quickly seen to that) – well, they'd had a laugh.

They had agreed, Prue and her mother, not to say in their stilted, badly spelled letters how much they missed each other: it would be too painful. But they both knew. God, how Prue longed to hear her voice, to be back in the *smallness* of things at home: the salon, the small terraced house, the back row of the picture palace just down the road. Here, there were such houseless miles, such silence – except for the tractor, whose grunting Prue found a comfort. And indoors, for all Mrs Lawrence's hard work, there were no . . . what Prue would call *nice touches*: no aspidistra in a copper bowl, no crochet antimacassars, no wooden clock carved to look like a setting sun, no Victorian tins with their Christmas pictures of ruddy children with toboggans and holly, or coaches and horses. For some reason, Prue missed the sterile little kitchen with her mother's collection of biscuit tins more than anything.

She raised her hand, sniffing, to be dazzled by the beam of a powerful torch. It quickly moved to one side. Prue could make out the figure of Joe standing by the tractor.

'So there you are,' he said. 'Tractor covered, I see. Coming down?'

'Soon.'

Joe banged one of his jacket pockets. 'I've got a Mars bar.'

Prue giggled. Her tears dried. Biscuit tins fled.

'Where did you find that? There aren't any in the village.'

'I have my sources. I'm stocking up against sweet rationing. Come on down and I'll give you a bit.'

'You come up here. Why not? It's warmer.'

'If you insist.'

In a few huge, climbing steps, Joe was beside her. It was almost completely dark: she could only just make out the blunt edges of his profile. There was a strong smell of

94

animal on his boots. Vaguely, she could see him take the Mars from his pocket, strip off its paper wrapping which crackled thinly as finest taffeta, and hold it out to her. She felt almost faint with desire for a taste of the chocolate.

'Got a knife?' she asked.

'No. Can't you just bite a bit off?'

He pushed it at her. Duskily, their hands met. She took it from him. Unable to see how far she was biting, she aimed for a modest length. The sweetness of the toffee, malt and chocolate was more delicious than any taste of Mars she had ever known.

'Thanks,' she said, smudgily, mouth full. 'That's absolute heaven on earth, that is. That'll have me working, resting, playing, *dagging*, like nothing you've ever seen.'

For the third time, Joe laughed, firing Prue's confidence. Somewhere in the dark she recognised the outline of her chance.

'Aren't you cold?' he asked, after a while.

'Not really.' Prue shivered, not entirely from the cold. 'Where do you go most evenings? We've all been trying to guess.'

There was a long pause before Joe answered.

'Walk up to The Bells, have a couple of pints with my friend Robert. We talk. Nothing very exciting.'

'That all? I imagined something very different.'

'I bet you did. Robert owns a farm nearby. Like me, he can't be called up for medical reasons. Like me, he's stuck on the farm all day, no one to talk to.'

'There's us, now,' said Prue, after a while.

'I suppose there is. But I'm not used to that idea, yet.'

'You're not easy to talk to, actually, are you? Pretty surly, on the whole.' Prue turned on him with a sweet smile, hoping his eyes had grown accustomed to the darkness and it would not be wasted.

'Surly? Me? Strange idea. Reflective, more, I would have said. More Mars?'

Again their hands briefly touched as she took the half bar, bit off another modest share.

'Thanks. Well, you're not at all surly tonight. First time.'

'I expect you find it all a bit strange, don't you? There's so much to do, I dare say we're all rather preoccupied. It must be very different from your normal life.'

'It is, of course. But I rather like it.'

'It's tough work.'

'I don't mind that.'

'Some pretty disagreeable. Wait till it's your turn to do the pig.'

Prue was colder, now. She clutched her arms more tightly about her.

'What I wanted, you know, was to be in a circus. That was my childhood dream. I used to practise little bits of acrobatic stuff from about five onwards. I used to put a plank between two chairs and call it my tightrope. I could do a backwards somersault from standing, when I was eight. I'd go to every circus I could – not many, mind – and long to be one of those acrobats in sequins. But my dad put his foot down, said no daughter of his was going into a circus. I went on practising whenever I had a chance, but then the enthusiasm sort of went.'

She sensed Joe turning towards her, interested.

'I walked a plank about twelve feet high, once. Never a real tightrope.'

'Could you have gone higher?'

'Easy. Just never had the chance.' She gave a small sigh.

'Here's your chance, then.' Joe stirred. He switched on his torch, lighting a crossbeam high above their heads. 'Bet you couldn't walk that.'

Prue studied the huge beam of blackened wood. It was wide enough, but many times the height of anything she had ever tried before. Disturbed by the torchlight, pigeons in the rafters broke into murmurous complaints.

'Ooh, Joe. How'd I get up?'

96

'There's a ladder. If you fell you wouldn't come to much harm – all this hay and straw. Besides, I'd catch you . . .' He swung the beam of the torch so that half Prue's face was lighted. 'Don't do it if you don't want to. I just thought it might be a lark.'

Prue looked into the deep, complicated shadows of his face.

'What would you think if I said yes, if I had a go?' she asked.

'Well, I don't know. I suppose I'd think you were rather brave.'

'Switch off the torch, then.'

'Why? I'll have to light your way very carefully.'

'Just for the moment. I want to take my shoes and socks off. I don't want you watching that.'

Joe turned off the torch. The darkness, renewed, seemed deeper. While Prue fumbled with her laces and pulled off her woollen socks, she heard Joe finish the Mars.

'Right?'

'I'm ready.'

'I'll help you down, put up the ladder. Sure you want to do this?'

' 'Course.' Prue's voice was light.

Joe jumped down to the ground, put out a steadying hand to help Prue scramble after him. They landed close together by the tractor. Prue touched its mudguard, steadying herself. Her heart was battering. She was no longer cold.

'Pity there's no fanfare of trumpets,' Joe said. 'Really, you need trumpets.'

Prue cocked her head, again hoping the wan light of the moon would be just strong enough to illuminate her devil-may-care expression.

'That's the nicest thing you've ever said to me,' she said. '*You need trumpets*. I shall always remember that: *you need trumpets*.' She was surprised by the shakiness of her voice.

'Come on, silly.' Joe touched her shoulder. 'I'll get the ladder.'

Here on the floor of the barn she was better able to see the large dark figure of Joe as he collected the ladder and propped it up against one end of the beam. Then he lit his torch again, flashed it up the rungs.

'All right?'

'Fine.'

Prue moved to join him, straw and rubble of the floor troubling the soles of her feet. She trembled with excitement, with fear.

'Don't worry about the ladder. I'll hold it firm. Then I'll keep the beam of the torch just ahead of you.'

'Okay.'

Prue took hold of the ladder's sides, put a foot on the first rung.

'Imagine the trumpets,' said Joe quietly.

Prue began to climb.

For the first time since she had been at Hallows Farm, Ag felt restless. Neither the news nor her book could fully engage her attention. In the sitting-room, where Mrs Lawrence made progress with a pair of socks for the troops, and Mr Lawrence sat with head tipped back, eyes shut, Ag studied the mauve-blue of the flames as they hissed up through a pile of damp logs. It was too early to go up to the bedroom. Besides, she did not want to disturb Stella in her letter-writing. Ag believed in protecting people's need to be alone: she was always at pains not to intrude. She could not be sure of what she wanted to do, where she wanted to go. Some vague anxiety about Prue assailed her, and then a larger worry seared: she had shut up the chickens, but not the bantams. Dear God, how could she have forgotten? Just like Prue, she had failed over a vital matter. Dreadful pictures flashed into her mind: the corpses of fox-chewed bantams littering the yard in the morning: Mr Lawrence's anger, Mrs Lawrence's sadness, disappointment . . . they would be unbearable. She would never forgive herself, such stupidity . . . *Never disappoint* had been her father's unofficial motto, branded deep into her since childhood. Here she was, just one week into her job, about to disappoint deeply.

Ag put down her book and swiftly left the room, whispering goodnight to Mrs Lawrence.

Outside, she found the denseness of the night confusing. No stars were visible. The moon, elusive in wandering clouds, would give ghostly light for a moment, then disappear again, leaving total blackness. Ag had a torch in her pocket, but determined not to use it till she reached the bantam house. You had to be so careful about light after dark, Mr Lawrence had warned them. She made her way cautiously through the garden. Unseen branches brushed at her face and snagged her arms. Despite the firmness of the ground, there was a sense of drowning. The sudden hoot of an owl made her heart race: she dreaded what would surely be a long hunt under hedges for the bantams.

Far sooner than she expected a familiar smell of creosoted wood came to her out of the darkness and she ran to the henhouse. She switched on her torch, slid the door of the peephole to one side. Inside were all ten roosting hens, heads drawn down into raised neck feathers, giving them a look of unconscious indignation. A couple of them, disturbed by the torchlight, began a minor, sleepy clucking. Ten pairs of wrinkled eyelids quivered, but none of them quite opened.

Ag moved away to the bantam house. She switched off her torch at the sudden return of the moon. In its brief light the wire netting, nailed to the wooden frame of the run, looked fragile as cobwebs. There were no birds in the run. The door was ajar, just as she had left it when she had let them out this morning. Ag closed it, shone her torch through the peephole of the house. To her amazement, there were birds inside, huddled more closely than the chickens, their feathers a grainy sheen. Five of them had returned to the fold on their own: just one was missing.

Ag's feelings of relief at the safety of the five were clouded with anxiety about the missing one. She hurried back through the garden, torch beam discreetly sweeping the ground, but with little hope of finding the bird here. The barn, she thought, would be the most obvious place. The bantams always congregated in the barn by day. It often took a while to flush them all from their hiding places when it was time to shut them up at night.

According to the restless rhythms of tonight's sky, it was the turn of darkness again when Ag reached the farmyard. She made swiftly for the barn. From halfway across the yard she saw a slash of torchlight inside. She stopped, straining to hear muted voices. *Have you seen a bantam in there?* she wanted to shout: but then her concern for the bantam was overwhelmed by curiosity, fear, dread. What was happening? She slowed her steps.

By the time she gained the barn's entrance, Ag could hear exchanged words clearly.

'Sure you're all right?'

Long pause. 'I'm fine. It's fun up here.'

It was *Prue*, for heaven's sake, with Joe.

'You're doing well. Not much further.'

Ag flattened herself against the outside wall of the barn, peered round. She saw Joe, back to her, looking up, torch trained to somewhere high above him. As her eyes grew accustomed to the dim scene she could see shadows huge as sails flapping at the walls of the barn, their shapes cut into by the expanding beam of torchlight that showed Prue – dear God, the fool, the fool – engaged on some flight of madness in the rafters . . .

Ag turned away, clasping her hand to her mouth.

'Well done, you're over half way,' she heard Joe say.

Ag turned to look again. She saw Prue more clearly now, creeping along the crossbeam, arms stiffly outstretched, awkward, determined, brave. Her thin white legs were lit by the torch. Far below, Ag caught sight of thick regulation socks and heavy brown shoes cast into the hay.

She saw Prue pause, flutter, not daring to look down. Her left foot wavered, suddenly unsure where to land. The toes panicked. She was nearly at the end, where a ladder waited. But she could not make it.

She saw Prue fall into the darkness, heard her scream.

No one in the house could have heard because at the same moment a distant siren began to wail. Its mournful voice and the ragged shriek coiled together, then were split by a sound even closer to Ag as a terrified bantam ran squawking from the barn across the yard. To save? Or to protect? Ag found herself running towards the house before she had time to make a decision. She saw the door open, the figure of Mrs Lawrence holding a candle.

'I was looking for a bantam,' she cried.

'Never mind the bantam: straight down into the cellar.' Mrs Lawrence slammed the door behind Ag. 'You didn't see Joe?'

'No.'

'He must be at The Bells. Either there or on his way back.'

The siren was fading. Ag followed Mrs Lawrence down the cellar steps. Stella was already there, sitting on the floor beside a small rack of ginger wine, a pad of writing paper and a pen on her knee – scarcely interrupted, it seemed.

'You didn't see Prue?' Mrs Lawrence was brusque in her anxiety.

'She might have gone to The Bells, too. She was upset about that tractor business,' said Ag.

Mrs Lawrence gave a sharp sigh. 'Little fool,' she said.

Ag sat on the cold stone floor beside Stella.

'You all right?' Stella asked, smiling, still half-entangled by the thought of her letter.

Ag nodded. She wrapped her arms round her bent knees,

101

pressing them against her body, trying to extract the various feelings: the fear of bombs, the guilt at lying, the worry of the Lawrences' scorn at her inefficiency about the bantams. But far more disquieting than these was the horribly familiar feeling, experienced all too often in Cambridge when she had caught sight of Desmond in the distance – on the Backs, or passing through a quad – with another girl. *That*, at least, was understandable, loving him as she did.

But with Desmond miles away, unaware of her love, hope of anything ever bringing them together almost dead . . . why had jealousy followed her to Hallows Farm? And what, when the horror of the night was over, would it mean?

To Prue, falling into darkness, the siren was part of her own scream. How could such a huge and terrifying sound emerge from her own small throat? In the immeasurable moments as she plummeted down into the hay, that was her only thought.

Part of her thumped against another body. There were arms supporting her, though her legs seemed to be far away, detached from her body, one knee spinning in agony. Then the arms encased her more firmly. She was lying on her back. Hay spiked through the fragile crochet of her jersey. The knee had become a gold disc in her mind, spitting fire. The scream petered out, a horrible sound skulking into the distance. So it was a *siren*, not her . . .

'I caught you. I've got you.' A man's voice from somewhere, alarmed.

Who caught her? Ah, that was it! Bloody hell: *Joe* caught her. She'd wanted to be caught by Joe for a whole week, hadn't she? Hadn't imagined it would happen this way. But here he was, waterproof crackling against her bare arm. Not exactly on top of her, but she could feel his heaviness at her side.

'Thanks.'

Her head was full of sparks from an invisible anvil. They danced confusingly in front of an accumulation of shadows that was Joe's face, low over her own. One of his eyeballs was ignited with a small shard of white, then the flash of moonlight outside was gone and all was dark again.

'You all right?'

'Think so. Bit dizzy. My knee . . .' Prue tried to shift. Joe ran a hand along a corduroy thigh, stopped at the knee. 'Think I may have twisted it. But it's my heart I'm worried about, banging away overtime.' She gave a faint giggle.

Joe's hand slipped back up the thigh, over the stomach, ribs, found its place on her heart.

'It'll calm down,' he said. 'I'm sorry. I'm really sorry. It was a stupid challenge. You could have –'

'I could've said no. Don't worry. It was fun.' Prue let his hand continue to cover her breast, calming the flurry of heartbeats. It was huge, warm, heavy as a flat-iron. 'What about the siren?' she asked.

'Raid somewhere. Or could be a false alarm.'

'Hadn't we better . . .?'

'No. They'll be in the cellar. They'll think I'm at The Bells.'

'Won't they wonder where I am?'

'Let them wonder. We'll think of some explanation.'

At this nefarious suggestion, all Prue's anxiety about the raid and her own disappearance fled. She wanted to lie in the hay with Joe for ever, not caring about anything. She put a hand on top of his, feeling the enormous rough fingers.

'Anyway, I couldn't possibly walk across the yard with this knee, could I?'

In truth it was no more than a small stab of pain now, nothing that a brisk rub and a measure of determination could not deal with – though none but a fool would assure Joe of the unserious nature of her injury just at this moment.

'I don't suppose you could, you little minx.'

103

The word fired her, just as it had in the cowshed. No one had ever called her a minx before. It meant pert, a flirt, a hussy – she'd looked it up, once. It was a compliment, in her book. The mass of Joe's head seemed nearer. She could feel his breath on her face. He smelt of melted chocolate.

'Are you really all right?'

'I'm really all right. Did I fall far?'

'Twenty feet or so. You'll see when I find the torch. I dropped it, struggling to catch you.'

'So much for my circus act.'

Joe withdrew slightly, moved his hand. Prue quickly retrieved it, returned it to its place.

'Don't go,' she said.

'I won't go.'

They listened to the black silence. After a while it was stirred by the churring of a rafter pigeon. They heard the distant squealing of a small plane.

'Bombs?' asked Prue. 'It'll be my first raid. Crikey: I'm terrified, Joe.' She kneaded his hand.

Then his mouth was on hers, plundering the worry. He whipped up the cobweb wool of her jersey, tugged at the stout cotton stuff of her brassiere, pulled forth a wild breast. Acting like a man in a hurry, he grabbed at the waist of her breeches. Prue wriggled to help, wires of hay burning her back with each impatient movement.

'I thought . . . you'd never get around to this.' Prue's legs, now bare, were scratched by the hay, too.

'Had to give it a week, didn't I? Little temptress, you . . .' Joe smudged the words with kisses. 'Batting your pretty green eyes at me over the udders your very first morning . . .'

'With a war on, there's no time to be lost. That's what I think.'

Prue was in a state of total deliquescence now, pliant, quivering, flaming cheeks, icy impatient limbs.

'I knew the moment you arrived exactly what you thought . . .'

Joe's mouth clamped on to Prue's again. He made a pillow under her head with one arm. His free hand worked miracles wherever it brushed, spinning her skin into whirlpools of such intense pleasure she found herself cooing in tune with the pigeons. The wondrous hand, firm as a piece of farm machinery, parted her legs. The cooing turned to whimpering as the vastness and the weight of Joe crushed the breath out of her and he, too, began to chortle and pant like a powerful engine on a cold morning. In some small independent corner of her mind, despite the state of desire to which Joe had brought her, Prue thought of the tractor and wanted to laugh.

Had bombs fallen, the lovers in the barn would have been too preoccupied to be concerned. As it was, the all clear merged with their own cries, joined the dying fall that faded into eventual silence.

'Crikey!' said Prue, at last, shifting under Joe's full dead weight.

'Your first raid. Plenty more to come.'

'Should hope so. There's a war on, isn't there? Where've you put my breeches?'

'Lost in the dark.'

'Come on, Joe. We'll be in trouble. I'll be sent away. Not having it off with the farmer's son is the land girl's number one unspoken rule.'

'If you don't tell the others, no one'll ever know.'

'Promise.'

'Tomorrow night, when they're asleep, you can creep back out here again.'

'And how'll I ever get up at five, night after night at it in the barn with you, tell me that?'

'You'll get used to it,' said Joe, stroking her hair, kissing her eyes. 'Keep still. I'm not letting you go just yet. We've only just begun.'

Some hours later, when the first light scratchings of dawn

105

appeared in the sky, they gathered up their clothes, dressed, and crept through the mists in the yard. Only Ratty saw them. Disturbed by the sirens, he had risen earlier than usual, and was making his way to the barn for an early pipe before breakfast.

Ratty managed to avoid direct confrontation by mere seconds. When he saw the couple emerge blurrily from the barn, he ducked down behind the dung heap. He could hear voices, but no words. Once they disappeared through the farmhouse door, he completed his journey to the barn. The first thing he saw, poised like a pale, windless flag in the gloom, was a white handkerchief hanging from a pile of hay. Ratty removed it, put it in his pocket. *Idiots*, he thought.

Then, settled on one of the lower stacks, pipe lit, he turned to musing about Joe. Joe had always been quite a lad – something he, Ratty, regretfully, had never been. No land girl would be safe from Joe: Ratty had known that from the start, soon as the idea of employing girls had come up. But of course it would not have been his place to have warned the boss and Mrs L. Funny they didn't think for themselves. Maybe they reckoned that Janet girl would keep Joe on the straight and narrow. Huh! some hope. Then when the girls arrived – well, Ratty guessed straight away it would only be a matter of time, Joe and the flirty flighty one. And good luck to them . . . They should fit in all they can, the young, before they're bombed to bits, was Ratty's opinion. So long as Joe stuck to that one . . . What Ratty wouldn't fancy, come to think of it, would be if he laid his hands on the tall one, Ag, the one with the holy face. If Joe had the cheek to touch *her*, and Ratty got to know about it, there'd be no accounting for his reactions. He could imagine doing something terrible to Joe: something he hadn't thought of yet, but it would come to him. It would definitely come to him . . . He clicked his pipe against his teeth, watched the paling of the sky over the farmhouse roof – going to be a fine day. Going to be a fine clear day for thinking. Why, already a plan was beginning to form in Ratty's mind.

The girls caught the two o'clock bus from Hinton Half Moon to Blandford. It was the first half-day. Each had fourteen shillings in her purse – half of their first week's pay: the other half went to Mrs Lawrence for board and lodging.

The ancient bus bumped along yellow-leafed lanes, jostling the girls in their various moods. Prue's lack of sleep was well disguised: in honour of the shopping trip she wore an emerald skirt and matching bow, and flamingo lipstick – on the grounds, she had explained to the others while they were changing, that you should be prepared for any eventuality. The eventuality she had in mind in Blandford was a chance encounter with an off-duty soldier or airman from a nearby camp.

'And what would you *do*, exactly, if this mythical man ran into us in the street?' Stella asked, intrigued.

'Get to know him before the bus back, of course,' giggled Prue, jabbing her eyelashes with thick mascara.

Ag was in unaccountably low spirits. As they chuntered through showers of falling leaves (*Yellow and black and pale and hectic red, Pestilence-stricken multitudes* came automatically to mind) she could not extinguish the picture of Prue falling from the crossbeam into the darkness, her terrified scream curdling with the siren. She could not understand why she had lied to Mrs Lawrence before there had been time to think. Nor could she understand why she had lain awake hours after the all clear, and then found the sight of Prue creeping in at dawn, dishevelled, ravished, scintillating, so disturbing. Perhaps it was envy of Prue's ability to make the whole business of men seem so easy: if a man is your target, go for him, get him. Ag could never behave like that. On further reflection, she put her melancholy down to disillusion. How could Joe, a man whom she was coming to respect, be so easily misled by a shameless young hussy like Prue? It was not as if he was a *free* man, after all: he was engaged to Janet. Did Janet not come into his considerations as he gave vent to his lust in the barn?

Ag smiled to herself, knowing her weakness for the schoolmistressy phraseology that came to her in moments of disapproval: *gave vent to his lust,* indeed. They probably had a wonderful time. And was that, perhaps, the trouble? The thought of Joe and Prue achieving something she and Desmond would never have? Or was it – and here surfaced the question Ag hated to contemplate even as she saw it coming – was it because, despite her love for Desmond, she would like to know she had at least the *power* to attract Joe: to feel they were soulmates, intellectual equals, friends? Somehow his skirmish with Prue managed to scatter the normal calm of her mind. It both repelled and excited her. It also alarmed her on Janet's behalf. What would happen to Janet? Ag's mind was a whirl of questions and unsatisfactory answers. Thus preoccupied, she kept her silence, barely nodding when Prue squealed about some new item she remembered for her shopping list.

Stella, too, was quiet. The ragged autumn landscape, bronzed golds and flame yellows against mole-dark earth, was lost upon her. She was concentrating on God.

'Please make HMS *Apollo* need a boiler clean soon,' she prayed, 'because if I don't see Philip soon I don't know what I'll do . . .'

They straggled round the streets of Blandford, disappointed. The old film *Rome Express* was on at the pictures, but there was no time to see it before the bus back. Prue insisted on visiting the chemist immediately, only to be greeted by a notice on the door saying *Sorry, no lipsticks or rouges.*

'How *can* a war affect lipsticks and rouges?' she wailed,

108

suddenly feeling her sleepless night, and almost in tears.

Her anticipation of Revlon's new colours shattered, she trailed dismally after the other two, uninterested in their quests. Ag could not find the book she was hoping for in the library, but bought a bunch of shaggy-headed chrysanthemums for Mrs Lawrence instead. Stella gloomily stocked up on writing materials. They all felt cold: the sun's brightness concealed the raw edge of a rising wind. By four they were sitting in a tea-room of dark wooden tables and checked cloths, the windows running with condensation, passers-by outside flattened into pearly ghost shadows. Ag and Stella chose savoury mince with greens, and stewed apples and custard, for sixpence. Prue scorned their economy.

'I'm going to lash out,' she announced with a flutter of her incredible eyelashes. 'I need energy.' She ordered toad-in-the-hole, butter beans in white sauce, prunes and junket for sixpence halfpenny. They all drank orangeade. 'What I wouldn't give for a gin and lime,' sighed Prue.

The fuggy warmth of the tea-room and the steaming food revived their spirits. They threw off their cardigans, lolled back in their wheelback chairs as if, on their day off from the land, they could resume a sophisticated nonchalance. After the main course Prue offered round her Woodbines and the others, usually non-smokers, accepted. They pecked inexpertly at the wizened little cigarettes, coughing and spewing smoke in all directions. Prue, with her superior habit, was laughing by now, sipping her orangeade as reverently as if it were the dreamed-of gin and lime.

'I've got news for you, anyway,' she said, when the cigarettes were at last finished, their lipstick-printed butts squashed into the ashtray, and the stewed fruits, junkets and custards trembling in bowls before them. 'Can you guess?'

Ag concentrated on polishing her spoon with a clean handkerchief. Stella shook her head.

'I made it! *Joe.* In the barn, last night. Told you I would.' She giggled. The emerald bow bobbed in the brownish light.

'Goodness,' said Stella, in some awe.

'Should you be telling us?' asked Ag, unsurprised.

'Blimey! You're right there.' Prue clamped her hand over her mouth. 'Don't suppose I should. Though he couldn't expect me *not* to tell you.'

'He could,' said Ag. 'What about Janet? I told you you should think about Janet.'

'Enough of your lectures, Ag. *He* didn't mention Janet.'

'What did you feel about her?' Ag heard the disapproval in her voice, sharp as it had been on the Sunday walk.

'Can't say I gave her a thought. None of my business. Think that's very wicked, do you?' Prue turned to Stella.

'I think,' Stella said, thinking fast, 'you should stick very carefully to your philosophy of not upsetting apple carts. You don't want to be thrown out by the Lawrences, and cause difficulties between Janet and Joe.'

Prue shrugged. 'It's not as if they're *very* engaged, is my way of seeing it. Besides, all's fair in love and war, like I *keep* saying. What Janet doesn't know won't hurt.'

'That's not entirely the point,' said Ag. 'What if you got pregnant?'

'Don't be daft. I know how to take care of all that. Haven't been caught out yet, have I?' Prue hailed the waitress, asked for another round of orangeades. 'Anyway, now we're over the serious bit, d'you want to know what it was like?' She looked from Ag, who blushed deeply, to Stella, who could not quite disguise a look of interest. 'It all happened easy as pie. According to plan. My plan. His too, if I know anything about randy farmers' sons. And I have to tell you –' she drew herself up, squashed the bow with an emphatic hand – 'Joe Lawrence is quite a man. If you're ever feeling like it, he'd be a good start. Set a high standard to go by in the future, know what I mean?'

'Prue! You're dreadful!' Ag felt sweat on her forehead.

'You're wicked!' added Stella, laughing. 'Go on.'

'Well, he's no miniature, that's for sure. More like a bloody great stallion.'

Prue put out her hands, measuring a width to match the side of the table. Her huge, green, mascara-spiked eyes opened wide, her tiny, manicured hands were held up in angels-bending-near-to-God position. For a second she looked more like something by Fra Angelico than an oversexed land girl, and Ag, despite herself, began to laugh. Stella joined in. Prue, looking from one to the other, seeing they were not mocking but enjoying her account, was fired to further revelations.

'Mind you, he sounded like a bloody tractor, and cor blimey am I *crushed* this morning! But it was all good fun. Wouldn't mind a bit more any time . . .'

'You're completely incorrigible,' said Ag, still laughing.

For some reason Ag's heart had lightened: must be something to do with the fact that, whatever had gone on between Joe and Prue, she couldn't believe it was serious.

Prue was about to ask what incorrigible meant, but her attention was snatched by a young man in RAF uniform who came through the door. He had very short, gleaming fair hair and a shaven neck, features that were enhanced by the severity of his cap. Assaulted by Prue's admiring stare, he hesitated, but then made his way to a table in the window – as far as possible from the girls – and ordered a cup of tea and a scone.

'How about that?' asked Prue. 'Quite promising, I'd say.'

'Stop staring,' whispered Stella.

'Your manners, Prue!' Ag heard herself being prissy again, even in laughter. She also felt reckless. In a strange way she wanted to urge Prue on, see if she would live up to her boasting. 'So what are you going to *do*?'

'Look friendly, that's all,' said Prue. She turned her head in the airman's direction, fluttered her huge lashes.

'You're shocking,' said Stella, smiling, aware of a certain admiration in her admonishment. 'Last night you seduce Joe; how could you even contemplate someone else not twenty-four hours later?'

'It pays to notch them up.' Prue slowed down the fanning of her lashes, gave a dimpled smile at the airman. 'Specially in a war.' She picked up her bag, searched for her purse. Ag, alarmed at the thought of Prue taking the next logical step, and moving to his table, asked for the bill.

'We ought to be getting back,' she said. 'We don't want to miss the last bus.'

'I wouldn't mind.' Prue dreamily counted her share of coins. 'By the way, did either of you see Joe this morning? I did the milking with Mr Lawrence. Didn't like to ask him where Joe was.'

'Mrs Lawrence said he had an asthma attack,' said Ag. 'He was in his room.'

The thought seemed to amuse Prue. 'Must have been the hay,' she said. 'We'll have to find somewhere he's not allergic to. His bed, perhaps.'

'Are you completely off your head?' Stella stood. She took Prue's arm. 'Come on, we're going. Fast.'

Dragged by the firm Stella, Prue, unable to linger at the door, cast the airman a final, signalling glance.

'Spoilsports!' she complained once they were outside.

But the complaint had no depth and once more the three of them were joined in laughter. They hurried along the streets through the sharp evening air, arms linked, drunk on orangeade and an afternoon's freedom from toiling on the land. Stella and Ag refused to let Prue pause by unlit shop windows awaiting their blackout.

'I'll come on my own next time,' she protested, 'buy some new ribbon, find my way to the RAF camp . . . Why do you think, after all Mr Lawrence's threats, there was no dagging this morning after all?'

'He was probably too busy, with Joe off,' said Stella. 'Probably be tomorrow.'

'I'm going to be the best bloody dagger in Dorset,' sang Prue. 'You'll see.'

And then all thoughts of dagging were blasted from her mind: in the bus shelter was a poster announcing a dance at a nearby RAF camp, in aid of the Merchant Navy Fund.

'Stone the crows, girls, do you see this?' she gasped. 'We're in luck! Here's something to look forward to, isn't it? Here's a chance for the diamanté, or would diamonds in Dorset be too much?'

The others bundled her up the steps of the bus and into a seat on her own. But there was no escaping her bubbling anticipation. She twisted round, lay her chin on the back of the seat that divided them, restless hand running through her curls, plucking at the wilting bow.

'What's the betting we run into Romeo of the tea-room, eh? Come on, you two fuddy duddies . . . Imagine . . .'

The bus started with a reluctant growl, moved out of the town and into dark lanes. Over the hedges and shaven fields a gun-metal sky glowed behind a grid of green-black clouds. The first evening star – the 'slippered Hesper' in Ag's mind – was bright. A dance in an RAF camp was the last thing she wanted to imagine: nothing would persuade her to go. She would have liked to have been alone in the bus, watching the darkness gather, then walking silently back from Hinton to the farmhouse. She was suddenly tired. For the first time since she had left home, she ached for the silent privacy of her own room, a quiet evening with her father. Until now, she had been too busy to think of him often. Now, imagining his domestic struggle without her, a disquieting anxiety caused her a private tear beneath closed eyes.

Stella, too, sat with head tilted back, only half listening to Prue's daft expectations. Fragments of Prue's description of Joe came back to her: *stallion*, indeed. Such a crude word for a man. Stella gave a small shiver, knowing it to be inappropriate for Philip. Philip was no stallion, thank God, was he? What *was* Philip, in fact? Did she know? And where was he this very minute, and why, again, hadn't he written?

'I'll lay a sixpenny bet with the two of you,' Prue was saying, head still bobbing over the seat, 'that at the RAF dance I'll have tracked him down in the first half-hour, and we'll have made it by midnight.'

'Do pipe down, Prue.' Stella wanted to be at peace with her own fantasies: Philip on boiler-cleaning leave, weekend in a hotel, a double bed, a bottle of wine . . .

'I mean the funny thing is,' Prue went on, 'this war does at least offer a lot of opportunities, especially for a girl like me who can't resist a uniform. I mean we have to do our bit for our country: plough the land, entertain the troops, make them feel wanted, so we're entitled to some fun in between – don't you agree, Stella? Oh crikey: you're not asleep, too? What a couple . . . Old before your time.'

Five

When Prue returned from her second visit to the barn, at three in the morning, she bumped into a piece of furniture while stumbling to find her bed.

Her yelp of pain woke Ag, who said nothing. The next sound to be heard was the unscrewing of a jar. Even in complete darkness, it seemed, Prue was determined to take off her mascara.

Rigid in her bed, Ag lay fighting against pictures of Prue's night. Details were blurred in her mind. She was too shy – too prissy, she thought with scorn – to ask even herself how they did it in the hay. But the general imagining of their flailing joy, combined with feelings of shameful envy, sickened. She hated Prue for so easily achieving what she herself might never have with Desmond. She despised Prue's silliness, her vanity, her preoccupation with material things. More confusingly, she admired her, too: the rough wit, outspokenness, warmth, energy, sense of fun. Ag would willingly sacrifice all her literary knowledge for an ounce or two of Prue's sex appeal, she thought. Silent tears, for her own inadequacy, dampened the pillow.

Unable to go back to sleep, she got up at four and dressed in the dark. There were lights on downstairs. Ag was surprised. She crept along the passage to the kitchen door. It was slightly ajar. Peering through, she saw Mrs Lawrence at the stove pouring boiling water into a teapot.

Ag went in. Then she saw Joe sitting at the table, which was bare of everything but the jug of flowers. There was a muddied silence – the kind of silence in which angry words had been spoken and had run out, or remained unspoken between them. Joe was pale, unshaven. He wheezed slightly with every breath.

'You're early,' said Mrs Lawrence.

'I'm sorry. Shall I –?'

'Get yourself a mug.'

Ag put three mugs, milk, sugar and spoons on the checked oilcloth. Thus furnished, it seemed more familiar. But the customary warm ease of the kitchen was missing. With the blackout still in place, there was a night-time feel to the room. Ag had no idea whether her presence was a relief, or made matters between Joe and his mother more difficult.

The three of them sat at one end of the table. They listened to the rhythmic hiss of Joe's breath. They stirred their tea quietly.

'Are you better today?' Ag turned, after a while, to Joe.

'Thanks.' Joe nodded. 'Dagging this morning,' he added.

It was no time to smile. Ag concentrated on her tea. She saw that Mrs Lawrence stirred hers with a hand that slightly trembled – round and round, far longer than was necessary, eyes cast down at the small milky whirlpool she made with her spoon.

'I doubt Prudence will be up to dagging,' she said. There was more silence. Joe did not respond to the challenge of her look.

'I'll take down the blackout, Ma,' Joe said then.

'You do that, son.'

Joe got up from the table and pulled the stuff down from the window. There was a flat grey sky outside, and a transparent sliver of moon. The two collies, half alert on the rag rug, tapped their tails as Joe passed. He left the room.

'It's his asthma,' said Mrs Lawrence, when he had gone. She looked hard at Ag with her tired eyes. 'Sometimes he

116

goes for weeks on end all right, then he has two bad nights.' Her voice defied Ag not to believe this.

There is justification in lying if it's to protect those you love, thought Ag. She was moved by Mrs Lawrence's fierce dignity, what sounded like the truth of her conviction. Conviction? Perhaps she really did think Joe's two sleepless nights had been caused by asthma. Was it maligning Mrs Lawrence to suppose that she knew what Joe had been up to? Or was it granting the strength of her instinct?

'Rotten for him,' said Ag, quietly.

'Still, he's better today than yesterday.'

Mr Lawrence, Stella and Prue arrived. There were black smudges under Prue's eyes. Despite her rouge, she looked pale. It was the first morning she had not bothered with her make-up though perhaps, thought Ag, this was from carelessness rather than lack of spirit.

'So it's dagging, this morning, is it?' Prue asked Mr Lawrence, helping herself to a thick slice of home-made bread.

'That's it.' Mr Lawrence gave a small smile. 'Your time's come.'

Mrs Lawrence brought a new pot of tea to the table. The sky was paling beyond the barn. A few yellow leaves blew across the window.

'You're going to be as surprised by my dagging as you were by my ploughing,' grinned Prue.

'We're not, actually,' said Mrs Lawrence. She stood at the end of the table, fingers of both hands stiffly digging into the oilcloth, denting its surface. 'Because you, Prue, are going to do the pig this morning.'

The grin left Prue's face. A whiplash glance was exchanged between the Lawrences. It was evident Mrs Lawrence's decision had been made on the spur of the moment, and her husband knew better than to query it. In the long silence, Prue decided to conceal her disappointment.

117

'Very well,' she said. 'I don't mind.'

'And then you can do some muck-spreading,' Mrs Lawrence added, 'and this afternoon, the cowsheds need a good scrub down and a limewash.'

Prue looked at Mr Lawrence: his nod meant he concurred with his wife's plan.

'Anything you say.' She gave a small shrug. Her back and legs were aching. The inside of her lips were swollen. She could taste tiny specks of salt blood.

'Ag and Stella will do the morning milk, then Joe'll supervise the dagging,' Mrs Lawrence went on. 'John will show you what to do with the pig, Prue: I'll be busy all morning with the laundry.'

This was the first morning Mrs Lawrence had been the one to initiate plans and she listed them with unusual ferocity.

Prue pushed away an unfinished slice of bread on her plate.

'I'm sure the pig and I will get on very well, any road,' she said, plumping up the yellow bow in her hair.

No one responded.

When the three girls and two men had hurried away from the uneasy gathering, Mrs Lawrence remained at the table, still stirring her tea, jaw muscles working. She watched the gathering light seep across the oilcloth, ignite the sides of the old mugs and teapot with small pale flames. After the last door had banged, and there was complete silence except for the dogs' faint snoring, she pressed her head into the darkness of her hands and said a quick prayer. Then she rose to begin her morning's work.

'Hello, Pig,' said Prue. 'Hello, Sly.'

She leaned against the wall of the sty, wondering what first move she should make. Mr Lawrence had left her with a pitchfork and yard broom, and instructions which, the moment he left, ran amok in her mind. The pig lay in its

118

sleeping quarters under a corrugated iron roof, on a bed of straw that gleamed a sodden gold. It appeared to be dozing. Eyes shut. The occasional soft grunt made the whole jelly-bristle fabric of its body quiver.

Apart from disliking roast pork, Prue had never before given any thought to pigs. She had scarcely seen one alive. Now, postponing the dreadful moment when she had to try to move the animal, she fell to wondering about its life.

In her tired state, small blisters and pricks of blood still troubling the inside of her mouth, she found herself full of pity for its boring captivity, and less repelled than she had expected by its ugliness. There was something rather dignified, she thought, about Sly's swollen pregnant belly of mauve-pink skin, the stubby sprawling legs, the ridiculous tail and huge alert ears. Animals, she was learning from her week of closeness to the cows, are without vanity, and she admired that. Although – she smiled to herself – Sly's appearance would be much improved with a touch of mascara. The white lashes stubbing round the tiny eyes gave the sow a pathetic, spinsterish look. In fact, Sly was far from a spinster. She'd been mother to dozens of piglets in her time, Mr Lawrence said. Did she enjoy being pregnant again? Prue wondered. Was she lying down out of boredom, fatigue, happiness or misery? Men would do well to concentrate harder on the subject of whether animals had thoughts, rather than how to make bombs and endanger the whole world, reflected Prue, to whom procrastination brought multitudes of thoughts.

She opened the gate and squelched along the muddy floor of the concrete run. A powerful smell came from the straw. The lattice of mud that spurted over her boots was slimy, disagreeable, unlike the dark fresh earth of the fields. The pig opened her eyes, looked without interest at Prue, shut them.

'Hello,' she said again. 'Sorry, but you've got to move.'

To give herself further time, Prue thought about what

Mr Lawrence had told her concerning the severe shortage of pig food. Many pigs were being slaughtered, he said. For the time being, Sly was in no danger: the Lawrences had a good supply of Silcock's Pig Feed No. 1, which was supplemented with leftovers from the house and semi-rotted fruit. But what of the future of the unborn litter? Tears came briefly to Prue's eyes at the thought of killing innocent piglets. She moved nearer to the sow, tapped her with the broom.

The pig heaved herself up so fast, with such a loud and hideous squeal, that Prue leapt back in surprised fright.

Sly gave an ungainly jump off the dented bed of steaming ammonia straw. She skidded towards Prue, who cowered in the corner of the run, planting broom and pitchfork in front of her in pathetic defence. The sow was grunting loudly, intent on something terrible, Prue could see. More than anything in the whole world, Prue wanted to be in the salon at this moment, warm and steamy, cosily surrounded with all the ingredients of a permanent wave.

Don't annoy her, whatever you do, Mr Lawrence had said. But he hadn't told her how to avoid this. Plainly, she'd done something wrong. Sly was definitely annoyed. She stuck her great head between the two handles, looked up at Prue, and furiously wiggled her obscene great snout.

'Go away!' screamed Prue, jabbing Sly's head with the handle of the broom. Then, more quietly, 'Just let me by, please . . .'

The pig's scrubby ears flapped back and forth. One of them brushed Prue's bare hand. The skin was pumice-hard, cloudily transparent, matted with purple veins.

'Bugger off!' Prue shouted again, as the snout now jutted into Prue's thigh. 'I'm not a bloody truffle.'

Suddenly bored, the pig turned away. Prue stayed where she was for a moment, contemplating the purple backside, the indecent meeting of bulbous thighs, the swing of dugs already swelling in anticipation of the forthcoming litter.

120

With extraordinary speed, adrenalin racing, Prue tossed the old bedding over the wall of the sty. Later, should God grant her the strength, she would have to load it into the barrow and put it on the dung heap. Later still – today, of all days – she would then have to spread it in some field, Mrs Lawrence had said. Now the danger was over, her thoughts no longer fled for comfort to the salon, but to the plough. She would like, this afternoon, to go back to ploughing. But no chance of that. What she would like best of all, of course, was the entire afternoon on one of the highest stacks in the barn with Joe.

The sty cleared and swept, Prue spread a pile of sweet-smelling wheat straw. Sly immediately returned to her newly made bed and slumped down on her side, ungrateful as a cantankerous patient. At least the way was clear for Prue to tackle the mud in the outside pen, and sluice down the drain with a bucket of Jeyes Fluid.

'Doing all right?'

Prue looked up to see Joe.

'You know she bites if she's annoyed.'

Prue shrugged. Her shoulders, arms and back were aching. The thought of transferring the muck from where she had thrown it to the dung heap depressed her so much she was unable to answer. She wanted Joe to lift her over the wall, carry her off somewhere – anywhere – and soothe her aches, kiss her, crush her, blast her with his extraordinary explosive force from the reality of pigs and dung and farm life.

'You look a bit weary,' he said. 'I think we should give tonight a miss. Get some sleep. The hay doesn't do my asthma any good. We're going to have to change locations.'

'All right.'

Prue gave a weak smile. She was aware of smelling as pungently as the pigsty. *Nuits de Paris* stood no chance in such circumstances.

*

An hour later, Prue realised to her relief and astonishment, the first part of her job was finished. Sly's dirty straw was piled high on the dung heap. There wasn't a stray straw in the entire yard: Prue had taken the precaution of sweeping it – Mr Lawrence was obsessive about the neatness of his yard. Now, with squelching triumph, she climbed to the top of the dung heap, leaned on the pitchfork for support. There was no one about, no one to condemn her for a few moments' rest. The words of a song she'd learned on the training course came back to her. She began to sing.

She volunteered,
She volunteered to be a land girl
Ten bob a week – 'not true'
Nothing much to eat – 'not true'
Great big boots
And blisters on her feet,
If it wasn't for the war
She'd be where she was before –
Land girl, you're barmy.

'Too bloody true, that bit,' she added, as she began to sink into the dung. She could feel its heat coming through her boots, and the ammonia smell rose powerful as incense. Prue leaned more heavily on the pitchfork. She felt quite faint.

After the milking was finished, Stella took the cows back to the pasture by herself. Ag went to let out the hens. On her way back to the house she passed the laundry room – a minimally converted old cowshed close to the kitchen – and happened to glance through the open window. There, clouded in steam, she saw Mrs Lawrence at work. The place was littered with sheets and shirts, some soaking, some hanging. There were pools of water on the stone floor. On a slate shelf, two old-fashioned irons were reared up on their backs, their steel underbellies a pinkish bronze in the smeary light. Mrs Lawrence stooped to pick a sheet from an enamel bowl of water. She wrung it out fiercely, the sinews in her thin strong arms pulled taut as cords. Then she manoeuvred the sheet into position in the mangle, and began to turn the handle furiously. Water poured into a bucket below. When there were no more than a few drips left, Mrs Lawrence slung the sheet on to a pile of others. She paused to wipe sweat from her forehead, push back a wisp of grey hair from her eyes. Her apron, faded to a pot-pourri of indeterminate flowers, was damp. She contemplated another bowl containing another coil of cotton to be wrung, but seemed to decide against it. Perhaps her hands needed a rest from the cold water. Instead, she pulled a huge, rough man's shirt from the pile and threw it over the ironing board. She picked up one of the irons – its custard-coloured back, Ag could see, was so chipped it reminded her of a monster ladybird – and thundered it down the length of the sleeve. Her mouth was a single hard line.

Ag took a step back. She had wondered whether she should offer to help, but decided Mrs Lawrence would not have wished anyone to see her working out her private rage. It was then Ag felt sure that there had been no words concerning Prue between Mrs Lawrence and Joe at dawn. Mrs Lawrence was in lone battle with her instincts, her suspicions. She was in a turmoil, no doubt, about what, if anything, she should do. Ag longed to help. But she knew all she could do was to remain alert to any indication that Mrs Lawrence might want to discuss the troubles on her mind, which was unlikely. She was a strong, proud woman who would judge the sharing of private matters a deplorable weakness. Without a sound, Ag went on her way. She had to find Mr Lawrence, put from her mind the pictures of his wife's battle in the laundry, and concentrate on rounding up the sheep.

*

Stella, returning from the field in which she had put the cows, heard singing. She paused, listened. Prue? A harsh, tuneless voice, but some passion behind the words. Stella walked round the side of the barn into the beautifully swept yard. By now the singing had stopped. Prue, on top of the dung heap, rested hands and chin on the handle of the pitchfork.

'Prue!'

'I'm resting between jobs. Pausing between *mucking* out –' she gave a chorus-line twist of her hips – 'and muck-*spreading*.' The blobs of rouge, bright as sealing wax, emphasised the whey colour of her cheeks.

'You all right?'

'Fine, all the muck-raking considered. I came over a bit dizzy a moment ago. Must be the bending.'

'You're not going to join us with the sheep?'

'Seems not. Instructions to spread this stuff over about a hundred acres.' She gave a grim smile, digging her pitchfork into the wet straw. 'To think that once I thought two perms and a colour rinse was a hard day's work. Well, in a war you learn, I suppose.' She sighed. Stella, looking up at her, smiled too. 'You know what I dream of, Stella? Up here – everywhere? I dream that when it's over I finish my apprenticeship and this man comes along. This *final* man. I tell you: I'll recognise him soon as he puts his head round the door. He'll be a great big hulk, something like Joe, except he'll have pots and pots of money. We'll get married and live in a huge big house on the outskirts of somewhere posh like York – no more Manchester, thanks very much. We'll have a marble bath with gold taps and lots of marble shelves where I can line up all my powders and lotions – many as I like. We'll have wall-to-wall carpeting *all through*, a wireless in every room and one of those big new radiogram things in maple wood that looks like a cupboard, and the maid will bring us *cocktails*, Stella, I'm telling you, on a silver tray every evening, and we'll be happy. In the day' – she prodded the dung again – 'I'll lie on a sofa like a film star, reading romances and eating chocolates, and all this muck will be a far distant thing, almost forgotten, and every night my husband will come back from his factory – or wherever it is he's made his money – in a Rolls-Royce. That's my dream.'

Stella laughed quietly. 'Children?' she asked.

'Kids? Three or four. That'd be nice. But only with a nanny.'

'What a dream. You'd be bored out of your mind.'

'No, I wouldn't. Not for a while, any road. Do you imagine anything like that for yourself?'

'No, my dream is more modest,' said Stella.

'Might as well aim for the big time.'

'What's going on?' Mr Lawrence strode into the yard just then, surprised to see a figure more like a cabaret singer than a land girl on top of his dung heap. 'Pig done?'

'Pig done, Mr Lawrence. And yard swept, Mr Lawrence, as you can see.'

'I don't want any of your cheek this morning. You'd better get this dung on the trailer and take it down to High Field. Sharp.' His look swerved to Stella, softening. 'Come and help me get the stuff, Stella, then we'll give Ag a hand with bringing in the sheep.'

Prue ostentatiously loaded a heavy lump of dung on to her pitchfork. 'Do you ever have time to dream, Mr Lawrence?' she asked.

'I'm warning you, young lady . . .'

Stella, following him to the shed to collect shears, knives and clippers, saw a dark flush spread up through his neck and wash over his weathered cheeks.

'Cocky little film star'll get her come-uppance one day,' he said. 'Though it's not her work I'm complaining about.'

An hour later Stella and Ag were grappling with their first sheep. The ewe lay on her back on a bench designed to make control of the animal easy. When Mr Lawrence had been there to demonstrate, it had looked simple enough. Left to themselves, the girls were struggling.

Ag had volunteered to hold the animal still while Stella, armed with her paring knife, examined its feet. Hands plunged deep into its greasy wool, Ag sympathetically contemplated the ewe's unease. The delicate black neck, jutting out of the great rug of its body, spun about, twisting the bony head with its roman nose and indignant yellow eyes. It cried out pitifully, lips drawn back to show long dun teeth scored with green, spittle thick as marshmallow spurted from its gums, flecking Ag's overall.

'Steady, old girl,' she soothed, feeling the frantic shoulder muscles writhe queasily in her hands. 'It's all for your own good . . .'

She remembered drawings of a sheep in a childhood book: anthropomorphised into a stern teacher, it was, with glasses on the end of its nose and a cane in its hoof. She thought of her father's love of boiled mutton and caper sauce, rainbow bubbles of fat in the gravy. Sunday after Sunday they would lunch alone together, the bowl of wax fruit between them, using their spoons to gather up the last grains of pearl barley swollen with the mutton juices.

'I think this one's okay,' said Stella. 'No rot, far as I can see. Just needs a trim.'

She clutched a waving leg, flushed with the effort. The horn of the hoof was splayed at the edges. There were two small splits. Biting her lip, Stella dug in the sharp knife and started to peel off a strip of hoof just as she would peel a potato. The ewe struggled harder, but in a moment a black half-circle of stuff like hard Plasticine fell to the ground.

'There – triumph!'

Stella let go of the frantic leg and was promptly kicked in the stomach. Ag laughed so hard she released her hold on the ewe's shoulders. If Stella had not then thrown herself, sack-like, over its belly, the animal would have escaped.

'You're a natural hoof trimmer,' was Ag's praise to Stella when the long job of manicuring all four hooves was completed. It was time for the dreaded dagging.

By now the sheep was weary, easier to handle. Stella bent over its head, hands plunged into the sticky matted chunks of its wool. She watched with some amusement as Ag picked up the clippers and assessed, with a look of mock wisdom, the dung-knotted expanse of the animal's hindquarters.

'Here goes.'

She took up a length of wool, rigid with dried mud and dung. Carefully, she snipped. It hit the ground with a small thud, like the shell of an empty nut. She chose another lump, snipped with more confidence. It was like cutting through pebbles, she thought, not half as revolting as she had expected. She worked faster. The animal scarcely twitched by now. Soon its hindquarters were shorn and clean. Ag felt pleased with herself. She and Stella gently helped it back to the ground. It went bleating away to join its companions in the pen Mr Lawrence had rigged up in the yard. Its head pecked the air like a great black beak, the spittled lips flung into a grimace of relief.

'Philip wouldn't believe it,' sighed Stella, rubbing her back. 'Only fourteen more to go.'

'We must try to get them finished by dark.'

'Easy,' said Stella. 'We're experts, now.'

At the end of the afternoon Joe drove the tractor to the field where Prue was muck-spreading. He had to pick up the empty trailer and tow it back to the yard.

He found Prue standing in a sea of tawny dung, the limp straw just lighted by dwindling sky. Her pitchfork moved feebly, twitching at the stuff she had already scattered. She heaved a clump from the small pile that was left, and threw it carelessly. When she saw Joe she stopped and gave up all pretence of effort.

He jumped down from the tractor, climbed the gate and strode towards her. She put out her arms. He held her, lightly kissed her hair. The satin bow had slumped over sideways, lying among the curls like a dead canary.

'You've done well,' he said.

'But Joe,' she said, 'I'm all in. Never, ever been so exhausted.'

His chest, where she lay her head, was saturated with sour farmyard smells. She found them more comforting than any bottled scent. The stuff of his waterproof crackled beneath her cheeks when she stirred.

'You go to bed very early tonight,' Joe said, 'and you'll be fine in the morning. Tomorrow, when the others are asleep, come down to my room.'

'But surely that's mad? I don't want to be sent away.'

'We'll take care.'

'There was something up, today – your mum and dad. All the rotten jobs they gave me. They were being tough: sort of testing me.'

'They have their ways. Best not to question them. Shall I run you back in the trailer?'

'I haven't quite finished – that small pile.'

'Leave it till tomorrow.'

'I'd like to get it finished.'

'I'll do it for you.'

'No.'

Joe lifted Prue's face, gave a wry smile. 'You're a deter-mined one, I'll say that for you.'

'Might as well do my bit for my country well as I can.' She giggled, energy returning. 'God, I smell awful. I stink.'

'Not so awful that I couldn't take you right here on this sodding bed of straw, if we had the time,' said Joe. 'Kiss me.'

Their mouths clashed. Behind Prue's closed eyes she saw that their heads had merged into one huge flower of inter-locking petals that spurted with light, like sparklers. She felt herself sway. She felt Joe hold her more tightly, to stop her falling. She dropped her pitchfork. It fell to the ground.

Mr Lawrence saw them as he passed the field on his way back from looking at a sickly cow. A mist had begun to rise, making them legless. They looked like the top half of a statue on a fragile plinth, swaying slightly, loosely soldered.

Mr Lawrence felt the burning of his face. He walked on, quickening his stride.

Ag and Stella failed. It was too dark to see clearly, and there were still five sheep left.

'We can't go on, we could hurt one of them,' said Ag. Both girls' backs ached badly. It was chilly, dank. Their last sheep skittered away to join the small flock. 'Still, we haven't done badly.'

They gathered up the tools, then each took an end of the heavy bench and moved it back to its place in the shed.

'What I'd love more than anything in the world is a long, hot bath,' said Stella.

'Me, too. Followed by some sort of silly cocktail in front of an open fire.'

When they returned to the yard, they found Mr Lawrence, flanked by the two collies, had already let the sheep out of the pen. The creatures pivoted about in the dusk, followed first one of their number then another, bleating with articulate monotony.

'Silly animals, really,' said Stella.

'Best as part of a landscape,' said Ag.

Mr Lawrence whistled to the dogs. In a trice they lowered their backs, nosed swiftly off towards the scattered flock, and formed it into an orderly bunch.

'We didn't quite finish, I'm afraid,' said Stella. 'Five to go.'

'Never mind. Tomorrow. We'll leave the pen up overnight.' Mr Lawrence seemed unconcerned, moved off to the gate.

'Can we help?' called Ag.

'I can manage.'

A few yards down the lane Joe, on the tractor, met the flock. He switched off the engine, watched them divide in confusion each side of the machine. The dogs skilfully kept them from running into the ditches – barking, pausing and sprinting with a subtle bossiness. Mr Lawrence, crook in hand, followed a little behind them. When he drew level with the tractor, Joe called to him.

'How did it go, the dagging?'

'Fine.'

Mr Lawrence strode past, not able to look at his son. Joe started the engine, drove into the yard. Ag and Stella were still there, leaning against the sheep pen – laughing, he thought. One of them waved: hard to tell which one. He drove into the barn, jumped down. The thump of gumboots warned him the girls had come to join him.

'It wasn't at all bad,' said one, with a happy voice.

'We became quite expert,' said the other. 'We managed almost all of them.'

'Good.'

One of them helped him unlock the trailer. The other threw a piece of sacking over the Fordson's engine. Then they found themselves looking towards the black hump of the house.

'One of the things I most miss in this war,' said Joe, 'is lighted windows. Imagine how it would be if we could walk towards a lighted kitchen window.'

'Never mind,' said Stella – he thought it was Stella. 'We're getting pretty good at finding our way in the dark.'

Joe put a heavy arm across each of their shoulders. 'I'll guide you all the same,' he said.

Prue, her muck-raking finally finished, tottered towards the gate. She decided to sit on it for a while, summon the energy to walk back up the lane. She would have done anything to accept Joe's invitation of a lift in the trailer, but some sense of pride insisted she finish the job completely before leaving the field.

She sat on the top bar of the gate watching the last light fade from the sky, trees change into black hoods, the ground mist stretch higher. She put out a foot, dipped it into the silvery skeins as if trying the water of a ghostly sea.

Prue didn't much like the dark. A shiver went down her spine. She feared an owl might hoot (something she had never heard, always wanted to hear, but not *now*). If a bat brushed past her, she'd scream bloody murder.

There was silence. Then, the distant shuffle and thud of sheep, anxious bleats, dogs barking. Prue swivelled herself precariously round, using the pitchfork for support, to face the lane. She could just make out a rumbling wave of fat woollen bodies, spectral cushions lumbering past, the occasional glint of an eye. Bloody hell, she said to herself, this is what I'd call *spooky*. What's more, they came with a phantom shepherd and his crook. Not till the shepherd reached the gate could Prue see it was Mr Lawrence.

'Finished,' she called. 'I done the lot, Mr Lawrence.'

Perhaps he did not hear, for he gave no answer. He strode past her, legs lost in the mist, whistling to the dogs.

'Old mean face,' she said out loud, jumping down.

With the last of her energy she hurried up the lane. She was very cold by now. She craved a hot bath in a bathroom like the one in shampoo advertisements – soaking in asses' milk or pine essence, gin and lime to hand. And what would she get? Three inches of tepid water, if she was lucky, in the Lawrences' mean and icy bathroom, followed by a glass of water and rabbit pie.

'*Land girl, you're barmy*,' she sang.

Her eyes had grown accustomed to the dark. When she reached the yard she could make out, quite easily, three figures walking towards the house. Joe seemed to be in the middle, arms slung across Ag's and Stella's shoulders. Prue stopped for a moment, to make sure.

Blimey, she thought, a week ago he was hardly speaking to any of us, and now he seems to *like* land girls. Very peculiar, men, as her mum always said.

Mr Lawrence strode into the kitchen without stopping to wipe his boots.

His wife, heeding the warning, glanced up from the pudding she was making at the table.

'Little hussy,' he said.

'What's she done now?'

Mr Lawrence frowned. He had meant to keep his silence. Calculations circled swiftly in his mind.

'Nothing you could put your finger on,' he said eventually. 'I told you. I always said land girls wouldn't work.'

'I don't know what we'd do without them,' she said. 'I'd begun to think you were getting used to them.'

'That Prudence girl. She's a menace.'

Mrs Lawrence put the dish in the oven, took her time to answer.

'I thought she might have been a threat – Joe. But I've come to the conclusion she's harmless. And she's a worker. It's Stella I worry about.'

'Stella?'

Mr Lawrence, on his way to the doormat, looked back so sharply the movement could have been taken for guilt. 'What's the matter with Stella?'

His wife coolly met his eye. 'Pining for the lover at sea. She seems so troubled by his lack of letters.'

'Is that all?' Mr Lawrence kicked off his boots with some relief. 'She'll get used to it. Pining'll get her nowhere. Hankering for what is not – stupid waste of time.'

'Quite,' said Mrs Lawrence.

Was it a smirched conscience, the farmer wondered, that caused him to think Faith knew he was addressing himself?

He felt a sudden desire to be far from the house – a house so full and changed by its new occupants. He wanted no part of the bustle, the chatter, the evening ahead. He wanted to get away, collect his thoughts in peace.

'I'll be out tonight,' he said. 'There's something on Ratty's mind and I've had no time to listen to him this past week. He needs an hour or two to unwind. Said I'd meet him for a pint in The Bells.'

'You'll need a shave, then. There's a clean shirt in the drawer.'

'Thanks.'

Mr Lawrence was convinced he saw a shadow of incredulity in his wife's tired eyes as she looked up at him. He left the kitchen too perturbed to drink the mug of tea waiting on the stove. It was the first time in their married life he had ever lied to her.

The others, at supper, were subdued by fatigue, but not uneasy. Joe got up after the cottage pie, saying he was going to his room to read. Before leaving he kissed his mother lightly on the top of her head – something none of them had ever seen him do before, and patted her shoulder. She did not respond.

Some moments later, Prue, with schoolgirl politeness, asked to leave the table: she didn't fancy any pudding and feared she would fall asleep in her chair. Mrs Lawrence nodded her assent, mouth reduced again to a thin line of disapproval.

Stella and Ag, on their way upstairs when the washing-up was finished, heard the thin sad sound of the Brahms cello concerto coming from Joe's room.

'Good heavens,' said Stella, pausing on the stairs. '*That*. I didn't know Joe liked music.'

'Do you? Do you play?'

'I play a little. I sing a bit, dance a bit. I'd like to teach one day, but at this rate I'll be far too rusty.'

133

They found Prue on her bed, the cover crumpled beneath her, fully dressed. She had fallen asleep even before taking off her shoes. She wore the crochet jersey again: the crystal beads on the collar sparkled like two inanimate smiles round her neck. Her bow-mouth was slightly open, two child-like front teeth resting on the bottom lip. Even in sleep she looked tired.

Ag struggled to pull off the regulation shoes. Lumps of dried mud fell to the floor. Stella began to tug at the breeches.

'What about the bow? The make-up?'

'Nothing we can do.'

'She'll be horrified in the morning. Panda eyes for milking.'

'She'll cope.'

When they had relieved Prue of her breeches, shoes and socks, they managed to bundle her under the bedclothes.

'More important, I hope she'll cope with Joe,' said Ag. 'The whole thing seems to be fraught with danger.'

'With any luck it'll burn itself out very quickly. No one will come to any harm.'

'Hope you're right. Apart from anything else, what land girl could find the time and energy for sex *and* farm work? They're not physically compatible, I'd say. Though maybe Prue will prove us wrong.'

'She's so pretty.' Stella studied the blonde head nestled in the pillows. 'You can see why Joe, alone here for so long, finds her irresistible.'

'He's an odd one, Joe.' Ag went to her own end of the room, turned down the bed. 'I didn't take to him at first. Now, I rather like him.'

Stella, as she did every night, picked up her framed photograph of Philip. 'As long as we all keep on liking him,' she said, 'we'll be all right. We'll be fine. We'll have a good friend.'

*

134

In The Bells Mr Lawrence found Ratty, as he guessed he would. The sight of the old man by the fire, tankard in hand, released some of his guilt. He had lied about a planned meeting, but at least Ratty's presence meant there *was* a meeting. The full weight of the lie was thus eased.

Mr Lawrence ordered himself a pint of bitter and joined Ratty by the fire. They nodded at each other, felt the warmth of the flames on their hands and shins.

'Poison day coming up soon,' said Mr Lawrence at last.

'This ruddy war.' Ratty shook his head. His eyes, the colour of tea, rolled about. 'Messes up everything. Girls ratting! Changes the nature of things.'

'Girls dagging, hedging, ploughing . . . odd, I agree. But something we'll have to come to think of as normal.'

Ratty's thin brown mouth stretched into an approximate smile. 'You've come round pretty quickly, then? Not two weeks back you were full of doubts, you said.'

'There's only one causes a bit of trouble.'

A growl of a laugh came from Ratty's throat. 'They're nice enough girls. The tall one puts me in mind of my mother.' Brightening, Ratty finished his drink. 'Then there's the floozie – you want to mind her. Then there's the – other one.'

'Stella.' The pleasure of saying her name, Mr Lawrence noticed, registered like a tiny graph moving upwards in his heart.

'That's right.'

'Another drink?'

'Thanks, no. Must be going.' Back to the furious darning Edith, thought Ratty. She'd managed to burn the single saucepan this evening. Potatoes abandoned, he had had to quell his hunger with drink.

'Couple of weeks, then, the ratting. I'll leave you in charge. You can explain to them, can't you?'

'Dare say I could if I put my mind that way.'

Ratty stood up, reluctant to think about it. He arched his

135

back, stiff. He didn't fancy the idea at all. Women screamed when they saw a mouse, in his experience. Lord knows what they'd do at the sight of a rat. As for explaining: words weren't easy on that sort of occasion. Still, he could *show* – like the day he'd shown the Stella girl to harness Noble. She'd learned surprisingly quickly.

'Night, Ratty,' said Mr Lawrence.

'Night, guv.'

Ratty touched his head with a kind of smudged salute. However close they had grown over the years, Ratty would not consider abandoning this deferential gesture. They were boss and hired hand, and nothing would persuade Ratty to alter his ways: he knew his place, and had no intention of changing the behaviour that was customary in his job.

'There's two things we must talk about, Joe, you and me,' said Prue. 'Two things we must talk about *first*.'

She stood just inside the door, dressing-gown clutched about her. It was the following night. After a long day lime-washing the cowsheds, she had had some difficulty waiting for the others to fall asleep before she crept downstairs to Joe's room. But she had promised to keep this date. He had reminded her several times during the day, assured her there was no danger providing she did not put on her torch. His room, luckily, was at the bottom of the attic stairs, the far side of the house from his parents.

It was lit by a dim lamp on the bedside table, knights in armour cut out from a scrapbook stuck on its shade. Even in the poor light, Prue could see it was still a schoolboy's room: pictures of trains and aeroplanes on the wall, a stack of board games in old boxes under a table. The bed was narrow, covered with threadbare candlewick. Pallid wool slippers stood neatly on the mat, a wooden chair was heaped with untidy clothes. Records in paper sleeves were stacked everywhere on the floor. Wedged in among them were piles of books that overflowed from the many shelves. There was a smell of toothpaste and dung, and it was cold.

Joe sat in the only comfortable chair, in an open-necked shirt and no shoes. 'Have this chair,' he said, rising after a long silence.

'I'd rather sit on the bed.'

'Sure?'

'Sure.'

Prue climbed on to the bruise-coloured cover. The springs whined. She curled her legs beneath her, hoping to warm her feet. She would have given anything for a Woodbine, but knew that was not possible – smoke brought on Joe's asthma.

'So what is it you have to say – first?' Joe gave a small smile.

Prue shivered: combination of cold and constraint.

'First: there's a party at the RAF camp in a couple of weeks' time. We all want to go. I mean, we must have a bit of fun.'

'So?'

'How do we get there?'

Joe rubbed his jaw, mock-serious. 'There's the Wolseley, I suppose.'

'Exactly. But it needs a driver. Would you – might you . . . be able?'

'I could see what I can do. There's a pretty tight rein on petrol, but we haven't used much lately. Dare say I could swing it.'

'Joe! You're a bloody angel!' Prue hugged herself.

'Of course, it would mean my having to *stay* at the party to bring you back. Dad would never agree to a lot of to-ing and fro-ing.'

'You wouldn't mind that, would you?'

'I'm not much of a party man. But no, I wouldn't mind for once.'

'We could *dance*.'

'It would take a lot to get me on a dance floor. A very large reward.'

'Promise you that!' Prue fluttered her eyelashes.

'And what was the other thing?' Joe began to take off his socks.

'The other thing was Janet. I think we should talk about her.'

'No need for that, is there?'

'I think there is.'

Joe undid the two top buttons of his shirt. 'You're at liberty to go back upstairs. I won't lay a finger on you again if it troubles your conscience.'

'It's *your* conscience I'm thinking of.'

'For various reasons that I won't bother you with, my conscience is having no troubles at all. But thanks for thinking about it. And come here.'

He put out a hand. Prue took it and slid herself off the bed. Joe guided her on to the floor between his legs. She put a hand on each corduroy knee. Her cheeks were scarlet. She wanted to laugh, but knew she must contain herself.

'Would you be terribly cold if you took off your dressing-gown?'

'Probably.' Prue giggled. She untied the cord, slipped it from her shoulders. Joe shifted forward in his chair.

'You realise,' he said, 'I could never see you properly in the barn. I could only imagine.'

'Well, here you are,' said Prue, giving a small wiggle so that her breasts shimmered. 'All right, are they?'

'All right? My God, come here.'

Joe took Prue's head in his enormous hands. She opened her shining pink mouth in readiness, the fluttering eyes not quite innocent. Suddenly fierce, he pulled her down.

Some time later Prue slipped out of the small, awkward bed. She felt exhausted by constraint. They had had to stop themselves from shouting. They had had to curb the instinctive wildness of their movements because of the singing bed springs. Prue longed to be back in the barn. Now, Joe put a warning hand on her arm.

'Listen,' he whispered.

Prue could hear footsteps in the passage. They hesitated. She quickly slipped into the small space between the wardrobe and the window, dressing-gown slung over her shoulders, heart battering. Joe struggled into his pyjamas. There was a small tap on the door.

'Joe?'

'Yes?'

'I thought I heard you coughing.'

Joe went to the door, opened it a few inches. His mother stood in the passage clasping a candle in a tin holder of cobalt blue. She wore a long cream nightdress of frayed wool: she had worn such nightdresses for as long as Joe could remember.

'Would you like me to put on the kettle? Do you a bowl of Friar's Balsam?'

Her sad beige mouth was drawn down, a tail of long dark hair hung over one shoulder. The slight trembling of her hand made the candle's flame to sway, and shadows to tremble on the walls.

'No thanks, I'm all right.'

'Very well, then.'

'Night, Ma.'

'Good night, Joe.'

Joe shut the door. Prue came out of her hiding place.

'Cor blimey,' she said. 'That was a near one.'

'Ma's always on the alert,' said Joe. 'Always worrying about my health. But she didn't have a clue – honestly.'

'I'll be going,' said Prue. She put up her cheek to be kissed, then on tense bare feet felt her silent way up the stairs. Night three: and complications, she thought. Trouble with Mrs Lawrence was the last thing she wanted.

Perhaps Joe wasn't such a good idea after all. Perhaps things would be easier all round with the RAF man in the teashop. At the thought of his severe blue cap tipped so neatly over his shaven head, Prue gave a small shiver as she climbed into her cold, dark bed.

Six

Stella's prediction that Prue's infatuation for Joe would burn itself out very quickly was proved right: just a fortnight after the affair began, it came to an end. Prue was exhausted by nights of scant sleep and dangerous journeys to Joe's room. She was fed up with the constraint, by day, of having to conceal her feelings. The impracticalities of illicit passion were too daunting, she found: she had had enough. For her, as always, the pleasure had been in the snaring. Once in the bag, the familiar melancholy feeling of having won too easily came upon her. Excitement waned. For some, affairs are flamed by enforced secrecy. For others, like Prue, it's a corrosive element that quells magic in a very short time.

'That's it, Joe,' she said, after an encounter in his unconducive room that had lasted till dawn. 'I can't be doing with any more of this. I'll collapse.'

She stood by the door in her dressing-gown, shivering. Joe scarcely shifted in his mean little schoolboy bed.

'Anything you say.'

'You're not bothered?'

'No.'

Prue hesitated before she smiled. His take-it-or-leave-it attitude was both a relief and something of an insult – mostly a relief, she quickly decided. There was nothing she would fancy less than Joe pouncing on her in the milkshed once she had said *enough*. In fact, his behaviour was so decent she felt she owed him something of an explanation.

'I can't take all the worry of creeping back upstairs expecting to run into blooming Lady Macbeth with her candle, night after night,' she said. 'It's a strain on the nerves.'

'I can understand that.'

'Besides, they've been giving me a hard time, your parents. Why should I be the only one who does the muck-spreading? It's not fair. Still, it's been fun – you and me, I mean.' She paused. 'I only hope all this won't change your mind about driving us to the dance . . .'

'It won't, no.' Joe turned away from her, pulling up the bedclothes. 'You have my word about that.'

Upstairs, careless in her strange sense of release, Prue made more noise than usual. The others stirred. Prue kept on her dressing-gown as she climbed into her cold bed. She sat with her arms round her knees. There was no point in trying to sleep for the half-hour before it was time to get up. Stella's voice came out of the dark.

'What's going on?'

'We've packed it in, me and Joe.'

'What?'

From the other end of the room, the squeaking of Ag's bed indicated she had sat up with some interest.

'Well, it couldn't go on, could it?'

'No,' said Ag.

'I think you've done the right thing,' said Stella.

'Pointless,' said Prue. Their voices, small chimes of agreement in the dark, were followed by a long silence. 'So what I've got to concentrate on now,' said Prue at last, 'is collecting jugs of rainwater. What I need is *rain*.'

'Whatever for?'

'The dance, of course, stupid. We're going to have Drene shampoos and rainwater rinses. I've got it all planned. You won't know yourselves by the time I've finished with you. The RAF boys'll think we're Rank starlets.'

Stella laughed. Ag lay down again, cold. In the darkness she touched her short, unremarkable hair. She wondered if, had she known about Drene and rainwater at Cambridge, it might have made all the difference.

There was no rain, that day, but the autumn weather had turned dank and misty. Ag, deputed to move the sheep from one pasture to another, strode through the long, grey grass, each blade tinselled with dew. She had no fears about the job: it was simply a matter, Mr Lawrence had assured her, of opening the gate between the two fields. The dogs would do the rest.

The collies swished along beside her, crouched with intent, tails low. Their bodies made dark paths through the grass. Overhead the sky was a dense grey, distinct from the earth only in its lack of sparkle. Earth and sky were divided by indistinct hedgerows, neither green nor brown nor grey, but a colourless density of bare wood. The only points of sharpness in the landscape were the few trees whose branches were raised like charred fans, brittle against the sky, awaiting a breeze to make them flutter.

As she made her way through this patch of land, silent and enveloping as a cloud, she should have felt at peace, thought Ag. It was the sort of surprising moment in nature that she loved, when a shift of weather transforms a familiar landscape so completely that the wonder of it fills the viewer with profound awe.

In fact, she was full of dread. Mr Lawrence had announced at breakfast that later this morning there was to be a rat hunt. Ag suffered an old fear of all scurrying creatures. She remembered the nights she had lain in fear listening to the sound of obscene little claws scraping against the wooden boards in the attics above her bedroom, terrified they would find a chink in the floor, hasten through it like lemmings and fall upon her. She had imagined them tearing at her with their eager paws, baring their teeth to shred her eyelids to morsels. Their overhead clatterings were at times so noisy she was positive they were rats and squirrels, though her father had assured her they were only harmless mice. She hadn't been able to tell him of her fears. After dinner, he would sit in his leather armchair fiddling with his pipe, listening to a concert on the Third Programme. He would not have welcomed a child disturbing his habitual evening peace. Kind, he would have been reassuring, patient. But secretly scornful. Afraid of mice? What nonsense, child, he would have said. Back to bed with you, go to sleep. So Ag had never gone down, but had remained rigid in her bed. She would long for the comfort of a mother she could not remember. On many such nights she prayed tearfully to God to show her just one picture of that mother's face. She willed her subconscious to pluck a single image from her babyhood. But none came. She would block her ears against the attic noises, and long for morning.

Ag opened the gate, its wood soft and wet under her hand. The dogs sped off to the distant huddle of sheep. She strained her eyes to observe their skills through the mist. The flock began to move. She could make out black heads jerked backwards, sensed their feeling of mass indignation at the disturbance the dogs were causing. An occasional bleat shredded the damp silence. Then they were close: a glint of yellow eye, the smell of acrid wool. The dogs crouched, swayed their tails across the dew, barked. On such a morning the sheep had no heart to resist the old routine. They spurted through the gate, muffs of dun wool puffed over skinny legs, their bleats turned to what now seemed to be pleasure at the small change of scene. Ag noted with some satisfaction the still-pristine condition of their hindquarters.

When the last sheep had skittered through, she pulled shut the gate. The dogs returned to her side, panting. Their breath rose in pale bulbs, lingered, vanished. Ag stayed where she was for a few moments, watching the sheep's indeterminate decision to make for the west corner of the field. Soon they became again as she had first seen them, an indistinct, distant skein. Her job done, dread of the next part of the morning returned with greater force. She could feel the beating of her heart.

'Desmond!' she said out loud, and the dogs looked curiously up at her.

When at breakfast that morning Mr Lawrence suggested Prue help Stella load the trailer with mangolds, Prue wondered whether her new innocence was as visible as her previous guilt.

'Bloody marvellous – no mention of muck-raking. Miracle,' she said later to Stella.

Side by side in the murky yard, they bent, picked up a mangold from the pile, swung it into the trailer. There was a huge pile to be loaded in the hour before they were to be handed over to Ratty for instruction. They worked fast, bending and throwing with easy rhythm. Their backs and shoulders soon ached with the grainy pain that had become a familiar, everyday occurrence. Prue paused, fingers exploring the knobbled muddy skin of one of the vegetables.

'Can't imagine fancying one of these even if I was a hungry cow,' she said. 'Do you think they know, or something? The Lawrences? I mean, why am I suddenly not muck-raking this morning?'

'Conscience,' said Stella, 'plays all sorts of funny tricks on the imagination. I expect there was just no more muck-raking to be done.'

'I didn't have a conscience.' Prue flung a mangold with some force. 'Well, not much of one, any road. I gave Joe some fun. He doesn't get much of that with Janet. He'll have something to look back on. Years and years of boredom with Janet, and he'll have me to look back on – the land girl who rogered him to a standstill in the barn.' She giggled, pushed damp curls out of her eyes. Stella laughed. 'What about you and Philip?' Prue asked, then, still resting, arms folded.

'What d'you mean, what about me and Philip?'

'Done it yet?'

Stella felt herself blush. 'Get on, Prue. I'm five mangolds ahead.'

'Go on, tell me.'

'I'll tell you if you do ten while I take a rest.'

'Done!' Prue bent at once.

'One, two, three . . . very good. You're doing well.'

Hands on hips, Stella watched Prue's small figure bending, straightening, throwing. In the grey air, her blonde curls were alive with light from an invisible source.

'Now come *on*, or I'll stop,' chided Prue. 'I want to *know*.'

Stella bit her lip. 'We haven't yet, no. No opportunity.'

'Poor old you, rotten luck,' said Prue. 'Still, only a matter of time. Once you get down to it you'll not want to stop, I'm telling you.'

'We'll only have a night or two, when his ship gets a boiler clean.'

'When's that?'

'Wish I knew.'

Stella returned to work. She hoped her voice conveyed a lightness she did not feel. The strain of waiting for a second letter was sometimes deflected by hard manual labour but, increasingly, even that antidote was often ineffective. The job of transporting cold heavy mangolds from yard to trailer on a damp and gloomy morning did nothing to raise her spirits. She wondered, as she so often did, how *so much love*, transported on air waves towards its object, was not felt and instantly returned.

'Don't envy *him* his job on a morning like this,' Prue was saying.

Stella followed her look to the yard gate. The postman pushed his dulled red bike through the mud, heavy canvas bag slouched over the handlebars.

'Silly to hope,' said Stella.

'You might as well,' said Prue.

To avert his mind from the dreadful prospect ahead – the instruction of the land girls in the art of ratting – Ratty allowed himself to daydream as he applied an extra polish to his boots and gaiters. He had been listening to a discussion on the wireless about the employment crisis in munition factories. Last September it had been announced that an extra 1,750,000 men and 84,000 women would be needed for the three Services and the Civil Defence by the end of this year. Therein the problem: if half a million men were withdrawn from the munitions industries to fight, and the industries had to expand by one and a half million, who would work in the factories to equip the newly swollen forces? Answer: women. A million and a half of them would have to leave their children, their kitchens, their darning, jobs such as running a local post office, and go into the factories. It was here that Ratty's dream brightened: he polished the toe of the second shoe with renewed vigour. For it might just be possible, it had occurred to him, to persuade Edith to go to work in a factory. He let a small scene, planned for the near future, run through his mind.

'*You ought to consider it, Edith. You're a fine worker. It would be an honourable way to do your bit for your country.*' (She'd be bound to like the idea of honour.)

'*And how would I do that? Where's the factories near here? Besides, my age . . .*'

'*You're a fine strong woman upon whom the years have left no trace, my dear.*' (If he really spoke to her like that she'd clout him about the ears in disbelief. In his dream she smiled pinkly with modest pride.) '*You could lodge with your sister Nancy: plenty of work in Southampton. You might have something of a social life. Forces' dances, that sort of thing. It would be a much livelier war than staying here with me . . .'*

'*Ratty!*' Her face lighted just as it had, once or twice, as a girl. '*I do believe you've hit on a good idea . . .*'

After that, the daydream swerved into other areas of pleasure: the cottage to himself, freedom from her tyranny, the luxury of being able to think uninterrupted. Best of all, the possibility that she might never come back.

Ratty put his brushes, dusters and polish neatly back in their tin. He straightened up to see Edith in the flesh at the door. In a nasty mood, this morning, she was – sort of mood where she'd rather give her loaves to the hens than let her customers buy them.

'What's all this polishing for?'

She was sharp, though. Had to say that for her. Nothing escaped her.

'Nothing special.'

'Huh.'

The meeting of dream and reality had come a little too quickly. Ratty knew that to say anything now would be foolish. Dregs of his fantasy would blur his powers of persuasion. On the other hand, he was impatient to try. If it worked, he could be rid of her within the week.

'They're saying on the wireless they're still wanting more women in the factories. Urgent,' he added, seeing the suspicion that instantly clouded her face.

'What's that got to do with me, pray?'

'It occurred to me you'd be a good woman on a factory line, all your energy, Edith. Wonderful sort of war effort. Greater sacrifice than any amount of saucepans . . .' He trailed off. His eyes lumbered over the whole rigid edifice of his wife's body, only avoiding her eyes. 'Plenty of work near Nancy. Livelier life for you than here. I could manage fine on my own.'

Edith began to laugh, a nasty cackling sound. Ratty was

filled with regret for his decision – such mistiming. Judgement distorted by disappointment, he wondered for a moment if she really was amused. He smiled in uneasy complicity. Would she stop that dreadful noise in a moment and say she agreed to the idea? Confused, Ratty put the tin of shoe-cleaning things on the table. Edith uttered a piercing scream.

'You can't get rid of me as easily as that, you can't! Have to try something better than that. And take that tin off my table! How many times have I told you . . . ?'

Over the years, Ratty had learned the advantages of appearing calm in the face of her hysteria. He let himself out of the room without a word, screams of abuse following him down the garden path. Once through the small gate, he turned to secure the latch. He was aware of Edith's contorted face at the kitchen window. As he moved away with a polite wave, the window opened. You wouldn't credit so small a woman with such strength of insult, such powerful lungs, thought Ratty. And then he saw an object flying through the grey air.

Ratty paused for less than a second to confirm the object, landed on the grass, was what he most feared it might be – their last saucepan. He hurried down the lane, determined not to think what kind of an evening this would mean. His knees were shaken by the scene: they always reacted first to Edith's outbursts. But then, rounding the corner, he saw in the distance the tall figure of the one with the holy face. She waved, friendly. As they drew closer Ratty saw her hair hung lank in the damp air. There was something hesitant, unwilling, in her step.

What then occurred was the kind of thing Ratty would rate as a small miracle. She smiled at him, the girl, and it was as if all the troubles of his life with Edith ceased to exist. Instead, the only thing that engaged his mind, indeed his whole shaky body, was a deep longing to convey to this gentle creature the skills, the joys, of hunting rats.

'Morning,' he said, weak with a gratitude she would never know she had caused. They walked together into the yard.

'You may sit,' said Ratty. He stood before his audience of three in the barn. The girls sank on to piles of hay. Ratty observed Ag's kindly look, her half-smile.

She was thinking of this time last year: the undergraduates in the lecture hall would stand as the Professor in Elizabethan Literature shuffled in, never less than ten minutes late, dropping his many notes on metaphysical poetry as he climbed the platform. He would survey them all for a very long time in silence, nodding his head as he silently counted how many had bothered to turn up. Small pieces of coloured papers covered with illegible writing sprouted from his pockets and the books he carried. It often seemed that he was so preoccupied with some erudite problem that he had forgotten his job was actually to speak. Sometimes he would leave his students standing for as much as three minutes before murmuring *You may sit*. Then, shaking himself free of all the notes, he would begin, and hold his audience spellbound for the next hour.

Now the girls were sitting down, Ratty felt more at ease. He could see over their heads to the tractor and the sacks, cast his eyes up to the familiar rafters and the mysterious darkness beyond, stirred now and then by the pale fluttering of a pigeon. It had been his idea to speak to the girls in the barn. Mr Lawrence had suggested that round the kitchen table would be most convenient – but no, Ratty had thought. That would be too close. He would like to stand while they sat. The barn was the place he had retreated to, for shelter and private thought, for so many years. It was the fit location for his first attempt at formal instruction.

He leaned on his stick, more for moral support than physical, kneaded its smooth wooden knob in his hand.

150

One knee still shook slightly, but he doubted any of the girls would notice. With his free hand he patted his jacket pocket, checking the huge ball of his handkerchief was there: these days drips from his nose and water from his eyes would appear without warning. The pert little film star shifted, impatient. The bow in her hair was the nastiest colour he had ever seen.

'Come on, Ratty,' she said.

Bugger you, you little floozie, he thought. Then he lifted his chin, as he did in church before the first hymn, and began.

'You may have been expecting a whole team of pest exterminators here today, girls – handsome men, real professionals: tour the country, they do, enjoy themselves. But what's the point of employing them, Mr Lawrence says to me, when we've got you here, Ratty? Truth is, I've been ratting all my life, though matter of fact that's not the reason for my nickname.' He paused. The girls all seemed to be listening. 'It could be said, what I don't know about ratting isn't worth knowing. Now, what you have to be to become a good rat hunter is something between a murderer and a detective. Like a detective, you have to be good at looking for clues. Like a murderer, you have to face a nasty job at the end – gassing and poisoning are the most effective. And I may say you don't get used to that, not really.' He paused, fumbled for his handkerchief, to deal with a rush of dampness irritating his nose.

Prue watched the distant figure of Joe, carrying two buckets, cross the yard. She wondered at the fickleness of her own nature. Just a week ago, a single glance from Joe in the milking shed or on the tractor turned her guts to flame – it was all she could do not to assault him on the spot. Now the sight of him left her cold. She felt nothing. She didn't ever want to touch him again. He was too big, too gruff, too unobservant, somehow – never seemed to notice what she wanted once the love-making was over.

That wasn't to say he was not a nice enough bloke: rather sad, what with the prospect of Janet, the fact he could not go either to the war or to university, and being stuck here with his parents working as a farm hand. Poor old thing, Joe. With any luck he'd meet some girl more suited to him and get rid of Janet.

Prue turned to look at Ag. Ag's hair was in a bad way: lifeless in the damp. Thin and dreary as old curtains. Still, come the day of the dance, Prue would do her best. She'd bought the curling tongs and a whole bag of kirby grips. She had good supplies of setting lotion and enough Drene to last six months – her mother had warned her that Dorset was most probably not rich in Drene shampoo. So all Prue had to do was to secure Ag's trust. Ag only had to give the go-ahead and Prue would transform her – waves, a little fringe perhaps to soften the wide expanse of her forehead. By the time Prue had finished, Ag wouldn't know herself. She might even look rather beautiful, in a quiet sort of way: she had good bones, a friendly smile, what could be lovely eyes if Prue could persuade her to try a little spit and mascara, and a dab of True Blue eye shadow . . .

'What you must never underrate,' Ratty was saying, 'is the *intelligence* of the rat. In my opinion, there are many more intelligent rats than there are human beings. But that's only my opinion, you understand.' His small joke was rewarded by another smile from the holy one. The floozie was fiddling with her hair ribbon. The other one, hands in her pockets as if she was cold, looked interested. 'So what you have to do is outwit them. It's a slow process. It could be said it's not a fast process. But it's interesting and it's a challenge. That's what it is. It's an interesting challenge. The rat has skills we don't have. For instance, he can camouflage himself by hiding behind his own shadow. The glint in his eye is the only thing that betrays him. You have to look for that glint, that tiny speck of light. You have to look for clues: tail trails running over heaps of grain, empty husks on the ground, tunnels through ricks or piles of loose hay or straw – that sort of thing.'

In her right pocket Stella's hand lay flat against the new, unopened letter from Philip. There was a picture in her mind that had been building in detail for the last few days: a grand Edwardian hotel by the harbour in Plymouth, crimson carpets of soft deep pile, chandeliers. The bedroom would be so large they could dance. They could order up a gramophone, put on some Glenn Miller, draw the curtains, turn out most of the lights. They would recapture the way they had danced at the party. But there would be no siren to interrupt them, this time. God willing, they could dance until they fell exhausted on to the huge bed, carry on where they left off . . . to the end. In the morning there would be the cry of gulls outside their window. No reason to get up until they felt like a soak in the deep marble bath, tons of hot water – breaking all rules of economy just for once – and back to bed, smelling of pre-war lavender soap from the small collection Stella had brought to Hallows Farm and husbanded so carefully . . . Ratty caught her eye. She struggled to put aside her thoughts of Plymouth.

'First day, we lay the bait. We lay bits of bait all over the place – here in the barn, the sheds, the yard. But don't expect a rush of rats. They'll take their time. They'll have their suspicions. They won't go near it the first day. Second day, much the same. Note where it is, they will, but leave it. Third day, we lay fresh bait. Temptation becomes stronger than caution, now. The word goes round. There's definite interest. But still some instinct holds them back. As I said, a rat hunter must be patient.'

Ratty stopped to shift his weight on to the leg that had been shaking. It now felt surprisingly firm. He tapped his stick on the ground a few times, no longer feeling the need to lean on it for support. In explaining the nature of a rathunt he had almost forgotten the girls were listening.

When he saw their eyes intent upon him, the warmth of encouragement flowed through him. He would have been quite happy to carry on a long time, now he'd got going – he had a hundred theories about the ways of the rat. But it would be foolish to presume upon the depth of their interest. He must come to an end in a moment or so.

He would have made an excellent Professor of Ratting, thought Ag, entranced by his lecture as she had been by the Professor at Cambridge. She alone of the girls admired his timing, the rhythms of his West Country voice – above all, his ability to convey enthusiasm for the subject he had studied most of his life. So few are blessed with that gift. She wondered if she had it herself. Could she inspire others with her own love of literature? Could she ever convey it to Joe? There he was, crossing the yard again . . . Or is a love of poetry as impossible to describe as a love of music? One day, she would like to try. It would take courage. It would take Ratty's kind of courage. Here he was, by nature a taciturn man, talking to three almost strange girls about a subject in which he was an expert, a subject he loved. His own enthusiasm was contagious. Stella hadn't moved, Prue had stopped fiddling with her hair. Ag herself would have liked him to go on and on.

But she could see he was bracing himself for the end. He straightened his bent shoulders, wiped his moustache with a huge handkerchief. On his fine, battered old face, pebbled with small shadows beneath jutting cheekbones and deep-set eyes, there was a look of confidence, enjoyment. He may never have fought a war, been in command. But something of a natural soldier in him seemed to be taking over. Rallying his troops for the fight, or hunt, came to him with almost Churchillian inspiration.

'On the fifth day,' he said, the whole length of his handkerchief having been stuffed back into his pocket, 'we put down fresh bait again. But this time it's *poisoned* fresh bait.' He paused, while the seriousness of the fact resounded. 'By this time, the little devils are impatient. Out they come, eager.' He broke off again, glanced up at a pigeon side-stepping along a rafter, cooing in time to its own movements. 'And here it wouldn't be honest, girls, if I didn't tell you the next part is not very agreeable. The poor buggers come snucking out of tunnels half dead, gasping for air. The effects are horrible, but no one can afford a farm overrun by rats. They have to be finished off . . .' He noticed a jerk of the holy one's head. She'd gone very pale. 'But don't worry. We won't ask you to take care of that. That's a man's job. Joe and Mr Lawrence and me will deal with that side of things. Now, no more talking. Sorry if I've kept you too long. I'm not much used to this sort of thing, explaining. Would one of you care to help Mr Lawrence lay the bait? The others can collect the orchestration, I call it, from the kitchen. A good percussion is what we want – banging saucepan lids together, spoons in pans, anything to frighten the buggers out of their hiding places. I wish you good luck.'

When the girls had gone, Ratty lowered himself on to the place vacated by Ag. The hay was warm through his breeches. He clasped his stick with both hands, leaned his chin on his knuckles. He was exhausted, drained, astounded, elated. He had done it. It was over. It seemed to have gone down with the girls better than he could ever have expected. They hadn't laughed or sneered or shown lack of interest. It was extraordinary . . . Edith would never believe it, not that there was any point in telling her. Matter of fact, he could scarcely believe it himself.

'You all right, Ratty?' Joe was beside him, smiling.

'Never strung together so many words in my life. I'm all right, just need a few moments to recover.'

'Ag said you were terrific.'

'Did she, now?'

'Do you want to come in for a cup of tea?'

'That I don't. Soon as my knees have brightened up I'll

be out to show them some of the clues. There's a good tail mark in the grain in the stable.'

When Joe had gone, Ratty felt tears in his eyes. He reached for his handkerchief again. What was such snivelling all about, he wondered. Perhaps something to do with a private victory. But no matter. It was time he returned to his duties – marshal the troops, alert the rats, get on with the day.

Out of sight of the others, Ag banged her saucepan lids with little enthusiasm. Despite her enjoyment of Ratty's talk, the last thing she wanted to do was to encounter a rat, especially on her own. To keep out of the way – Stella and Prue were enjoying themselves making a terrible din in the milking shed and yard – Ag went to an old stable, now used as a grain store. She opened the door, let herself in. If anyone found her taking a rest from clashing these cymbals, she would say she was looking for clues. Ratty had said nothing about having to make a noise while you were looking for clues.

She stood quite still, eyes travelling up and down the piles of grain. On one of them, she saw, there was a curved indentation that ran from the floor halfway up, then stopped in an untidy swirl of grain, as if the rat had changed its mind about going to the top, and jumped down. Was that what Ratty had meant by the trail of a tail? Had she found the first clue?

Heart beating fast, she backed her way quickly to the stable door, put a hand on its lower half for support. Then, on the ground between two piles of grain, she saw it – the glint of an eye Ratty had described. A moment later another speck of light joined the first one: Ag could now clearly see two red eyes, pink-rimmed. The ears lay flat back on the head, making the animal's face seem longer and meaner. Whiskers twitched. The whole body – large and oddly flabby – was poised to flee, or to attack. Ag held her breath, too scared to move. The rat, lifting its head, took a few steps to one side. In the silence Ag could hear the high-pitched scraping of its claws on the floor. With horror she watched the obscene way in which the small toes parted, revealing the slithers of pink flesh lining between them, as the claws gripped. The terror of her childhood nights returned. She screamed. Black moments later, she opened her eyes. The rat had gone. Ag edged herself from the door to the limewashed wall so that she could lean her whole body against it: she feared she might faint. Then she heard the thud of hurrying boots, and turned to see Joe leaning over the door.

'You must have seen a rat!' He was in cheerful mood.

'I did! I did!'

'First one?'

Ag nodded. Her head was beginning to clear. She could see Joe was smiling.

'Everyone screams when they see their first rat,' he said, and came in.

Ag turned to face him. 'So silly of me,' she said, unable to control the quaver in her voice.

'Ratty should've told you not to come in here. It's one of their favourite places.'

'He couldn't have known I didn't want to see one.'

'Are you all right? You look a bit shaken.'

'I'm . . . fine. It's just that I've always had this silly sort of thing, this phobia, about scurrying things. Rats, mice – hamsters, even.'

Joe nodded.

'When I was a child they used to make a terrible noise in the attic above my room at night. Even now, when I go home, I don't like it. Funny how long it takes to overcome such silly fears. I thought it might have gone for my throat.'

'That's an old belief, I know. Can't say I've heard of a single case where it's actually happened. Tell you what, I've just said to Dad I need some help unloading the mangolds

157

for the cows if he wants me to see to the tractor before this afternoon. He said I could ask one of you. Not much of an offer, but perhaps better than ratting. How about it?'

Their eyes met: his anxious, hers relieved.

'Do you think anyone else heard me scream?' Ag asked.

'No one, I'm sure.'

Joe took the saucepan lids from her and put them under his arm. His gentle concern was not lost upon her.

On the Saturday afternoon of the dance, Mrs Lawrence sat at the kitchen table polishing the silver handle of the salt and pepper holder. It did not need a polish: she had rubbed it up not long ago. But for once, free time on her hands, she was at a loss what to do. From upstairs came the squeals and giggles of the girls preparing themselves. The sound of their high spirits did nothing to ease her own feelings of melancholy.

She had agreed to their taking their half-day today, to give themselves time for all the beautifying Prue had been planning for the last few days. At first, Ag had said she had no wish to go to the dance. For a moment, Mrs Lawrence had envisaged a quiet evening in conversation with this calm, agreeable girl. But Prue had been persuasive. Ag gave in, albeit reluctantly. She even agreed to let Prue do something to her hair. Stella, too, had shown no particular enthusiasm to go, but had agreed to for Prue's sake. But then Stella was so in love with her absent sailor that she never minded what she did. The intensity of her love protected her completely from the ups and downs of reality, that was clear. Mrs Lawrence could remember such feelings herself.

Polishing finished, she stood up, restless. No task appealed to her. What she would like was to see the girls, join in a little of their fun. She might be needed, she thought: a placket to be done up, a necklace fastened. Surely they wouldn't mind her asking if they wanted any help . . .

Climbing the stairs, she heard music coming from Joe's room. The song , on his old gramophone, was scratchy, shaky. But it did something to her limbs, her head.

> *Gee, it's great*
> *After sitting up late*
> *To be walking my baby back home . . .*

Mrs Lawrence caught herself half smiling. Joe's door was ajar. She could see him grimacing into the small mirror on the wall, struggling with a tie.

'You look smart, son,' she said.

'Mustn't let them down,' he said.

He had not complained at all about his job as chauffeur. Mrs Lawrence privately thought he was rather looking forward to the evening. Well, he didn't get out much, deserved the occasional break. And this dance caused no worries. Joe may have been quite the ladies' man in his time, but with three girls to chaperone him there was no danger. Prue, the wicked little flirt, had done nothing but talk about some RAF lad she had seen in the tea-shop – her sights were clearly not on Joe tonight. It was only a pity Janet wasn't here.

She stood in the shadow of the girls' doorway, unnoticed for a while. The attic room was hilariously untidy, unrecognisable from the neat and spotless place it had become after days of scrubbing and painting before the girls had arrived. Now, it was like a communal dressing-room in a theatre, ravaged by a series of quick changes. Clothes were flung everywhere – signs of several dresses being tried on and rejected, Mrs Lawrence guessed. Coloured shoes and shiny stockings were strewn over the floor. Lipsticks clustered on the top of the chest of drawers, and every surface was sprinkled with a fine dust shaken from a box of Pond's powder decorated with its comforting design of floating puffs. The war seemed to have made no difference to the extravagance of youth, thought Mrs

Lawrence. She remembered the meagreness of her own wardrobe even when she was young.

Ag sat on a chair under the central light, feet together, hands folded primly on her lap. Prue twittered round her, dabbing and pulling at Ag's transformed hair – a mass of scatty curls and waves that twinkled in the light from the low-watt bulb.

'We're getting somewhere at last,' assured Prue, tottering on her high-heeled black suede sandals, their ankle straps fastened with ruby buckles. 'You won't know yourself. No, you can't look till I've finished.' Ag gave a trusting smile. She touched a thin gold chain round her neck, from which hung a small gold heart. 'That doesn't do much for you,' said Prue. 'Haven't you anything *sparklier*?'

'No,' said Ag. 'I like this. It was my mother's.'

'Very well.' Prue gave the small sigh of one who knows best but is forced to agree to less sure taste for tactical reasons. 'Tell you what, then: I'll lend you my chiffon leopard scarf – cheer your shoulders up a bit.' She tweaked the dark green stuff of Ag's quiet dress.

'Thanks,' said Ag. Prue passed her a hand mirror. Ag studied herself in silence before handing it back. 'Good heavens, what *have* you done to me?'

'One more thing,' said Prue, 'and the transformation'll be complete.' She moved to the chest of drawers, picked up an open lipstick. '*Fire and Ice*,' she threatened, holding it dagger-like towards Ag's mouth.

'*No.*'

'*Cherries in the Snow*, then?'

'No! Prue, please. I'm not going to wear lipstick. I never do.'

'*Spoilsport*! It's yourself you'll be letting down. No hope of wowing the RAF without a bit of lipstick.' Prue pouted. Her own mouth was a squealing pink, designed to seduce an entire squadron, thought Mrs Lawrence, smiling. 'How about a touch of Vaseline, then?'

160

'Just for you,' agreed Ag.

Prue giggled, rummaged through a tangle of scarves in an open drawer. Ag stood, saw Mrs Lawrence at the door. She was immediately embarrassed.

'Mrs Lawrence! Goodness knows what I look like . . .'

Mrs Lawrence came further into the room. Prue leapt at her.

'What d'you think of my handiwork, Mrs Lawrence? God, do I need a fag. *Shine on, shine on harvest moon,*' she shrilled a tuneless snatch of song. 'There.' She knotted a wisp of chiffon round Ag's neck, searched her dressing-gown pocket for a packet of cigarettes. 'And what about Stella, here?'

Stella, sitting on the edge of her bed, concentrated on putting on her own lipstick. A red spotted skirt was drawn up over a pair of sharp little knees, pressed together as if for comfort. Her legs splayed out like two sides of a triangle: the feet, in pink slippers, turned in, ankles bent. There was something childlike in the pose, thought Mrs Lawrence, as if Stella had no interest in trying for sophistication when Philip was away at sea. Stella looked up, blotted her lips, smiled.

'You all look very nice,' said Mrs Lawrence. In this scene of frivolity she felt herself a symbol of dourness, awkward. She did not know where to put her hands, wished she had taken off her apron. 'I wondered if there was anything I could do to help . . .'

'*Please*, Mrs Lawrence.'

Prue flung off her dressing-gown, which sank into a foam of blue on the floor behind her. With a shimmy of her wiry little body, she defied them all not to observe the breasts that swelled above the peach petticoat, the lean hips to which the bias cut of the satin skirt clung. She stepped out of the foam, ankles jigging in their straps, waved a thin arm above her head.

'Who would believe this very arm has spread ten acres of

muck, milked five hundred cows, fought a pig, frightened a rat? *Land girl, you're barmy,*' she sang.

The others laughed. Encouraged, Prue stubbed out her half-smoked Woodbine, and stepped into her dress with a single fluid movement whose natural grace Mrs Lawrence could not but admire.

'Please, Mrs Lawrence.' She presented her back. Faced with a plummet line of small gold buttons, Mrs Lawrence raised her hands, wondering at the sudden clumsiness of her fingers.

'All this just for the RAF,' said Stella. She looked admiringly at Prue. 'Now, if it had been the Navy . . .'

'I'm not fussy,' said Prue, bending about, impatient.

'Keep still,' said Mrs Lawrence.

'Army, Navy, Air Force, Home Guard, anything. Ag, give me that bottle and I'll treat you all to a spray.'

Ag handed Prue a cut-glass bottle of scent. 'Not for me, thanks,' she said.

'Don't be daft, Ag. You don't want to smell of sheep.'

Prue pressed the small bulb in its filigree cover of golden thread. A spray of vapour hit Ag's chest. She laughed, backed away, clutching at herself. Prue swerved round to Stella, sprayed her, too.

'I said, keep *still*.' Mrs Lawrence found herself smiling.

'And last of all, me. Ears, throat, cleavage, wrists. There.' With each steamy puff the smell of tuberose thickened the air. 'No: not quite last – here, Mrs Lawrence!' Prue snapped round on her heels, aimed a squirt of scent at Mrs Lawrence's apron.

'No! Not for me – please, Prue.'

Mrs Lawrence, to her own surprise, joined in the others' laughter. She tugged Prue round again to finish the last of the buttons. A picture came to her mind of dancing in a summer barn, years ago: a harvest supper, perhaps. John coming up behind her, putting his arm round her waist. Streamers looped from the rafters, a small band that made her feet tap long before they reached the dance floor.

'It's magic, I'm telling you,' giggled Prue. 'It'll *do* something for you, Mrs Lawrence.'

There was a shout from downstairs to hurry. With one accord, the girls swerved about the room gathering up scarves, bags, coats. Mrs Lawrence moved about trying to keep out of their way. The sugar smell of powder, combined with the sickliness of Prue's favourite scent, could not quite disguise a sharp, sour smell of sweat.

'Excitement!' shouted Prue, the first to run to the door.

Mr Lawrence and Joe stood side by side in the hall, waiting. They heard the patter of feet on the stairs, saw three pairs of silky legs make a brief moving trellis among the stair bannisters, followed by flashes of coloured skirts. Then they were there, swirling about in the dim milky light of the hall, filling the air with the overwhelming sweetness of cheap scent. Stella's hand clutched a dark oak bannister as she paused for a moment, laughing, catching her breath. Mr Lawrence, staring at her, met her eyes, more visible than ever before now her hair had been caught back each side in combs. He quickly looked away. The curve of a pearly lid, the curl of thick lashes, seared in his mind. Ag – he vaguely noticed something different about her – was struggling into an old grey coat. Joe was helping her.

'I've brought the Wolseley to the door,' he said.

'Joe, you're wonderful.' Prue spun over to him, kissed him quickly on the cheek. 'What would we do without you? Can I sit next to the driver?'

Mr Lawrence undid the bolts on the front door. He meant to wish them all a good evening, but could not manage it. As they crowded past him to the car, Stella saw the sudden paleness of his cheeks.

'Good night, Mr Lawrence,' she said. 'Thanks for the use of the car. Have a peaceful evening without us.' She put a hand on his arm, brief as a bird touches water, sees nothing there, and soars away again.

163

' 'Night, Stella,' he said.

When they had gone, Mr Lawrence shut the door. Mrs Lawrence came downstairs quietly in her slippered feet. Fearful she would recognise his infidelity in the murky place full of horrible scents that the hall had become, he hurried into the kitchen. His wife followed him.

'Just eggs and bacon, tonight,' she said.

Mr Lawrence took a bottle of ale and a glass from the dresser. He sat down at the table. Mrs Lawrence leaned up against the range, the dogs at her feet. She undid her apron, took it off, folded it, hung it over the back of a chair. Such a pale, worn thing, the binding coming unsewn round the edges.

'Did we have anything like that, in our youth?' she asked.

'Not exactly, no.' Mr Lawrence stood up. 'Can smell that filthy stuff even in here. Don't say you . . . ?'

Mrs Lawrence smiled. 'Prue squirted it over all of us: very generous . . .'

'God forbid. You'll have to have a bath.' He moved over to his wife, lowered his head to sniff at the brown wool of her shoulders. 'It reeks.'

Mrs Lawrence half raised her arms, as if to encircle her husband's neck, then thought better of it. It wasn't Sunday, after all. Instead, she undid the top button of her cardigan. Mr Lawrence watched her, puzzled. Their eyes remained locked for several moments, the disparity of their thoughts almost tangible.

'Reach me down a frying pan, will you,' said Mrs Lawrence at last.

'You're a good woman,' her husband said. 'You're a good woman, you are.'

A plane squawked overhead, shredding the sound of the RAF band. They did not miss a beat, but a few of the dancing couples gripped each other more tightly. Stella, at a small table with the other girls and Joe, clasped her glass of ginger beer.

'It feels more as if there's a war on, here, somehow,' she said.

She looked round the large, rather cold hall. The organisers had tried to disguise its dreary walls with paper chains and clumps of tinsel. Flakes of cottonwool snow had been stuck to the blackout stuff over the windows. At the far end of the hall, next to the bar, someone had struggled to make the buffet look tempting. Coming in, Stella had noticed piles of bridge rolls filled with fish paste, and plates of sliced Spam lay with an exhausted air on lettuce leaves. There were several bottles of salad cream and what must have been a pre-war jar of French mustard. A second table was reserved for a small townscape of castellated jellies. Bright primary colours, some flecked with tinned fruits; they rose out of dazzling white imitation cream skilfully piped to look like shells.

Prue had no interest in the surroundings: her eye was busy on the crowd of uniformed pilots at the bar with their soft, young faces, red necks and noisy laughs. The cheering thing was there were at least three men to every one girl in the room. Prue tossed her curls, tapped a foot under the table – quite Glenn Miller, really, she thought – impatient. She would have to make a break soon, waste no more time. Finish this first gin and lime, kindly bought by Joe, then she'd be off. But there was no time to finish the drink – *for there he was*, the tea-room flight lieutenant, even more handsome without his cap. Prue jumped to her feet.

'Sorry, folks,' she said, 'but I have to go. Don't want to miss my chance. See you.'

The others watched her spraunce off towards the crowd at the bar, hips waggling, hair bouncing, hands on hips. Many heads, they noticed, joined in observing her progress.

'Same performance as in the milking shed the first

morning,' said Joe. Stella and Ag laughed, then they fell into the awkwardness engendered by a trio. Ag, conscious that Stella was looking extraordinarily attractive in a very different way from Prue, folded her hands. tried to assume a settled sort of look.

'If you two want to dance,' she said, 'I'm quite happy sitting here just looking.'

'I don't want to dance,' said Stella, without conviction.

At that moment, a short, heavily built wing commander approached their table, gave a little bow in Stella's direction.

'Might I have the honour,' he said, with a teasing smile, 'of the next one?'

Stella hesitated.

'Go on,' said Joe. 'You can't rely on me.'

'Very well, thanks. I'd love to.'

'My name's Stephen,' said the wing commander.

'My name's Stella.'

'You look to me like a girl who *can* dance.'

'Oh, I don't know.'

He put out his hand, led Stella towards the floor. They were quickly lost in the crowd.

Ag felt all the humiliation of failure. There was no one, she noticed, on the way to ask her to dance. The agony of teenage parties, when the same sort of thing had happened so often, returned. She felt a fool in Prue's silly chiffon scarf and the ridiculous curls: she wished she hadn't come, she wished Joe didn't look so bored.

'Your curls seem to be falling out,' he said.

'The damp.' Ag managed a smile.

'Much better your usual way.'

'Prue enjoyed doing it.'

'I bet she did.'

A small, irrational pain skewered Ag's heart. She watched Joe looking into the distance – remembering Prue, she supposed.

'Who are the other girls here, do you think?' she asked.

Joe stirred himself. 'Some from the Services. Probably quite a few other land girls.' Then he smiled at her kindly. 'Can't say any of them look as if they've made the same effort as all of you.'

'It's a pity Janet can't be here,' said Ag.

'She wouldn't like this sort of thing. She doesn't like dancing.'

'Then you have that in common.'

'I suppose we do have that, yes. Shall I get you another drink?'

'It's my turn. I'll come with you.'

'I can't let you buy me a drink . . .'

'You can in a war. Besides, how can I spend my vast wages? My fourteen shillings a week?' Ag jumped up, suddenly carefree. She would enjoy the sensation of walking across the hall with Joe behind her.

When they reached the dance floor, he said:

'Shall I surprise you?'

Without waiting for an answer, he took her loosely in his arms. Neither was a skilled dancer: they shuffled awkwardly, others twirling past them. 'Are you as much in love as Stella, with someone far away?' asked Joe.

Ag felt herself blush. She spoke the truth. 'I dream about someone who scarcely knows of my existence,' she said. 'He was a graduate student, medicine. We did once have tea, with some other friends. For some reason, I found myself telling him my name was really Agapanthus and he didn't laugh. But I don't suppose he'd remember.'

'Agapanthus? Well, it's hard not to laugh.' Joe suppressed a smile. 'You are an odd lot, you three. Not at all as I imagined land girls.'

By now they had reached the bar and gave up all pretence at dancing. Ag bought Joe a pint of beer and an orange squash for herself. They made their way back to the table.

'I like your *deportment*,' teased Joe. 'You walk so straight, ramrod back like a gym mistress.' He pulled out her chair.

'I went to a very strict convent,' said Ag. 'We had to train with books on our head.'

Joe smiled. A jitterbug number had started. 'Lucky we missed this one,' he said.

Their eyes were drawn to the dancing. It was an exuberant crowd on the floor, some skilled at the steps, others merely jumping about, not caring. Then it became apparent there was unanimous recognition of a couple of stars among them, and they were being given space. Lesser dancers had drawn back, still moving, but their concentration was on the stars: Stella and her partner.

The wing commander's short, bulky figure, lightened by the music, was transformed. His jitterbugging had all the vitality of a younger man's actions, but also a precision that was astonishing to watch. He flung Stella hither and thither and she followed, sure as Ginger Rogers, adding her own inventive little flurries – a flick of the head or skirt, a sharp circling movement of her hands. The band, aware they were playing for experts at last, stepped up the tempo: the rest of the dancers fell away, leaving Stella and her unlikely Astaire on their own till the end of the number. Stella kicked off her shoes. The combs fell out of her hair. Her cheeks were scarlet as she spun faster and faster.

When the music stopped, the wing commander lifted her easily above his head, like a ballet dancer. There was cheering all round the hall, applause. Stella dizzily returned to earth. She hurried back to the table, followed by her smiling partner. Her hands rushed through her now wild hair. She was panting.

'You can *dance*,' said Joe. He stood up in acknowledgement. His clear admiration spurred Ag to rise, too, and turn to the wing commander.

'*You* must have been jitterbugging all your life,' she said.

'I like to dance,' he conceded. 'Your turn. Shall we?'

'I can't do anything like that,' said Ag.

'It's a nice slow number. Come on.'

I'm in the mood for love was rising and falling through the hall. Ag followed the wing commander to the floor. He clasped her with such expertise, his lead making the slow steps so easy to follow, that she began not to mind the fact she was a good head taller than him. She looked down, studied the intricate waves of his Brylcreemed black hair, then averted her eyes. All round them, other couples, on just an hour or so's acquaintance, clung to each other as if to make the most of the last moments of life on earth: eyes shut, whispering things inspired by the rarity of such occasions. One of these couples was Prue and her tea-shop flight lieutenant. His chin nuzzled into the bow in her hair, her arms were clasped round his back. Again, Ag felt a pang of a sensation she despised. How did Prue manage it, every time?

At the table, Stella finished her ginger beer in one gulp. Her face shone, excited.

'You were amazing,' said Joe.

Stella shrugged. 'I've always loved dancing, singing.'

'Is that what you're going to do, eventually, be a dancer?'

'Heavens, no. I'm nothing like good enough for that. I'd like to teach the piano – though I'm so out of practice I may never get it back. Where's the nearest piano to Hallows Farm?'

'There's always The Bells,' said Joe. 'There's an old one there, very out of tune.'

'Anything'd do me.' Stella leaned back in her chair, eyes shut. 'That was fun,' she said. 'You don't find many men as good as that. I'd have done anything tonight. Celebration.' She opened her eyes, smiling.

'Might I guess? Something to do with the sailor?'

Stella nodded. 'I heard at last. Two weekends from now he's got several days' shore leave. He wants me to join him for forty-eight hours. Do you think your Ma . . .? Mr Lawrence?'

169

Joe rubbed a huge hand across his face, straightening out a frown. 'Dare say that could be arranged. It seems very unfair, land girls only entitled to a week's holiday a year. Ma appreciates that.'

'I'd make up for it.'

'I'll put in a word for you.'

They sat listening to the music, watching the dancing. Prue and her partner had by now ceased to move at all. Ag and the wing commander were nipping expertly through the more statuesque dancers, Ag with a tight little smile.

'Do you know what Prue wants in the end?' asked Stella. 'She wants a rich Yorkshireman, gold taps, cocktails on silver trays. She told me her dream, standing on the dung hill.'

Joe smiled. 'What Prue wants, Prue'll get. She's a determined little thing if ever there was one.'

Their eyes met. They laughed.

'Jesus, I was rash,' said Joe, 'but it didn't seem worth resisting, offered like that on a plate. Couldn't have lasted long – too dangerous, under my own roof. I like her spirit, though. And I don't know any girl better at ploughing a straight furrow.'

Stella smiled, honoured to have been taken into Joe's confidence.

She watched his eyes, suddenly dulled, trail round the hall.

'Times like this,' he said, 'it hits you. Being one of the very few not in uniform. You feel such a rotten shirker.'

'Well you certainly shouldn't,' said Stella. 'Everyone knows if a man doesn't join up it's for good reason.'

'Not much comfort in that sort of logic, I'm afraid. The day I failed my medical was the worst day of my life. Never forget it: this icy room with that poster on the wall – you know the one, *Your Country Needs You*. This cocky little doctor. Afraid your country doesn't need *you*, my lad, he said. You can't expect to fight the enemy if you're fighting for

170

your own breath. Stands to reason. I told him – I told him I was much better than I had been as a child – growing out of the asthma fast. But nothing would change his stubborn little mind. Same thing happened to my friend Robert – his lungs are seriously rotten. They laughed at him wasting their time, turning up for a medical. But Robert's a pacifist at heart. He didn't give a damn that he was ordered to stay at home. My ambition was to join the HAC.'

'I'm sorry,' said Stella. She paused, knowing the inadequacy of any sympathy. 'But think about what you are doing. Someone's got to organise the massive job of feeding the country. Hallows Farm is making the sort of contribution you shouldn't undervalue.'

Joe shrugged, looked Stella in the eye.

'I don't,' he said. 'You're wise and you're right. But I can't help the guilt, the shame. I'd rather be fighting.'

Ag and her partner returned to the table. The four of them sat talking over more drinks. The wing commander was a married man, his wife at home in Edinburgh. In civilian life, they had won prizes for dancing. He missed regular dancing, he said.

As midnight drew near, the evening sloped into a minor key. The music slowed. Couples disappeared. Prue and her flight lieutenant were nowhere to be seen.

They reappeared just in time for the national anthem. Intent on reaching the table, Prue's progress across the hall was uncertain. She leaned heavily on the flight lieutenant, his scant baby hair a pinkish gold under the harsh lights. Her ankles gave way several times, but he supported her nobly, rewarded with a constant, lipstick-smudged smile.

'Rather overdone the gin and limes, I have,' she said. 'This is Barry.'

Barry had just time to shake hands all round before his body was flicked to attention by command of a thunderous chord from the band. *God Save Our Gracious King* boomed

171

out. All the uniformed men, moments ago so slack and soft on the dance floor, now adopted unblinking rigidity. Prue, through the gin-induced silvering of her mind, somehow appreciated that to cling to Barry at this solemn moment might be unwise. Instead, she leaned against Joe with the lack of inhibition of an old friend who dares to impose. She then found herself firmly guided to the door between Ag and Stella.

They supported her in the doorway of the hall while Joe went to the Camp car park to fetch the Wolseley. Cold night air ripped through their bones. Barry, still in his upright national anthem position, boldly stayed close enough to the trio of girls to plant a kiss on top of the sagging head of the one in the middle.

'See you, Prue,' he said. Saluted. Left.

'What did I tell you?' Prue giggled. 'Mind out – your feet! I think I'm going to be sick.'

After supper at Hallows Farm, Mr Lawrence went out to check a sick cow. Mrs Lawrence settled to a pile of darning by the wood fire, listening to a concert on the wireless. When her husband returned, he slumped in his usual chair, tipped back his head and shut his eyes.

'Strange, having the place to ourselves again for an evening,' ventured Mrs Lawrence.

Mr Lawrence nodded, but did not answer. He slept for a while, then roused himself to go to bed. Mrs Lawrence knew that if she followed him she would not sleep. She stayed where she was, put more logs on the fire as the night grew colder.

Sometime after midnight, she heard the car. Quickly she switched off lights and went to the window. She pulled back a little of the blackout stuff, peered through a chink. The girls and Joe were getting out of the car: there seemed to be some confusion. By the light of a full moon Mrs Lawrence could see a discussion between Joe, Stella, and

172

Ag. Then Joe bent down to the front passenger seat. He emerged with Prue in his arms, awkwardly propped her up against the open car door. Mrs Lawrence had a brief glimpse of a floppy blonde head, smudged lips. Then she saw Joe pick up the girl, sling her over his shoulder like a sack. The thin legs and silly shoes twitched against him but Prue made no protest.

Mrs Lawrence stood in the darkness of the room watching the last flames. She heard Joe and the girls make their way upstairs.

There was laughter, urgent whispers as they urged each other to be quiet. Mrs Lawrence waited till she heard Joe return from the attic to his own room, shut the door. She wondered if there was any chance of waking John. Her own wakefulness, alone, was almost unbearable.

After the house had been silent for some time, she made her way to the sitting-room door, crept upstairs through the darkness to the bedroom. Would any of them tell her how the evening had been? She wondered, too, at her own curiosity, and the impatience she felt for the morning.

Seven

In the wake of his success as a lecturer, Ratty found himself newly impervious to Edith's unreasonable behaviour. When she claimed it had been his fault the saucepan had flown through the window, and his fault it was lost, he did not offer to go and look for it (knowing quite well in which patch of long grass it lay) or attempt to extract himself from the blame. In silence, he ate fried vegetables and bacon, gleefully aware of Edith's own distaste for fried food. Give her a few days, he thought, and the saucepan would be back, no explanation.

The girls, he was bound to admit, had grasped the nature of the sport better than he had supposed they would. The floozie swore she had seen a right great bugger of a rat hiding in its own shadow. Here, Ratty felt, was an element of exaggeration – it wasn't something he often saw himself. He had a feeling she was trying to please, worm her way into his good books. The holy one, he must confess, had not come up to scratch. She reported one tail trail in the grain store – right enough – but tapped a wooden spoon on the side of a pan with such feebleness Ratty could tell her heart was not in it: the pathetic noise wouldn't have scared a mouse. In a word, though Ratty hated even privately to recognise this, when it came to ratting the holy one was a disappointment.

The Monday after the RAF dance was the fifth day of the hunt. Ratty took it upon himself to lay the lethal bait before dawn: he had no wish to be responsible for the girls doing something silly with the poison. He crept about, torchless in the freckled dark, slipping scraps of food, well marinated in ensearic zinc phosphide, under bales of hay, by piles of grain and hen food, the dung heap – all their favourite places. Now, it was just a matter of waiting. Ratty was a satisfied man: the buggers would come sneaking out today, not knowing what had hit them, begging to be clobbered on the head. He could never relish that part, as he had told the girls. But it had to be done.

At breakfast, Mr Lawrence warned the girls to be on the look-out. Should they come upon a dying rat, he said, they were to call Ratty, Joe or himself to deal with it.

Ag hoped her job for the morning would be spraying the fruit trees, a place far from the rats. But her luck was out: Faith wanted the eggs gathered early so that a collection could be taken into Dorchester, where the WVS distributed them to the old. The other two were assigned to a morning's hoeing.

Armed with her basket, Ag went first to the barn. She calculated that, as Ratty had laid the bait only a few hours ago, chances were the rats were exercising their habitual caution, and had not yet been tempted. She put a gloved hand nervously into the small holes between piles of loose straw that she had come to know were the bantams' favourite places for laying. Then, in one of the secret nests, she came across a gristly piece of lamb, just recognisable from a stew some days before. Ag quickly backed away, revolted, to battle with her conscience. Should she continue in her egg hunt in the normal way until she had gathered a dozen or so eggs? Or should she call it a day? The poisoned bait had unnerved her.

Tense and self-despising, she left the barn, walked towards the harness room. It housed an old horse rug that had been left folded on the floor for countless years. Stiff and mildewy underneath, its top had been moulded into a

175

nesting place by some long-ago duck, whose descendants still took the opportunity to lay in this ancestral nesting place. Eggs were to be found there most days.

A few yards from the tack-room, Ag saw Ratty come out, a pleased look on his face. He held up a large dead rat that swung from a hairless tail. In the split second before a blurring of vision came to her rescue, Ag observed a glimmer of obscene tooth and claw. She shouted to Ratty not to bring it near her, then clamped a hand over her mouth to stifle a scream.

Ratty, in his own pleasure, was confused. He had imagined she would share his triumph, gloat with him over the monster. He could not understand her incomprehensible cries, nor why she turned away from him and fell into the arms of Joe.

'Take it away, Ratty,' said Joe, over Ag's shoulder. 'She doesn't like them.'

Ratty at once turned away and shuffled off fast, reduced from his few moments of uprightness to his old stoop.

When he had gone, Joe gently unclasped his arms and stepped back from Ag.

'All right?' he asked her.

Ag pushed back her hair, tossed her head. She was pale, ashamed. 'Fine, thanks. I didn't think I'd mind a dead one so much, but the revulsion is just the same.'

'They're obscene, dead or alive. Like me to make you a cup of tea?'

'What, and earn your father's medal for utter feebleness?' Ag managed a laugh. 'No, thanks. I'll go down to the orchard, help with the fruit spraying.'

'Right.'

'And thank you for rescuing me. I felt dizzy for a moment. Where were you? You appeared from nowhere.'

Joe looked at her for some time without answering, his brows drawn into a frown.

'I was about,' he said. Then he patted her on the shoulder, and strode off to the barn, own shoulders hunched, preoccupied by some private thought.

He had offended and alarmed the holy one, and regret swung within him heavy as a cast-iron bell. Desolate, Ratty had fallen from the heights of the morning to the murkiest of depths. Pride came before a fall, he muttered to himself. Oh, to have undone the morning: to be given the chance to start again, act with more sensitivity. All the signs of Ag's aversion to rats had been there to read, and he had ignored them. Ratty spat on the hard ground, cursing himself. Would she ever forgive him? What could he say to her? How could he ever explain his regret for causing her such a fearful moment?

Once he had disposed of the dead rat – and no rat had he ever loathed so much for causing all this trouble – Ratty had little heart to continue his search for others. The joys of rat hunting had vanished. He wandered down to Lower Pasture, leaned over the gate to watch the cows. So often he found their indifference a comfort. But another horrible thought assailed him: Joe and Ag. The holy one in Joe's arms – Joe, who'd turned up like some bloody magician on cue – sure way to a girl's heart, being there at the right moment.

Exactly what Ratty did not want to happen between Joe and Ag was not clear in his mind. But the old unease he had felt some days ago, which had died down, now returned. He had not liked seeing the girl fall back spontaneously against the great hulking figure of Joe, and the swift comfort of Joe's arms. He did not want to see any such thing again. He did not like the ease between them. Besides, the holy one should be protected, be warned: Joe was no bloody good. Not to be trusted, relied upon. Ratty had witnessed many wild couplings in the lad's youth, seen many a girl with a broken heart whom he had left without reason. The holy one was as innocent and vulnerable-look-

177

ing a creature as Ratty had ever met, inspiring him with protective feelings that were new, in this his eighth decade, and troubling. His old plan of revenge returned. Any hint of Joe's selfish intentions towards the girl, and he, Ratty, would step in and rescue her from a far graver situation than the event of the dead rat this morning. He was not sure, yet, what measures he would take, but a pitchfork would probably come in useful. Joe should have learned by now the cruelty of dallying with an innocent girl's feelings. Besides, there was Janet. Ratty had no great respect for Janet, but she was Joe's fiancée, and had done nothing to deserve this deceit. So Joe had better mind his Ps and Qs, thought Ratty, and with his new resolve strength returned. He saw on his watch almost an hour had passed in contemplation. He must return to the farm, keep searching for dying rats, before the light faded and he would be forced to go home.

'I don't know what a girl's supposed to do, this clothes rationing,' grumbled Prue. 'Sixty coupons a year! *One* complete outfit. What makes those idiots in the government think we can get by on that? They're barmy.'

'You've got more clothes than anyone I know,' said Stella.

'Luckily, I stocked up before June. I'm all right for *now*, but what if Barry and me take off? You have to keep a man surprised. Something new for each time you see him. Keep up the interest.'

The girls hoed side by side. Deserted in the weeks the farm had been short of labour, before their arrival, the field was waist-high in thistles, mutton dock and charnock. As usual, they suffered aching backs. They found the long handles of the hoes difficult to manoeuvre. Their work was slow and clumsy. After a couple of hours they had cleared a disappointingly small amount of ground.

'Don't know why they don't just let me plough this all

in,' sighed Prue, straightening up for a pause. 'God, what I'd do for a fag. Look at my hands. Scratched, purple, fingers swollen. Lucky if anyone ever looks at me again.'

'You should wear gloves.'

'Hate gloves. Bloody hoeing. I'm exhausted. How come Ag always gets the orchard?'

'Spraying the fruit trees isn't that much fun. The stuff blows back into your face in the slightest breeze.'

'I'd rather do the *pig* than hoe. I've grown quite fond of Sly, matter of fact. But ploughing's my best thing. Wouldn't mind ploughing every day. Joe did finally admit, you know, he was impressed by the straightness of my furrows. Joe, I said, my apprenticeship in hairdressing wasn't for nothing. I been well practised in giving clients straight partings, haven't I? Course I can plough a straight furrow.'

Stella laughed. She, too, straightened up, leaned on her hoe.

'This time tomorrow,' she said.

'Where'll you be?'

'On the train to Plymouth, any luck.'

'That's good.' Prue took a packet of Woodbines from her pocket, lit one in the cup of her hand. 'Mrs Lawrence easy about letting you go?'

'Very understanding. It's only two nights. I said I'd stay here over Christmas to make up.'

'I'm going home, Christmas, whatever.' Prue inhaled deeply. Then she puffed a ribbon of lilac smoke into the cold, clear air. 'Don't suppose I'll ever get used to this silence,' she said after a while. 'Ag and you – you seem to find it all less surprising than me – the mud, the dogs, the cold house and everything.' She wiped a gleam of sweat away from her face, leaving muddied cheeks. 'Suppose it's been less of a leap from Surrey than from Manchester.'

'Oh, I don't know. It's just that with Philip on my mind I don't care what I do, where I go. When I'm not with him I seem to be indifferent to everything. In fact, I'm enjoying it all more than I expected, despite the hard physical work. But perhaps that's just because Philip *exists*.'

'You really *are* in love,' said Prue, in some awe, inhaling again.

'I am,' said Stella dreamily.

The sour, pinkish smell of Prue's cigarette spumed above the deeper smells of earth and weed.

'Well,' said Prue, after a while, 'I just might be on the way to join you. There was something very nice about Barry. Not just a handsome face, I'd say.' She flung down the butt of her cigarette, stamped it fiercely with her boot. 'I'll be ready, Barry, I said, any time you want me.' Giggling, she angled her hoe towards the root of a large thistle, tapped at it with little effect. 'I suppose you're thinking I'm promiscuous.'

'More, just your way of trying to find the right man,' said Stella. 'I do the same. The only difference is I don't sleep with them. I'm too scared. Instead, I fall in love. Not very deep love. I'm such a hopeless romantic, the very idea of love is almost enough for me, though I know in my heart most of it's make-believe and I'll be disillusioned. I nearly always am. Though this time, with Philip, I think it's different.'

'I'll keep my fingers crossed,' said Prue. 'I don't go for all that soppy romance stuff myself. Especially with a war on – no time. Get your knickers off as fast as you can is my belief, before the poor buggers are shot down. Bit of quick fun, then off to the next one. End of the war, when we're all a bit older and wiser – that'll be the time to look for a husband. That's when some unsuspecting millionaire's going to come in handy. Meantime, I get my fun where I can find it. Not as easy stuck out here as it was at home, of course. But I'm not off to a bad start. Joe's a good bloke, bit of a dark horse, pretty good lover by my standards. But what was he? Just a challenge. Seduce the farmer's son was my number one priority, then start searching out the local talent. I think he quite enjoyed it, mind: holding out for all of a week, then shagging me stupid. One morning I actually fell asleep propped up against Marybelle, teat between my fingers . . . Not practical, me and Joe, really. Besides, Mrs Lawrence was beginning to have her suspicions. I didn't want to be sent anywhere else, one of those land girl hostels or anything. It's a good place, here. I wrote to my mum only last night. I said: Mum, we're lucky. Then I said, I've got my hopes pinned to this Barry. I wouldn't half mind if he came looking for me, I said.'

They returned to their hoeing, their silence. The only sounds for a while were the chinking of tools against stony earth, the distant crunking of rooks and crows restless in the bare trees of the copse. Then, a piercing whistle startled them: the whistle of an experienced shepherd commanding his sheep. Both turned towards the gate, some fifty yards away, expecting to see Ratty or Joe. Instead they saw a young airman on an old bicycle, smiling.

'*Blimey*!' hissed Prue. 'It's Barry. *Talk* of the . . . Mind if I go? Wonder how much time he's got. Don't go back to the yard without me, *please*. I'll come and get my hoe.'

She flung it to the ground, automatically ruffled a hand through her hair, muddy fingers checking the state of the blue satin bow. Then she began to run through the weeds, waving, shouting Barry's name. Barry dismounted his bike, opened his arms, smiling, blushing – even from so far away Stella could see the sudden ruddiness of his cheeks. When Prue reached him, they kissed frantically, oblivious to the gate between them.

Stella turned away. She wondered if Philip's welcome tomorrow would be as ecstatic. The nervous anticipation, which she had been trying so hard to conceal, returned. Its force made her feeble. With a great struggle, she returned to her hoeing, knowing that with Prue gone she must do double the work.

*

When Prue and Barry's first embrace, and its encores, finally came to an end, Prue climbed over the gate and took the flight lieutenant's arm. They quickly reached the entry to the copse, some yards along the lane, and found themselves a comfortable place in the densest part of the wood. Barry sat on the trunk of a fallen tree, having assured himself its fuzzy yellowish moss would not stain his trousers. Prue placed herself in an alluring curve on the ground ivy, positioned so accurately that when the time came she could rest her head on his knee without having to move.

Barry's scarlet face was smeared with the deeper red imprints of Prue's lipstick. His shorn gold hair, released from the forage cap folded in his pocket, stood straight up as if in alarm. Prue herself, purring in the knowledge of her own allure, was the epitome of a rural pin-up: a blending of mud and rouge on her cheeks, blonde curls a chaotic nest on which her satin bow clung like a wounded bird. They both trembled. Prue reached for her cigarettes. Barry found a match. He lit her cigarette with great finesse, as if it was a skill he had been practising all his life: cupping his hands round the flame, touching Prue's wavering fingers for no more than a second. Then he took a cigarette himself, lit it with equal precision. They blew smoke in each other's faces, then scattered it with floppy hands, laughing. Barry looked at his watch.

'I wasted a lot of time,' he said, 'biking from field to field, looking. Didn't like to ask up at the farmhouse. An old boy with gaiters eventually said I'd find you down here.'

'Ratty,' said Prue.

She wondered if Barry appreciated the faint traces of her own scent beneath the sweet smell of the mingling smoke. Barry looked at his watch.

'So I can only stay ten minutes,' he said. 'Then I'll have to ride like blazes to get back in time. It's a good seven miles.'

Prue exhaled very slowly. Stupid, it would be, to reveal any show of disappointment.

'Pity,' she said.

'It's a pity, all right. You're so gorgeous.'

Prue had never liked the word gorgeous, but it wasn't Barry's adjectives she was after. She looked up at him from under her lashes.

'Moment I saw you,' she said, 'in the tea-room, I thought pretty much the same. I thought: he's the one.'

'I knew you thought that. It made me quite nervous.' Barry laughed.

'Couldn't let a man like you get away,' said Prue. 'That's why I made them all come to the dance.'

'I saw through your planning, of course, and I was lost.' He gave a small, contrite smile, like a schoolboy. 'I thought: I'm a pushover. I'm going to say yes to whatever she suggests.'

Prue smiled. She put a hand on her battering heart. Barry stretched down and put his hand over hers.

'My loins are on fire,' he said, solemnly.

Prue giggled. 'Oh, Barry,' she said, 'you're the sweetest thing. Well: I'm here for the asking, aren't I? I'm here for you to take, to do what you like with.'

'We've only got eight minutes now,' said Barry.

Prue pouted. 'We could just make a start,' she said. 'We'd have longer next time.'

'But there's so much I'd like to do to you. It's been haunting me, all the things . . . Shall I tell you? I'd like to start kissing you at the top, go round and about, everywhere, very slowly . . .' The blush had by now suffused his neck. He grasped the heavy wool of Prue's jersey, that strained across her breasts, with a hand that was as red as his face. 'I don't know if I can wait, sweetheart.'

Prue saw his desperate state. She removed his hand from her jersey.

'You might have to wait, old cock,' she said nicely. 'Six

183

minutes being really too much of a rush, trying to fit in everything you have in mind, as it were. You'd have to exceed the speed limit. We might not get the full benefit, such pressure of time.'

Barry gave an agonised sigh. 'You're probably right.'

They both stubbed out their half-finished cigarettes, threw them into a thorn bush.

'What's your actual job?' asked Prue. Take his mind off the matter that was obviously causing him a lot of pressure would be the kindest thing, the best way to calm him down, she thought: though God knows that was some sacrifice, considering the wicked way she fancied him.

'Mostly night flying.'

'That's terribly brave.'

'I'm not brave. I'm terrified every time we take off. Every time, I think this is it. My number's up. I could come again Friday,' he added. 'Two o'clock, free afternoon. Could you make it?' Prue nodded. 'It's nice here in the woods.' He looked at her, trying for calm. 'That land girl uniform does something wicked to me. Christ, those breeches. Come here, sweetheart. I must kiss you again, at least.'

Prue knelt up, startling a nearby blackbird which flew away with a thin hollow sound of wings. Barry's face, against hers, was hot and damp. This time, kissing, she felt none of the excitement she had felt at the gate. Barry's urgency was almost apologetic, as if life itself might be running out, chance must be taken. But in their very few moments together this afternoon Prue had worked out that, for all his sweetness, Barry was not to be her Philip. He was too young in his ways for her: he reminded her of a choir boy, the angelic blushing face and golden baby hair. In her post-Joe afternoon in the tea-shop, and in her gin-fired dreams at the dance, enthusiasm had caused her to miscalculate. Still, he'd do nicely for a while.

She could sense him raising his watch above his head, glancing at it through her hair.

'Just under three minutes left,' he said.

Prue felt a kind of sadness.

'No time for the *actual*,' she told Stella and Ag later that night, 'but a good beginning. He's a real charmer, Barry, in his way – brave as anything. He'll be my fourth pilot.'

On the train next morning, cold in her third-class carriage, Stella thought about Prue. She pondered her gather-ye-rosebuds-while-ye-may approach to men, and wondered at its benefits. She could not imagine herself flitting from one state of intense carnality to another, in Prue's light-hearted way; she could not imagine the swift cutting off from one man, apparently no untidy trails left, followed so quickly by a new and untarnished keenness for another. Prue suffered no disillusions because she had no illusions in the first place. Her short-term goals were sex and fun. Conquering was the stimulus. Endings were of no consequence. She acted with the confidence of one who knows the ruling power of her own heart. Her heart would not be touched until it was convenient – until, when the war was over, it was the right time for the millionaire to provide marriage and security.

Stella could not but admire Prue's philosophy, even though the thought of quite so many casual men disturbed the depths of her puritanical psyche in a way she would never admit. She wondered if Prue ever missed the vicissitudes of other ways: the highs and lows of constantly being in love, the anticipation, the excitement of waiting for letters, for declarations, the general shimmering of daily life that love of a man can bring about. In her brief experience, if she had to be honest with herself – a difficult process Stella rather enjoyed – most of her own 'loves' were figments of an optimistic imagination. Her feelings, so eager to bestow themselves upon someone, were often – for lack of choice – bestowed randomly. She would stamp upon the love object the required attributes so clear in her mind. The reality behind the resulting picture, when it burst through, caused many a downward spiral in her heart. But she was not one to succumb to melancholy for long. She would never blame a man for letting her down. Rather, she would admit her choice had been mistaken. There would be others, she felt. And somehow there always were. To those who believe there is little point in being alive without being in love – Stella's creed – there is no shortage of objects upon whom the cloak of fantasy can be flung.

In her short acquaintance with Philip, Stella had had more rewards than usual. His heart-breaking handsomeness combined with a lack of vanity, his sense of fun balanced by a serious side of his nature, his prowess at dancing, his way of making her believe his declarations of love – all these things were new and wondrous to Stella, a spur to the idea that life ever after, with him, was a strong possibility. And perhaps his letters would improve. Their love was crystallised by the uncertainties of an insecure world: fear of an unknown future, an unknown amount of time, possible death that would snatch away their chances – such things were common to so many wartime lovers, Stella knew. All the same, she was convinced this was very different from the majority of desperate, unstudied wartime affairs. This had a lasting quality . . . didn't it?

Stella turned to look out of the window. Through the strands of rain, looped and pearled across the glass, she saw small hills of reddish earth. Devon, she thought it must be: names of stations were no longer displayed, just as signposts had been taken down. England had become a mystery place in which you had to find clues, guess where you were. But apart from that, here, as in Dorset, the only evidence of war was the sight of women working in the fields. She caught a glimpse of a row of land girls bent over hoes in a mangold field, and smiled.

The guard who came to check her ticket said they were half an hour from Plymouth. Stella's heart constricted. She thought for the thousandth time of Philip waiting for her on the platform, of his dear face breaking into a smile as she ran towards him. Except the face in her imagination was suddenly a blank. It had gone.

In her panic, another picture came to mind, horribly clear – Mr Lawrence's. *His* face, as he turned in the Wolseley to say goodbye to her, she would remember for ever. His look had been a mixture of anguish, sympathy, regret. He had briefly patted her knee, wished her well, assured her he would be there to pick her up on her return. He had opened the passenger door, handed her the suitcase and said goodbye at the ticket office, his face so stricken Stella had been tempted to ask what troubled him. He was an odd one, Mr Lawrence, she thought, but she liked him. She then remembered that he had mentioned at breakfast his brother, terminally ill in Yorkshire, was worse. No wonder he had looked so unhappy, and the power of his unhappiness had touched her own high spirits.

Stella took out her wallet, searched for the small Polyfoto of Philip. At the sight of the familiar features, her moment of amnesia was forgotten. Relief and rising excitement made her heart beat crisply, as if it was a razor-edged organ thumping with peculiar precision in her chest, hurting the parts nearby. She took out her silver compact – a legacy from her grandmother – and dabbed at her nose with a piece of swansdown fluff. No point in lipstick, she judged, and smiled to herself at the thought of the cosmetic preparations Prue would have been making in the circumstances.

The rhythmic grunting of the train began to slow. Stella closed her bag, folded her hands on her knees. She studied the sepia photograph of St Ives, Cornwall, framed above the opposite seat. Maybe she and Philip would go there for a holiday one day. It looked an unspoiled place. Maybe

187

she and Philip would travel the world. Then come back to a suburban house (they shared a love of suburbia) with spotted laurels, two cats, room for a piano so that she could give lessons . . . three, no, four, children.

The train bucked, throwing her forward. There was a screech of steam. Through the rain-blurred window, a misted view of the large station, dozens of troops crowding the platform.

Plymouth. Philip.

Stella, trembling, stood up.

Meeting can be like drowning. In the moments leading up to the encounter, a whole life can flash by. As Stella jostled her way through the army greatcoats, the stamping boots, the cloudy breaths gathered like small parachutes in the air, she realised she had only ever seen Philip at night. This would be her first view of him in *daylight*. Their three previous meetings (was it really only three?) had all been at parties: low lights, drink, dancing, the pitch dark of the old nursery. Any moment now she would see him in the cruelty of this grey light.

His head was suddenly there in the distance, the familiar photograph coming alive, cracking into a semi-smile, the dark blue of his uniform handsome against the crush of khaki. They pushed towards each other, fell into each other's arms like dozens of couples in wartime movies. Stella could taste rain on his cold lips, smell the damp of his hair, and the brown musky wood scent of his skin, peculiar to him, that she had forgotten.

Outside the timeless cavern of their kiss, she heard the train pulling out and hundreds of cheers and calls of encouragement – envious laughter. Extracting herself from Philip to see what was happening, she realised that they were the objects of derision. Philip took a moment longer to realise this. His reaction was to laugh. But Stella saw his rain-smudged face had turned a raw red, and knew her own cheeks were the same colour.

'Jealous bastards,' he said, and waved back at the troops leaning from the train windows, a merry-faced lot who had latched on to an unknown couple's moment of joy to hide whatever they themselves were feeling.

Suddenly, the train gone, the station was quiet. Philip picked up Stella's case from the damp platform.

'Come on,' he said. 'Food. You must be famished.'

He took her hand. The high tap of Stella's shoes made small unsynchronised chords with the deeper sound of Philip's boots. They made their way to the ticket barrier, and the city beyond.

They sat in a small café, a place with none of the refinements of the tea-shop in Blandford. There was cracked oilcloth on the tables, covers of *Picture Post* stuck randomly on the walls to disguise a web of dirty marks. The place was empty, but for a slack-mouthed, greasy-haired waitress whose weariness, almost tangible, seemed to be smeared thickly over her like lard, hindering her movements. Philip ate scrambled dried eggs, so gritty and gristly-looking Stella wondered how he could swallow them. She herself, not hungry, toyed with two slices of bread and marge. They both drank strong cups of tea, which they sipped with great concentration, each waiting for the other one to choose a beginning.

'We're booked into quite a decent room,' said Philip, at last.

Stella smiled. She saw the hotel lobby of her dreams: chandelier, the ruby carpets soughing up the swirling staircase leading to their suite. And, somehow, a gramophone.

'We're asked to check in at five,' he added.

This was puzzling. But Stella imagined there were wartime rules in hotels. Regulations about which she knew nothing.

'That's fine. I'd like to look round Plymouth.'

'We'll go down to the harbour, take a look at the ship. Journey all right?'

189

Stella nodded. The days of waiting for this moment, the agony of anticipation, had turned, like all past pain, to dust. She wondered if Philip had been through any of the same agonising moods of impatience, and wondered whether she dared to ask.

'It's so good to see you,' she ventured at last. 'I thought I'd go mad, waiting, sometimes.'

'It's good to see you, too,' said Philip, after some thought. 'Very good.' But he went no further, gave no clues as to how the wait had been for him.

They ordered another pot of tea. Philip decided to try the jam roll. The single nicety of the café was a small china jug, patterned with morning glory, for the custard. While Philip struggled to hold back the skin with a fork, and encourage the thick flow of custard beneath with a spoon, he asked Stella to marry him.

Stella stared hard at the jug, the delicate pattern of flowers engraving itself on her memory for the rest of her life. Such havoc of thought skittered through her mind she wondered if she had heard right, if she was imagining the question. This was so far from the picture of where and how the proposal would take place, she found herself in a silent, desperate struggle to appear composed.

'I thought,' said Philip, eventually alerted to Stella's confusion, 'if we made it clear marriage was on the books, things would be easier tonight . . .'

'How do you mean?' Tears skinned Stella's eyes.

'I didn't want you to feel any guilt, any apprehension . . . any nervousness that I might be one of those chaps who makes love to a girl then leaves her.'

'Nothing like that had entered my mind.'

'No, well. We don't know each other terribly well, do we? I wanted you to feel sure. Anyhow, what's the answer to be?' He sounded almost impatient.

Stella put down her cup, blinked back the tears. She had only a few seconds in which to straighten out the surge of feeling that had rendered her physically useless. She looked down at her own shocked hands lying dead on the oilcloth, the nails painted a pale pink by the insistent Prue last night. She tried to sort out the muddle in her brain. The main factor was one of relief, an out-of-focus sort of joy that what she had been planning, hoping for, had happened so fast, so easily. But clambering about this main sensation were small, worrying shoots: the profound sense of bathos, the disappointment that Philip had not engineered so important a moment with more skill.

'You look surprised,' he said. 'Surely it's no surprise. I thought . . .'

Stella braced herself, managed a small laugh. 'I'm only surprised by the time, the place,' she said. 'Being a hopeless romantic I somehow thought the proposal was bound to happen with champagne and music.'

'On bended knees, I dare say. You've seen too many films. I'm sorry, I don't work like that.'

Philip took one of Stella's hands. The electric shock between them revived her. The familiar love that had so consumed her while hoeing fields, milking cows, spreading dung, returned. Ashamed at her sense of disappointment, she gripped Philip's hands tightly, leaned towards him. The moment of her humility was accompanied by the sickly smell of suet and hot jam sauce.

'Am I to be turned down?' Suddenly anxious, Philip's voice.

'Of course not. Of course I'll marry you. I love you.'

'I love you too. That's all right, then.'

Philip extracted his hand from Stella's, pushed away the plate of unfinished pudding. He signalled to the waitress for the bill, pulled a handful of change from his pocket with which he made three small towers of sixpences.

'When I'm back at sea it'll be good to know there's a future wife waiting at home. Sometimes, on the night watch, especially, staring out at those miles of sea, you begin to think nothing else in the world exists. You think you're the only ship on the only sea. Your mind plays all sorts of funny tricks.'

'Hope the idea of a wife will make that better.'

'I think it will. Let's go.'

Down at the harbour a thin sun was breaking through a taut, colourless sky. Gulls shrilled overhead, their indignant cries dying away into low, tattered, affronted notes. Small groups of sailors trailed back and forth with no apparent purpose. There was a smell of salt and tar, a suspicion of fishy depths to the wind.

Stella and her sub-lieutenant stood looking up at the massive sides of HMS *Apollo*, a powerful ship built with the sharp sleek lines of an attacker. For some reason she reminded Stella of a pointer she had once seen at work when her father was out shooting – nose to the ground, cutting through a field of long grass. She could imagine the *Apollo* scything through the endless waves with the same sleek determination as a hunting dog – but that was a silly thought, not worth putting to Philip. She linked her arm through his, looked up at him, so handsome in his cap, the gold braid gently fired by the sun. His head was back, eyes on the White Ensign fluttering at the mainmast.

'So lucky I got a destroyer,' he said. 'A lot of my friends were appointed to drifters and trawlers. I wouldn't have wanted that.'

'You'll be a captain one day,' said Stella. 'Perhaps even a rear-admiral.'

Philip transferred his look of devotion from the White Ensign to Stella. He gave her the friendliest smile since she had arrived.

'The future wife of the sub-lieutenant speaks,' he said. 'Look at those.' He pointed up to a row of wickedly snouted guns – menace in waiting.

Stella shivered. 'I can't really imagine a battle at sea,' she said. 'A destroyer of this size snapped in two like a toy, burning, sinking. What I'd like' – a sudden boldness gripped her – 'is to know *exactly* what your life is like . . . I want to know your daily routine, all the details, so that when I'm back at the farm I can imagine you accurately. Up to now, I've just been guessing.'

'I wouldn't be very good at describing all that,' Philip said.

They moved away from the shadow of the *Apollo*, walked hand in hand further down the harbour. Several ships were at anchor, unmoving on the flat water.

'Awesome things, they seem, to someone not in the navy,' said Stella. She thought that by making any observation, quickly enough, she would not have time to reflect on Philip's lack of cooperation. 'Whole, strange worlds.'

'By the time we get to Hamilton Road,' said Philip, looking at his watch, 'it'll be five o'clock.'

Mrs Elliot, the widow who ran The Guest House in Hamilton Road, was a woman of such deep suspicions that she was not ideal material for a landlady. Her pessimistic imaginings were fired at the very sight of strangers walking up the concrete path, and lingered long after they had gone. Her mind, filled with the possible activities of past guests, was thus always ready to come up with some point of reference. When Philip had come round to book the room, Mrs Elliot was able to inform him that not only had she had many lads from the forces staying under her roof but also, of particular coincidence, a sub-lieutenant from the *Apollo* had once stayed two nights. Her veneer of friendliness was calculated to make the new incumbent forthcoming with the sort of information she could pass on to the guests of the future.

As Stella and Philip walked in uneasy silence up the street of identical semidetached houses, Stella struggled to put aside her picture of a uniformed doorman ushering her through huge glass portals into a hotel lobby of rococo magnificence. Approaching Mrs Elliot's establishment up the sterile little path, she had her misgivings – but then put them quickly to one side, because nothing, she told herself, now mattered except that she was here *with* Philip at last. While they waited for the door to open, Stella studied the grey stucco walls of the house, the windows veiled with thick net curtains, the highly polished brass knocker on the nasty green paint of the front door. She was aware that a kaleidoscope of material images was collecting in her mind where they would retain a significance for the rest of her life, simply because they were part of the weekend when, as Prue would say, she finally Did It.

The door opened. Mrs Elliot, from her superior position in the hall, was able to look down on Philip and Stella on the path. Her glance told them she was well appraised in all tricks of human nature – there was no point in any pretence. Stella was curious to know how Philip would deal with her censoriousness: silly old bat, she thought – what we are has nothing to do with her. The woman's silent, instant disapprobation was intrusion into a privacy that meant much to Stella. She felt sudden anger, but said nothing.

Inside, they were greeted by smells that had never escaped the tightly closed windows: years of soup, cabbage, gravy, tea, had combined to thicken the airless atmosphere like invisible cornflour. The place was spotless, immaculate: the front room was crowded with a three-piece suite covered in rust rep, a material Stella's mother had always sworn she would never resort to, no matter how long the war lasted. Starched white lace antimacassars hung over the back of the chairs and sofas indicating their owner was a connoisseur of such refinements, and woe betide any brazen member of the forces who dared lean his head against them. Despite the warm, claustrophobic air, Stella shivered. What on earth would they do, all evening, she and Philip, in this dead room?

Mrs Elliot was studying an appointments diary. 'Sub-Lieutenant Wharton, that's right, isn't it? The two nights.'

'That's right.'

'And . . .?'

Stella saw Philip turn pale. She saw his hands shake.

'I'll soon be Mrs Wharton,' said Stella.

'Soon as the war's over,' added Philip.

'That's what they all say.' Mrs Elliot snapped shut the diary, waved a grey-skinned hand towards the window ledge. 'You may be interested in my collection of corn dollies,' she offered; 'most of my guests are. You'll have the opportunity to study them before the evening meal.' She took them upstairs and delivered a little speech concerning house rules – blackout, locking-up time, essential economy of bath water, and absolutely no alcohol on the premises. Finally, in consideration of others, she would ask that they refrain from undue *noise*. This last rule, calculated further to inhibit young seamen bent on nefarious activities with a future 'wife', was accompanied by a bang on the bedroom wall: the dull echo of plasterboard proved its thinness. Perhaps to counter-act such fierce warnings, Mrs Elliot pointed out that their window, thickly clouded with netting, overlooked the 'front'.

When she had gone, leaving them with a knowing smile, Stella went over to the window, pulled back the net curtain. The view was of houses on the other side of Hamilton Road, identical to Mrs Elliot's.

'So where's the promised front?' she asked.

'I think she meant the front of the house rather than the sea.'

Stella turned back to Philip who was sitting on the bed. She began to undo her coat. Smiled.

'Nothing matters,' she said. 'Absolutely nothing matters except that we're here at last.'

'I suppose not,' said Philip. He rose and came over to Stella, helped her off with her coat. 'We'll eat here tonight,

195

but tomorrow night we'll go to some big hotel.'

'That would be lovely.' Chandeliers began to retwinkle on some faint horizon: the possibility of champagne. Philip looked at his watch.

'We've exactly an hour till Mrs Elliot's gourmet feast at eighteen hundred hours. And what we've got to remember is no noise . . .'

They both laughed. Philip tipped Stella's head back into the gathering of net curtains so that it rested against the window pane. He began to kiss her with an eagerness which Stella would have shared had she not been anxious about cracking the glass behind her.

Exactly an hour later they sat at a table in a back room eating corned beef salad and – speciality of the house, Mrs Elliot had assured them – baked potatoes.

The silence was stifling. Fatigue, readjustment and a sudden dread of things to come had deprived Stella of all ideas to entertain the blank-looking Philip. Joined only in mutual hunger, they ate their etiolated salads fast, and spread extravagant amounts of salad cream on their potatoes to counteract the tiny wafers of marge Mrs Elliot had laid on a small saucer. In the quietness, Stella contemplated for a long time the inspiration behind the salt and pepper pots – crude china mushrooms painted with identical spots. Whose idea had it been to create such objects? What pottery had agreed they would catch the discerning landlady's eye, and set about their manufacture? Stella always enjoyed asking herself such unanswerable questions, and added the mushrooms to her list of memorable things in this unforgettable weekend. She smiled.

'What are you thinking?'

'I was thinking about the salt and pepper pots.'

Philip showed no flicker of understanding her train of thought.

'*I* was thinking we ought to get out of this place for a

drink somewhere. We can't just sit in that room waiting to go to bed.'

'No.' Stella finished her glass of water.

'There's a pub just down the road.'

'There is,' said Mrs Elliot, coming in from the kitchen, 'but locking-up time is nine thirty and I'll not tolerate any incidents of drunken behaviour. They've been known to happen in the past, especially able seamen.' She knew how to fling an insult: watched Philip stiffen. 'There's butterscotch shape to follow. They've quite a reputation, my shapes. I've not had a guest yet who's not complimented me, that I can tell you.'

Philip and Stella, still hungry, could only accept her challenge. Mrs Elliot fastened the blackout across the small window, and switched on a dim central light. Scene set for triumphant entry of pudding, she brought in a beige mound on a cut-glass plate.

'You'll like that,' she said, 'or I'll be blowed.'

When Mrs Elliot left the room, Stella gently moved the plate. The shape wobbled very slightly. They both laughed.

'Come on,' said Philip, 'out of here as soon as possible.'

They smeared a little of the butterscotch stuff on the bottom of their pudding plates, spooned the rest into the two unused paper napkins, and stuffed the squashy package into Stella's handbag.

Ten minutes later they were back at the harbour. In the winter dusk they threw the pudding ceremoniously into the black water, joined in laughter, relief, sudden new excitement. From now on, Stella knew all would be well. She took her future husband's arm, rested her head against his shoulder as they walked. A full moon lighted their way to the pub.

It was warm, light, crowded with seamen and their girls. Too noisy for conversation, Philip and Stella had their drinks at the bar. They leaned against each other, the thrill of proximity piercing through their coats. Stella, on Prue's

197

advice, drank gin and lime. Unused to alcohol, she felt delightfully out of focus after two glasses. Philip chose neat whisky. But even in their alcoholic state of careless rapture, Mrs Elliot's threats hung over them with a penetrating chill. They left at nine fifteen.

Stella's steps were a little unsure. Philip supported her with a firm arm the short distance along the street. Back in the house, they braced themselves for a silent passage up the narrow stairs, determined Mrs Elliot – surely awake and listening out for the slightest sign of trouble – would be thwarted. In their stark little room they found the blackout had been drawn, and the vicious lilac walls were muted by the low-watt light.

Stella was grateful for Prue's advice. The gin had done much to improve the setting for her seduction. She sat on the bed and longed for music, candles, dancing. But, thanks to the gin, the hideous carpet and curtains and the designed meanness of the room could not really touch her. These were merely another cause for laughter, should they dare laugh . . .

Philip left the room carrying a sponge bag and dressing-gown. Stella took advantage of his absence to undress quickly and put on her dressing-gown. In her slightly inebriated state the regular nightly duties of brushing teeth and hair did not occur to her. She climbed into the small hard bed with its scant blankets and firm pillows, and waited.

After what seemed a very long time, Philip returned. He slapped his jowls, a watery sound in the quiet.

'Thought I'd better shave,' he said. He hung his uniform neatly in the upturned coffin of a cupboard, and placed his shoes by the door in a strict to-attention pose, as if his feet were in them for the national anthem. Then he flung himself on the bed, smelling of toothpaste, aftershave and whisky. They drew quickly towards each other, wool dressing-gowns pulled open by the roughness of the blankets.

'Remember,' said Philip, 'no noise, no cries, no laughing. We'll have to save all that for the rest of our lives.'

Stella, in her eagerness to get on with the event in hand, would have sworn eternal silence.

'Think we'd better put out the light,' she whispered smudgily. 'If I see you, I might cry out in wonder.'

In the absolute dark, they giggled nervously. As their hands hesitated over each other's bodies, and their lips met and parted, met and parted, Stella was aware that the quality of their desire had shifted since the night in her old nursery. It was as if a premature familiarity, an unwanted sign of how it would be for untold future years, had emerged unbidden. A little afraid, but wanting more (more what? she kept asking herself), she lay wide-legged in the blackness, waiting for the moment in her life she had been taught was so important and must not be given lightly. She was glad Philip could not see her, glad she could not see him. The confusion in her mind was between the imaginings of how it might have been and how it actually was. *This.*

Here he was, very sudden, unexpectedly heavy. There was a moment's pain. A burning in the depths of her. Then there was nothing. Just the emptiness of darkness.

It was over. She knew this because Philip rolled off her, panting. Now, not even their hands touched.

'The first time, always . . .' Philip murmured eventually.

'I know.'

'I didn't hurt you?'

'No.'

'She won't have heard a thing, bloody woman.'

Stella, puzzled by the extent of Philip's concern about their landlady, heard him turn away, shift himself comfortably. He slept very quickly. She herself remained on her back. There was much she would have to ask Prue, she thought. There was also much she would have to keep from Prue, for fear of her laughter.

*

199

They were woken by a tapping at their door next morning: Mrs Elliot called out that breakfast was on the table.

'Silly old cow,' murmured Philip. 'Her only pleasure in life must be spoiling others' fun.'

Stella studied his sleepy face, less familiar than the photograph she looked at every morning. He drew her towards him, kissed her on the forehead.

'Don't let's give her any satisfaction,' he said. 'Let's get up.' Ten minutes later they faced a scant breakfast. Philip seemed in much better spirits than the day before. He dabbed a knife in the minuscule ration of marmalade.

'There are some economies not worth making,' he said, 'and this place is one of them. I've decided: we're *moving*. We're going to book in to your glamorous hotel. My godmother sent me ten pounds for my birthday. We're going to spend every penny . . .'

'The two nights we agreed, they'll have to be paid for.' Mrs Elliot, who had been listening behind the door, strode over to the table and picked up the empty metal toast rack with a vicious flick of her wrist. 'I'll not be replenishing the toast,' she said, 'neither.'

Philip produced a crumpled ten-shilling note from his pocket and slammed it on the table.

'Keep the change,' he said.

Mrs Elliot could not help gasping. 'I dare say I could do another slice if you want one,' she said.

Her offer was firmly declined.

They sat in the sun lounge of the Grand Hotel in wicker chairs, a tray with coffee laid on a wicker table between them. Outside, destroyers lay motionless on a sun-petalled sea: the cry of gulls was dulled by the domed glass roof, the palm trees in pots, the condensed warmth of the place. No one else was there. The hotel was so short of visitors that when Philip had asked for a double room and bath, the receptionist offered a suite for the same price.

In the lobby, Stella had found her chandeliers, her ruby carpet and swirling staircase. There was a wireless in their sitting-room, a vase of dried honesty, comfortable chairs, and a view of the harbour. Stella took so long to examine every detail of her dream that Philip had to urge her to hurry if she wanted coffee before lunch.

In the sun lounge, he asked her to marry him again.

'But I said yes yesterday. Did you doubt me? What makes you think I might have changed my mind?'

'I just want to be absolutely sure.'

'You can be.'

Philip frowned, but still seemed to be in high spirits. 'Then I have a confession to make.' He was silent for a while. Stella waited, curious. 'Those girls I mentioned when we first met – those girls in the past . . .'

'Not that many of them, as far as I remember.'

'Two. Two especially. The thing being . . . I may have exaggerated. Whatever I may have indicated, I was boasting. I didn't actually . . . with either of them.'

'Well?'

'So . . . last night was the first time for me, too.' He looked down.

'Does that matter?'

'I thought it might. I hadn't the courage to tell you. I rather fancied the idea of your thinking of me as an experienced hand . . . I was ashamed of being such an amateur. I mean, I'm twenty-three. Most men, by then . . .'

Stella's love, which had waned a little in the darkness of her lonely night, returned – a small poignant gust in her chest. She reached for his hand.

'You don't mind?' Philip asked.

'Of course not. I'm rather pleased.'

'Rather?'

'Very.'

'It'll get better. It probably wasn't any good for you. It'll get better and better, I promise. And also, I love you. I love the way you don't mind about that awful cafe yesterday, the dreadful guest house. I don't know why we didn't come straight here. Mustn't give into her dream too soon, I thought. Silly confused thoughts, something to do with showing who's boss.'

Stella smiled. 'I wouldn't have minded where we'd gone, what we'd done. Though I confess this place is . . . the sort of thing I was rather hoping for.'

'Good. Let's give that bored waiter something to do. Let's have sandwiches in our room for lunch. Let's turn on that wireless –'

'– and dance,' said Stella.

'Don't imagine there'll be much time for dancing.' Philip grinned.

They spent the afternoon in the large double bed, a bright winter sun lighting their bodies, hours flying in the concentration of each other. They bathed together in the deep cast-iron bath, revelling in six inches of very hot water and Stella's lavender soap. They dined, along with only two other couples, in the silent cavernous dining-room crowded with ghost tables of white napery. The underemployed waiters made much of trundling the meat trolleys to their table, pulling back the silver-domed lids with a grand flourish, and serving two minuscule cutlets with the kind of solemnity that must have applied to vast joints of pre-war beef. With a pudding of jelly, given status by a frill of imitation cream, they drank half a bottle of champagne. Stella made Philip laugh with stories of Hallows Farm.

Aware of the shortness of time left to them, they climbed back up the red stairs at nine thirty. Blackout in their rooms was concealed behind thick curtains: pink lamps had been lit, the bed turned down. They heard on the news that the Allied Armies had invaded French North Africa. But their concern was the few hours left: their last chance for God knows how many months. They hurried back into the bed, leaving on the lights. They spent the kind of night that would have shaken Mrs Elliot and her prim Guest House to their foundations.

'I knew very early on,' said Philip the following afternoon, at the station, 'that I loved you – or at least that I *thought* I loved you: you were the sort of girl I'd always had in mind. But – I don't know how to put this: I don't think I *felt* the kind of love you're meant to feel when you ask a girl to marry you. I think what I felt was the urgency of war, the need for firm plans.'

'I expect a lot of couples feel the same: such an unreal, unsure time.'

They sat on a bench on an empty platform. The train was due in two minutes.

'I have to admit I'm not really sure I loved you properly even when I first proposed, the day before yesterday.' Philip spoke rapidly, wanting to say so much before the departure. 'But now I *do*. I do. Believe me?'

Stella nodded.

'Since the nights, I suppose. That's why I proposed twice: once, semi-sure, once absolutely sure.'

Stella smiled. Philip glanced at his watch.

'Hope I've not spoiled anything, confessing. It was just terribly important you should know the truth. Will you tell me just once more? Will you tell me you'll marry me as convincingly as you can?'

'I will, yes.'

'Whatever happens?'

'Whatever happens.'

'Thank God for that. That means the weeks apart, however long, don't matter so much. I mean, being sure.'

'No.'

'I love you, I love you.'

'I love you, too.'

They kissed. They hugged, tears in their eyes. Then the

train, horribly punctual, came roaring up to stop their shorthand promises, and remind them it was now time to brace themselves, as Churchill had urged, to their duties.

Stella slept on the journey. She had never known such tiredness. She wondered how she would manage to stay awake through supper, fend off Prue's curiosity. She dreaded the dawn rising tomorrow, milking the cows in the freezing darkness. Sleepily, it occurred to her that, for all her stories of Hallows Farm, she had not told Philip the place was beginning to feel like a second home.

At the station she found light snow. A few flakes were falling from the dark sky, but they quickly melted on the windscreen of the Wolseley.

It was very cold in the car. Mr Lawrence had brought a scarf and thick jacket for Stella to put over her coat. She was touched by his thoughtfulness.

'All went well, I hope,' he said, after a few miles of silence.

'Philip asked me to marry him. I said yes.'

She could hear Mr Lawrence grinding his teeth.

'Good,' he said eventually. 'If he's the right one, you won't regret it.'

Eight

A few weeks after Stella had returned from Plymouth, Mrs Lawrence fell ill. She struggled for a couple of days with a bad cough and a temperature. Then Mr Lawrence announced one morning at breakfast he had insisted she spend the day in bed.

'It'll be the first time for twenty years she's done any such thing,' he said, 'but I told her if she didn't I'd call the doctor – an even worse threat, in her eyes. One of you will have to take over from her today. Which shall it be?'

Prue's reluctance was instant. She had an assignation with Barry. She busied herself spreading plum jam on a second piece of bread to avoid meeting her employer's eye.

Stella, since her official commitment to Philip, had discovered that she had become less indifferent to any duty that was required of her on the farm. Being engaged, it seemed, had altered the frizzy nature of love. Now, knowing she was secure, her thoughts were not, curiously, permanently with Philip. There was no longer a glazing of indifference between herself and whatever the matter in hand. She found herself better able to concentrate on the animals, the fields, and actively enjoy them. Secretly, she was missing Philip less than she imagined possible. Instead, what she now craved was music – a piano, a concert on the wireless. She wondered if there was a need for some kind of craving, at all times, in human nature, and spent many hours contemplating the subject of solace. If the thing you most want is missing, where do you turn for comfort? A line from Keats, vaguely remembered from school, came to her in answer. 'Glut thy heart on a morning rose . . .' Well, she thought, in her job as a land girl she was brutally exposed to Nature: she would try. She began to observe more accurately, find strange pleasures in the smell of earth newly turned by the hoe, the gilt-edged clouds of winter skies, the feeling of awe within a wood. She confessed these new sentiments to Ag, who had understood at once.

'I'll have to get you reading Wordsworth,' Ag said. 'No one better on the partnership between Man and Nature. He's pretty well convinced me of the compensations of the earth. Hope he's right, because if Desmond doesn't come about it'll be all I'm left with.'

She had sounded so solemn, envisaging a spinster life with Nature her only lover, Stella wanted to laugh.

'I'd be happy to do whatever's needed, Mr Lawrence,' Stella now offered, 'though I'm not much of a cook.'

She had been looking forward to a day freeing a gate from a tangle of brambles. Yesterday, she had begun the job armed with thick gloves and powerful secateurs. Surprised by her own skill in disentangling the thorny mass, she was eager to finish. Also, it was a solitary task – one of the occasions on which, without inhibition, she could sing as she worked.

'I'd positively *like* a day indoors,' volunteered Ag. 'I've been watching Mrs Lawrence making bread day after day – I'd like to have a go.'

'Ag it is, then,' said Mr Lawrence. 'Up you go for instructions from Faith, and we'll be expecting lunch at the usual time, two courses.' He smiled at her nicely.

'*At least* two courses,' giggled Prue. 'Canary pudding and syrup, if you can manage it.'

Prue found she needed especially large lunches the days of Barry's visits, to keep out the cold, and to give her strength for the acrobatics in their bed of leaves under the trees.

*

206

When they had all gone, and Ag had cleared and washed up after breakfast, she allowed herself a few moments by the stove, hands resting on the dogs' heads, to accustom herself to the strangeness of staying indoors. She was by now so used to spending most of each day outside, it seemed very curious, tame, to be left to the world of the housework. But this is what it must be like every day for Mrs Lawrence, she thought: sudden silence, the looming of domestic plans, lists of tasks to be accomplished by night-fall. There was no freedom from the discipline of deadlines: food must be on the table by midday, no matter how much ironing. The pile of socks to be darned must be kept under control; the grading of eggs, in the stone-chill of the scullery, was necessary before sending them off twice a week. For the first time, Ag began to reflect on the life of a housewife, doubly hard if you were married to a farmer. She wondered how it would be, how she would like it, when her time came – if, that was, she was not left entirely to Nature.

Stirring herself with a sigh, Ag went up the dark stairs to the Lawrences' bedroom – a side of the house she had never visited before. Mrs Lawrence called to her to come in.

Ag took a moment or so to adjust to the duskiness of the light in the bedroom, with its beamed ceiling and small windows. Then a few objects, touched by the grey sky out-side, began like just-lit lamps to burn into view – a set of silver-backed brushes on the dressing-table, a framed sepia photograph of a girls' lacrosse team, a jug of dried thistles. Mrs Lawrence lay propped up on pillows in a high bed made of dark wood. Her hair was bound in a plait that lay over one shoulder; her face was flushed the colour of a bruise. She wore a long-sleeved calico nightdress, folded hands emerging from frilled cuffs and lying on the bed-spread, stony as the hands of an effigy. The sight of her was a reminder of mortality: death from illness and old age, not just death from slaughter in the war.

There was a faint smell of cough sweets and honey. Despite a one-bar electric fire, it was very cold. Mrs Lawrence stirred.

'Do you mind, Ag? So silly, this. But John insisted . . .' Her voice was painfully hoarse. Shadows under her eyes scoured the drawn cheeks. Ag wondered whether she was seriously ill, or suffering from exhaustion, or both. What age was she? Probably early fifties, but she looked sixty. Affection for this contained woman, with her silent strengths, swept over Ag with renewed force.

'Don't worry,' she said. 'Just tell me what there is to do, then I'll bring you a cup of tea.'

'Sausages and mash for lunch, stewed apples and custard. Corned beef hash tonight, perhaps – whatever's there. I'm not thinking very clearly.'

She gave a small, self-despising smile, shut her eyes. *Tired eyelids upon tired eyes* . . . Pith-white skin stretched over the deep eyeballs. Open, the lids were crinkled as aged tissue paper. Closed, an illusion of youth clung to Mrs Lawrence's strong features.

'I'll have a go at making some bread,' said Ag.

'There's enough left from yesterday.'

'I'd like to try.'

'Very well. Don't overdo the salt. John doesn't like much salt.'

Their quiet voices chimed, church-like, in the soft brownness of the room. Then Ag crept away, leaving her employer to sleep.

It was the strangest morning since she had been at Hallows Farm, Ag later told the others. Working in the cold and silent house, her main anxiety was that she would not have done all the normal morning tasks, besides cooking the lunch, by twelve o'clock. Where was the Hoover, the dusters? What should be polished? Was it the day to scrub the stone flags of the kitchen floor? What rewards were there in doing such things *every day*? Guiltily she realised, as she buffed up the bannister rails in the icy hall, rewards did not come into it: Mrs Lawrence would never think in terms of rewards. Keeping house was merely a job to be done.

In the sitting-room, a forlorn place in the daylight, Ag turned on the wireless. The jaunty tunes on *Music While You Work* spurred her to polish the brass fender in time to the music, trying to keep herself warm. Then she listened to the news. It was announced that the Japanese had attacked Pearl Harbor.

Ag sat back on her knees, twisting a duster – slash of yellow in the dull light – in her hands. She tried to imagine the distant carnage, the destruction, the horror, the terrible suffering and pointless loss of life. She felt impotent anger, fear. This was followed by feelings of equally impotent guilt at her own lot, which was comparatively safe. There was never a day she could take for granted her luck in being here, a place where the war scarcely touched them, but there was also never a day when she did not wonder if she should not volunteer for some less protected field of action. Should she not join the Red Cross, or drive ambulances in the Blitz, rather than milk cows and feed off Mrs Lawrence's secure stews? Should her courage not be tested? And yet, while the men were fighting, girls to work on the land were vital: she had chosen the job, she loved it. But when news came of disasters, Ag was racked by the thought she should be helping the wounded rather than sweeping a safe yard or tending to the sheep.

She turned off the news, returned to work. Dully she set about preparing the lunch – at least the kitchen was warm. She was haunted by imaginings. Never having seen a photograph of Pearl Harbor, she had no idea of its scale. Visions came to her of gentle harbours on the East Anglian coast, crowded with pretty sailing boats. She tried to swap the familiar scenes for a more massive place, with destroyers at anchor. The paucity of mental pictures caused tears in her eyes.

When the others came in to eat they found her kneading a large lump of dough at the kitchen table. They wondered at the fierceness of her thumping, but made no comment. Ag's first loaf, which later rose magnificently in the oven, was filled with the stupidity of mankind, the futility of war, the helplessness of one individual such as herself to enable the world to come to its senses.

Ratty, too, heard the news on the wireless. It was one of his days off from the farm – never a good time, the hours would stick to him like mud, nothing would shake them off – petty chores in the house or woodshed were useless at accelerating the long minutes. What Ratty missed, in this state of semi-retirement, was the discipline of long hours at work in the open air. Alone in the front room, tapping his pipe against the grate, the news increased his restless state.

'Poor buggers,' he muttered. 'More trouble to come.'

He needed to be with someone. Anyone. Even Edith.

The kitchen was unusually welcoming: warm from baking, and filled with the sweet smell of dough. Edith, at the table, was regimenting troops of scones into neat lines on wire racks. Ratty was suddenly, piercingly, hungry.

'Will you spare me one?'

'That I won't.'

Ratty shuffled a little nearer the table, watched his wife's floury hand whisk among the crinkled edges of the beautiful scones, moving them into pure lines.

'Japanese buggers have bombed Pearl Harbor,' he said. 'Ah.'

Edith, devoid of all imaginings beyond the confines of her own life, was immune to most of the horrors of the war. She could only believe in what she read in the papers – her faith in the printed word had always puzzled Ratty – and then only if there was a photograph to prove the story. Thus it was a picture of Beaverbrook waving an armful of saucepans that had fired her own wartime effort, and she conceded the Blitz took its toll because the photographs 'said so'. Any wider understanding of the war, particularly 'abroad', was beyond her. Of late, Ratty had begun to wonder whether her lack of interest in the state of the world, affecting millions of lives, was some kind of disease. But then it occurred to him that solution was merely a figment of his own vivid imagination, and the real answer was that Edith's professed ignorance was a defence against intense, private fear.

'One thing after another. They're for tea, then, are they?' Again Ratty looked longingly at the scones.

'They're not for tea. They're for the shop. Got to keep the customers happy. Got to make a living.'

A new tack to deny Ratty the odd luxury, he thought. Usually, her concern was to cause unhappiness among the customers in their fight for her few loaves. Ratty looked at his wife carefully. Sighed.

'What's for dinner, then?'

'Thought I'd boil up a couple of parsnips.'

On such a grey day, so full of bad news, Ratty did not feel like boiled parsnips.

'Don't think I want any,' he said, knowing his rejection would cause a disproportionate measure of offence.

'Get yourself a sandwich, then. It's not the Ritz here, you know. I'm not bothered.'

Ratty had expected worse. But Edith's concentration on her scones, he noticed, was out of the ordinary.

He cut two slices from the loaf of hard, dark bread, and spread it thinly with shrimp paste scraped from a small ribbed jar. He knew better than to ask for butter: Edith had obviously availed herself of his carefully hoarded ration for her scones, and was in no mood to be confronted with her thieving. *Yes*, said Ratty savagely to himself, he would definitely call it *thieving*. If the point came he would, in all honesty, have to call his wife a thief.

'Think I'll take my dinner out,' he said. 'Sky's clearing.'

'Up to you if you catch your death,' said Edith.

Ratty pottered about making himself strong tea which he poured into a thermos. Edith, so preoccupied, failed to notice his stirring in two forbidden spoonfuls of sugar: that was at least one triumph. He wrapped the leaden sand- wich in greaseproof paper.

'Mind you fold it up carefully, bring it back; it can be used again,' Edith snapped. She had been listening to the crackling of the paper, though she had not bothered to raise her eyes to check how much Ratty had taken.

'It's only a scrap, for Lord's sake.'

'Every scrap counts in a war.' When it came to the petty necessities of war, her perverse mind worked well enough. She raised her eyes. 'I suppose you're going off to join those girls.'

'That I'm not.'

'One of them, anyway.'

'No.'

'That's not what I've heard.'

'What d'you mean, Edith? Whatever are you talking about?'

'I keep my ear to the ground.'

Guilt seized Ratty's heart. Despite his innocence, and knowing he had never uttered a word to anyone, or made any kind of untoward gesture, he wondered how his wife could have guessed at the admiration, the secret *esteem* in which he held the holy one. In a moment of panic, he thought that maybe he had confessed this to Edith, and amnesia had blotted out the occasion. But no, that was mad. Surely . . . the mere sense of wistfulness – for that is what it was – he felt about Ag, was an absolute secret between Ratty and his God, and would always remain so.

'You're being ridiculous, woman,' he said. 'You know you are. You know those girls mean nothing to me. We're just fellow workers.'

'Huh. And since they've come, your working hours are

almost back to full time, aren't they? That's what everyone's noticed. That's what they're all saying to me.'

There was a long, incredulous silence. Then Edith began to brush flour from the bosom of her apron. It fell in a light dust on the cracked linoleum floor. If her snappish movements indicated a nefarious imagination could be called upon by his wife when necessary, Ratty did not notice.

'You're a wicked woman, Edith, that's what you are,' he said at last. He picked up his stick from the corner and thrust the thermos into his free pocket. Then he left the kitchen before she could answer, moving faster than he had for several years.

The heavy lunch and a strong cup of tea left Ag feeling calmer. She longed to do the afternoon milk, clean out the pig, anything rather than face the huge pile of ironing, but praise for her cooking had given her heart to face the domestic afternoon, and as soon as the lunch was cleared she went to the laundry room and set up the cumbersome ironing board.

Ag was an unpractised, unskilled ironer. It took her a long time to negotiate the difficult points of collars and spaces between buttons: compared with them, the stretches of sheets and tablecloths were easy, though the ancient iron was heavy. Within an hour her arm ached and her feet were icy on the stone floor. She began to recite to herself every long narrative poem she could remember, and was pleased to find there were few blanks. By the end of *Lycidas*, there was a pile of neatly folded clothes on the table – very professional-looking, she thought, and could not decide which gave her more satisfaction: remembering the long poem, or finishing the first basket of laundry.

The window of the laundry room was misted with condensation, but she could see the vague figures of Prue and Stella in the yard, driving the cows back to the field. She could hear the beasts' lowing – a different, deeper sound of relief, once they had been milked – and the squelching of dozens of hoofs in mud. Ag looked at her watch. Amazingly, two hours had passed. She finished the last of Mr Lawrence's shirts, allowed herself a brief image of ironing shirts for Desmond in some eternal future, then decided to pause for a while. Here she was, mind on *ironing*, when Pearl Harbor had been bombed . . .

She put a tray of tea beside Mrs Lawrence, who was sleeping, then went downstairs to sit at the kitchen table. Clasping cold hands round a mug of tea on the bare stretch of oilcloth, she listened to the muggy silence of mid-afternoon. Suddenly the quietness was split by the screech of a plane overhead. Within seconds the alarming sound had withered back to nothing, and Ag could hear the dripping of a tap again, and the beating of her own heart. She looked up to see Joe, in gumboots – not allowed in the kitchen when his mother was there – standing at the door.

'Hasn't been one like that for a long time,' he said.

'Come to shake us out of our complacency, perhaps. Pearl Harbor –'

'I know, I heard. How's Ma?'

'Asleep. I took her some tea.'

'How are you managing?'

'Fine I think.'

'I've got to walk down to River Meadow, look at a sheep. Like to come?'

Joe poured himself a mug of tea from the pot. Ag took her time, weighing things up.

'There's the bread to come out, the rest of the ironing.'

'I said would you *like* to come.'

'Yes.'

Ag smiled. She carried the tea things to the sink, moving with the kind of languor that assails those who have been indoors for many hours and now face the prospect of a walk in the cold.

'I'll get my boots,' she said.

The fronds of a plan, so indeterminate she could not be sure of its meaning, began to pulse in her mind. She felt suddenly courageous. Or was it reckless? As she followed Joe through the back door, Ag could not be sure: nor did she care.

'The wicked, wicked woman,' Ratty muttered to himself. He stomped down the lane, slashing at the verges with his stick. Sometimes he spat ahead of himself, a hard ball of sputum that sizzled out and died by the time he strode past it. His anguish was twofold: Pearl Harbor, poor buggers, and himself: deprived of a single scone by a wife who also – with no scrap of evidence – accused him . . . of what? And how was it she managed to undermine his innocence? What made her suspect there was more respect in his heart for the land girls – yes, even the floozie, a gallant little worker for all her silliness – than there had ever been for her?

The winter sky was heavy on Ratty's head. His temples throbbed, his arthritic hip ached. He needed shade, shelter from the cruel glare of the heavens. He turned into Long Wood that ran half a mile beside fields, then straggled on up the hill. In the path between the trees he found some relief. The purplish light that clings to winter branches, and the myriad shadows scattered finely as broken glass, confused his eyes in an agreeable way. He was in no mood to see things clearly. The muffling of his own footsteps was a blessing, too. Here, the only sound was an occasional soft snapping of twigs, mushy from rain, breaking underfoot. No birds sang.

Then the aeroplane, from nowhere. Ripped from the bowels of silence, it screamed invisibly overhead. Interrupted in their winter husbandry, birds rattled out of the undergrowth calling in alarm, and fled to high branches that trembled in the wake of the monster. Ratty peered up. Was it ours? Theirs? It had gone too fast for him to see. Knees trembling, he moved off again more slowly. After a while the wood returned to its old quiet and he came to a clearing, a junction of paths.

Ratty had intended to walk to the top of the hill – thus keep safely out of the house for a couple of hours. But, shaken by the plane and the mess of anxieties in his head, he took the wrong path. He progressed some fifty yards before realising this, but decided to carry on. Then, rounding a bend, he saw the distant figures of Joe and Ag coming towards him. A thumping and boiling of blood in his temples told him this was the last straw . . . Joe and the holy one . . . Such anger scorched his being he came to a halt, stood helpless in the path. They waved, *waved*: the cheek of it, thinking they could deceive him, no doubt. They smiled, *smiled*: how dare they! Ratty stood glowering back at them, his look signalling their time had come. By the time they were just a few yards from him, Ratty had made up his mind. Pity he hadn't got his pitchfork, but his stick was solid enough. He would thrash the life out of Joe: teach him to stop mucking about with the feelings of innocent girls.

With a gesture that might have been less fierce than he intended, Ratty raised his stick in the air, shook it threateningly. Even as he did so, he felt his free hand automatically touch his cap.

'Ratty!' The bugger Joe was smiling. The girl, too, happy as a lark. 'About to show Ag a nice bit of foot rot,' Joe said. 'We must keep on before the light goes.'

' 'Bye, Ratty,' said the holy one.

They passed each side of him like a tide that divides effortlessly round a rock in its path. If only he'd been quicker, silly old fool. Now he'd missed his chance – and Joe would have his way with the holy one, like he had with all the rest. Though in truth, and here Ratty began to potter on, even more slowly, Joe did *seem* bent on his mission with a sheep. Didn't look as if he was up to any funny business, but you never could tell. The art of deceiving, as Ratty well knew, is to wear a look of innocence with such ease that suspicion is never ignited, never has reason to flame.

The sheep were gathered together in the far corner of the field – probably suffering from shock of the plane, Joe said. Sheep panicked more easily than cows, he explained: nervous, silly creatures – but, all the same, he would be sorry to see them go, next spring, after lambing.

'But, like everyone else, we have to turn most of our acreage over to plough,' he said to Ag. 'Price of living in a country that produces a third of its food. Come a war and animals must be sacrificed. We'll probably have to reduce the cows, too: just keep one or two for house milk.' His eyes travelled over distant fields. 'It's odd to think that in 1939 there were eighteen million acres of grassland, twelve million of plough. The rate things are going, in a couple of years that'll be reversed. But I don't suppose we'll be here to see the complete changeover at Hallows. We may have to move to Yorkshire.'

'Yorkshire?'

In the fast-fading light, they walked slowly towards the flock.

'My uncle, Dad's brother, isn't going to recover. His farm's the Lawrence family home. My aunt and cousin can't manage it on their own. They're struggling, even with the help of two land girls. When Jack dies, Dad'll have to take over. He'd rather be here than there, but he hasn't much choice. He feels he can't sell a place that's belonged to the family for a couple of hundred years. Rotten time to try to sell Hallows, middle of a war. And after all he's put into this place. But it can't be helped.'

'I didn't know any of that,' said Ag quietly.

'I'd be grateful if you didn't tell the others. I probably shouldn't have said anything.'

'Of course.'

'There's the one I'm after.'

Joe pointed to a dejected-looking ewe. When the rest of the flock swerved away and began to run, she hobbled so badly she was soon left behind.

Ag held the animal's shoulders while Joe examined the rotten hoof. The great black head worried about, bleating pathetically. Ag spoke soothing words, trying to calm her, but not succeeding.

'Treatment first thing in the morning,' said Joe at last, lowering the painful hoof to the ground. 'Off you go, old girl.'

They watched the ewe limp to join the rest of the sheep, who showed no recognition of her plight.

'You can become fond of them, somehow,' said Joe, eyes anxiously following the animal's progress, 'especially if you've known them from birth. I never forget the circumstances of a single birth, don't know why. Maybe you'll see what I mean, come the spring. We'd better hurry back, or you'll not have tea on the table in time.' He smiled.

'I don't much want to hurry,' said Ag.

For twenty-four years Ratty had been walking the woods on Mr Lawrence's land. He could find his way about them on the darkest night, learned – folly of a distant youth – by snaring the odd rabbit or pheasant, when he and Edith had found it hard to make ends meet. But today, in the gathering dusk, at the end of so disagreeable a day, he was confused. He turned down a small path that he thought would eventually lead back to the lane. He then realised he was again mistaken, and knew it would take him deeper into the wood. Ah well, he thought, he'd keep ambling aimlessly about: anything better than going home.

By now it was almost dark. It was hard to see where grass and brambles met roots of trees. The millions of individual bare branches had turned into solid, dense shapes. A tawny owl cried. Then there was the sound of a human cry, followed by laughter.

Ratty paused, listening intently. The laughter came again, from behind a holly bush. Ratty knew the holly well. Years ago, there had been a badger sett beneath it. He had taken Joe there, one night, to see the badgers play. Joe, at seven or eight, was a real one for wildlife. Ratty had often thought he might become a naturalist . . .

There it was again – the human cry clashing with the lugubrious note of the owl. Ratty took small side steps closer to the bush. He peered round. He saw a pile of something on the ground – a collapsed tent, perhaps. Trespassers? Poachers? Maybe, worst of all, *picnickers?*

He narrowed his eyes, forcing them to focus through the gloom, and saw that it was no tent but a pile of clothes. He could just make out the bluish jacket of an RAF uniform, forage cap tucked neatly into the pocket. Then he saw, slightly to one side of the general pile, a pair of corduroy breeches. He caught his breath, edged closer still to the place from which wild shouts and laughter were now coming.

What Ratty focused upon then caused him for a moment to think that he was hallucinating: two spectral melons rising and falling with beautiful rhythm in the darkness. As he watched, entranced, the ghostly fruits turned into the human flesh of buttocks. These buttocks, pale as moonstone, flew up and down so fast that Ratty, following them with incredulous eyes, soon found himself dizzy. He dug his stick deeper into the ground for support. A small hand had slithered up on to the buttocks, and was frenzying about in excited patterns, the fingers fluttering, fast. The air was suddenly filled with cries of abandon that, like the plane, frightened hidden birds. They flew up into the darkness, wings stirring the air near Ratty's face.

He could bear no more. He stepped backwards. Blindly, he moved down the path, tapping the roots of trees. The noises grew fainter behind him. An early moon, he saw through a gap in the trees, had just slit the sky, forcing a

219

strand of light down through the branches that enabled Ratty to see he had arrived back at the main clearing.

There, he sat down on an old tree stump, a place where for many years he had paused in his walks. He could hear no more sound from the lovers . . . *lovers doing it on the earth, rutting like rabbits under the trees* – a dream so deeply secreted away that only the sight could have brought it back. The floozie and her airman: God forbid, the floozie and her airman were experiencing something he, through decades in the marital bed, had never known, would now never know. Oh Lord, he envied them.

For their pleasure, and for so many things he himself had never known, Ratty wept in the darkness.

'Can we go round the long way?' asked Ag. 'It'll be dark in the woods.'

With matching long strides, they moved across the field to the path by the hedge that divided the grassland from the wood. They walked in easy silence for fifty yards, then Joe came to a halt.

'Listen,' he said.

From somewhere distant in the trees came a thin trill of laughter, familiar in its running cadences.

Ag smiled. 'Wood spirits,' she said. 'They must be terribly cold.'

'Hope one of the spirits remembered to sterilise the bottles this time,' said Joe, with good humour. 'On Monday she was in such a hurry she forgot. I had my work cut out trying to cover for her.'

They began to walk again.

'If Ratty comes upon them,' said Ag, 'he'll have a seizure.'

'Poor old Ratty. He's ageing fast. Gets pretty confused these days – waving his stick at us like that, as if we were poachers.'

'Prue says he unnerves her, his silence. Stella and I are

220

his fans.'

'How was Stella's weekend in Plymouth?' asked Joe after a while. 'I never heard.'

Ag took some time before answering. 'I suspect something happened,' she said at last, 'but I'm not sure what. She said it was all wonderful and she's pleased to be actually engaged. But I don't know. I privately think there was some kind of . . . disappointment.'

'She's not quite her old exuberant self. She seems to have come down from the clouds.'

'She does. That's just it. She concentrates more on the matter in hand now. Her dreamy look is gone. She talks in practical terms about marriage, houses, children, life after the war. It's almost as if spurred by just three meetings with Philip, before she came here, her imagination superseded the reality. She's always saying she has to be in love, Stella. She can't live without being in love. So there she was, in love with this almost imaginary figure, goes off to meet him and, well . . . But I'm only guessing.'

They had reached the gate that led to the lane. Joe leaned on its top bar. He seemed in no hurry to open it, or climb it. Ag imitated him, fingers of one hand drumming the damp wood. By now a dew was falling. The darkness, characteristic of a late winter afternoon, seemed to cascade inefficiently over what was left of the daylight, so that the struggle between impending night and departing day was visible. In an hour or so, the transparent quality of the ensuing gloom would have thickened, become dense. A skeletal moon was stamped on the sky, the most fragile of seals, which gave no light.

Joe turned to Ag. 'And you, Ag,' he said, 'do you have a secret, imaginary love, too?'

'As I think I told you, there was this research graduate at Cambridge.'

'Was?'

'Never *was*, really. Still *is*, in a way. I still cling to the idea

221

of him, though I knew him even less well than Stella knew Philip. Just saw him in the distance a few times. Had one tea in a café with him and a few friends. Listened to him. You'll think this mad, but if, that evening, he'd asked me to go anywhere in the world with him, I would have gone without further thought.'

'Highly romantic. Good thing he didn't give you the chance to be so unwise.'

Ag smiled. 'I wouldn't expect anyone to understand,' she said, 'but I felt a kind of *certainty*. I felt such certainty, such conviction, that here was my other half, or whatever the silly phrase is, that in some strange way my life changed absolutely from that day on. From June the sixth, 1941, I've been borne along by the indescribable sensation that . . . everything I do is significant only in that it's a step nearer to the inevitable outcome . . .' She sounded solemn, shy.

'And what's that outcome?' There was a trace of sceptical laughter in Joe's voice.

'Him and me. Together in some form.'

'Ah.'

'I suppose you think all that's ridiculous?'

'No. Most people need their fantasies. I rather envy you such a dream. What happens if it doesn't work out?'

'It will,' said Ag, 'but if it doesn't I'll be all right – just lesser, somehow.'

She glanced sideways at Joe, could just see a smile twitching the corners of his mouth. Suddenly she felt the warm rush of an unfamiliar feeling: skittishness, she thought it was. Confidence, ease. And the vague shapes of the plan that had come to her earlier in the afternoon returned, beating faster.

'But if it's all a disaster, doesn't happen, I never see him again, then I'm quite prepared to live a solitary life.'

'For a clever graduate with a face which won't go unnoticed, you're talking a lot of nonsense,' Joe laughed. 'Aren't you cold? Shouldn't we be getting back?'

'Not very. In a moment.'

Scarcely aware of what she was doing, Ag, inspired by some peculiar boldness, stepped on to the gate and sat on the top bar. She faced Joe.

'Here's some more nonsense,' she said. 'If it *does* go right, and we meet again one day, I want to go to him *experienced* . . .' Her face blazed in the darkness. Wondering at her own recklessness, she went on. 'I don't want him to think I'd been pathetically keeping myself for him.' She paused. 'I'm quite keen to be shot of my virginity . . . There: I've said it.'

In the silence that followed, Ag realised the extent of her impropriety. But, still fired by her inchoate aims, she went further in her madness, and rested her arms on Joe's shoulders. He did not protest, or move, but kept his silence.

'I knew I'd go too far eventually,' Ag murmured at last. 'I've made a complete fool of myself. Please don't tell the others.'

She removed her arms, climbed back off the gate to the other side. Joe followed her.

'I think I could probably oblige,' he said.

'*What?* I didn't really mean you, Joe . . .' His reaction caused her such confusion she turned from him, began to walk.

'I think you did.'

'I've been in a terrible muddle. Waiting, waiting: it's a sort of canker. It does things to you.'

Joe caught up with her. He took her hand.

'I can imagine that,' he said.

They walked in silence up the dark lane, so fast that the cold that had bitten into them was replaced by an almost feverish heat beneath their thick clothes. As they turned the corner to the farmyard gate, Joe released Ag's hand. She felt briefly deprived of warmth, comfort, understanding. The expectation that his offer had provided was a calm, sweet thing: no desire attached, just curiosity.

'When?' she said.

'Soon,' said Joe.

Two days later, Mrs Lawrence, recovered but weak, was up
and resuming her usual duties. The first evening of her
return to normal life, she stirred the Christmas pudding in
a huge bowl.

'It'll be a thinnish pudding, this year,' she said to Stella,
who was chopping vegetables at the other end of the
kitchen table. 'Rich only in sixpences. I've been saving as
much dried fruit as I can, and John's let me have a bottle of
brandy from the cellar. But it won't be like the old days.'

Stella smiled. In her pocket was an unopened letter from
Philip – the first since Plymouth. Curiously, her impatience
to read it was manageable. The idea of keeping it till she was
in bed throbbed no more fervently than the idea of a minor
luxury. Her chief feeling was one of a childlike excitement
about Christmas. Earlier in the day Mr Lawrence had
brought in a Christmas tree, and set it in the sitting-room.
Mrs Lawrence had brought down a box of decorations from
the attic, and given them to Prue. As the experienced win-
dow-dresser of a leading Manchester hairdresser, Prue had
said, she was the most qualified to dress the tree. No one
had quarrelled with this. She burst into the kitchen now,
twigs in her hair – there were twigs in her hair most days,
Stella quietly observed – starfish lashes blinking wildly.

'It's done, it's beautiful! No one's allowed to go in and
see it till after supper. Only thing that's missing, Mrs
Lawrence, are small candles. I'll get some in Blandford
tomorrow. You coming, Stella? It'll be good fun. We could
get Christmas cards and presents and things, and go back
to the tea-room. Then we could see what's on at the picture
house, have a drink somewhere, catch the last bus . . .
couldn't we, Mrs Lawrence?'

Mrs Lawrence nodded. She passed the spoon to Prue.
Prue stirred the uncooked pudding.

'Shouldn't I be making a wish?' she asked. She shut her eyes for a moment. 'I know what I'm wishing.'

Stella thought she had a pretty good idea of Prue's wish, too: she wondered what her own should be. For a return of the old impetus, perhaps.

'I always wish the same, every year,' said Mrs Lawrence, taking back the spoon. What could *that* be? Stella wondered.

'You just keep on,' giggled Prue. 'You just need enough faith, and anything'll come true.'

'I hope so,' said Mrs Lawrence. 'Come on, Stella, your turn. Where's Ag?'

Ag, her three days of intense domestic duties over, had returned with some relief to her tasks outside. She was pleased to be reunited with the bantams and hens. Collecting eggs, feeding and cleaning their houses, had become one of her regular jobs. She had come to learn the birds' various moods, their stubborn ways, their flights of stupidity, their sense of detachment. While the others stirred the pudding in the kitchen, Ag searched the barn for two missing bantams: the rest were shut up in their houses for the night.

She held a hand over her torch, released a few bars of almost useless light. But she knew her way about well by now: knew their favourite corners, far from the tractor – they had separate places for sleeping and laying. As Ag felt among the sacks she could hear the familiar churring of pigeons high in the rafters. Then, from a place near her, the higher, tremulous clucking of bantams. She uncovered the face of the torch, swept its dim beam over a cluster of nesting places. In a comfortable dip in the hay, croodled the two lost birds.

'Come *on*,' she chivvied. 'You're late.'

In an obedient mood, the bantams flopped to the ground, squawking and flapping. They ran towards the farmyard, heads jabbing furiously. Ag switched off her torch. Turning to follow them, she saw the dark silhouette of Joe. Her heart quickened. The arranged seduction, whenever that was to be, was not going to take place here in the barn, copy of Prue's experience. Of that, Ag was determined.

'I need some books, Ag,' said Joe. 'I've finished everything. If I take you all in to Blandford tomorrow afternoon, would you help me choose some?'

Ag was glad of the darkness. Glad he could not see her blush. Glad it was only books he wanted.

'Of course.'

'Then,' said Joe, 'we could go out to tea.'

'Fine. Anything. I must make sure the bantams have gone back, shut them up.' She hurried past him.

'Hurry in and stir the pudding,' Joe shouted after her, 'and wish us luck.'

Five minutes later, it was Ag's turn with the spoon. Screwing up her eyes, she saw a picture of Desmond's face, and wished to do the right thing. When she opened them, she found Joe looking at her. This unnerved her. She had been strangely calm since their conversation two days ago at the gate. Now, her usual composure left her.

'I think we all need a drink,' said Mrs Lawrence. 'Joe, there's a bottle of whisky in the cupboard.'

Joe fetched glasses and the bottle. Stella and Ag exchanged looks. Apart from the ginger wine on the first night, it was the first time an alcoholic drink had appeared since they had arrived. Ag drank hers, neat, in one gulp. It would steady her, she thought. She needed something to dissipate troubling thoughts of Janet. Her own conscience was not loud enough to halt the planned deed, but planned betrayal, she was finding, is full of noisy rebuke.

'Joe,' Mrs Lawrence was saying, 'Janet rang earlier. She says she can get off midday on Christmas Eve, be here by supper time.'

Ag took a quick look at Joe's face. The neat whisky had

226

had its impact already: his features spun like a Catherine wheel. Indeed the whole room, all faces, trembled with uncertainty. Joe had no time to answer his mother before Prue dashed in singing *I'm dreaming of a white Christmas*. She wore garlands of tinsel round her neck. Silver balls hung from her ears and gold paper stars were wedged in her hair. Everyone laughed: Joe poured her a drink. Ag, to her own amazement, found herself moving right up to Prue and putting her hands on her shoulders – the same gesture she had so curiously made to Joe by the gate.

'Prue,' she said, 'you look *marvellous*. You should be on top of the tree.' The words, like the glittering vision before her, were a little unsteady.

'Good heavens, Ag,' said Prue, 'whatever's got into you?' There was more laughter.

Joe answered for Ag. 'The Christmas spirit,' he said.

My dearest darling Stella, Stella read in bed later that night. Well, at least he's upped the tempo a little, she thought. A good start.

> *That was a lovely weekend. I keep thinking of so many bits of it, and it's a good feeling knowing you're as sure as I am about getting married. It's frustrating not being able to make any plans because of the war. We must just hope it's over soon and then we can make arrangements very quickly. We're escorting a convoy to Liverpool tomorrow which will make a slight change. Hope you're happy back with the others and the animals. Forgive brief note.*
>
> *In great haste.*
> *With all my love, Philip.*
> *PS My friend Michael and I are planning a day trip to London in the New Year. Perhaps you might be able to come and join us?*

Stella folded the letter, returned it to its envelope, put the envelope by the photograph, still in its same place. She sighed, turned out the light.

'Letter from Philip?' Prue's whisper came out of the darkness. She never missed a thing, Prue.

'Yes.'

'Anything the matter?'

'No. I'd just hoped it would be a bit longer. A bit –'

'Don't worry. Practically nobody in the world can write a good letter.'

'True,' Ag joined in, from her end of the room. She had been wondering, now the spinning of her head had calmed down, whether or not she should buy a Christmas card for Desmond in Blandford tomorrow. She turned this way and that, making the bed creak. Yes, she decided. She would.

'Stella?' It was Prue again.

'Yes?'

'Are you coming, tomorrow?'

'If you like . . .'

'Ag? How about you? Do our shopping, have some fun?'

'As a matter of fact,' said Ag, 'Joe mentioned that on condition I helped him choose his books he'd give us all a lift.'

Prue giggled. 'Blimey! You mind out. Choosing books is as good a way as any.' There was a brief silence. 'Shall I tell you something? Barry says he's not sure how much longer he can keep up all this cycling.' Prue giggled again. 'So, obviously, I've got to be on the lookout for a replacement, for when he's finally exhausted. We could go to the pictures, Stella, couldn't we? Always a chance, there. Will you come, too, Ag?'

'Think I'll come back earlier, if Joe will give me a lift,' Ag answered carefully. 'I've got letters to write, Christmas cards.'

'Anything you say.' Prue gave a final giggle. 'Tell you what, I recommend the barn. One of those stacks up on the right – very comfortable.'

'Don't be *silly*, Prue,' said Ag. 'You know there's Desmond.'

'Well, there *isn't*, exactly. Desmond, I mean. Is there?'

There was another long silence. Ag thought the other two had gone to sleep. Then Prue had the last word.

'Ag, you awake? Because let me tell you something. What you're going to be shocked by, this time, is *yourself*. I bet you.'

Ag put her head beneath the bedclothes. She had no wish to hear any more truths from Prue. She had no wish to think further about the extraordinary resolve to behave badly that seemed to have overwhelmed her.

While the others went off for their Christmas shopping, tea, and the hunt in the cinema for a Barry replacement, Joe and Ag spent a long time searching the shelves of a small bookshop. Joe was keen to buy the entire works of Gissing. Ag persuaded him that to start Balzac would be more rewarding: the compromise was *Eugénie Grandet* and *Born in Exile*. Joe began to enjoy himself. He randomly chose a disparate selection of Penguins: *Can You Forgive Her?*, Chekhov short stories, Hardy's poems (Ag's strongest recommendation), various books that had slipped through the net of his reading, as he put it. It took over an hour to fill the large shopping basket Ag had brought.

They then went to a grocer, where Joe bought a bag of ginger biscuits, two anaemic iced buns and half a bottle of red wine. Ag, curious, but determined to ask no questions, helped him carry the purchases to the car.

It was three o'clock when they drove out of the town. The light had not yet begun to fade.

'Poor Stella,' said Ag, 'I bet she would have liked a lift home with us.'

'Probably,' said Joe, 'but Stella wasn't part of my plan.'

His plan, he explained eventually, as they drove into deep country of small wintry hills, was for tea in Robert's cottage. Robert was his oldest friend, unable, like Joe, to be called up, because of weak lungs.

'Before you all arrived,' Joe said, 'we used to meet most nights in The Bells. Have a drink or two, talk about anything except the war and farming. It was something to look forward to at the end of the day. But since you've all been here . . . I don't know. I've grown used to Prue's mindless chatter, your serious little head bent over a book, Stella's dreamy look while she keeps up polite conversation. There's more to the evenings, now, somehow.' He smiled. 'When I rang him last night, he reminded me we hadn't spoken for a week. Some friend, he said. What Robert needs is a woman, a girl. He's lonely. I was rather thinking –'

'I know exactly what you're thinking.' Ag laughed.

'Think she'd do? Save her a lot of scouring the streets and cinemas of Blandford.'

'I don't know Robert. How can I judge?'

'He's a good man. Funny. He'll make an uxorious husband one day.'

'Rich?'

'Far from it.'

'Temporary measure only, then. Prue's set on her gold taps. But you could try.'

They turned off the lane into a muddy, uneven track between high hedges, and reached a grey stone cottage. Its moss-clad thatched roof, in danger of slipping off, was only held in place by the frailest netting. Paintwork was peeling. Windows were thick with cobwebs and grime.

Joe took an old iron key from the lintel above the front door. He led the way into a dark, damp room. It smelt of past cats and rotten fruit. There was little furniture, but for an old sofa in front of an empty grate. Dozens of books were piled on the floor, some of their covers smeared with mildew.

'He doesn't have much chance to be domestic,' Joe said. 'You go and boil a kettle while I organise a fire.'

Ag took some time to find her way round the unpleasant kitchen. She had to wash dirty tin mugs under the single cold tap, and she could only find one plate. By the time she returned to the sitting-room with tea things on a rusty tray, Joe's fire had brightened the place a little.

'So when's he arriving, Robert?' Ag asked.

'Don't be silly. He's not.'

'I see.'

'Biscuit? Bun?'

'I'm suddenly not hungry.' Ag sat at the far end of the sofa.

'We needn't go through with this if you've changed your mind,' said Joe, gently.

'Last night I was awake for hours, thinking I was mad, immoral, wicked, a ridiculous fool. I was going to say I had changed my mind. But now I'm here . . .'

Joe took two cloudy glasses from a shelf and a corkscrew from his pocket. His pre-planning was exemplary, Ag thought. He opened the bottle of red wine. 'This'll take the edge off things for you.' He handed her a glass.

'Thanks.'

Ag took a sip. It was cold, bitter. She forced herself to keep drinking, treating it as medicine. A flicker of warmth came from the fire. She began to feel better. The outrageousness of her behaviour seemed slightly less outrageous. By the time she had finished the wine, there was only one real worry left.

'I fear you may not find me very attractive,' she said. It came out sounding prim as a governess. To obliterate the taste of the wine, she tried the nasty tea. She could not meet Joe's eyes. 'So if . . . it doesn't work, I'll quite understand.'

Joe touched her hot cheek. 'In a few years' time, when this roundness has fined down a little, you'll be more striking, more original-looking, more *arresting* than either Prue or Stella.'

231

'Do you really mean that?'

'I do. Prue's prettiness, her kitten looks, won't last. Stella can look beautiful – that night at the dance she was stunning – but she doesn't take enough trouble. But you've got the bones. Somewhere. Waiting to emerge.' They both laughed. 'I said to Robert how lucky we were. Imagine the three land girls we might have been sent, I said.'

'We're the ones who've been lucky. We might have been landed in one of those hostels – not much fun, I hear. Or with some tyrannical farmer. Hallows Farm, the kindness of your parents – no land girl could ask for more.'

'It was Ma's idea.'

They finished the wine. The second glass Ag found less difficult. It had, as Joe predicted, taken the edge off things. The bleakness of the room, the apprehension of the act they were about to commit, lay more gently on her spirits. Joe stood up, took Ag's hand.

'I think we should go up.'

Ag stood, too. She was as tall as Joe. Their eyes met on the level. He kissed her on the forehead.

'Just one more thing,' she said.

'What's that?'

'Janet.'

'What about her?'

'Isn't all this very immoral? What about your conscience – and mine, for that matter?'

Joe sighed, impatient. 'It's not the time to discuss Janet, is it? You should have said something about her before if she troubled you. I can't tell you why, but for some reason she's not on my conscience. I've given her my word: I'm going to marry her. Until that time I feel free to do what I like. All right?'

Ag nodded.

Joe led her out of the door and up the narrow wooden stairs. Ag wondered how many other times he had made use of his friend's house: how many other girls had

232

followed him up those stairs, and into the little cold bedroom with its sloping black wood floor and crooked
window. Joe drew the scant cotton curtains. Dead moths
fluttered to the ground. Then he pulled down the bed
cover. Two blankets lay folded on an ancient mattress.
Stained pillows were slumped, caseless. He switched on an
exiguous bedroom light. The low-watt bulb smeared the
walls with a dun light, increasing the gloom. Ag stood by
the window, taking in the scene of her impending
seduction.

'Not exactly a honeymoon suite, I'm afraid,' said Joe,
'but I don't think we should use Robert's room, which isn't
much more cheerful anyway.' He sat heavily on the bed.
The springs yelped. 'Why don't you get undressed?' He
bent down to untie his own laces.

Ag wanted to say that she had imagined a lover would
help with this process. But then she remembered Joe
wasn't a proper lover, just a friend about to oblige her in
her irrational request. So, in silence, she slipped off jersey,
skirt, shoes, let them slide to a heap on the floor. She
paused before raising her petticoat above her head. There
would be something either comic or distasteful, she felt, in
the sight of her knickers, suspenders and brassière. But
Joe must be used to such things. The glance he gave her
did not indicate surprise.

'You've the body of a ballet dancer,' he said. 'Degas
would have liked to have painted you – the blue lights on
your skin.'

Ag smiled politely, rolled off her stockings. A moment
later she was completely naked. This time Joe's look was
appraising. She stood to attention, knees touching, a blade
of light between her thighs. Her cold fingers curled about
in small whirls over her thumbs. She told herself this would
probably be the only time in her life any man would sit
looking at her body, taking in the thinness of her legs, the
smallness of her breasts.

But even as Ag enjoyed Joe's silent approbation, a worrying thought came to her. What if she became pregnant? It would be a dreadful irony, that – to conceive a child in a single sexual experience designed (in a fit of madness, she now thought) to impress the stranger of her fantasies, Desmond, with her past 'experience'. In some alarm, still not moving, she tried to remember what Prue had said. One night, just before Stella had gone to Plymouth, Prue had volunteered to advise them on the matter of birth control. Something about making quite sure the man either used a french letter or – a bit riskier – 'unplugged', as Prue called it, before the vital moment. But what was the vital moment? Ag hadn',t liked to ask Prue, and she certainly wasn't going to ask Joe, displaying even further her pathetic naïvety. She remembered, too, Prue declaring that sometimes, at safe times of the month, she couldn't be bothered with any of the whole boring palaver, and, touch wood, she'd been lucky so far.

Ag put a hand on the chest of drawers. When was the safe time? Anxiety clouded her swift calculations. She wished she had listened to Prue – whose advice was chiefly aimed at Stella – more carefully. But she'd fallen asleep, probably missing important details. There was nothing for it, now, but to take a risk. If this was to be her one and only sexual encounter, possibly *ever,* then it should not be complicated with technicalities. It should be as uninhibited and enjoyable as possible in the peculiar circumstances. Screw your courage to the sticking place, Ag told herself, privately relishing the aptness of the self-advice, and get through the whole business with as much dignity as possible. She gave the faintest smile of encouragement.

Joe rose from the bed, came towards her. The fact that he had taken off only his shoes seemed to Ag unfair. She was curious to see his body, too. The nearest she had come to the study of a naked man's body was her study of Michelangelo's David. She had judged that Joe, with his height, his broad shoulders, narrow hips and firm thighs, would be something like that. She wanted to see the private parts. She was curious to learn what happened when stone turned to flesh. But this she was to be denied.

Joe picked her up. In a concave position, slung over his arms, she knew he was studying the flatness of her stomach, the hands modestly placed over the Mons Venus. He laid her on the bed. It smelt of cat, like the sofa downstairs.

'I'm going to put out the light,' he said, 'and we can pretend we're somewhere better.'

A murky dusk clogged the room. Joe, his face a clutch of indistinct shadows, bent over Ag. He rested on stiff arms placed each side of her shoulders.

'Are you sure . . .?'

Ag nodded. Joe moved to lean on a bent elbow. With one hand he began to unbutton his shirt. With the other he traced a gentle path from her neck to breast, to stomach, to thigh. Ag closed her eyes.

Later, lying stiff and cold in his arms, the experience reminded Ag of a visit to the doctor. It had been efficient, clinical, easy, swift. It had not hurt. Neither pleasure nor displeasure had been present: all Ag could think about, feeling the bulk of Joe upon her, was *this is happening*. It did not differ from the imaginings, because she had never been able to imagine exactly what it would be like. How it felt, in the end, was not very exciting. Perhaps, with someone you loved, it would be different. The only really curious thing about it all, she thought, was her lack of concern about what she called her wickedness. Thoughts of betraying Janet – for which she had berated Prue – existed no longer. Perhaps, it occurred to her, such callousness is a sign of maturity.

In a matter of moments Joe was swinging his legs off the bed, sitting up. He switched on the lamp, glanced at his watch.

'We'll be back in time for supper, complete innocence. You all right?'

'Fine. Thank you.'

Joe patted her leg with an uninterested hand. 'There,' he said. *There*, she had heard him say, so many times, at the end of a task: milking, muck-spreading, parking the tractor. *There*, he would say, meaning *a good job done, and now it's time to eat.*

He stood up and reached for his clothes, his back to Ag. Gone was her last chance to view the sight she had craved for so many years.

'Hope it wasn't too disappointing.'

'No. Thank you.' Ag shook her head. It wasn't disappointing: it wasn't anything. So she could not bring herself to say the deflowering had been either satisfactory or happy. It had been merely interesting. He had efficiently performed a function she wanted, needed, for her own esteem. And the best thing about it was that it was now over. The small web of deliquescence that had netted Ag as she lay in his arms, due more to fatigue than fulfilment, now broke. She leapt up and scurried to her pile of clothes, dressing with her back to Joe.

Ten minutes later they were in the Wolseley, on the way home.

'Now that's over,' said Joe, 'we can spend our time with more important things, like books.'

Ag smiled. Really, he had been – was being – very kind about the whole thing. Her only concern now was that her new status would not be observed.

Joe carried the basket of books into the kitchen. Mrs Lawrence was pouring soup into bowls, inspiring Ag with unusual hunger.

'Very literary afternoon,' Joe said, 'advised by my tutor, here.'

He gave Ag an open smile.

*

236

Ratty spent the evening in the front room, smoking his pipe by an unlit fire. He wanted to listen to the news, imagine the war. Edith did not. She darned peacefully – it had been a strangely peaceful evening, not a single argument – at the kitchen table.

At ten o'clock, she opened the door, stood looking at Ratty slumped in his chair. She always liked to keep bad news till late, to ensure Ratty would have something to trouble him in bed.

'There's a stomach upset going round the village,' she said. 'Seven or eight down with it.'

'Ah. Hope it won't clobber us.'

'Don't suppose it will.' Edith sounded oddly definite.

She went on standing there, not moving, arms folded defiantly under the bolster of her bosom.

'I forgot to tell you,' she said at last, 'my batch of scones went like greased lightning, everyone wanted more. Fighting over them like cats and dogs, they were.'

They returned to silence. Ratty could think of no appropriate answer. He could hear the tick of the grandfather clock in the hall. Its rhythm set something off in his brain: a thought so vile he must quickly speak – say anything – to block its progress.

'How many customers did you have, in the end, then?' He tried to give the question lightness.

'Seven or eight in all,' said Edith, without hesitation. She moved away.

Fear spread over Ratty like a cold dew. From now on, for survival, he knew he must keep a close watch on Edith. Driven by some cankerous demon, there was no knowing how far she would go in her bitter hatred of mankind.

Ag went up to bed early. She was almost asleep when Stella and Prue returned from the late bus, string bags full of Christmas presents. Prue, flinging herself on her bed, chattered excitedly about the outing. She hadn't a penny left, she said, but had bought all the presents she needed. No: they hadn't found a Barry replacement in the tea-shop or in the pub, but a friendly old farmer had bought them two gin and limes and told them there was to be a New Year's Eve party in the town hall to raise money for the Red Cross.

'So there's hope *there*.' She giggled. 'Barry'll do till then.'

She lay on her back on the bed, lifted her legs, admiring the rayon stockings and dove-grey suede shoes, with their neat little pattern of holes, and thick platform soles.

'So let's hear about your news, then, Ag. What were you and Joe up to?'

'We bought a lot of books, we had tea,' said Ag.

'Come on. You don't expect Stella and me to believe that, do you? Not with two hours on your hands, Joe plainly keen for you.'

'It's the truth.'

Prue sighed, mock impatient. 'We don't want details, do we, Stella? We just want to know how it was. What it was like.'

Ag imitated the mock sigh. 'Don't go *on*, Prue. I'm almost asleep. I tell you, it was shopping and books. If you don't believe me, I can't help it.'

Prue screeched with laughter, squirming on the bed, clutching her knees to her chest. 'I can see by the look on your face. Okay, you go to sleep. But we'll get it out of you one day, see if we don't.' She winked at Stella.

It wasn't till 1947, their second lunch after the war, that Ag confessed. By then the activities of the afternoon had turned to such fine dust in her memory that secrecy was no longer of any importance.

Nine

S tella had never intended to go home for Christmas. She had had her two nights away and her mother, who drove ambulances for the Red Cross, was to be on duty in London. Ag had planned long and complicated train journeys to King's Lynn. She would arrive home, after many hours waiting on cold platforms, late on Christmas Eve, and have two days with her father. She, like Prue, would return the day after Boxing Day. Both promised to undertake unpaid overtime when they came back.

On the night before their departure, Prue lighted the candles on the tree. She had devoted an entire half-day off to finding them. After several long bus journeys, and a ride in a farmer's cart, she had returned triumphant with two dozen small red candles, and tin holders shaped like daisies. General appreciation made her declare her terrible afternoon had all been worth it. Mr Lawrence produced a new bottle of ginger wine, which they drank, from the pink glasses, round the fire. Small presents were exchanged. Ag came in with a tray of white hyacinths – a single flower for everyone, in a pot tied with a red bow. Mrs Lawrence gave Ag a parcel to take home with her. To Prue she gave a flat white envelope.

'I know I shouldn't, now,' Prue said, 'but I'm that intrigued I can't wait.'

She sat down and split open the envelope. Dizzy blonde curls jumped excitedly round the tinsel star, left over from the decorations, on her head. She pulled out a Christmas card. A page of clothing coupons fell to the floor. She leapt up, incredulous, scarlet with pleasure.

'Oh, Mrs Lawrence – I don't believe it! Better than *diamonds*, better than anything you could possibly have thought of. Thank you ever so much.'

Prue hugged her employer, who stood stiffly by the tree. Small shadows from the candles flickered over Mrs Lawrence's brown dress, softening the rigidity of her thin body. Unused to such celebration – for years Christmas had been just the three members of the family – she smiled at Prue's delight.

'When I get back,' Prue gabbled on, 'I'll be off to some great town, kit myself out with a whole new wardrobe – you wait!' The others laughed. 'Can you really spare them?'

'What would I do with them?' asked Mrs Lawrence, glancing at her husband.

Joe refilled glasses. There was the sound of a hand-bell ringing outside. Then, singing.

> *It came upon a midnight clear*
> *That glorious song of old . . .*

'That'll be Ratty and his carol singers,' said Mr Lawrence, going to the door.

Ratty trudged in, thickly coated and scarfed, carrying a church candle.

'No lantern again this year, blackout rules, blasted war,' he said, 'and only these members of the choir willing to come with me.'

He was followed by two young boys, also holding candles. Each cupped a hand round the flame, so that their palms shone pinkly as shells, and a visible incense of cold blew off all three of them.

'What'll it be, then?' asked Ratty. 'Come all this way up the lane, we got to give you your pie's worth.'

240

'"In the bleak mid-winter",' suggested Ag.

This time last year she had heard it sung at King's College. She had spent every minute of the carol service looking round for Desmond. She did not see him.

'*In the bleak mid-winter,*' the small choir began. Ratty's deep growl made an unharmonious base to the boys' pure voices. After a line or so, the others joined in. They stood in a semicircle, eyes filtering from flames of the fire to the miniature flames on the tree. They stood very upright, as if for 'God Save the King', private thoughts hidden behind the familiar words. A particularly sweet female voice stood out from the rest. Mr Lawrence let his eyes glide towards Stella. Tonight, as on the night of the dance, she was so beautiful in her unadorned way that he felt his heart contract, and a pricking behind his eyes. He quickly dashed his look from her face, left the room to fetch more glasses.

The evening passed with more carols, and hot mince pies sprinkled with sugar that Mrs Lawrence had been saving all autumn. Two bottles of ginger wine were drunk. The room had never been so warm. The candles on the tree burned down to their stubs. Prue extinguished them with an expert pinch of her fingers dampened with spit. Brief wisps of smoke replaced the flames. Ratty, confused by several drinks, observed to no one in particular: 'Look at that! The floozie's gone and filled the tree with smoke!'

He swayed slightly, pleased to find laughter at his comment. Had he said anything so foolish at home, Edith would have struck him. Joe took his arm.

'And leave me be, thanks, Joe. The boys here'll see me home. Sober up in the midnight clear, I will.'

He smiled for the first time since his lecture on ratting all those weeks ago. And, heaven forbid, bless her lovely heart, the holy one smiled the sweetest smile back. That made his Christmas, that did.

Not till after midnight did Ratty and the boys leave. Mrs Lawrence pulled back a corner of the blackout to watch

241

their departure. The girls crowded round her. They could just make out the trio – dark figures against dark – moving across the yard, the boys each holding one of Ratty's arms. With their free hands, they held up their candles, which made firefly lights to guide their way under a sky devoid of stars.

Prue and Ag left early next morning. Janet arrived in the evening.

She came in the Austin Seven, carrying a utility suitcase and a string bag of presents wrapped in Christmas paper. Mrs Lawrence was shutting up the hens, Joe was out somewhere, Mr Lawrence was affording himself the rare treat of an evening bath. Stella found herself the one to welcome Janet, who looked cold, pale and tired. She led her upstairs to the attic, where Janet was to sleep in Prue's bed.

'Goodness me . . . Aren't you frozen up here? And no privacy. I wouldn't like that.'

'We've grown used to it,' said Stella. 'In fact I think we'd miss each other if we had separate rooms.'

'Well, well. Better than a hostel, I suppose.'

Janet took off her grey coat, to reveal a grey skirt and matching jersey – clothes no more alive on her dull body than they would be on a coat hanger. She sat on Prue's bed.

'At least it's comfortable,' she said, with a grateful smile.

'Why don't you unpack your things? Prue's cleared two top drawers. I'll go down and make a pot of tea.'

'I haven't brought much. I'll come with you. I'm not here to be waited on.'

'Don't be silly. You must be tired after the journey.'

'Well, my goodness, I did get a little lost once it was dark, I must say. No signs make it so confusing. Don't tell Joe: he'd think me so stupid. He'd never get lost.'

She pulled some hairpins from the roll of hair that coiled round the back of her neck. Shaking her head, she stirred her hair with cautious hands. Lustreless locks fell on to her shoulders, altering her face: the pale eyes seemed to retreat, while the nose gained prominence.

'After I was here last time,' she said, 'seeing all of you . . . I thought maybe Joe would like me to let it loose over Christmas.'

Stella nodded kindly, unable to find an answer.

In the kitchen Mr and Mrs Lawrence were stuffing the turkey. Mr Lawrence held the bird's thighs while his wife spooned in a coarse mixture of chestnut and onions. They greeted Janet without pausing in their task, leaving Stella to fetch the girl bread and tea.

'What a lovely sight, very Christmassy,' said Janet shyly. Stella observed a small shiver under the grey wool.

Then Joe came in, the dogs behind him. He did a swift double-take, for a second confused about the creature with forlorn locks. To mask his hesitation he hurried over to her, gave her a peck on the cheek.

'Good journey? I've put the car in the barn.'

'Oh, Joe. Thank you. Four and a half hours. Sorry I was a bit late.'

Joe was already far from her, washing his hands in the sink. He returned to the table, picked up the bread knife.

'I'm famished,' he said.

'Let me,' said Janet.

'You never cut it thick enough.' Thin smile.

'Then let me get you a mug of tea.'

Janet stood up, awkwardly bustled between stove and table. Her desire to please was so blatant Stella found it painful to watch.

'I mean, goodness me, I'm here to help, you know.'

'That's very kind, Janet,' said Mrs Lawrence, after a silence which no one else attempted to fill, 'but I should think you could do with a couple of days' rest.'

She pulled a flap of skin across the stuffing-filled cavity. Mr Lawrence let go of the bird's legs, wiped his hands on

243

his corduroy trousers. His eyes drifted over the grey figure of his future daughter-in-law before swerving to Stella, healthy-cheeked under the kitchen light, messy hair lit with reddish gold. She gave him so faint a smile he understood it was private. In acknowledgement, Mr Lawrence returned her sign with so slight a movement of his mouth that it, too, went unobserved by the others.

None of the gaiety of the previous evening prevailed. The hours were long until it was time to go to church. They sat by the fire listening to carols on the Third Programme: Mrs Lawrence with her usual darning, her husband stretched out in his customary position, eyes closed. Janet placed herself close to Joe on the sofa. He concentrated on a crossword puzzle, only half listening to her news about life as a sparking-plug tester.

'It's getting so cold, the work, now, we freeze to the bone,' she was saying. 'We take turns in getting the sniffles, although none of us ever takes a day off. I'm still hoping to become a radiographer, but the path doesn't seem clear. I talked to Andy Barrett – he's our boss – about it the other day: he said he'd bear it in mind but didn't hold out much hope.'

Janet's prominent ankle bones just touched each other: she always sat with her feet together, as if for security, Stella noticed. Her hands were in their habitual position, too – tense on her lap, fingers of the right one rubbing knuckles of the left.

'Actually,' Janet went on, with a coy look at Joe, 'Andy called me aside last week.'

She paused, waiting for the impact of this information. Joe carried on with his puzzle. The small attempt to arouse jealousy, or at least interest, was pathetic. Stella felt acutely for her.

'But don't worry, Joe – it was nothing, really.' Janet, suddenly bold, nuzzled one of her fiancé's knees with a screwed-up fist. 'It was just that apparently his wife was having trouble setting up their Anderson shelter. Would I take a few hours off and help her, he said. Of course, I could tell he didn't approve of the whole idea, anyhow. "I said to Marion," he said, "what do you want with an Anderson shelter out here? We're not London. It's not the Blitz, here." But she's apparently the nervous type, Marion, and insisted. So, anyway, off I go. At least it made a change, an afternoon digging up earth in their back garden, trying to stop it sliding off the roof of the shelter. We did quite a good job of it together, Marion and me. But was Andy grateful? Huh! We'd made a b-awful mess of his Brussels sprouts was all he said.' Janet returned her hand to its place on her own knee. '"People like Marion go to pieces in a war," he said, which I thought was rather unkind, don't you?'

Stella nodded, to make up for lack of agreement from anyone else. From the hall came the unusual sound of the telephone. It had not rung more than a dozen times since the girls' arrival. The older Lawrences regarded it with misgiving. For them it was an instrument that conveyed either bad news from John's brother in Yorkshire, or dull information. None of them stirred. Puzzled by their peculiar reluctance to answer it, Stella – to whom the telephone had been a wondrous link with the love objects in the past – offered to do so herself.

In the cold of the hall she picked up the receiver, heavy as a hammer, and held it curiously to her ear. Philip's voice. Her heart gave the merest flutter.

'Stella?'

'Philip!' She was pleased, of course. But wondered why she wasn't more pleased.

'Sorry it's so late. I've been waiting in a queue for ages. Everyone wants to ring home.'

'Of course.'

'Everything all right?'

'Fine –'

'Got my card?'

'I did.'

'They're laying on quite a show on board, Boxing Day. Vera Lynn herself, the rumour goes.'

'How wonderful.'

'I'm looking forward to that, I must say.'

'I can imagine.'

'This time next year, perhaps it'll all be over.'

'Quite. Now America's joined –'

'This time next year, you'll be Mrs Wharton, any luck.'

'I hope so.'

'Must go, now. Chaps behind me getting impatient. I think about our weekend a lot. Gosh, I do. The nights.'

'So do I.'

'Love you, Stella. Love you, darling.'

'Love you, too.'

Conversation over, Stella remained sitting on the stairs in the dim hall. The mean thought entered her mind that Philip was no better on the telephone than he was at letters. Perhaps talking across distances was an art not yet much practised, and future generations would take to it with complete ease, laughing at those who still regarded the telephone with dread and awe: a machine which had the power to make articulate men stumble, and those less talented with words cause endless disappointment.

She was aroused by footsteps, and the appearance of Joe.

'Boyfriend?'

Stella nodded.

'All well, I hope.'

'Fine. They're expecting a Vera Lynn concert on Boxing Day.'

'Lucky old them. It's time to go to church.'

As Stella watched Joe rummaging about through the mess of scarves and gas masks hanging from a row of pegs, she heard herself making a spontaneous declaration. It was one of those peculiar moments, she thought later, when an unpremeditated thought surprises its owner as much as it does the receiver. The sudden idea was not part of the plan she had put to Mrs Lawrence.

'Joe,' she said, 'I couldn't find anything I thought you'd want in Blandford. So I thought my Christmas present could be a lie-in tomorrow morning. I'll do the entire milk, scrubbing down, sterilising, everything. You sleep.'

Joe turned to her, winding a scarf round his neck. She could see the struggle on his face as he grappled to try to decide how to react.

He smiled.

'Heavens! That's the most imaginative Christmas present I've ever been offered,' he said at last. 'It'd be very churlish of me to turn it down. I can't sleep late, ever. But an extra hour or so in bed, reading . . . what a luxury. Thank you.'

'I'd do the same in the afternoon,' Stella went on, 'so that you and Janet can have an hour or so to yourselves. A walk, whatever.' Joe's eyes avoided hers. 'Well, yes, perhaps, thanks.' He pulled on a jacket. 'But it can't be all one-sided, this present giving, can it? I've done hopelessly by you – hideous little scarf. So my real present can be identical to yours to me – but on Boxing Day. All right?'

'Lovely.'

They both laughed.

Outside, the cold was bitter, dry. Snow in the air, Mr Lawrence thought. The sky was clear, full of stars. A bright moon lighted their way up the lane.

Stella walked between Mr and Mrs Lawrence. Some yards behind, the engaged couple followed – Janet with an arm tucked firmly through Joe's. She was prattling on, though Stella could not hear what she was saying. As they neared the church a quiet bell began to chime.

247

'Ratty'll be strung up if anyone in charge gets to hear about this,' smiled Mr Lawrence. 'Breaking rules again.'

But as they walked through the porch and saw Ratty at the back of the church pulling on his bell rope, Stella could see Mr Lawrence's look was one of admiration. Ratty waved. Pulling on the rope lent his old limbs a balletic quality: if he had suddenly alighted from the ground, swung up to the sixteenth-century rafters, clinging monkey-like to the rope, it would have been no surprise.

'Christmas Eve, bugger the war,' grinned Ratty. 'Christmas isn't Christmas without church bells.'

The echo of his single bell sounded with unusual urgency, thought Stella: a warning of mortality. Just two weeks ago today, HMS *The Prince of Wales* and HMS *Repulse* were sunk. Since then, pictures of a flaming *Apollo*, disappearing between mammoth waves, had been haunting her. They came to mind now as the bell insisted. She had always feared the ability of bells to stir unwanted imaginings. But then a woman at the organ – who wore a badge saying *Dig for Victory* among the speckled feathers of her hat – launched into 'Jesu Joy of Man's Desiring', her plump fingers chomping at the notes with surprising skill, and the flames faded.

The Lawrences, Stella, Joe and Janet filed into a pew near the front: there were only six others in the congregation. Stella knelt on a tapestry stool made, it said in cross-stitch, in 1916: by someone's mother or wife waiting for a son or husband to return from that war, no doubt. Stella prayed for peace, for those who were fighting for their country, dying for their country, the wounded and the grieving. She prayed for the safety of her mother, and for Philip, the prayers slipping mechanically through her mind. She glanced at Joe, hands jabbed right over his face, fingers running into his hair, and Janet, mouth pursed, fingers a gloved temple beneath her chin. One last mechanical prayer that they should be happily married, though God knows . . .

248

The vicar, wounded in the last war, came limping up the aisle. The congregation stood. Stella looked at the red-berried holly on the altar, the mistletoe that dangled from the pulpit, the jug of white chrysanthemums squat and defiant on the chancel steps. Someone had gone to the same effort as Prue to find candles: they stood lighted on every ledge, their flames making leaf-shadows across the old stone. The thought of all the time that villagers had invested to ensure the church would be the same as ever at Christmas, despite the war, Stella found deeply moving. She sometimes wondered at people's lack of appreciation of invisible effort: effort that, in the context of the larger world, is of small importance, but whose ultimate results – a decorated church, an embroidered fabric – give so much pleasure. To Stella, such effort, made by what her mother called 'the unsung saints of England', could be as disturbing as music.

O come all ye faithful . . .

The party from the farm joined in.

At some point Stella felt Mr Lawrence's eyes upon her, and saw they sparkled with the kind of embarrassed tears that strong men fight at a funeral but cannot completely control.

'I'm not sure he noticed,' said Janet. She dabbed a sad hand at the slabs of loose hair. 'What do you think? Should I put it back to normal tomorrow, what Joe's used to? I'll feel easier like that.'

It was almost one in the morning. Janet sat once more on the edge of Prue's bed. She made no effort to undress. Stella, in her dressing-gown, put her working clothes into some order on a chair ready for the morning.

'Do you know something?' Janet said. 'Joe's never kissed me. I mean, not properly. Not what I call a full-blown kiss like you see at the pictures.'

249

'He will,' said Stella. 'You haven't had much chance.'

'We've had the odd chance – he's just never taken it. What worries me sometimes is I think his mind hasn't been on that sort of thing at all. Not with me.' She gave a small sigh. 'I suppose it'll all be different when we're married. I expect he's just holding back, not wanting to alarm me. He knows I . . . Well, I wouldn't want that to change, of course, till we're married. But I wouldn't mind just a bit of, you know. All the girls at work go quite far with their boyfriends. They all tell each other what they do. I have to pretend Joe and me do much the same.' She pulled the grey jersey up over her head, revealing small breasts encased in a stiff pink brassière, its surface a complicated pattern of white stitching. 'Sometimes I think I just don't understand men at all.'

'None of us does, really,' said Stella, getting into bed. She looked at her watch. 'The thing is, I have to be up in about four hours . . .'

'Goodness me, I'm sorry.' Janet stood up, attempted to complete the rest of her undressing, but was distracted by the photograph of Philip.

'Your fiancé?'

Stella nodded.

'My, he's handsome. Do you really love him?'

'I do, I think, yes. It's difficult ever to be quite sure.'

'I don't agree with that at all,' said Janet. 'I'm quite sure of my love for Joe. Always have been since the moment we met, years ago, not much more than children. Any little bothers in my mind are all due to this b-war. They'll all be sorted out when we're married, that's what I believe.'

'I'm sure they will,' said Stella, almost asleep. 'Do you mind if I turn out the light?'

'Oh, I am sorry, chattering on – you go ahead, go to sleep.'

In the darkness, Stella heard Janet get into bed, churn about, making the springs squeak.

'Just one more thing, Stella: it's lovely being here. You're all being so kind. Christmas Day! My goodness, it's Christmas Day at last. I think what I'll do is give Joe the surprise of his life. I'll put on some lipstick, make him *want* to kiss me . . . What d'you think? Would you lend me some of yours?'

'Of course.'

'D'you think it's a good idea?'

No answer to this question told Janet that Stella had fallen asleep. Still, it didn't matter: she was quite confident so sympathetic and beautiful a girl would agree with her. Yes: Janet liked Stella.

A few hours later, in a clear, cold dawn, Stella let herself out into the empty yard. She tried to determine whether this morning held the childlike excitement she still felt every year on Christmas Day, whether it was different from normal days. It was, in a way, she decided, on account of the silence. There was no Mr Lawrence trumpeting into his handkerchief, as he did first thing outside every morning. There was no Joe clumping about the place with his long strides and preoccupied face. Besides, the extra exhilaration of having decided to do everything herself added to the especial feeling of the day. Joe had been pleased by her idea just as she had been delighted by his. Tomorrow, her turn for a few extra hours in bed, would be bliss.

She was about to turn into the lane, make for the cows' field, when she heard a bellow from the shed. Puzzled, she turned and hurried back, wondering if Joe had changed his mind and come to help her after all. In the shed, she found the animals in their stalls, chains clanking with their familiar heavy sound. Steam was rising from muddied hindquarters, strained wide by bulging udders. And hobbling down the aisle came Ratty, in his bell-ringing clothes, looking very pleased with himself.

'Thought I'd get them in for you, at least,' he grinned.

251

'Knew you were planning to do them on your own. Takes a very long time, no help at all.'

'Ratty! Thank you. But your best clothes . . .'

Ratty's smile disappeared. 'Didn't bother to go to bed, as a matter of fact, after the service.' He paused, wondering whether to confess further. 'Edith, she doesn't – well, she doesn't hold with Christmas. We had words.' He gave a rattling cough. 'Better be on my way. Get a bit of sleep before *Christmas dinner*, if you can call it that. Edith's got in a tin of Spam and a Mrs Peek's Pudding . . .'

'I'll make sure you have some of ours.'

'They're all ready to go.' Ratty's cloudy eyes dragged along the rows of black and white rumps. 'A happy Christmas to you.'

Stella knew that to wish him the same would only encourage further thoughts of his own bleak day, so said nothing.

It was mid-morning by the time she had finished the sluicing down and the sterilising. Pale sun, colourless as a Christmas rose, slanted through the open door, gilding a patch of watery concrete floor. Stella couldn't deny feeling a certain satisfaction. She had completed the long job all alone, efficiently, and was undaunted by the thought of repeating the whole process this afternoon.

Mr Lawrence appeared. 'Happy Christmas, marvellous job, Stella, thanks. But I think you'd be appreciated indoors now. I'll take them back to the pasture.'

In the kitchen, Mrs Lawrence was stirring a pan of gravy on the stove. Janet, her back to Stella, was at the sink washing the pink glasses very slowly. Stella sat at the table, where she began to prepare the sprouts. Janet turned, dishcloth in hand, back-lit by the winter sun. Her hair had returned to its usual tight roll and she had, as threatened, put on a red lipstick (it must have been Prue's: Stella did not own such a colour). In the whey colour of Janet's face it resem-

252

bled a crude line drawn by a child. When she smiled it emphasised the primrose tint of her long teeth.

'What do you think, Stella?' she asked, licking at the gash of red with a nervous tongue. 'Improvement?'

'Definitely,' said Stella.

'Christmassy, I thought.' She held up the pink glass, blinked at its crisp shine, gave it another fussy polish.

No wonder more hands were needed indoors, thought Stella, who had been looking forward to the walk down the lane with the cows.

Joe came in, then, his face blurred by unaccustomed sleep. Janet, in her excitement, almost dropped the glass.

'The best Christmas present ever, Stella,' he said. 'Christ, I only woke up ten minutes ago. Unbelievable.'

Janet's red mouth fell for an instant, then winched itself into a terrifyingly bright smile.

'Happy *Christmas*, Joe.'

She moved towards him, dishcloth and glass still in hand, head positioned for a kiss. Stella observed the varying emotions that crossed Joe's face. First, blankness, as if he had forgotten Janet's existence. Then, surprise at her being present. Finally, horror at her appearance. Janet seemed not to notice any of these reactions. By the time she had reached Joe, he had organised an expression of greeting, and obliged with the required kiss on the cheek. This brief affair over, Janet kept her head tilted back, this time awaiting an opinion.

'So – what d'you think?'

'What about?' Joe looked puzzled. The ruby bar brooch, which Janet had pinned to the neck of her beige cardigan, in celebration of Christmas, or some more private reason, caught his eye. He touched it. 'Very pretty,' he said.

'No – not the brooch, silly.' Janet smiled. She found the smallest measure of attention from Joe intoxicating. It made her daring. 'The lipstick.'

'It'll take some getting used to,' he said. 'You know what

I am: man of habit. Slow to change.'

This, in Janet's eyes, was approbation enough. Suffused with pleasure, she nuzzled her head against his shoulder, a dreamy smile slipping this way and that.

'I thought you'd like it.'

'Come along with those glasses, Janet,' snapped Mrs Lawrence. 'They're needed on the dining-room table.' She gave an impatient stir to the gravy. Spots flew over the side of the pan and landed with an angry sizzle on the top of the stove.

'Sorry, Mrs Lawrence,' Janet murmured, still impervious to the sharp voice of her future mother-in-law. 'I'm all of a dither, this lipstick.'

After Christmas lunch – which, due to Mrs Lawrence's careful husbandry turned out to be a pre-war affair – Stella excused herself as soon as possible to start on the afternoon milk. She could not bear to watch Joe undoing the parcel Janet had brought him – a pair of Fair Isle socks she had taken months to knit in between working on socks for the Forces. She had no wish to watch Janet's reaction to the box of four handkerchiefs Joe had bought her, nor witness the struggle over plans for the afternoon. She knew having a few hours alone with Joe was Janet's intention, and sensed the reluctance to comply with any such thing on Joe's part.

Stella devoted most of her Christmas afternoon to hard work with the cows. By early evening she was exhausted. She went upstairs to lie down for an hour before changing out of her working clothes for supper. Janet was sitting in her now customary position, ankles just touching, on Prue's bed. She was near to tears.

'Oh, Stella. I'm glad you're back.'

'What's the matter?'

'We went out in the car. Joe likes driving the Austin. After a while I said, why don't we stop, Joe, study the view?

254

He looked at me, honestly, as if I was mad. He said when he had a chance to drive a nice car, he wanted to drive, not look at a view. I think he must have guessed what I was hinting at . . . Well, eventually we did stop, in a gateway, not at all private, no view. I gave him the box of chocolates I'd brought – I wanted it to be a small, private present, and my goodness, it went down much better than the socks. He seemed really pleased. You're a good girl, Janet, he said, and patted my knee. *There*, he said. He began on the chocolates. I refused to have one. I wanted to take my chance.'

Here, a single tear ran down Janet's cheek. She quickly wiped it away with one of the childish handkerchiefs that had been Joe's present to her, and gave a brave little grin.

'Anyhow, I said, things don't seem to be going too well, Joe. We never seem to have the chance to talk, and you hardly ever write. I'm not complaining, I said, but I always supposed when people were engaged they wanted to be in touch. And then, when they met, they were pleased to see each other. Joe was on to his fourth chocolate, by now, a rose cream. You must give me time, he said. I'm *sorry*, he said. But somehow it didn't sound very convincing. After that, he concentrated on that little map – you know, saying what's inside the chocolates. Then he said, the thing was he had a lot on his mind, or words to that effect, that he didn't want to talk about. Not even to me, Joe? I said. Not even to you, he said.' Another tear appeared. 'But I do understand, I said. Of course I understand. I know how fed up you were not being able to go and fight. I know how disappointed you were not to be able to go to Cambridge. They're big things to cope with. But you could always go to Cambridge at the end of the war: we could *live* in Cambridge, I said, and he just looked out of the side window so I couldn't see his face.'

Janet paused, made sure of the sympathy still in Stella's eyes.

'Then – and please don't tell the others – I made my mistakes. I said, Joe, have things changed because of the land girls? I'd quite understand if you'd fallen in love with the Prudence girl. She's so pretty and bright . . . He looked at me again, as if I was off my head: quite comforting, I suppose that was. Don't be ridiculous, he said. I like them all in their different ways and I don't know what we'd have done without them. But I'm not in love with Prue – the idea has never crossed my mind. He gave a kind of a smile at such a ridiculous thought, which sort of cheered me up. But I could see that I'd also annoyed him. So then I said, trying to sound bright and light-hearted: and how did you like my lipstick? You couldn't really say, earlier, in front of the others. Silly of me to have asked then. This time he turned to me quite fiercely, his mouth full of chocolate. There's no point in trying to ape the others, he said. You're not that kind of girl. I like you best as you always are, unadorned. A scarlet mouth doesn't suit you, if you want the truth. I just thought, I said, it might make you want to kiss me . . . It did just the reverse, as a matter of fact, he said, so cruelly – I know he didn't mean to be cruel – I had to hold myself in not to cry. So I took out this handkerchief' – she held up the damp, pinkish screwed-up ball – 'still fresh from its box, and wiped all the lipstick off in one go. There, I said, is that better?'

There was a long silence. Stella could see Janet no longer fought to ward off tears. Her struggle, rather, seemed to be to find the right words.

'So he did kiss me. No words. Just a kiss on the mouth, his arm awkwardly round me. All the time, though, I felt there was something not quite right. I mean, I'm not experienced like I expect you and the others are. I don't know about kissing. But I'd always imagined it would sort of be . . . warmer, somehow. I began to open my lips, like I've seen them do at the pictures, and he backed away. I didn't let him see I was disappointed, of course: after all, it was the longest kiss we've ever had. I was very grateful. So I told him I loved him and he said, again, that I was a good girl, and started up the engine. On the way home I said that I thought it would be all right once we were married; waiting gets everybody down. And he said yes, once we were married everything would fall into place.'

'So you must be happier,' said Stella, after another long pause.

'Well, I am and I'm not. I have faith in Joe, I don't think he'll let me down. Just be patient, I keep on telling myself, and we'll end up married. But it's hard not to suspect he doesn't love me half as much as I love him, and never will. He doesn't ever say how he feels, he just says he won't let me down. Perhaps that's all I should ask. I mean, goodness, I know how lucky I am – not exactly Veronica Lake and far from brilliant, and still a rare man like him, who could have anyone, chooses me. So all I can do is go on being sure, chasing away doubts while waiting for the war to end – there must be so many couples feeling just the same. I'm ashamed of feeling sorry for myself.' She gave a dim smile. 'And once we *are* married, not a day will go by when I don't prove to him how much I love him. I think he'll come to feel the same. I pray he will.'

'It's time,' said Stella, 'to go down to supper.'

Janet jumped up, smoothed out her skirt. 'Do I look as if I've been crying?'

'Let me put a touch of powder . . .' Stella dabbed a powder puff under Janet's eyes, and rouge on the pale cheeks. 'If only Prue was here. She's much better at this sort of thing. There, you look fine.'

Janet took a nervous glance in the hand mirror. 'You've been so kind. I told Joe how kind you've been.'

'I haven't at all.'

'You've listened. Hardly anyone listens. I wish I didn't have to be off so early in the morning. It's gone so fast, my stay. And there won't be another moment to be with Joe alone. Mrs Lawrence says there's a tradition of gin rummy on Christmas night, so I'll have to put a brave face on for that.'

'No cards for me,' said Stella. 'I'm going to bed straight after supper. I want to make the best of my luxurious Christmas present from Joe.'

'You mean the long lie-in while he does the milking? He can be very imaginative, sometimes, Joe.' Janet looked so melancholy Stella feared more tears.

'Come *on*,' she said. 'Devilled turkey and mince pies.'

'At least Joe'll be pleased,' said Janet following Stella downstairs, 'that I'm back to no lipstick again. That, at least, should make his Christmas. Funny old Joe.'

On Boxing Day morning, Stella slept till midday, unaware of Janet quietly packing her bag and leaving. She came down in time for lunch to find a lightness in the air: it could well have been her imagination, but the tension of the last two days, while the sad grey figure of Janet hovered about trying to help, doing her best to fit in, had lifted. The Lawrences chattered more easily. Joe, who had gone to visit Robert when he had finished with the cows, returned with the news that he had invited his friend to supper on New Year's Eve.

'I told him about the Red Cross party,' he said. 'With any luck, he'll suggest to Prue they give it a try.'

His mother gave him a look.

In the afternoon, Stella helped Joe with the milking, and the delivery of the churns to the village. Mr and Mrs Lawrence went for a long walk with the dogs – another of their Christmas traditions. Joe invited Stella to his room to listen to some music but she said she must write a letter to Philip. The break in routine and the strangeness of a few hours' rest during the daytime had begun to wane. She looked forward to the return of the others tomorrow, and the return to normal, disciplined days.

After supper Mrs Lawrence suggested that Joe went for a drink at The Bells, taking Stella.

'It's often quite cheerful up there, Boxing Night,' she said, 'and you haven't had much fun.'

A couple of hours in the cold air had ruddied her wan cheeks. Stella guessed she would like an evening alone with her husband.

'It's been a lovely Christmas, but I'm all for a drink, if that's what Joe would like,' Stella replied.

They walked quickly up the lane. It was much colder than Christmas Eve, deep shadows sharp-edged under a full moon.

The bar at The Bells was warm and crowded. Paper chains and silver bells swooped between the low beams, and the landlord wore a paper hat.

'Almost everyone from the village here,' said Joe, looking round, 'except Ratty and Edith. That augurs badly.'

He carried two glasses of mulled wine – seasonal speciality at The Bells – to a table near the fire, where a child, the landlord's son, was roasting chestnuts. Joe helped Stella off with her coat. She sat back in the old oak chair, looking about, smiling. She felt no need to talk, as she had done in the pub in Plymouth, with Philip. Joe was not a man to be provoked by others' silence. He remained unspeaking himself, eye on the door, hoping Ratty would appear. After a while he leaned towards Stella.

'This bloody war,' he said.

She knew, for him, all the things that meant, but judged it best to make some neutral reply.

'You know,' she said, 'I've only had one real sighting of it. My mother – she works for the WVS as well as the Red Cross – was on duty at Victoria Station when the soldiers were returning from Dunkirk. She said I should come and help on her tea stall, it would be something I would never forget. At the station, there was chaos. Hundreds and hundreds of soldiers wandering about so shocked and exhausted they seemed almost to be sleepwalking. Many of them were bandaged up, wounded – the strong helping the weak. I handed a cup to one man, and he gave me twopence. No need, I said, it's free. *Free?* he said, and tears poured down his stubbly cheeks. It was the first time I'd ever seen a man cry, the tears spilling down his greatcoat, running into the buttons . . . that was my only glimpse of the war. Otherwise, the nearest I've got to it was listening to my mother's stories of the Blitz. At home we only had to go down into the cellar a couple of times during a raid. Here, at the farm, there's such extraordinary peace it's hard to believe the horrors of London, the big cities, the remote world.'

'There's always the tension, the uncertainty.'

'There's always that, yes. You remember it first thing every morning; you're reminded by the odd screaming plane.'

'Has its effects – the feeling nowhere is absolutely safe.'

'Of course.'

'Though, here, I think I'd be right in saying the arrival of you girls has been something of an antidote. It was a bad time before you came.' Joe broke off at the sight of Ratty coming through the door. 'Thank God for that,' he said quietly, signalling to Ratty to come and join them.

The old man pushed his way through the crowd, Adam's apple working furiously above his scarf, troubled eyes blinking. He drew up a chair. Joe went to fetch a pint of beer, and two more glasses of wine.

'I'm later than I should be,' said Ratty. 'Edith's on about something or other.'

'You couldn't persuade her out, then?' asked Joe, on return, with a teasing smile.

'You can say that again. She's in one of her festive moods, all right. Thanks.'

The three of them sat quietly drinking. Their silence was broken by a sudden commotion in the crowd. There were shouts of encouragement. Stella saw an elderly man being hustled towards an even more ancient piano.

'Told you.' Joe smiled at Stella. 'There's music at The Bells. Hugh Wadley, there, is the keenest pianist for miles. He used to teach at a school in Dorchester.'

The sprightly old man settled himself at the piano, laid his hands on the keys. The notes were bruised, out of tune. At the sound of the imperfect chord, a frisson zipped down Stella's spine. It was a long time since there had been any possibility of a musical evening. She was enjoying herself.

It's a long way to Tipperary, the drinkers round the piano began to sing. Stella, Joe and Ratty joined in. There was applause at the end of the song: much slapping on the back and cries of *Down with bloody Hitler*. Mr Wadley took a sip of beer, and looked towards the fire.

'Is there anyone here with a real voice?' he asked.

General laughter.

'Stella?' whispered Joe.

Stella shook her head.

'If there was, I'd be much obliged,' said Mr Wadley. 'All this shouting you lot call singing can damage a man's ears.'

'Go on,' urged Joe.

Stella hesitated, tempted. Her cheeks were warm from the wine. Happy in the crowd of strangers, she was filled with an unexpected longing to sing.

'You know what I'd like to hear?' Ratty bent towards her. 'I'd like to hear "They Can't Black Out the Moon".'

'All right, Ratty, just for you.'

Stella was on her feet, elated by her spontaneous decision. She moved towards the piano. The drinkers – mostly men – made way for her, eyes curious. Regulars at The Bells were not used to such a sight. They disguised their stares with cheers of encouragement.

Bending over Mr Wadley, Stella hummed the first line of Ratty's song. Mr Wadley, overcome by the response to his request, was bowed over the stained keys in a position of great reverence for the instrument, as if his concentration would magically clean their ivory.

'Anything you like, dear. G major do you?'

Stella nodded. The noise died away. A moment's silence was chipped only by the soft shuffling of logs among flames. Stella clasped her hands, let them hang against the skirt of her red dress. She looked up at the smoke-grained ceiling, felt twenty pairs of eyes upon her.

She began. Quietly, for a few lines. Then, encouraged by smiles, she increased the melancholy power.

> *I see you smiling in the cig'rette glow,*
> *Though the picture fades too soon*
> *But I see all I want to know*
> *They can't black out the moon . . .*

When the song came to an end, there was another moment's silence before rough applause and shouts for more. Stella, blushing and bowing her head, could see that the only two people who sat unsmiling, and not clapping, were Joe and Ratty. Confusion: what had she done wrong? They had been the ones to encourage her – how had she let them down? Anxiety flooded her enjoyment. She moved to the piano, leaned on the cracked maplewood of its top.

'You know what that pose reminds me of?' Mr Wadley laughed. He played a few notes. More shouting as Stella smiled. It was the introduction to one of her favourite songs. She would sing it, she thought, then go. Find out what she had done to cause Joe's thunderous look. She glanced over at him, caught his eyes.

'*Falling in love again,*' she began. Her pure, husky, sweet voice curled through the smoke, the warmth, the nostalgic faces of men and women reminded of their own love stories that had begun before the war.

While she sang, Joe stared.

Ratty, watching Joe, saw before him a man transfixed: a man within whom some life-shattering process was taking place. With his keen eye for a rat's trail, Ratty could not fail to observe what was happening to Joe: something he thought Joe could never mention, a secret he, Ratty, would take to his grave. Whatever the nameless experience was, Ratty felt he understood it long before Joe himself. It was not often a spectator had the privilege of witnessing any such private rite of passage: it was as rare as coming across the mating of a wild animal, the hatching of a bird's egg, the closing of a daisy's petals at dusk. Ratty wiped an eye, moved, suddenly very tired.

Stella was coming back to the table, cocooned in more applause. She was smiling, sparkling, one hand on the white skin visible above the low white Peter Pan collar of her red dress.

Dear God, Joe said to himself, *here she was*: how could it have happened that she'd been under his nose all this time and he'd never thought twice about her? From time to time he had reflected on the flirtatiousness of Prue, the gentle melancholy of Ag, the kindness of Stella – but it had not occurred to him that any of them was destined for him. Unlike Robert, he had never tried to envisage the perfect girl. He didn't believe she existed, he used to say. Or if she did, well – he'd recognise her when she appeared.

He recognised her now.

He stood up.

'Was I all right? You didn't mind, Joe, did you?'

'You were very good. They loved you.'

He sat down again, not daring to put out a hand, not daring to touch her. He did not even dare to smile, lest he should give himself away.

Someone handed Stella a glass of wine with the landlord's compliments. As Joe sat watching her modestly accepting congratulations, revelling in her success, he tried to fathom what it was that gripped him with such physical force it was all he could do to breathe normally. Time, that night, was a smashed globe too complicated to reconstruct. But at some point an explanation of his feelings came to him, blindingly: *certainty*. Ag's words, he remembered. *I felt such certainty, such conviction, that here was my other half; or whatever the silly phrase is, that in some strange way my life changed absolutely from that day on* . . . She was a wise old thing, Ag. He hadn't understood at the time. He did now. This was *certainty*, all right. This was certainty as he had never known it. This was iron conviction, this was light from heaven, this was something so utterly devastating that, on return to the real world, it would take all his strength to hide.

'Is there anything the matter, Joe?' The sweetness of Stella's voice . . . why had it not reached him before? He cursed the lack of poetry in his soul, longing for words he knew did not exist. Like a man bemused, he kept on looking at her, unable to answer.

'I'm just a farmer,' he said at last.

Stella laughed. 'Farmer Joe! You've had several glasses of wine, Farmer Joe. I think it's time we were going home.'

He could not blame her for thinking him intoxicated. On the walk home, under the arc of freezing stars, he kept his distance. Had not the extraordinary thing happened to him in The Bells, and had he still felt about Stella as he had only an hour ago, he would have taken her arm in polite, friendly fashion. Now, fear of the slightest physical contact was too great. In the silent night he tried to deflect his thoughts by imagining a ghostly gas balloon in their path: their entering it and soaring up to the heavens to the music of its flames . . . Christ, Stella was right about the wine. Perhaps he *was* suffering merely an alcoholic fantasy. All the same, having opened the back door, he moved quickly away for Stella to pass, making sure even their coats should not brush.

'That was such fun,' she said in the hall. 'I haven't sung for months. Thank you for taking me.'

So young, so careless, she sounded. Sometimes, at the end of a long day's work, Joe now remembered, Stella was subdued as well as dreamy. She ran up the stairs. In the wake of her smile he thought she looked happier than she had for some weeks. But then, completely sober, he remembered that a mind diseased – whether by good or evil – plays tricks. And the possessed lover – what he now felt himself to be – sees what he most desires to see, and foolishly sets store upon it.

Joe gave up all hope of sleep that night. He sat in his room, cold, battered, perplexed, entranced. He put his favourite Brahms clarinet quintet on the gramophone to calm himself. But when the first side of the record was finished, he found himself too preoccupied to turn it over and wind the machine. So he sat in his chair in silence, cogitating upon unconsciously stored pictures of the girl who had blasted his senses: Stella the dreamy one, Stella crying in the orchard over her boyfriend's letter, Stella surprising them all with her extraordinary dancing, Stella the modest, helpful, quietly cheering one, so kind to Janet . . . then Stella this evening, casting a spell over a crowd of strangers with those two wistful songs. Why had her perfection not come to him before? The Lord is devious in his revelations, he thought. He keeps a man in the darkness of no expectation, then sends light blindingly. Joe had never expected what he had always regarded as impossible – the force of certain love so great that it changes all perceptions. If he had believed such a thing existed, beyond the poets' imaginations, he would never have committed the treacherous deed of proposing to the wretched Janet. That was the most unaccountable act of his life, he now reflected, lethargically committed in a moment of misplaced desire to please his parents. And now what could he do?

Nothing. There was nothing to be done. Go ahead and marry the unlovable Janet. Carry on as if nothing had happened. Keep his word. And yet, knowing what he now knew, would that be humanly possible?

Joe pulled back the blackout to watch the first silvery snail-tracks of light trail across the sky. He'd read his Byron: he knew the necessity of keeping a hopeless love secret. His priority must be not to burden Stella with the knowledge of his feelings. She was in love with Philip . . . wasn't she? Her feelings for Joe were of friendship, nothing more. To make any indication of the chaotic sentiments within him would be unfair, unwanted. All he could do would be to try to come to terms with the agony caused by such mistiming, to attempt to quell fears and desires. After the war, or whenever Stella and the others left the farm, he would have to try to forget. *Forget* . . .? He fumbled among a pile of clothes for his working things. How could it be possible to forget an event as important in its mystery as birth, as death? Joe began to hurry. He wanted to get the cows in before Stella came down. He wanted her to find them all in the shed when she arrived, to surprise. He wanted his first act for her in his new state to be as soon as possible. He smiled grimly to himself, thinking it was hardly a romantic notion, herding the cows. But there was no alternative. Surely she would be as pleased with waiting cows as with red roses . . .

Soon after four o'clock Joe crept downstairs.

The magic of change in ordinary things, brought about by the existence of another human being, acted with a power, that day, that Joe found as moving as it was remarkable. As the extraordinary hours shifted in their new form he realised, in wonder, what he had been missing until now, and was humbled. The change, he observed, touched everything. It was a heightening of the world that the poets and writers of loves songs are inspired to convey – whether through genius or trite skills – in coded words only understandable to those in a state of love. Nowhere was too lowly for its reach. The kitchen – the kitchen he had known all his life – was almost unrecognisable because at any moment Stella was about to appear. He had found the cowshed, the fields, the farmyard, all equally unfamiliar. He sensed a kind of static in the air, a trembling of solid things, a feeling of glorious hallucination. And the exhilaration of the new feelings, he quickly realised, was an illness both of body and mind. He trembled as he planned how to cross Stella's path many times during the day without arousing her suspicions.

Suddenly, he could not bear to continue his wait in the kitchen. He was not yet ready to deal with the proximity its size would force upon them. He hurried out to the cowshed, forced himself to concentrate on work. He had already started to milk Nancy, the oldest of the herd, when Stella came in.

'Joe! You beat me to it. You shouldn't have – my treat was yesterday.'

Joe kept his head against Nancy's flanks, not looking at her. He felt her hand, for an infinitesimal moment, on his shoulder.

'I woke early. Thought I might as well get going.'

'Well, thanks. I'll start the other end.'

Joe allowed himself a glance at her retreating boots. His fingers shook against Nancy's teats. *I'm a crazed man . . .* It was far from an unpleasant feeling.

As he listened to the whine of milk shooting into the bucket, and struggled once more for calm, he became aware of a certain sense of objectivity. By the time he rose, the bucket full of warm froth, and glanced down the cowshed for a glimpse of Stella's head leaning against the infinitely fortunate Belinda, he realised there were now two look-out posts within him: one with which to observe Stella at every possible moment; the other to study his own peculiar behaviour.

*

That evening Prue and Ag returned. For different reasons they were both in high spirits. After supper there was a merry reunion in the attic, a chance for private news.

'Nice, quiet Christmas with my father,' said Ag, '*but* . . . this. Waiting for me.'

She held out a Christmas card for the others to examine. It was an ink drawing of Trinity College under snow. Inside, under the printed wishes, was the signature *Desmond*.

'I couldn't believe it,' smiled Ag. 'I still can't. In the train I kept taking it out of my bag and looking at it. It must mean, surely, he hasn't quite forgotten me, don't you think? It must mean something.'

'Well,' said Prue, her attention not entirely on Ag, 'look what *I* got!' She rustled among tissue paper in her case, pulled out a dress of ruby velvet with a white fur collar.

'My mum found this old curtain material in a market, ran it up for me. Isn't it just heavenly? She swears the fur is rabbit: I say it's ermine. It's the most beautiful dress I ever saw . . .' She held it up in front of herself, danced about the room glancing in various small looking-glasses as she passed. 'When can I wear it? That's the only problem.'

'New Year's Eve,' said Stella. 'Joe's asked his friend Robert to supper. There's the Red Cross dance you could go to.'

Prue's face relighted. 'Gosh! How about that? I've been thinking . . . Barry's time is up. Maybe this Robert . . . What about you, Stella? How was it having the beautiful Janet in my bed?'

'We had a quiet time. Nothing much happened. I enjoyed it. I sang in The Bells one night.'

'You didn't!' Prue laughed. She curled up on her bed, hugging her dress, rubbing the fur against her cheek, childlike. 'It was so strange going home, you know. Did you find that, Ag? So small. Noisy, our street, too: funny how I'd never noticed that before. Lovely being with Mum, of course. She said, Prue, what on earth's happened to your hands? I said, you try mucking out Sly and keeping your hands in good shape, Mum. I rather missed Sly, actually, though I didn't tell her that. Anyway, she gave me a shampoo and set. Very odd, with a proper basin and dryer and everything again. Took some getting used to. Funny thing is, I'm quite glad to be back. What about you, Ag?'

Ag murmured agreement. She was concentrating on arranging her Christmas card on the chair by the bed. She found a position which allowed her, from her pillow, to see Desmond's signature. When the lights were out she secretly kissed the card, just as Stella used to kiss her photograph of Philip. That, Ag noticed, had been moved to the chest of drawers.

On New Year's Eve, Robert arrived promptly at seven for supper. Just a year older than Joe, he looked like a man of thirty who had suffered illness all his life. He was small, thin, cowered over a concave chest. There were bluish shadows under deep eyes, and his skin had a pale, skimmed look that made it hard to believe he spent most of his life in the open.

The girls, curious about Joe's friend, arrived in sparkling line to shake his bony hand in turn. Prue had insisted on being the last. She wore her new dress, had curled her eyelashes into spikes of unbelievable length.

'I'll give you a kiss, too, Robert,' she said, 'seeing as it's New Year's Eve,' and his arms went round her in automatic response.

Later, she told the others, she fell for Robert as soon as her mouth touched his deathly cheek. The attraction was mutual. Prue concentrated her full attention on him during supper, fluttering the absurd lashes, her dimples and pouts working overtime. Too preoccupied to offer any help, she smiled, duchess-like, as Stella and Ag acted as waitresses. Supper over, she and Robert left at once for the Red Cross dance.

269

'So that's worked,' said Joe, smiling at Ag. 'I thought it might. No more Barry. Hope Robert enjoys himself.'

'*Really*, Joe,' said Mrs Lawrence, a note of wistfulness beneath her stern look. 'It's a very unlikely match. What could a girl like Prue give Robert?'

'Fun,' said Joe. 'Nothing wrong in that, for a time.' He felt the strength of one to whom the emptiness of mere fun, nothing else, is a thing long past.

Stella and Ag sat with the Lawrences listening to the wireless, waiting for Big Ben to strike twelve. They raised their glasses to each other, conveyed polite formal wishes – but were not the sort of people to seal those wishes with random kisses. This was a relief to Joe. The proximity of Stella this evening – beautiful, a little subdued – was both an ecstasy and a torment. His own, private wish for the New Year, as he raised his glass briefly in the direction of the girl who had ungrounded his life, was for strength.

Ten

P rue, alone in the cowshed, no one around to complain, was taking her chance to sing.

> *If you want to go to heaven when you die*
> *Wear a pair of khaki breeches and a tie.*
> *Wear an old felt bonnet with WLA on it*
> *If you want to go to heaven when you die . . .*

She was doing her best to whitewash the battered walls.
Bloody awful job, but at least better than carting loads of
mangolds down to the cows, like Ag. Or harnessing the stubborn Noble, like Stella. *They* would have rain gushing down
their necks, sodden hair, soaking wool gloves. It had been
raining hard for the first week of the New Year – Prue had
collected enough buckets of rainwater for a month's hair-
washing. Also, it was freezing. Bloody freezing. Prue was the
only one of the girls still awaiting a greatcoat. Shortage of
cloth for land girls' coats had still not been overcome: there
was no saying when hers would arrive. Mrs Lawrence had
made several enquiries to the district commissioner, who
held out no hope of a coat in the near future. So Prue had
to make do with three jerseys under one of Joe's old macs,
and still the cold cut through her bones.

But Prue had learned as a child that hardship is a
challenge. She remembered her mother's advice: when
the going gets tough, remember Winston Churchill.

Remember everything you can that he says. He's an inspiring man. Prue's mother was given to muttering *Now is our finest hour* as she strove to overcome the shortage of solution for permanent waves. Now *is* my finest hour, said Prue to herself, sloshing whitewash over a daunting new area of dirty brick wall. Her arm ached so badly she wanted to cry. But there was no use in crying, or stopping. Mr Lawrence expected the wall to be finished by midday.

Besides, there were thoughts to dwell on that made up for everything: Robert. She and Robert had made a swift start on New Year's Eve. Half an hour at the Red Cross dance was enough to convince them that his cottage would be a better place in which to celebrate the New Year. Robert had lit the fire and shaken out the rag rug in front of it. He had heated up a tin of soup, and found half a bottle of wine. Thus the setting for her third seduction as a land girl, while not perfect, was both slightly warmer and more comfortable than either the barn or the woods.

Prue found herself much taken by Robert's shyness. She liked the way he averted his huge, moth-like eyes when, halfway through the revolting soup, she considered it time to stop dilly-dallying, and remove the velvet dress. She laid it on top of the rug, pushing the fur neck into a kind of fairy bolster. For some moments Robert looked so charmingly embarrassed Prue felt herself inclining towards him in a way that immediately alerted her to its inconvenience. Just in time, she remembered that to go falling in love with an anaemic young farmer, penniless to boot, would not fit in with her ultimate calculations. She quickly placed his chilly hand (in all her experience she had never known such icy flesh) on the silken thigh beneath her slip, and was rewarded by an electric reaction.

'It's the bombs urge a girl on,' she said, fluttering lashes winged by three layers of mascara. 'I'm not forward by nature, but when it comes to a race against the bloody bombs I want to win.'

'Quite,' said Robert.

He hastened out of his own clothes while Prue languorously released her stockings from their suspenders, an art she had learned from close study of many film stars. She smiled at the sight of her new lover-to-be's feet – the smallest, most delicate men's feet she had ever had the pleasure of observing. Blue-white skin stretched over fine bleached bones. The miniature toes wriggled in the folds of red velvet – *crustacean* (a word she had recently learned from Ag), somehow, and making Prue giggle. She looked up to see Robert naked but for his watch.

'Five to twelve,' he said.

'And Big Ben ready to strike, I see.'

Prue collapsed into further giggles as Robert lowered himself beside her. As on many previous occasions, she was oblivious of the precise moment of the passing of the old year, but was able to rejoice, very early in the new one, at the presence of a new lover.

Now – the tiresome thought returned to her in the cold of the cowshed – the only thing that had to be *tidied up* was Barry. She thought of their last meeting – December the tenth. Quite a day for loss, as a matter of fact: Singapore, according to Mr Lawrence, who was a keen listener to the news, and her interest in Barry. She said nothing at the time, just promised she'd be in touch. This new turn of events meant she'd failed to keep her word. Perhaps she would write to him tonight. It wasn't fair to keep a man mooning about in hope. Hard to know what to say, though.

Dear Barry

I can't ask you to keep up all the bicycling any more and it wouldn't be much fun in the woods this wintry weather, we'd catch our deaths, and anyway it's difficult me slipping off so much even though Stella and Ag are kind and cover for me. So I think we shall have to call it a

day. It was good fun. When it comes to telling
grandchildren about wartime romances I shall say, well
there was Barry . . .

Nah! Soppy, that last bit. She wouldn't put that. *Love and good wishes* at the end, though: she didn't want him to think he'd been nothing more than a bloody good shag.

In the past week, there had been much meal-time talk about the end of the war. Now that America had joined the fighting, Mr Lawrence seemed to think there was some hope it wouldn't drag on too long. Prue herself thought such speculation pointless. She agreed with Ratty, who declared much worse was to come before victory. She had no wish to think about the future. She was happy – despite the cheerless rain and cold – with each day as it came: tough work, long hours, plenty of good hot food, and odd moments of reward in Robert's dingy bed. He was something of a mystery, Robert, Prue had often thought in the past week: no matter how passionately they made love his skin never warmed up. Quite a challenge, that. One day she'd like to be responsible for replacing his corpse-like temperature with a warm pink glow (Prue giggled to herself at the thought). She liked his company, too: dry little phrases, their academic references usually way over her head, shy little compliments, quaint little jokes. And the way he stroked the bridge of her nose when he was being very serious about the war or something. He said the bridge of the nose was an erogenous zone. Perhaps it was among academics, she had replied, but she could think of more erogenous places in the opinion of ordinary folk. All the same, she didn't try to stop him – tickle tickle tickle with his cold little finger.

'You've done well, Prue,' said Mr Lawrence.

Prue turned to see him at the door of the cowshed, appraising her work. Rain ran thickly down the raw-coloured runnels of his face. Swift as balls of mercury they slid down the creases of his neck. 'Not *exactly* my finest hour, Mr Lawrence,' she said, pleased, 'but I'm getting on.'

At times like this, it occurred to her, there was a darn sight more reward in being a land girl than there was in hairdressing. In fact – it had crossed her mind several times – when the war was over it might be worth trying to find her millionaire somewhere in the country, rather than in Manchester.

'You're not half as daffy as you look,' said the soaked Mr Lawrence, smiling.

Joe was avoiding her. This Stella noticed within a few days of their evening at the pub. At first she thought it was her imagination, and he was avoiding everyone. Certainly he seemed less forthcoming – the others had observed and remarked on that, too. Perhaps two days of the beautiful Janet's company had caused his despair, suggested Prue. Ag's view was that no end to the war in sight depressed everyone. But Stella knew it was neither of those things. It was something to do with her. She had inadvertently acted in some way to offend or annoy him, but could not imagine what it was she had done.

In the cold and gloomy days of early January, Stella puzzled over Joe's behaviour. It was definitely her he singled out for the cold shoulder (she noticed a hundred small occasions) and the worry of her unknown misdemeanour was beginning to blight the days. She would have liked to confront Joe: ask him what had happened, clear the air. But he was not an easy man to confront. He had become more and more elusive, always the one willing to undertake jobs far from the farm that could be done alone. Stella watched for her chance. But, as the dreary days dragged by, it did not come.

On the afternoon that Prue was assigned the unenviable but dry task of whitewashing the cowshed, Mr Lawrence asked Stella to take the milk churns to the village. Usually, this was a task he undertook himself. But the persistent heavy rain had taken its toll on the old roofs. There was a leak in the laundry room: water had poured down on to a basket of Faith's ironing. Repairing the tiles was urgent. Mr Lawrence apologised to Stella, said if he caught sight of Joe he would ask him to give a hand.

Stella, setting off for the field to catch Noble, leaned against the heavy slant of the rain. A dour mass of dark cloud was low in the sky, releasing no chinks of light to play among reflections. And yet the puddles in the lane dappled with inky blues and muddy pinks as Stella splashed through them. In the leafless hedges dishevelled sparrows cowered, unsinging. The thrumming of the rain would sometimes switch into an *adagio* passage, giving hope it would soon be stopping altogether. Then, like a tease who knows not when to stop, it would fall *prestissimo* again, defying all such silly hopes. The persistence of such weather had affected Stella's spirits.

Noble sheltered under a tree, darkened by the rain. He came at once when Stella called. She removed her sodden glove and gave him half a carrot, snorts of warm breath agreeable on her cold hand. In the next field she could see the drenched figure of Ag, sou'-wester falling over her eyes, throwing mangolds from the trailer behind the tractor on to the ground. The cows were hustled round her in a selfish crowd, a black and white puzzle whose individual pieces, at this distance, were indistinguishable.

Ag waved. Stella waved back. Ag had been much more cheerful since Desmond's Christmas card. Strange how thin a hope the human soul can survive on, Stella thought, gripping the soaking rope of Noble's halter. She and the horse sloshed their way through the long grass back to the gate. If Ag ever did secure this almost non-existent love, surely the stuff of fantasy, Stella would remind her of this rainy afternoon, January 1942, when she, Stella, had been quite convinced nothing would ever happen with Desmond. And with Philip? In his last letter, he had said that when he went to London he was going to buy her a ring. Then they would be engaged. Then they would be married. Then they would live together ever after. Wartime bride and groom. Romantic stuff. But happily? Stella supposed so, in some ways.

She tethered Noble to a post in the barn, made several journeys to and from the tack-room lugging the heavy harness. Her hands, wet and cold, worked inefficiently. She struggled to do up the hard old straps. She tugged at the stubborn leather, determined not to be beaten and have to call for help. As finally she led Noble towards the shafts, a thought came blindingly to her. It came with such terrible clarity that for a moment she was forced to lean against Noble's damp withers, bury her head in her arms so that she could be submerged in blackness. The suspicion that had been nudging her for some weeks, that she had kept at bay, had suddenly stormed her fragile defences. It was Philip, not the weather, that caused her dejection. The sprightly love she had felt for him when she came to the farm, which had protected her in the many bleak moments that manual labour produces in all those who would rather be engaged in some more intellectually creative activity, was gone. Absolutely gone. She was fond of him, respected him . . . she would marry him: *but she was not in love with him.* And, as she had so often said to Prue and Ag, what is the point of life if you are not in love?

Stella moved back at last from the warmth of the horse's body. She looked again at the swathes of rain that billowed across the yard. There was only one thing to do. The only antidote to any kind of unhappiness, her father used to say, was work. She must apply all her energies, all her concentration, on work: do her bit for her country to the best of her ability. She must remember that, while thousands of girls were suffering the premature death of their loved ones, her fortune was to be loved by a good man who, thank God, was still alive. The thought of Philip being *killed* sent a spasm of guilty horror down her spine . . . Should he be spared, she would make a good wife. Learn to come to terms with the kind of love, based on friendship and affection, that, buffed by marriage, lasts. She realised, as she tried to persuade Noble to reverse himself between the shafts of the milk cart, how young and silly she had been, hoping that the froth of love she felt so quickly for Philip, and others before him, was the stuff of permanence.

There was a helping hand, suddenly, on the bridle. Joe muttered a few magic words to Noble who instantly obeyed. The inexplicable discord with Joe was the other reason for her unusual depression, though minor by comparison. She looked up at his grim face, veiled by water that poured off the brim of his waterproof hat. Perhaps there would be a chance to confront him, discover what had caused his hurtful behaviour.

'Thanks,' she said.

'I'll give you a hand with the churns.'

When they had secured the shafts, Joe led Noble over to the milking shed, where the streaming silvery churns stood in a line. He swung each one easily into the cart, signalling to Stella not to help. She climbed into the driving seat, sat waiting. Joe, to her surprise, when all the churns were loaded, joined her. He looked at his watch.

'I'll come with you. Give you a hand the other end. They're buggers when they're wet.'

Stella relinquished the driver's seat.

They clattered out into the lane. The rattling of the churns, Noble's hoofs, and the drumming rain, made an orchestra of sweet sound. Branches of vapour drifted from the hedgerows, ghostly extensions of the hedges themselves. For all the discomforts of the wet and cold, Stella found herself enjoying exposure to such weather. She was awed by the mercilessness of the rain. She was fascinated to find so familiar a journey made unrecognisable by the gauzes of mist that filtered through it.

In no time, Joe unloaded the churns on to the wooden platform from which they were daily collected. The rain fell harder.

'Think we should shelter for a moment or two,' he said. 'This'll pass.'

He urged a reluctant Noble on a few yards, halted under the oak tree beside the gate to the church. There, they were protected from the main force of the rain, although it still managed to fall between the intricacies of bare branches. Joe, hunched on the seat, let the reins fall slack on Noble's back. He stared ahead at the cascade of water battering the dark stone of the cottages opposite, oblivious, it seemed, to Stella's presence.

'Joe? Joe, what have I done?' Stella broke a long silence between them. 'You've been so distant, since that night at The Bells. Did you mind my singing?'

She watched his profile carefully. Even in the poor light under the tree his skin gleamed with running rain. Drips trickled from his eyebrows to join drips falling from the brim of his hat in a squiggling journey down his cheeks. He frowned, causing a rush of more drips to scurry down the bridge of his nose. His dark waterproof, silvered with rain, creaked as he turned towards her.

'No,' he said, 'you haven't done anything. I liked your singing. You've a lovely voice.' He paused, sighed. The slight hunching of his shoulders caused another flurry of water to scuttle down his arms. 'I suppose it's just the thought of the long year ahead. Dark. Getting ill with asthma. The not knowing. The suspense. The waiting. The waste, for everyone. The utter waste.'

Stella, half appeased, half believing him, gave no time to the weighing of her next words.

'But you're just the same to Prue and Ag. It's only to me, I feel . . . I've felt you've changed. Unfriendly, somehow.'

'Really?' He shifted further round so that Stella could see both his eyes. The irises were the same colour as the rain, flecked with light. He gave her a curious look that quickly wafted away, light as a flake of ash in a breeze. 'Am I?' Then he turned away.

'You must know,' said Stella. 'It's not my imagination. There must be a reason, beyond the doom of war we all feel.'

'Maybe.' He went on staring at the rain ahead, falling so hard it bounced back off the road only to fall again. 'If that's so, and I dare say it is, then I'm sorry. I don't mean to be unfriendly.'

Stella was aware of the effort he made, then, to remedy things. He turned to her again with a teasing half smile.

'I could, I suppose, come back at you. Where've all your spirits gone? You're neither so dreamy nor so happy, seems to me. But I could be wrong. People's shifting moods, in a war, are almost impossible to keep up with. Hopes chasing fears: strain of broken rhythms, traumas, upheavals from the norm . . . What's happened to you?'

Stella shrugged. Now, dozens of tiny streams ran down her own sleeves.

'Perhaps a case of mistaken identity of a feeling. Perhaps I've been in love with an idea, instead of a reality . . .'

'Ah. That.' Joe looked as if he was attempting to concentrate very hard on the weather. 'Doesn't look as if this is going to ease up. I think we'd better brave it. I should be helping Dad with the roof.'

But as he picked up the reins, a cyclist came into sight. Head down, miserably hunched over the handlebars, his waterproof glinted dully as the feathers of a wet crow. 'That's Barry, isn't it?' said Joe.

The airman rode towards them, stopped at Noble's head. He raised his sodden forage cap, looked at them enquiringly. It wasn't Barry, but a man of similar physique: shaven head and ruddy countenance.

'Could you tell me where I could find Prue? Prudence? Hallows Farm?'

'Half a mile down the lane,' said Joe, pointing. 'We're going there. Can we give her a message?'

The young man bit his lip. He squeezed and released the handlebars of the bicycle several times, as if to some private rhythm. Tapped the ground with his heavy black boot.

'She was a friend of my friend Barry. I came to tell her he was . . . was shot down night before last. I thought . . . I thought she'd want to know. . .' He replaced his soaking cap. Stella thought she could distinguish tears among the raindrops on his cheeks. 'If you're going back there, if you know her . . . I'd be grateful. My name's Jamie Morton, should she want to get in touch. At the Camp.'

'I'm so sorry,' said Stella.

'Buggeration!' screamed Prue, when Joe told her Barry was dead.

She picked up a tin of whitewash and slung it at her newly painted wall. 'That's what I think of this bloody war. It's come here, now. It's hit *here*!' She dropped on to a milking stool, thrashing her heart. Began to sob. 'Poor Barry! He was so brave. He told me he hated night flying. I think he knew he was going to die. Oh God, he's the only person I've ever known to *die* . . .'

As she buried her head in her hands, the yellow satin bow slumped in her sad curls. The toes of her white-streaked rubber boots were turned inwards: so often there was a childlike innocent look about Prue, thought Stella, for all her superior experience. She put a hand on the shaking girl's shoulder.

'You just cry,' she said. 'That's the best thing.'

'I just hope the same thing doesn't happen to your Philip . . .'

Joe quickly picked up the tin of whitewash. 'Marvellous job you've done in here,' he said. 'Finished on time, too.

Why don't we all go in and have some tea?'

Any approval from her employers affected Prue deeply. Her wails stopped for a moment. She looked up, her stricken face a grid of running mascara.

'Heavens, you two – drowned rats! Whatever have you been doing?' She sniffed, brightening. 'Well, at least there's one good thing. I hadn't sent my farewell letter. I was planning it only an hour ago. So he died not knowing it was all over between us. I'm glad of that. Because he was a funny boy, Barry: I think he loved me.'

She stood, gave the faintest smile. The three of them made a dash through the rain to the house. When they had changed into dry clothes, and Prue had repaired her face, they gathered round the kitchen table with mugs of tea.

'I can't quite believe it,' sniffed Prue, who had exchanged her wet yellow bow for a new black one. '*Barry*. One moment you're with someone. The next moment they're dead – and for what? This bloody, bloody war . . .'

A couple of silent tears fell from her naked eyes, dampening the long soft lashes which, devoid of mascara, glistened. She wiped them away with an impatient hand, cocked her head towards Joe.

'This friend of Barry's, Joe, who broke the news – what did you say his name was?'

'Jamie Morton. He said you should get in touch, if there's anything you want to know.'

'What was he like?'

'Sad, and soaked to the skin,' said Stella.

'I must write to him. I'd like to know . . . where it happened. I'd like to thank him for his trouble.'

She gave such a minor smile that her dimples were only just stirred into action. As Stella and Joe both recognised, and acknowledged with a private look, even in the darkness of Barry's death Prue, with her resistant spirit, saw the light of some possibility in his friend, Jamie Morton.

*

That same afternoon of unforgettable rain, Ratty was at home making an attempt to celebrate his wife's birthday. He had given her a card in the morning; at tea-time he produced a present made bulky with many layers of newspaper beneath the final wrapping – a sheet of paper decorated with holly, left over from Christmas.

Edith, never a gracious receiver of presents, tore impatiently at the string.

'What's this, then? Who said I wanted my birthday remembered? I'm past all that sort of thing.'

Nonetheless, she scrabbled through the paper like an excited child. Eventually she found the present, a small porcelain robin perched on a porcelain tree stump. Edith had always had a fondness for robins, though no interest in other birds. Ratty had made several difficult journeys to local towns in search of the robin in his mind. He had been pleased to find it at last, dusty in a junk shop – lifelike little fellow with a bright eye, especially attractive for its bargain price of sixpence. He anticipated Edith's pleasure – stupidly, as he later reflected. He should have remembered there was nothing in the world he could give her that would please.

Except, curiously, the paper.

Edith picked up the robin with a sniff of disdain, put it on an empty shelf (previous home of saucepans) and said not a word.

Then she returned to the bundle of newspaper and wrapping paper, and began to flatten out the creases of each sheet with a trembling hand.

'Where'd you get all this? This'll be a help.'

Ratty was mystified. 'Here and there. Got a store of old newspaper in the back shed.'

'*What*? Storing up paper in the back shed without so much as a word? What for? Lighting bonfires? Don't you know the Government's asked us to save our paper? One envelope makes fifty cartridge shells, they say. They want every scrap. You bring me those papers, Ratty Tyler, or there'll be trouble.'

By now she had folded one of the sheets of newspaper into small, neat squares. She took a pair of kitchen scissors and began to cut the squares reverently as if they were finest silk, mouth pursed in concentration.

'What are you cutting them up for?' Ratty ventured. 'What's the use of that?'

Edith snorted at his stupidity. 'It's a lot more use than not cutting them up,' she said. 'I must have cut up thousands of squares this week,' she added, with some pride. 'They're all stacked away in boxes waiting to be collected. But I don't suppose you've noticed.'

'I haven't, no,' admitted Ratty. He wondered what sort of a man would instinctively know his wife wished him to hunt about the house for boxes of cut-up paper, and then to praise her for such husbandry.

'Trust you,' said Edith. 'But then you've never been like me when it comes to doing your bit for the country. All you do is hang about the farm mooning after those useless land girls. First you complain about the saucepans, now you make a fuss over collecting paper.'

'I'm not making a fuss,' said Ratty. He watched her cut up the second lot of squares, carefully balance them on top of the first. Some devil within him urged him to express his puzzlement once more. 'I still don't see the use of all this cutting up,' he said. 'Paper is paper, just as good not cut up.'

'That's what you think. That's what you would say, after I've spent all these hours doing my best.'

Ratty watched his wife's tense shoulders as she hunched over the piece of holly paper, smoothing it again and again with swift little strokes. 'The war's got to you, Edith,' he said gently.

'Some of us have to take it seriously,' she said. 'Now you just go and get those papers from the shed. I'd like to make a start on them.'

'What, in this rain?'

'Are you a man?'

Ratty stood, tapping out his pipe. 'Did you like the robin?' he asked, playing for time, dreading the downpour in his already soaked mackintosh.

'The robin?' Edith looked wildly round, eyes veering over the shelf where the ornament perched, but seemed not to see it. Then she returned to stroking the holly paper.

In the New Year, evening habits shifted at Hallows Farm. After supper, instead of the family and girls gathering in the sitting-room, they went their various ways. Stella, on Ag's recommendation, was reading the *Iliad*. As Homer needed a greater measure of concentration than she applied to her own choice of novels, and even the Third Programme was a distraction, she had taken to going up to the attic early and reading peacefully on her bed till the others came up. Prue went out with Robert several times a week. Joe had reverted to his old habit of disappearing. (Stella could see light under his door and hear faint music as she crept upstairs.) Only Ag stayed downstairs with Mr Lawrence dozing in and out of the news, and his wife upright on a chair beneath the standard lamp that cast a pale disc of light on to her darning. Ag herself, speeding through a pile of old *Telegraph* crosswords, reserved a small corner of her mind for further Desmond detective work: *why* had he sent a Christmas card? What could it mean? The answers never came. As is often the case when there is no evidence to the contrary, optimistic possibilities gathered strength.

On the evening of the news about Barry, with unspoken consent – perhaps to show support for Prue – they reverted to their old pattern and converged round the fire after supper. Prue, pale but calm, played Solitaire in a corner. She wore an unusually dark lipstick which, she had earlier told Stella, she thought appropriate to the occasion. When,

285

on the wireless, there was news of a bombing raid on London, Mr Lawrence quickly changed to a symphony concert. Behind the music they could hear the single, persistent note of rain shredding against the windows.

The telephone rang. Mrs Lawrence, to whom it could only ever mean bad news, physically started. She put down her darning and ran from the room. A moment later she returned, flustered by relief that it wasn't the call she dreaded from Yorkshire, but confused by another concern.

'Prue, it's for you. Robert. He wants to know if you'd like to go out for a drink.'

Prue's back still ached, her eyes stung, an appearance of small appetite at supper had left her hungry. She would have done anything for a drink with Robert: the smoky warmth of The Bells, his cold fingers on her neck, his awkward comforting ways. But there were rules that had to be observed when your ex-boyfriend had been killed. She was aware of disguised glances towards her. Her answer was awaited with curiosity.

'Not tonight, Mrs Lawrence,' she said at last. 'If you could explain . . .'

Further relief softened Mrs Lawrence's face. She went off with her message. Prue returned to her game.

Joe, who had been restless all evening, stood up.

'Ag,' he said, 'it was weeks ago you promised me some tutoring. I don't know where to begin on all those books. Could I ask you . . . could we mark a start?'

Ag's surprise was evident. Pleased to think that here was a sign at last that Joe was emerging from his gloomy mood, she jumped up, eager to help. The memory of their one strange afternoon was skeletal in her mind. She knew nothing like that would ever happen again. Joe had merely been obliging. She had no fear of going alone to his room and looked forward to their evening.

They left the room, causing Prue a private smile. She

liked the thought that she had been the *first* of the girls invited to Joe's room, albeit for different reasons.

Later, alone in the attic waiting for the others to come up, Stella was conscious of the kind of restlessness that physically chafes. She hurried into bed without kissing Philip's photograph, lay listening to the slurry sound of rain against the windows, the whining of the wind. Why this feeling of discomfort? She put it down to the events of the day: the puzzle of Joe's behaviour was not resolved – if it hadn't been for the appearance of Barry's friend, Stella would have probed further. The news that Barry had been killed. Prue's distress. The endless rain. And now Joe's invitation to Ag. Stella supposed, of all the disparate characters under this roof, Joe and Ag probably had the most in common. And maybe a little communing with books would cheer Joe up. All the same, for some reason she felt quite cross. She would like to talk to him – about music. Well, Prue and Ag had gratified him in their different ways. She would not like to be the only one who did not contribute to his life. Since she had been freed of the mists of romantic love of Philip, she had noticed Joe more often, and discovered she liked him.

His literary evening must have been a success because Ag came to bed unusually late. Stella pretended to be asleep.

It was long after midnight and still Edith had not come upstairs. Ratty, unable to sleep in a half-empty bed, stumbled to the kitchen. He found his wife standing at the table, as she had been most of the day, regarding a landscape of dozens of paper towers, made of hundreds of small squares of cut-up paper. The room was lighted by a single candle on the table. Shadows stretched darkly across the walls. The table of towers, each with its matching, paler shadow, was a picture of mad geometry, thought Ratty:

287

something he couldn't understand. Any more than he could understand the look on Edith's face. Bent over the candle, her turnip skin pocked and scored in the halo of the flame, she seemed to be going through some kind of private mystic experience.

'You'll have us burnt to the ground,' said Ratty at last.

'That I'll not,' Edith replied, her voice quite normal.

'Come to bed, Edith. It's nearly one in the morning.'

'Our country needs our paper,' she said. 'I'll come by and by.'

With extraordinary calm – Ratty had feared his interruption would mean one of her funny outbursts – she began to knock over the paper towers. She flicked each one with a finger, watched it tumble. He regarded her for a while. Soon the table was covered with a thick layer of paper squares. Still Edith went on standing there, running her hands through them. Ratty could bear the scene no longer. Afraid, he turned and went back up to bed.

None of the land girls could remember a time when, if they came upon Mrs Lawrence by chance, she would not be engaged in some form of work. She never grumbled about her endless duties. In fact, the disparate jobs that occupied her, both indoors and out, from early morning till late at night, seemed to give her pleasure. She was an example of a married woman totally preoccupied by the narrow confines of her life, and happy within them. This gave all the girls food for thought. Prue, whose respect for Mrs Lawrence was infinite, was not for one moment deflected by her example: to swap such a life for her own dream of servants and cocktails did not occur to her. Ag had been romantically tempted by the thought of ironing Desmond's future shirts (all that white linen, so Lawrentian). But of late she had begun to think about becoming a barrister: she would be willing to undertake household duties, but they would have to be arranged around a post-war life at the

Bar. Stella, too, was inspired by the loving energy Mrs Lawrence put into every loaf and pot of home-made jam: something her own mother, a useless cook, had never instilled into her. But, like Ag, she was determined to go out to work when she and Philip married. Life would certainly not consist entirely of looking after his needs. Perhaps, she thought, when the war was over, a new and enlightened breed of women would feel much the same.

On a cold February morning – rain had given way to bitter frosts – Ag came into the kitchen to fetch a carrot for Noble. She had spent half an hour trying to catch him – Stella was the only one to whom he came at a call. Mrs Lawrence was sitting at the table, unoccupied. This was so unusual a sight Ag felt a sense of shock, as well as surprise. On the table was one of the small churns in which milk for the house came straight from the dairy. Also, two opened letters.

Mrs Lawrence looked at Ag, unsmiling. There was a tide-mark of milk on her top lip, a comic moustache quite out of keeping with her grave demeanour.

'Oh Ag,' she said, 'good news and bad.' She patted the letters. 'John will have to go to Yorkshire tomorrow. He's been putting it off for ages. But they can't cope much longer. Things have to be sorted out.'

Ag sat down.

'What it means, of course, is deciding *when* . . . when we have to leave here and take over up there. John's brother will stay to the end. He won't go into hospital. But then we'll have to go. It's much bigger than here, several hundred acres, mostly arable. God knows how we'll manage.'

'Perhaps we could be transferred with you,' said Ag, touched by Mrs Lawrence's despair.

'Perhaps, perhaps.' Mrs Lawrence looked out of the window. 'We've been here all our married life.'

'It won't be easy, going.'

'No. Some people don't mind about houses, places. I

wish I could be like that. Rootless. A happy mover, a wanderer, with a desire to see new places. But I'm not. I love our small world. I love this place. John loves this place. Joe, I think, too.'

'Understandably.'

'Still, there's time left. Till the end of the year, I should think. We must warn you all. Give you plenty of notice so that you can make up your minds about what you want to do next. The immediate problem, John having to go tomorrow, is the lambing. We need all the hands we can get.'

'Don't worry, we'll help all we can,' said Ag. 'I expect Ratty wouldn't mind –'

'Ratty?' Mrs Lawrence smiled at last. 'Ratty wouldn't miss lambing for anything in the world. He more or less camps in the shed. We'll manage. Now: the good news.' She picked up the second letter. 'I've been in correspondence with the district commissioner. Believe it or not, you've been here six months: reward time, if the authorities think rewards are in order. Anyhow, there's to be a little ceremony next week. Nothing very much: tea and badges. I was asked for a private report of your progress, naturally. Apparently there have been quite a few problems with land girls round the country. One Agricultural Executive Committee had to take disciplinary action against fourteen girls who refused to thresh in twenty-five degrees of frost. I said, nothing like that here.' She paused to smile again. 'My girls will do anything, I said . . . I don't know what we'd do without them . . . But what am I up to? Sitting here chattering, the lunch not on. Go and tell the others, Ag. Best bibs and tuckers, four o'clock on Wednesday. Lardy cake, would you like? Egg sandwiches? Glass of ginger wine? We'll try to make it a small celebration, if I have a moment.'

She hurried to the stove, her old self again.

*

Mr Lawrence left for Yorkshire early the next morning. As his wife waved goodbye, Ag noticed a small pulse began to beat in her neck. In twenty-four years of marriage, the Lawrences had never been apart for more than a couple of nights.

Joe drove his father to the station. Mr Lawrence had planned a complicated and slow journey by train. He hoped to return in a week.

There was too much extra work to allow time for much reflection on his absence. Lambing had begun. The night frosts were so hard that Joe worked to divide the lambing shed into many small folds. As the entire flock of ewes and lambs was to be sold in the spring, it was essential to make sure as many lambs as possible survived. Other years, only problem ewes or sickly lambs were given shelter. This year, Mr Lawrence believed, cosseting was the best policy.

Ratty and Joe set up the folds. Prue tossed wheat straw on the ground, filled troughs with water. She had already seen a lamb born, an experience which had inspired a long letter to her mother concerning Nature's miracles: by comparison, she had said, even the most beautiful permanent wave was no great shakes. (*By that I don't mean I won't always admire your talent and skill, Mum,* she had added in brackets.) Her greatest excitement was for the forthcoming birth of Sly's last litter. Although Joe assured her they were not due for at least another week, Prue kept running to the sty to judge for herself the pre-natal state of the sow with whom she had come to have a very good understanding. She was determined to be present at the birth.

For all their fitness and strength, the girls found themselves tired by the extra work and went to bed earlier than usual. Joe, having completed the night check straight after supper, did likewise. Frequently he was called out by the indomitable Ratty in the middle of the night to help with a ewe. A few hours' early sleep was essential to the maintenance of his efficiency and temper.

*

At three o'clock one morning, Stella, eyes on her clock, happened to be awake. There was a bang on the attic door.

'Could one of you come and help? There's a lot going on. Sorry.'

Stella sat up in the dark. Silence from the other two meant they were deeply asleep. She fumbled as quickly as she could into her clothes. Crept out. What help did Joe need? She had no experience of lambing . . . She put on her coat and scarf, hurried across the freezing yard.

In the shed, she found biblical light from a few lanterns that hung from the walls, and were secured to the pens. There was a smell of hay, earth, blood. A discordant chorus of bleating filled her ears: tremulous notes from the ewes in labour, piteous high squeaks from one or two newborn lambs. In one pen Ratty was huddled over a ewe who lay on her side, mumbling comforting words to her as he dug a syringe into her hindquarters. He was watched by a tiny black lamb, its wool skin glistening like broken cobwebs. In another fold Joe was kneeling on the straw, one arm deep in a ewe's backside. Stella made her way towards him. He looked up for a moment.

'Oh, it's you. Ewe in the far corner over there: turning on her lamb. See what you can do. I've got a nasty mess here.'

Stella hurried away, wondering what she was supposed to do.

The lamb needing her help lay on wet straw, its head tipped back, alarmed eyes a milky blue. It was still covered with a translucent skin, silvery over the dun-coloured wool, that its unmaternal mother had felt disinclined to lick clean. Stella stroked its neck, watched the flaring of the small black nostril. She felt helpless, useless. But the lamb, encouraged by her presence, struggled to rise. On tottering legs it made a precarious journey to its mother who stood sulking in a corner. She sighed deeply, twitched her ears.

The lamb gently butted its mother's stomach in search of milk. With extraordinary speed the ewe lashed out with a hind leg, making the lamb jump back in fright. Then she turned and lowered her head towards her offspring with all the aggression of a ram. The lamb fell back on the straw from the fierce butt of its mother's head. Stella saw a flash of dun-coloured teeth: the ewe was going to attack further. She quickly bent and picked up the squealing lamb. The slime of its skin slobbered down her greatcoat. The lamb felt cold and tense. It struggled. Stella, keeping a tight grip, swung herself back over the side of the pen and returned to Joe.

He was standing now, fiddling with a syringe. His bare right arm and hand were skeined with blood, as was the straw on which the ewe lay panting on her side. Beside her stretched the unmoving body of a lamb, obviously dead.

'First one we've lost,' said Joe. He glanced at Stella holding the rejected lamb, which had grown quieter.

'Case of post-natal depression over there,' said Stella. 'Had to rescue this one. The mother was about to butt it.'

'Good timing, at least.' Joe put the empty syringe into his pocket. The upper half of his body was in shadow: she could scarcely see his face, but knew it was grave. Shadows flickered in the pen. Only a small stretch of straw bedding was illuminated by a nearby lantern. 'Hang on to it, for a moment,' Joe said, 'while I deal with this.'

Stella leaned up against the pen to watch the process of adoption. Joe knelt down, patted the tired ewe, then picked up her dead lamb. He took a knife lying beside him in the straw, tilted back the rigid little head with its unlit eyes. Carefully he dug the tip of the blade into the skin, began to pull down towards the chest. Then, very fast, the knife travelled this way and that, its blood-laced blade giving an occasional muted flash in the dim light. With a surgeon's skill, Joe began to ease the skin from the body and limbs. It came away all of a piece in his hands, a dishevelled old jersey, leaving a naked lamb behind. The small body, Stella could see, was an extraordinary blue – the blue of wild flowers, bluebells, forget-me-nots: the flesh iridescent between patterns of tiny veins. She burrowed her own icy hands into the warmth of the living lamb in her arms.

Joe picked up the corpse, slung it into a sack.

'Now, give me yours.'

He took the animal from Stella. Again, fascinated, she watched as he struggled to fit the dead lamb's skin over the orphan lamb. In a few moments he had succeeded. The creature stood beside its foster mother, bemused and shaky in its new ill-fitting clothes. The ewe, nostrils twitching, heaved herself up on spindly legs. She began to sniff the lamb, who stood patient, curious, wobbly. Then, with sudden confidence, it pushed and nuzzled towards the udder. Moments later it was sucking, a whispery, rubbery sound. Its tail wavered from side to side. The ewe, ears back, eyes half shut, did not move.

'Worked,' said Joe. 'Usually does. Thank God for that.' He threw the sack containing the dead lamb towards the door, glanced round the shed. Ratty had gone. The bleating had died down. 'All calm for the moment. I'd better hang on, though. There should be a couple of others by the morning. Thanks very much for your help.' From his side of the pen he patted Stella's shoulder. 'You'll have to clean up your coat,' he said, swinging a leg over the fold. 'And you should go back to bed. But let's sit down just for a moment.'

They sat on a pile of hay between two pens. Joe picked up a clump of straw from the ground, began to wipe the mess from his arm. Then he pulled down his sleeve, fastened the cuff, dragged a thick jersey over his head.

'I suppose it's freezing,' he said, 'but I stopped feeling the cold some time ago. *You* must be . . .'

He turned to Stella, whose hands lay flat on her corduroy knees. Like his, they were smeared with blood. Joe put a hand on top of one of Stella's, covering it. Then he snatched it away. The touch was as transitory as a V in water after a bird has passed. The coldness of its imprint, on Stella's own chilled skin, she could not feel.

'There. I knew it.'

'I'm all right.'

'It's a hard time, lambing.' Joe now ran both hands randomly round his face. Stella could hear the squeak of flesh as he rubbed his eyes. She felt him shudder.

'Stella?' he said, after a while.

'Yes?'

They listencd to the stirrings of the animals in the dark straw. The weak mewing of the lambs indicated they were well-fed, sleepy. Outside, an owl hooted. Candles in the lanterns were low. The small patches of light they made were murky as cloud. Stella wanted to go on sitting there, sitting there.

'I think it's time you went back to bed,' said Joe, at last.

'I could stay and help,' said Stella.

'No,' said Joe.

The unexpected appearance of Stella, followed by the cold night hours in the shed while lambs were born, dead and alive, very nearly blasted Joe's resolve. After the brief, foolish touch of her hand, he felt he could keep his silence no longer. In the few minutes that they sat – tired, bloodied, cold – listening to the sounds of new life among the sheep, a thousand good reasons for telling her how he felt dazzled his weary senses. Shc would never know the effort he summoned to say, instead, in a normal voice, that it was time for her to go. She further confused him with her offer to stay and help. Almost more than he could bear. He prayed that she would go quickly – which she did – before weakness overcame him.

Left alone, he remained sitting staring at the moonless

sky outside the shed. The darkness had that peculiar density, known to those who are up before dawn, before the first cracks of light, subtle as the camouflage of tiger skin, indicate the new day. Recent pictures of Stella shuffled across his mind: the anxiety on her face when he told her to deal with a ewe, the maternal relief as she stood by the pen holding the lamb. As he skinned the dead lamb her eyes, he knew, never left his knife's journey. Then, as he fitted the skin on to her orphan lamb, he saw a look of – wonder, was it? Admiration? Or, in the poor light, was he merely seeing what he hoped to see? In a state of acute love, misinterpretation is so easy. Most probably all that had been in her eyes was the normal fascination anyone would have on witnessing an operation they had not seen before.

Since Stella's accusation of unfriendliness, Joe had been doing his best to act as he had before his revelation and yet, for his own preservation, to avoid her as much as possible. For some reason, in the urgency of the moment, it had not crossed his mind she might be the one to answer his night call for help. And for all his concentration on the sheep, Stella's very presence in the shed, followed by the terrible proximity on the hay, had caused him new agitation. Wearied by a week of broken nights with the sheep, he had little energy to fight the feeling. He found himself succumbing to an idea that raced suddenly from nowhere. He knew, however unwise, there was no holding back from his next plan.

Long hours later, he walked into the attic bedroom without knocking, holding a mug of tea. He allowed himself a moment to look down on the sleeping figure of Stella, hair awash on the pillow, one shoulder showing above the sheet. He called her.

Stella woke quickly, struggling through shards of dream to focus on reality. There was still a knife in the air, skinning a lamb: there was a silvery-blue corpse on bloody straw, there was Joe's cold and bloody hand on hers. When the remnants of the dream dissolved and she saw the real Joe, tired eyes, small smile, mug of tea stretched out, Stella gave a cry.

'Joe? Whatever . . . ? What time is it?'

'Seven.' He passed the mug, stretching his arm rather than moving nearer.

'Oh my God. I'm *sorry*. I've never overslept before.'

'Don't worry.'

'Where are the others?'

'Milking.'

'They should've woken me.'

The sheet slipped down her shoulder as two hands cupped the mug. There was a glimpse of low-necked white nightdress. The slight humping of one breast as the arm she leaned on squeezed her side.

'I told them not to.'

'I'm sorry, I really am.' She shook her head. Hair surged about in natural waves.

'I've said. It doesn't matter a bit.'

'What about you?'

'There were two more lambs. Both fine.'

'So you've not been to bed all night?'

Joe shook his head. 'I'll get a couple of hours now. Would you mind doing Sly?'

' 'Course not. Where's Mrs Lawrence?'

'Gone to the village with the eggs.'

In the cold air of the room Stella and her bed were an island that smelt of warm sleep. Joe wanted to kneel on the floor beside her, tell her of his certainty. He held on to the doorpost.

'I won't be long. Down in time for lunch.'

'And what about all this luxury?' Stella lifted the mug. 'I don't deserve this.' She smiled at him. 'Thanks. I won't be a moment.'

She sipped her tea. Hair parted over shoulder. Eyelids, cast down, the colour of iris petals, blue-veined. Joe would have liked to watch her drinking tea for ever.

Stella quickly pulled on her breeches and thick jumpers. She ran across the yard to fetch a pitchfork from the lambing shed. Her special lamb, still wearing its adopted coat, was asleep beside its foster mother. Late, guilty, she did not linger to see the rest of the newborn lambs, but hurried to the pigsty. There she found Sly, in the last stages of her last pregnancy, in an irritable mood. First she refused to move from the bedding that had to be discarded, then she butted Stella's side with a complaining snout. Stella's usual patience was frayed. She wished she could swap jobs with Prue. Sly and Prue had a special relationship the others would never acquire. She did her best, flinging sodden straw into a barrow in the yard, to be moved later. While she tossed down the sweet-smelling new stuff, a wayward thought came to her: simply, she looked forward to lunchtime. She looked forward to Joe's being there.

Engaged in this small reflection, it was some moments before she realised Prue was leaning over the sty wall, a critical eye on her work.

'What's going on?' Prue asked.

'Joe said would I –'

'Sly's my special job.'

'None of us has special jobs, really, do we?' Stella paused in her work, leaned on the pitchfork. Prue, she saw, looked unaccountably put out. 'I'm sorry. I overslept.'

'We have special things we're good at,' Prue snapped back. 'Hedging and hens and the fruit for Ag. You're good at milking and Noble and the cows. I'm the plougher and the pig lady.'

Stella had never seen Prue so petulant. 'That's probably so. But we all swap about without making a fuss, don't we?'

'Don't you understand? Sly's about to give birth and *I*

298

wanted to look after her till it's all over,' Prue suddenly shouted. 'I don't want *you* interfering, taking my job, thanks very much.'

'Calm *down*, Prue –'

'I'm not calm, I'm furious.'

'I can see that. Here.' Stella handed over the pitchfork. 'You take over. I'll finish off the cows with Ag.'

Prue's outburst was quickly demolished by Stella's gesture. She entered the sty as Stella left it, ostentatiously rearranged the already well-tossed straw, gave Sly a proprietorial scratch behind one ear. Then she turned to Stella with an apologetic smile.

'If you think about it, there's not many hairdressers who fall in love with pigs.' They both laughed. 'Sorry. I didn't mean to shout. Everything's got on top of me. Nightmares about Barry. A letter this morning from his friend Jamie with details of how he died . . . Too many late nights with Robert. My nerves seem to have gone all to pieces.'

'You could do with a good night's sleep,' said Stella.

'You sound like my mum,' said Prue.

It was the first squabble Stella could remember in their six months at Hallows Farm. That, she reflected on her way to the cowshed, was an amazing fact that perhaps the war could account for. Civilians, horrified by the fighting, instinctively wanted to live in extra peace at home. And, in any case, they were too busy to indulge in petty quarrels.

At four o'clock that afternoon the girls, in clean jerseys and breeches, sat round the kitchen table with Mrs Lawrence and the district commissioner, a Mrs Poodle. There was an air of a children's tea party. The girls had brushed their hair: Prue, for the first time, for Mrs Lawrence's sake, had left off a bow. They had washed every trace of mud from their hands and nails, laid a cloth on the table, and arranged a lardy cake and two sorts of sandwiches. Beside each of the girls' plates lay three red half-diamonds, rewards for six months' satisfactory service, which they were now allowed to sew on to the sleeves of their jerseys and coats.

'The badges are usually just sent through the post,' explained Mrs Poodle, 'but I wanted to come and see how you're getting on in this remote spot.' She smiled round merrily.

'We wouldn't want to be anywhere else, would we?' said Prue. 'Stella and Ag and me.' Overcome by her badge, the first prize of any kind she had ever received in her life, Prue was close to speech-day tears. She fingered the half diamonds in disbelief, shuffling them together to make whole ones. 'My mum'll not believe this.'

'It's curious that the Land Army is the only one of the services in which there's no promotion,' Mrs Poodle went on. 'Seems very unfair to me. But at least the badges are some recognition of your loyal service. If you keep up the good work you'll be entitled to a special armlet in eighteen months' time, and a special *scarlet* one after four years. Think of that!'

'Good God,' said Prue, tear-bright eyes flicking to the ceiling, 'surely we're not going to be needed that long. Surely the bloody war's not going on for another bloody –'

'*Prue,*' said Mrs Lawrence.

'Sorry.'

'No one can say how long you'll be needed.' Mrs Poodle, unused to such feasts, was enjoying her third piece of lardy cake. She had cut it up into tiny morsels to prolong the treat. In return for such hospitality, she felt, her knowledge of how the WLA fared beyond Hallows Farm would be bound to interest. 'But enrolment is galloping ahead,' she said. 'In Dorset alone, by the end of last year, three hundred and nineteen land girls had signed up. I reckon there'll be twice that many by the end of this year.'

Mrs Poodle shook hands with each one of them, before she left, and wished them well in their long and hard service to their country that lay ahead. She, like Prue's mother, found the famous words of Winston Churchill invaluable when it came, as it often did in her job, to encouragement on formal occasions. '*We are moving through a period of great hope,* as our great leader put it, *when every virtue of our race will be tested and all that we have and honour will be at stake.*' Her eyes dimmed at the poignancy of her own rendering of the great man's words. She pulled on a pair of black kid gloves, adjusted her hat. '*It is no time for doubt* . . . Good luck, girls. And congratulations.'

'Bugger everything,' shouted Prue, as soon as she had gone. 'I'm going to sew on all my diamonds *now.*' But as she was about to turn back indoors, they all heard Joe's urgent shout from the pigsty.

'Prue! You'd better hurry. Sly's begun.'

Prue gave a shriek. Her half-diamonds dropped to the ground. Stella bent to retrieve them for her. Again, she felt a brief sense of annoyance. It was unreasonable. Unaccountable. But a fact.

That evening Robert came to supper and suggested that they should all go to The Bells to celebrate. Ag and Mrs Lawrence declined in favour of an early night. Joe said he could not leave the sheep. Stella volunteered to help him.

'Just you and me, then,' Prue giggled to Robert, the only one to accept a second apple dumpling and more Bird's custard – love never affected her appetite. 'But before we go you'll have to be introduced to every single one of Sly's litter. Help me give them names.'

The sow's late-afternoon lying-in had inspired Prue with unexpected maternal feelings.

'Never seen such a performance,' she had kept on saying to Joe. 'Look! There's another one! How does she do it? Good old Sly . . .'

She had stood for a long time watching the fourteen tiny piglets writhing and squeaking, snouting among their mother's dugs, their gristly bodies slipping over her panting belly – contemplating the miracle of birth. It was something to which she had given no previous thought: now, beguiled by Sly's piglets, the attraction of having babies seemed suddenly understandable. She'd like four, she decided, and looked forward to telling Robert this new decision. So she was relieved to find the others would not be coming to The Bells. The announcement that she wished to make should be private. There was much to tell Robert: it had been a memorable day, what with prizes and piglets and decisions about children. The kind of celebration she fancied was several stiff gin and limes, followed by wild activity in the hard and noisy bed, and bugger Stella's prissy suggestion about an early night.

As soon as the washing-up was finished, Mrs Lawrence and Ag went upstairs. Joe followed Stella into the sitting-room.

'Cold?' he asked, and put another log on the small fire before she could answer. Stella switched on the wireless. Rubinstein was playing a Chopin prelude. 'I'm not much of a Chopin fan,' said Joe. 'I've got things to do.' He left the room.

Stella curled up on the hard sofa, disappointed. She had spent the last half-hour looking forward to a short time alone with him. Why she wanted this, she found impossible to explain to herself. But somehow, she had discovered since Christmas, his presence was a luxury, a comfort, a warm pleasure. Watching him skin the dead lamb last night, and skilfully introduce the orphan lamb to its foster mother, had inspired her admiration. This morning, tea in bed, he had surprised her. Now, he had sort of . . . insulted, rejected her. The curious thing was, however he acted seemed to affect her. This was confusing. Stella, not wanting to understand for fear of discovering the truth, allowed herself to believe that the distortions of the war were more devious than she had supposed. They accounted for Prue's sudden temper, Ag's unflagging hope of a non-existent relationship, and her own jumpy reactions to one who had become a friend.

The warmth of the fire, combined with Chopin's sad and plashy chords, made her drowsy. She would make herself a cup of Ovaltine, go to sleep hoping Joe might call upon her again to help with more lambing.

Stella imagined he was already out in the shed, so was surprised to find him in the kitchen. He had spread paper over the table and was cleaning his shoes, chipping mud off a heel with a blunt knife.

'Job I most hate,' he said.

'I was going to get myself some Ovaltine before bed. Like some?'

Joe nodded. Stella poured milk into a saucepan, prepared the drinks.

'Good about the half-diamonds,' said Joe.

Stella smiled, brought the drinks to the table, sat down. She held her mug to her nose, sniffing the hot, beige-smelling froth, enjoying the warmth of the steam. Joe kept his eyes on brushes, polish, dull leather that began to gleam under the fierceness of his polishing. After a while, the swishing of the brush, like the music, induced in Stella a further drowsiness of the careless kind.

'Do you ever feel,' she asked, 'such total confusion that you don't know where to begin to untangle the various strands? You don't even know what the strands consist of? An amorphous confusion? Do you ever feel that, Joe?'

He glanced at her, saw the beautiful mouth turned down.

'Of course. Often. All the time.'

He held up a huge black shoe, admired its shine, took up a duster. One of the dogs, asleep by the stove, growled in its dream.

'We're the ones who've decided on marriage. Do you think we're right?' Again Joe glanced at her. 'I mean, why are you going to marry Janet?' Even as she asked, Stella realised the silly risk she might have taken.

Joe put down the finished shoe, sat down, picked up his drink. He fought for calm, forced himself to look her in the eye. *Oh God, please give me the strength not to let her see . . .*

'I could ask you the same question. Why are you going to marry Philip?'

Stella gave an embarrassed smile. She shrugged. 'I was in love with an idea – one of my weaknesses. I've been in love with lots of ideas. I thought he was the right person. Perhaps it was the urgency of war . . .'

'You *thought?*'

'I thought.'

'You still think?'

'I don't know. To confess any doubts would be too disloyal.'

'I know those feelings.'

'I've given him my word.'

'I've done the same to Janet. You never said how it was, your weekend in Plymouth.'

'It didn't occur to me you'd be interested.'

'I admit to being intrigued about the sort of man you love.'

Stella hid her face behind a structure of hands and mug. She tried for lightness.

'Philip's a good man. The weekend wasn't . . . entirely perfect.'

Joe nodded, began to chip mud off the second heel. It fell on to the paper in dark curves, like giant nail parings. Stella stood up, took her empty mug to the sink. She was not sure if Joe had heard her last remark. She hoped he had not, for it was a first act of betrayal.

'I must go to bed,' she said.

'We haven't really answered each other's questions.'

'No. Perhaps we will some other time. Call me if you want any help in the night.'

'You need your sleep.'

'Really. Please.'

Joe nodded. He did not watch her leave the room, but continued to work with manic concentration on the shoe. He polished and repolished till no brighter shine could be achieved. A possibility he hardly dared to think about added to the general morass in his mind. Surely it wasn't his imagination: surely, tonight, there was some indication . . .

Joe felt he had seen signs of something so small, so amorphous – in Stella's words – that she herself was perhaps innocent of its existence. But it was there, within her. It had taken root. The question was, should he stamp on it before it flared into consciousness? Or should he abandon all principles and encourage it to life?

Some days later, Ag finished her morning duties earlier than normal, so joined Mrs Lawrence in preparing the lunch. Joe came into the kitchen carrying a couple of dead rabbits. He slung them on the draining board. From the stomach of one of them purple blood oozed through the pale fur on to the dark wood.

'Thanks, Joe. Your father will be pleased.' Mrs Lawrence turned to Ag. 'John's expected home this evening. He'll be wanting his rabbit stew and boiled onions. There's suet left over for a treacle pudding – his favourite, too.'

The news came as no surprise to Ag. She had noticed early that morning that Mrs Lawrence's spirits had risen. Her inner life, always so carefully concealed, emanated in subtle hints of private exuberance. She moved faster between table, sink and stove. Her worn hands, sometimes slowed and dull with fatigue, fluttered happily among soapy plates. She buttered slices of newly made bread with extraordinary speed. Her beige lips, released from their usual cautious clench, kept breaking into a smile.

Ag had often thought how she would have liked Mrs

Lawrence for a mother: the idea was renewed this morning. She sensed that this strong woman, in her state of anticipation, exuded a kind of approachability which was rarely apparent. Ag, who loved as well as admired her, yearned to talk to her. She wondered if it would be untoward to try.

Mrs Lawrence darted to the sink holding a lethal knife. She began to skin one of the rabbits. Ag watched her firm hand grasped round the animal's neck: the head flopped over, an obscene bunch of fur, bone, tooth resting on stiff lip, blubbery balls of dead eyes.

'Could you do the other one for me, Ag? It's not difficult. Common sense.'

'I'm afraid I . . . I'm no good with dead things. Birds, fish, animals. For some reason, I can't touch them.' It was the first time Ag had had to refuse Mrs Lawrence any request. 'I'm sorry,' she added, ashamed of her squeamishness.

Mrs Lawrence glanced at her. 'That's all right. I used to feel the same. I had to get used to it. I was sick, I remember, the first time I drew a pheasant. I don't mind any of it, much, now.'

She tugged at the rabbit skin, turning it inside out as she pulled. It came off clean as a glove. Ag regarded the naked pink body beneath, the legs bent as if still running, their flight frozen by death. Feeling sick herself, she chivvied about, laying the table, not wanting to see more of Mrs Lawrence's butchery.

The rabbits were quickly chopped into a jigsaw of pathetic joints and piled into a large bowl. Mrs Lawrence poured in a dash of cider, bay leaves, juniper berries, pepper. Her movements were light, happy. When the bowl of hideous contents was complete, she carried it to the larder as if it weighed no more than an empty plate.

'John'll love that,' she said, on return. 'When we were first married, not a brass farthing between us, we ate a lot of rabbit.'

She sat down at the table, correcting the position of a

fork, a glass. She tweaked at the few sprigs of forsythia, still in bud, that Ag had arranged in a jug. She put one hand over her heart.

'Ridiculous! I ought to be ashamed of myself, at my age. I'm all of a flutter.'

Ag smiled back at her. Here, perhaps, was her chance.

'We'd be lucky,' she said, 'any of us, if we ended up with a marriage like yours and Mr Lawrence's.'

Mrs Lawrence looked surprised. 'Really? I don't know about that. I think if you're happy working together for the same end, it's a help. We've been so lucky in that respect, John and me. I wouldn't have wanted to marry a man who went off on a train every day. Like that, there's so much of your lives unknown to the other . . . Absence can mean a blurring of the rules. I wouldn't want to go away from home myself, either. I suppose I'm terribly old-fashioned. I can see an age, a generation or so ahead, when women will think it quite natural to go out to work. Mere housewives, like me, perfectly happy with their lot, will be scoffed at. Perhaps we are even today. But I'm too busy to dwell on things like that. I'm so out of the real world, I don't know much of what is going on. But what about you, Ag? Have you thought about what you want to do after the war?'

Ag thought for a silent moment, decided to confide.

'I've been thinking: I'd like to study law, go to the Bar. I'll go on being a land girl, or do some other war work, while I'm needed; then I'll try for law school. The ultimate plan – the old plan –' she gave a self-deprecating smile – 'is to marry Desmond.'

'The one who sent the Christmas card?'

Ag nodded. 'I sometimes think my dream of him is a stupid waste of time and energy. But then I remember the certainty I felt. Instantly. Positively. Mysteriously . . . Foolish, I suppose, but I'm relying on that.'

'You must. You should.' Mrs Lawrence sighed. 'I wish Joe felt such certainty.'

'Doesn't he?'

'What do you think?'

'Well, he shows no great outward signs of it. We don't talk of Janet. We talk about books. But he's a dark horse, Joe.'

There was a long silence.

'Perhaps I shouldn't say this, Ag, and I would ask you not to repeat my indiscretions to the others. But I think John and I may have made the greatest mistake of our lives over Janet. And I don't know what we can do.' Mrs Lawrence spoke quietly, unsure she should be saying such things but compelled, after so many months of silence, to tell this sympathetic girl for whom she had particular affection.

'Joe was such a daffy young boy, seducing every girl for miles, breaking hearts all over the place. We found ourselves lecturing him on the wisdom of looking beyond physical attraction, of choosing a good, solid girl for life. He used to scoff at such concepts, say the only *marriageable* woman he'd ever met was me!' She smiled to show she knew this admission of vanity was an indulgence. 'And of course he didn't change his ways. Then – I don't know how it came about, exactly, he never said – but he announced he'd proposed to Janet. *Janet*! Well, we'd known her for years – they used to live in Somerset. We liked her parents. She was a childhood friend of Joe's – plain, gawky, kindest heart in the world. He treated her like another boy; she loved him from the age of twelve. As I say, I don't know what drove him to his decision, but a lot of bad luck came at once – no Cambridge, no fighting. I suppose he felt bitter, a failure, useless, though he never actually complained.

'Anyhow, unofficially engaged, as it were, he stopped chasing girls. He spent most of his free time with Robert, talking, talking: they have a lot in common. Then, out of the blue, this proposal; entirely to please us, we now think. And at the time we were pleased. We felt, here was security.

Not very exciting, perhaps, but security, support, devotion.

'But then, in a way, he seemed to give up. The life went out of him. He said, "I've done what you want, you ought to be pleased." We said, "Joe, you must do what *you* want." Timing was against him, of course. Just as they'd announced their engagement, Janet was posted to Surrey. Joe didn't express any great sadness. I still have to chivvy him to write to her. As you've seen, they hardly ever have a chance to meet.

'Then, you girls arrived. John and I were worried, of course. Especially, when all of you turned out to be so . . . well, it would have been easy for Joe to fall back into his old ways. We trusted him, naturally. He's an honourable man, Joe. Once he's given his word, he sticks by it. What's happened, you coming, as you've probably noticed, is that he's come out of his shell. He's still tense, restless, full of regrets: but happier. Don't you think? I think you must be his first women *friends*, all three of you. I have to admit I had my suspicions Prue would get her pretty little hands on him, and I dare say she tried, but she wouldn't have succeeded. I know he enjoys *your* company so much.' To Ag's deep discomfort, their eyes met. 'Intellectual equivalent. With all the farm work, he's been denied so much of that sort of stimulus, apart from Robert. Prue amuses him – he's amazed by her capacity for hard work, hand in hand with all her silliness. And he seems to like Stella – their mutual interest in music. Really, you've done him the world of good, the three of you, in your different ways.' She paused, began to knead her knuckles.

'You've also shown him . . . But I don't want to be disloyal to Janet. Suffice to say that at Christmas the contrast between her and all of you . . . must have made him think. Besides which, Janet seems to have changed: jumpy, eager, *irritating* in her desire to be of use, to be liked, to be loved. The poor girl. She must see he doesn't love her, she must see he's merely trying to stick to his word.

'We blame ourselves, John and I. We blame ourselves. We taught Joe to stick by his promises and now, in doing that, he may have a lesser life. What can we do?'

Mrs Lawrence gave Ag a look in which desperation was bound with regret. Ag, astonished by the confession of her normally reticent employer, felt unable to advise. She could give no immediate answer. To play for time, she fetched the warm plates from the stove, stirred the pan of carrot soup. Then she returned to her seat.

'By strange irony,' she said at last, 'I think it's a case where maybe the war can *save*. I mean, as it twists and breaks so much anyway, perhaps it could be used as an excuse. Perhaps both Janet and Joe will just drift apart, and blame only the war. The end of their arrangement could come about for the same reasons as it began: *pressures* of war, decisions forced by an unnatural time.'

'You're not accounting for his honour,' said Mrs Lawrence.

'I am. But even honour, distorted by the events of war, can be seen as foolishness. So if a word is broken, it may be forgiven.'

'I hope that's so. Perhaps events will right themselves. Now: not a word of all this, Ag, please.'

'I promise.'

'Take out the potatoes, if you will. I'll call the others – only a few hours.' She was cheerful again. 'John'll be back about five.'

Mrs Lawrence put on a clean pinafore for her husband's return and her rabbit stew was appreciated by all but Ag, who could not bring herself to eat the running legs even though they were half disguised by gravy, having seen them in their naked form.

Mr Lawrence came back with the news he had expected. His brother's illness was in remission. The prognostication was that he might now live months rather than weeks.

Together they had agreed that the Lawrences would move to Yorkshire in the following new year.

He left no pause, after this fact had been announced, going on to explain his plans for Hallows Farm before their departure. He wanted as much as possible to be turned over to arable land before it was put up for sale. The cows – all but Nancy – would have to go within a few weeks. Sly likewise. At Prue's squeal of protest he refrained from mentioning the fate that would befall her litter. But pig feed was scarcer than ever, he patiently explained to the distressed Prue, and their supply was almost finished. He spoke of detailed plans concerning which fields would be best planted with which crops.

'I'm warning you,' he said, 'it'll be the busiest spring of your lives. Harrowing, ploughing, weeding, sowing: good thing you're all so fit. Half-diamonds well deserved, by the way. But I don't want you to underestimate the hard work ahead. Tell me honestly: do you think we can manage, six pairs of hands and Ratty, or should I think about more help?'

'We can manage,' said his wife quickly, for all of them.

Next only to ratting, Ratty loved shepherd's work. Lambing time was his favourite season, the nights away from home, the 'dozens of bloody miracles', as he called the births. Besides which, the night work afforded him the excuse of sleeping a few hours during the day, thus avoiding the increasingly irascible Edith.

The night Mr Lawrence returned home was a busy one for Joe and Ratty. Nine lambs, including twins, were born. It was six in the morning when he walked home – not tired, the adrenalin of wonder kept him going till the last lamb of the season was born – but hungry. There were signs of a fine day to come. Signs spring was not far away.

Ratty looked forward to an hour's peace in the kitchen, frying himself rashers of bacon in the one pan, and a slice of bread. But to his dismay he found Edith already down-stairs. She stood before a large box on the table, rummaging through deep litter of paper cut-up squares, as if searching for something in a bran tub. The squares, he noticed, had become smaller in the last week or so. Their symmetry took hours of her time.

'Out with the girls again,' Edith greeted him, a strange bleak look on her face.

'I've been lambing with Joe. Nine since midnight, including black twins. You know I've been lambing. I could do with some breakfast.'

'Breakfast!' Edith cackled. 'You can get your own rotten breakfast, or get one of those girls to get your breakfast.'

'Now, look here, Edith . . .' The pleasures and achievements of Ratty's night suddenly left him. They were replaced with a cold anger, spurred by hunger and the desire for peaceful sleep. 'You're being unreasonable,' he said.

'*Unreasonable?*' Edith snapped round. Her hands flew out of the box, scattering paper. She clutched its sides, threw its contents at Ratty. 'That's what I think of you, Ratty Tyler.'

The paper showered over Ratty: bright little sparks from old coloured books and postcards, dull flakes from news-papers, soft, clinging fragments of tissue. They chipped his coat, clung to his cap. Edith began to laugh.

'Confetti! That's it, confetti. We never had any on our wedding day, remember? You wouldn't run to confetti. I should've known then . . .'

Ratty began to shake the paper from his clothes. He was suddenly very tired. Empty. Cold.

'We did, didn't we . . . ? Surely?'

'That we didn't.'

Edith stomped over to the dresser and snatched up a small brass frame containing a sepia photograph. She thrust it at him.

'Our wedding day, right?'

Ratty blinked at the faded image of the young foolish hope in his own wooden smile. Had Edith ever really been like that, smiling too?

'No confetti. *No* confetti! See?'

'It wouldn't show, not in an old photograph. I'm sure we had. Pink stuff, petals.' He was confused, dizzy.

'I'm telling you. This is proof.'

Edith's old indignation died down in her triumph. She stepped back, replaced the frame. 'Well, what we didn't have, at least the Government's getting.' Ratty could not see the logic of this argument, but was too weary to contradict. 'I'll just sweep this lot up, get going on some more.'

'Is there a rasher?' Ratty tried to dodge the broom she had picked up.

Edith swept the kaleidoscope of paper pieces with peculiar relish, for some moments, before she answered.

'No,' she said at last. 'There's not so much as a slice of bread, Ratty Tyler, neither.'

Eleven

For as long as he could remember, Ratty's small patch of garden had been home to a dynasty of blackbirds. Close guardians of their territory, year after year different generations would sing from their inherited place in the lilac tree. They left the cherry tree to the chaffinches.

At the end of February, Ratty heard the first evensong from a couple of old males. Their prime over, he knew that all they would afford him was a run-through of melodies from time past, sung only at dusk, and lacking their former vigour. But this was a sign, too, that a member of the new generation would be shortly taking over. Ratty was keen to catch his first sight of the inheritor.

After a lone breakfast – Edith, for the first time in her life, had taken to staying in bed – Ratty pottered into the garden. There on the grass he found the chap he was looking for: a handsome bird, still the dark brown of its mother, its beak also still brown. The ring round its eye was a pale hint of the gold it would become in the next few weeks.

The bird showed no fear of his presence. Ratty stood quite still, studying it for some moments, then pottered off to the end of the garden past the lilac tree. He turned, leaned against the fence, looked back at his cottage. From the branches of the unpruned tree came the first ripples of familiar song: tentative at first, then swelling in confidence, accelerating among scales, showing off. If Ratty had been a man of sentimental disposition he might have thought the bird had followed him, read his thoughts, sung especially for him. As it was, the music which annually renewed optimism that had been frayed by winter merely reminded him spring was here at last: there was much work to be done. And that this time next year life as he knew it at Hallows Farm would be over. He would be finally retired, not semi-retired like the old blackbirds. God knows, then . . .

Ratty retraced his steps along the path that struggled to keep its identity through neglected grass. Every yard or so he paused, let the blackbird's song – riotous, rapturous, now – lock him into a present of nothing but pure sound. The past and the future were both places he had no wish to be.

He contemplated the back of his ramshackle cottage, not a thought in his head. The music of the bird excited the old skin of his arms into roughness beneath his sleeves. Then, it appeared. He saw ahead of him a monster. At first, he thought the horrible creature, standing there at his own back door, must be a hallucination. He had slept little of late, what with the lambing. Several times he had found himself confused, not remembering, seeing things that vanished into air. And yet he knew he was awake. The ground was firm beneath his feet. The blackbird went on singing.

The monster had one large glassy eye, oval-shaped, and the rubbery black snout of a giant pig. It stood on its hind legs, front legs folded, staring back at Ratty, no expression in the terrible eye. Then it took a few steps towards him and Ratty saw its skin – a horrible blue – was a familiar blue skirt, and its forelegs were human arms in the wrinkled sleeves of a brown cardigan.

It was Edith in her gas mask.

'Dear God, Edith!' Ratty cried.

So great was his relief that he had to lean on his stick to save himself from tumbling. He felt coldness gushing through the precarious joints of his knees. Sweat greased his temples. His hands shook.

'You gave me a fright, you did. Whatever are you doing in that thing?'

Edith pulled off the mask. Her face was pale, her eyes unsteady. Sprigs of white hair, normally caught back into a bun, allowed light to pink the skin of her skull.

'There's lambs in the fields, bombs in the sky,' she said quietly.

Ratty glanced up, unsteady. Two clouds moved across a stretch of silent grey-blue.

'There's never,' he said.

'The war's come here, now, you mark my words.'

'I'm going down to the farm.' Ratty shook his head. He didn't like the look of her.

'You take a gas mask, Ratty Tyler, or you'll regret it.'

'I'll never take one of those things.'

Ratty shuffled past her, eyes on the ground, heading for the lane. He was aware that Edith shrugged.

'We'll all be dead as cowpats, soon,' she said.

While Ag did not share Edith's fear of bombs in the local sky, she became increasingly aware of the war in parts of the world far from their own: fighting in Malta, the Philippines, Hitler's renewed attacks on Russia, the sufferings of the Eighth Army in Egypt. So long and busy were the days, now, that there was little time to keep up with the daily bulletins, and she rarely saw a newspaper. But Ag made a point of trying to listen to the nine o'clock news every night, with the Lawrences. The acceleration of war, even from this comparatively safe corner of Dorset, unnerved her more than it did the others. When she wasn't thinking of Desmond she found herself almost obsessively imagining battles, destruction, killing, corpses.

In contrast to – and perhaps because of – these dark reflections, this spring seemed of particular significance. Ag watched its slow beginnings. Mrs Lawrence had long ceased to tend the garden: priorities these days were fruit

trees and the vegetable patch. But Ag, knowing her
employer's love of flowers, had bought and planted a few
dozen bulbs in November. Now they began to appear,
much to Mrs Lawrence's surprise. First, snowdrops. Then
the 'rathe' primrose (Ag had never been able to discover
the meaning of Milton's arcane word, she admitted to Joe
one evening) in the orchard, where one of her tasks was
thoroughly to spray every tree with lime sulphur – protection against apple scab. In beds that edged the neglected
lawn, a dozen narcissi straggled through the unkempt
earth. By March a few scarlet tulips randomly glittered,
cold as glass among the weeds. Mrs Lawrence's delight was
touching.

'So kind of you, Ag,' she said. 'The pity of it is we shan't
be here to see how they've spread, next year.'

Rewards for Ag's autumn labours were beginning to be
seen in the hedges, too. She and Mr Lawrence observed
buds breaking on the carefully woven young hazel shoots.
They found a haze of new leaf on the long, neat thorn
hedge that protected two sides of Lower Pasture.

'Beautiful laying, I'm bound to say,' Mr Lawrence gently
boasted as they inspected the new growth. 'I think we did a
good job, Ag. The new owners, whoever they are, will find
themselves with a nicely cared-for parcel of land . . .'

They walked through the woods. Ag had the impression
that the farmer's eyes were scouring every view with particular vigilance, as if storing sights and sounds for the
future. He pointed out a blackcap, high in an ash tree,
paused to listen to its wild song. On the far side of the
wood they came across a gathering of fieldfares, preparing
for their journey overseas. On another occasion, inspecting
a newly sown field, they heard the croaking voice of a corn
bunting. And one fine afternoon, from out of an almost
eerie silence, the intense bubbles of a skylark's song
dropped like a waterfall on the ploughed earth.

'You see it, you hear it, you feel it, year after year,' said

317

Mr Lawrence, 'and it always catches you out, spring, the wonder of it. Makes you think: funny kind of God. On the one hand there's all this; on the other, thousands of armed men out to destroy each other. And now all this talk of an atom bomb, which could be the end. Doesn't make sense. Look: first woodpecker of the year, cocky bastard.' He placed a hand on Ag's arm to stop her moving. He thought how even now, despite the dimming of the tormenting flames, he would not allow himself to touch Stella in the same innocent way. Their eyes followed a brief flash of emerald feathers. 'Tell you one thing: if we get through this bloody war, if I eventually come to retire – know what I'd like to do? I'd like to write a book about migration. Something that's always fascinated me: something no one really understands.'

'I'd like to read it.' Ag smiled at him.

'You shall have a copy inscribed to the best hedging apprentice I ever came across. You've a real talent for hedging, Ag: there's not many have that. You're pretty smart when it comes to birds, too – not just the dry academic I thought you might be. But then, I was wrong about all of you. I admit that. I was against your coming. It was Faith who insisted. She turned out to be right, of course. You can count on Faith, in most things, to be right. To be wiser than anyone else.'

Mr Lawrence's approbation meant much to Ag. It cheered her for a while. But the underlying melancholy she suffered that spring never entirely left her. Hope that the end of the war might not be too far off began to fade. As did the possibility of Desmond.

While Ag struggled with the feeling of doom within her, Stella tried to understand why – with no prospect of seeing Philip for some time, and scant letters – she felt so content. Pieces of an incomprehensible puzzle kept appearing. There was the day when Prue sprained her wrist and could not drive the tractor: Joe tried to teach her, without much success, to plough a straight furrow. They laughed so hard at her attempts Stella felt weak and giddy, earth and sky spinning about as she leaned up against one of the great mudguards. There was the day Noble had to be taken to the blacksmith. Joe drew a map of how to get there, a simple route of some five or six miles. But then he suddenly changed his mind about Stella's ability to find the way despite his directions: declared if she was to return before nightfall he would have to accompany her. She rode the horse bareback, Joe cycled beside her. Somehow, it all took the best part of the day. They had spam sandwiches at the local pub while the shoeing took place, returned by a longer route through high-banked lanes, rhythmic sparky noise of the horse's hoofs making a bass for the breeze. The pieces of the puzzle all contained Joe.

Looking back much later, Stella could never say when it was exactly that the whole picture fell into place. Unlike Joe, she was not struck by blinding revelation. The building of her own certainty formed so quietly, so subtly, that its culmination was no surprise. What she saw before her – when, *when* exactly? she could not say – she knew had been there for ever, waiting for a cover to be drawn back. She calmly accepted its existence, knowing there was nothing to be done. She knew Joe liked her, had no idea if he felt more than that. They were both committed to other people. It was likely their friendship would come to an end when they left the farm. There was nothing that could be done. Stella's love for Joe was fated to die before it could ever live. He would never know about it. All she must do was exercise caution, contain her happiness, give no clue as to the heartbreak of her feelings. It was worthless to reflect upon the cruelty of mistiming. In the short months left to her, Stella decided, all she could do would be to imprint every possible moment in her mind, to feed on, sometimes, in the years to come: for it would surely never be like this again. This was so far removed from the old, frivolous, silly notions she had had in the past of being in love, based on nothing more than wishful thinking, that she laughed herself to scorn, felt suddenly old. This was certain love: the kind that spreads, and grows and, given the chance, can survive. Stella believed – when she allowed herself the luxury of thinking about it – that she had been blessed with a rare feeling, seldom repeated in a single life. To stifle any acknowledgement of this feeling would be the hardest challenge she had ever known. It would be a kind of murder, something she would live to regret always. But there was no alternative.

Stella did her best to contain herself. By the time the bluebells were coming out in the woods, and the cow parsley, she felt herself well under control. She divided her attentions evenly between everyone, was punctilious in her behaviour. No one, she was sure, could have any idea. All the same – and here was the ghost of a new puzzle – her eyes did inadvertently meet Joe's more than usual. Somehow, they often found themselves working together. Somehow, their paths often crossed. And all the while, to Stella in her confused happiness, the trumpetings of spring were no more than an abstract background of birdsong and new leaf and clear sky. Nothing in nature, this spring, was sharp-edged. Only Joe's face was clear. She tried to read in it any sign of something beyond close friendship, but failed. Her position was a solitary one, then: her secret the hardest thing she had ever had to bear.

For Prue, spring was a dizzying experience. It was the first year of her life she had witnessed it outside Manchester, and she found it a revelation.

'No wonder blood rises,' she observed, skipping about, marvelling at lush new grass and emerald leaf. Indeed, she found the whole process even more captivating than shopping. Several weeks running she chose not to go into the local town on her half-day, but to gather primroses or snow-drops, to stand gazing at a field of ewes with their lambs, until Mr Lawrence accused her of 'idling'. Stella and Ag became impatient with her constant wonder. After a while she kept it to herself.

Three things, however, disturbed the magic of the season. First, the Government's ban on embroidered underclothes and nightwear put Prue in a rage: she had been planning to surprise Robert with some Jean Harlow petticoats she'd seen in a magazine. Now, the shop would be banned from selling them. Second, Sly and her piglets were sold to a nearby piggery. Mr Lawrence took the trouble to apologise to Prue, but explained he had had an offer he could not refuse. He had planned for Sly to go anyhow: sooner was less worrying than later. The screaming, as mother and brood were loaded on to the lorry, was terrible – matched only by Prue's wailings. She was quiet, puffy-eyed, mascara-smudged for the rest of the day, but insisted on being the one to do the final clearing of the sty.

While the matter of the underwear was ridiculous and the departure of Sly sad, these two things caused only a few days of rampant gloom. The third matter was a constant flickering of discomfort that only sprang into clear life when Prue gave herself time to reflect: Robert.

Robert, she was fast coming to realise, was no match for her own rising sap. For almost four months she had enjoyed his company, his love-making, his dry little jokes. She had given up trying to induce warmth into his flesh, and had become used to his chilly limbs and lips. But the fact was there was no spur to continuing the affair for the rest of the year until Prue left. They were useful to each other, liked each other, but had nowhere to go. And no destination, in the curious love map that lived in Prue's mind, meant that a relationship could not and would not survive very long. She sometimes faced the fact that, beast that she was, the only real, lasting aphrodisiac for her was *money*: she could only sustain eternal interest if there was money in the lover's bank.

But she made no indication of her waning interest: pointless, when there was no one to replace Robert. They weren't thick in ploughed fields, the kind of men she fancied – or indeed any men at all. So for the time being, wistfully wishing there was a new challenge to be found in the mossy banks in the woods, she stuck to the arrangement of going out with Robert three times a week.

Some days after Sly's departure, and after the kind of low-key night which Prue found hard to forgive in any man, she was feeling more than usually melancholy despite the glorious spring morning. But at lunch, Mrs Lawrence broke some news which, as Prue saw it, was a once-in-a-lifetime remedy for any kind of tragedy. A letter had arrived from Headquarters of the Land Army in London to say that the King and Queen were to give a tea party, in the summer, for a selection of land girls from all over the country. A limited number of invitations was allocated to each county. Mrs Lawrence was required to send one representative. Prue's incredulous wail cut the reading of the letter short.

'*Buckingham Palace*? I don't believe it . . .'

'Obviously the fairest thing would be to draw lots,' said Mrs Lawrence. Prue's moment of dazzling anticipation collapsed.

'Of course,' she said, 'that would be the only fair thing.'

There was a moment's silence. Stella and Ag glanced at each other, looked at Prue's face, twisted by a mixture of feelings.

'I don't know about Stella,' said Ag, 'but I'd be happy not to go. I've been to London often and I don't like it. The outside of Buckingham Palace is good enough for me.'

'Same here,' agreed Stella, a moment later. She had no desire for a single afternoon away from Joe.

'So why doesn't . . . ?' Ag waved a hand towards Prue. 'There doesn't need to be a vote. I think it's a unanimous decision.'

'Are you sure?' Mrs Lawrence looked anxiously from Ag to Stella.

Both girls nodded. Prue let out another, exalted wail. She ran to hug and kiss each one of them in turn, leaving pink lipstick on their cheeks, and showering them with incoherent thanks for being the most generous, kind, and wonderful friends she had ever known.

Prue needed time to herself, of course, to think about the vital matter of what to wear. That afternoon, a half-day, she wandered off to the woods to marvel at the dog violets and cow parsley and stretches of bluebells, and to find inspiration about what colour and material, and who would make it and where . . . But, for once, she found difficulty in concentrating on the subject of clothes. Her excitement at the prospect of the far-off date at Buckingham Palace had made her more jittery than she would ever admit to the others. She sat down under a tree, struggled between thoughts of *pink* or, more original, *yellow*. She jumped up again, began to wander waist-high among the cow parsley, listening to a crowd of birds doing their nut, bursting their lungs. Restlessness increasing, she began to break off stems of cow parsley with the idea of putting a great jug of the stuff on the kitchen table – beating Ag at her own game – to give Mrs Lawrence the surprise of her life. Then, she came upon an intense patch of bluebells: spreading, they were, as far as she could see, a blue that no paint box on earth can contain, a blue that took her breath away. Prue stood still, marvelling. Then it came to her: *artificial silk this very colour*. Surely, somewhere, she could find it, if it meant searching half Dorset. Thrilled by her idea, she knelt on the ground, began to pluck fast at the flowers, amazed to find that some of the long stalks slipped easily from the ground, a shining purple-green, untouched by the earth they had come from. She would add these to the jug: they'd all think she'd gone potty, but she didn't care. She'd defy any of them to disagree with bluebell artificial silk . . .

Some time later, Prue walked back down the path, sheaves of flowers in both arms, their shadows speckling her shirt. A high afternoon sun needled through the trees: Prue was conscious of being warm, of being just right. This spring business, she thought for the hundredth time, was incredible. What she wouldn't give to have her mum here to see it: brighten the salon up a lot, a jug of blue-bells.

At the end of the path she could see the opening between two ash trees, where a gate led to the lane. The opening was a jagged, blazing patch of light. Prue quick-ened her step, looking forward to sun, unhindered by leaf and branch, on her bare arms.

Then she saw it. Across the patch of light cycled the ghost of Barry.

Prue screamed, and ran.

She did not turn back into the woods, but ran *towards* the apparition. Made for the gate. In her terror, she knew only that she must reach the lane, get back to the farm-house. Should the ghost enter the wood, face her there, among the shadows, she would pass out with fear.

She scrambled over the gate, shaking, dropping blue-bells on each side. As she turned towards the farm, she saw it again. The ghost was now straddling the bike, black boots firmly on the ground, hands kneading the handlebars, for-age cap tilted to one side, just as Barry always wore his. The sun dazzled Prue's eyes, confusing: but quickly she saw that this was no spectre. She screamed again, clutching at her heart and dropping the rest of the flowers.

'Lord, I'm sorry if I gave you a fright,' said the man, grinning. 'I'm looking for Prudence.'

'Who are you?' Prue felt foolish in her breathlessness. 'I could have sworn it was Barry, come back to haunt me.'

'I'm his friend, Jamie Morton. I came to say thank you for your letters, and I thought it was time we met. Talked about Barry, you know.'

Prue studied Barry's friend with curious eyes. By now used to the light, she could see that the likeness was superficial: this Jamie figure was larger, clumsier, with high-coloured cheeks and brown eyes. Only the short blond hair, scarcely visible under the cap, was the same. He had a friendly grin: rather sweet, she thought.

'Goodness: you didn't half scare me!'

'Sorry. Cigarette?' He took a packet of Players from his pocket. 'Someone down in the farmyard told me I might find you up here. Big man.'

'Joe.'

They both inhaled. Smoke, sharp-edged, trailed into the air. Its smell mingled with the scent of bluebells that were strewn at Prue's feet.

'Quite a ride, I must say.'

Jamie's eyes travelled up and down Prue like a blowlamp, appraising. She dabbed at her bow, the red spots, by chance: always Barry's favourite. She put a hand on one hip, smiled just enough to power the dimples.

'Want to come up to the farmhouse for a cup of tea, or what? Before you go back. I'm sure Mrs Lawrence wouldn't mind. Barry sometimes came in.'

Jamie looked at his watch. 'Thanks, but I mustn't. I'll be late if I don't go now. Took some time finding you.' The grin again: nice, fat teeth. 'We could make another time, if you'd like that. I could come another afternoon. Or we could meet in Blandford: cup of tea or a drink.'

Prue narrowed her eyes, made a great show of deep thinking. 'Personally,' she said, 'I wouldn't want to miss a moment of this fine weather in a tea-shop. It's my first spring in the country: could well be my last. Why don't we meet right here, this time next week? Two o'clock?'

'Fine by me.' Jamie swung a leg over the bike, turned it.

'I'll walk back up the road with you,' said Prue.

'What about all those flowers you dropped?'

Prue shrugged. The surprise jug for Mrs Lawrence had lost some of its importance. 'I'll come back later: don't want to hold you up.' Her heart was still beating fast, but no longer from fear.

With the coming of the fine weather, Ag and Stella, too, chose to spend their half-days quietly at the farm, reading, sleeping, walking. With the increase of work – harrowing, sowing, rolling, couching – they had little energy, in their scant time off, for taking the erratic bus to shops of little attraction. Most half-days, now, they chose to go their own ways, each feeling the need for a few hours of solitude in the busy week.

On the afternoon that Jamie had made his ghostly introduction to Prue, Ag made her way to the orchard with a rug and a book. It was her favourite place. Each tree was by now familiar to her, having spent so many hours picking fruit. She had sprayed almost every branch, laid potash round the roots. Now, they were in full blossom, the part of the cycle she had not seen last year. Ag spread the rug on the ground. She lay down. Her back ached badly. Last week, the automatic potato-planter had broken down. For two days, while it was being repaired, they had had to plant by hand. Bent over the furrows for hours on end, placing the potatoes at regular intervals – the view nothing but earth, earth – was the most physically exhausting task any of them had encountered since their arrival. Ag's back still had not recovered, still felt as if the muscles were pulled taut as Victorian lacing. She lay flat, feeling the relief of solid ground beneath her. The rug smelt musty. Above her was an arcade of blossom, and beyond it the wider arcade of clear blue sky. It would be easy to sleep, she thought, one hand on her books. Perchance to dream. Where was Desmond, now?

Stella, her ears always attuned to Joe's plans these days, had discovered that he was to drive to a farm some miles away to inspect a tractor which Mr Lawrence wanted to buy. To turn the farm over to arable land fast and as efficiently as possible, more machinery was essential. Stella calculated that Joe would be returning from his inspection at about three o'clock. She would therefore take a short walk – she, too, was suffering from a strained back – ending at Lower Pasture, where the cows were spending their last few days. She would sit on the gate, enjoying the sun. Joe would drive along the lane, see her. Stop, perhaps, for a few inconsequential words about the tractor or the cows. Oh, how devious is love, she thought.

Her wait turned out to be a long one, but Stella did not mind. She sat listening to birds, busy in the thorn hedge. A drowsy bee flew back and forth, indeterminate, as if waiting for some outer force to decide on its next action. The cows, gathered in the far corner of the field not far from the only rick of last year's hay, were lying down. Unsympathetic creatures, really, thought Stella. She enjoyed milking them, but felt no affection for them. Their sameness was dull. Cows, she thought, could never compare with horses (she was very fond of the surly Noble) or even pigs: Sly's eccentricity had great charm. No: she wouldn't miss the cows – only the sight of them, the personification of peace in a green field.

Stella looked at her watch. A Red Admiral flew past her, further confusing the bee. She did not care how long she waited in the warm silence of the afternoon.

Then, from nowhere, came a horrendous scream of machinery: the silence, suddenly split, seemed itself to scream in agony as a hideous black plane scorched across the sky. As Stella fell from the gate, holding her ears, she

327

saw a cluster of small silver incendiary bombs dropping from the plane's belly. By the time they had hit the ground, the plane was out of sight. Its terrible noise lingered, reverberated in its wake. The grass flattened, cowered.

Stella listened to the blistering noise as the bombs landed. Magnesium flames immediately spurted up, a terrible beauty in their many colours. The rick was on fire. She saw the sleepy cows leap wildly to their feet with one mass shudder, like the shaking out of a black and white rug. Their bellows joined the fading sound of the plane. Tails lifted stiffly in the air, they began to gallop about, panicking.

In the split second that all this happened, only one thought persisted in the numbness of Stella's mind: she must get the cows out of the field fast. They kept charging back to the rick, higher flames lapping at its base, now, and where one of their number lay, struggling on her side, stiff-legged, bleeding, roaring. There was no time to run for help. Stella had to act now.

As she was about to race across to the gate that led to the next-door clover field, she heard a squeal of wheels, saw the Wolseley rocking from side to side like a mad thing, and pull up with a great jerk. Joe was beside her, assessing the scene in a moment.

'I'll ring for the fire engine, be right back,' he said. 'Try to get them into the clover. Careful: they're hysterical.'

He was gone.

Stella, even in the panic of the moment, was pleased to think her idea was the same as Joe's.

She contemplated running round the edge of the field: in the shadow of the hedge she would be less conspicuous. But no: that would take too long. She set off straight across the field.

Immediately, two of the cows swerved towards her, heads down, ridiculous tails in the air. They followed her, screaming. Stella took a chance: she spun round, facing them, flapping wildly with white-shirted arms, shouting at them. Surprise penetrated their maddened state. They arced away, tipping sideways like clumsy boats in a wind. Stella registered a flash of wide black nostrils, four surprised eyes, before they careered off to join the rest of the herd, still bucking perilously close to the rick.

No cows followed Stella for the rest of her run to the gate. She struggled with it, back muscles an agony of protest, pushed it open: she had no idea whether all this had taken seconds or minutes. By chance, within feet of the gate, she saw a long stick, the kind Joe always broke off for himself when walking the land. She picked it up, turned.

By now she could see the rick was one dense mass of high flame. From it a shimmer of heat radiated among the jumping animals. They appeared to be a mirage of shattered glass, black and white skins flashing with sun and flames. Somewhere very near the flames Stella could see the figure of Ag, stick in hand, calling the cows' names in a calm voice.

As Stella ran across to join Ag, she saw that Prue had appeared from somewhere, too. And Ratty, hunched and excited, was shouting inaudible instructions from the gate by the lane.

When they reached the cows from their different directions, Stella and Prue slowed to a walk. They could feel on their faces the intense heat from the flames. They could smell the sour smell of the alarmed cows' excrement: shit-scared, Stella said to herself. They shimmered in each other's vision.

'Let's try to get behind them,' Ag called. She was scarlet in the face, but firm of voice.

The three girls, backs to the rick, waving their sticks and shouting encouragement, began to urge the cows towards the gate Stella had opened into the clover. They moved behind the animals towards the centre of the field, trying to avert their eyes from the bespattered corpse, black and white pieces fallen apart and gushing blood: Nancy, the old cow who was to have stayed.

Glad of any form of direction, the cows allowed themselves to be herded towards the opening. Every few moments one of them, in renewed panic, would spurt from the crowd, veer back towards the flames, and had to be chased by whoever was nearest.

The process of persuading the frightened but tiring cows towards the gate seemed endless. Ratty, shaking his stick from his safe distance, shouted more feebly. The girls were drenched in sweat, their faces red, hair sticky and flecked with ash. The cows, too, were dark with sweat. Slime ran from their nostrils. Their breath was hot, damp. Their wailing was a pitiful sound that echoed round the field.

At last they were all through the gate. They charged away through the long grass: relief in their antics, now. Their bellows petered out. Quiet returned over the landscape, but for the dull roar of the flaming rick.

'Christ,' said Prue, 'nothing but a bomb could've stopped my thoughts in their tracks.'

Ag and Stella were too exhausted, and concerned about the raging fire, to ask what she meant. They walked back slowly towards the rick – useless to hurry. A slight breeze cooled their faces.

Joe reappeared. He and Ratty swung open wide the gate on to the lane, ready for the fire engine. Then Joe hurried towards them.

'They'll be too late,' he said.

The rick was by now a fragile skeleton, pale among the crackling flames breaking off in large lumps that then burned on the ground. The heat was so great they could not stand too near. Ag thought of the autumn bonfire at the end of her first day's hedging: the crowd of them at ease around the small flames in a cool evening. This fire was so different in its savagery. Stella observed Joe's impenetrable face. She felt better now he was with them. Prue, now danger to the cows had passed, allowed herself the thought that *flame* red might be a possible alternative to bluebell blue . . . Scorning herself for such frivolity, it occurred to her this was the most dreadful, but most exciting, event she had ever witnessed. It would jolt them all out of any complacency about the war not touching their rural lives. Mr Lawrence, his wife not far behind him, was hurrying across to join the fire's spectators. Each carried pitchforks and rakes.

Joe was right. By the time they heard the pathetic little bell of the fire engine rattling along the lane, the rick was no more than a black smouldering mound. Ratty, still in his position at the gate to the lane, waved in the fire engine with a gesture of great impatience, dignified in its superfluity. The scarlet machine lumbered across the field, bell still ringing. It reminded Stella of fire engines in children's stories.

There was little the four firemen could do but hose down the scorched black earth with their limited supply of water. Wisps of smoke rose up from the bald patch and there was an acrid, powdery smell.

'Bastards,' said Mr Lawrence. 'Probably returning from bombing somewhere in the west, dropping their stuff on the way home for the hell of it.'

'Could have been worse,' said his wife. 'Could have been the house.'

'Your mother and I'll help rake this over: I'd like you to check the cows, Joe.' Mr Lawrence turned towards the lane. Ratty was still at the gate, still waving his stick. 'And I'd be grateful if two of you girls would escort Ratty back home. By the looks of things, he needs calming down.'

Ag and Prue immediately hurried towards Ratty. Stella offered to help Joe.

They crossed the field swiftly, in silence, climbed the gate into the clover. Hidden from sight by the thickness of the thorn hedge, Joe grabbed Stella's hand. With one accord they fell into each other's arms. Joe's chin rested on the top of Stella's head. Her hair smelt of smoke.

'You all right?'

'Fine.'

'I was so terrified that you . . . all I cared about was your safety . . .'

Joe pushed Stella slightly back from him so he could see her face. It was as black-streaked as he imagined was his own. They stared at each other with the kind of wonder that comes from acknowledgement, at last, of something long concealed.

'You must surely have known,' said Joe. 'You must surely have had your suspicions . . . I've tried so hard not to let you see. But you seem not to mind?'

Stella shook her head. Away from the heat, the sweat dried, she was suddenly, gloriously cold.

'That's good, because I'm going to kiss you, very briefly, very quickly, to show you that I love you, that I've been loving you to madness ever since Boxing Night.'

Their kiss was as brief as he promised. From the other side of the hedge they could hear miniature voices, the fire engine roaring its motor.

'We must check the animals.'

'Yes.'

'No time to talk. Don't let's try to talk – there's the whole summer to talk . . .'

'. . . the whole summer to talk.'

Stella heard, from a long way off, her own delirious echo. They parted to walk through the clover grass, sweet-smelling and full of bees. The cows were calm now, but wary-eyed.

'I see this as a beginning,' Joe said.

Edith was waiting for Ratty at her garden gate. Once again she had taken the precaution of putting on her own gas mask, and had brought Ratty's with her so that he might benefit from its protection on the journey up the garden path.

When she saw he was escorted by two land girls she sniffed, inconveniently steaming up the window of her mask. But it was not the occasion for the full force of her indignation. Rather, here was a good chance to show how right she had been. She took off the mask.

'What did I tell you, Ratty Tyler? War's all about us now. Thought the bombs might have got you.'

In truth she had thought no such thing. Terrified by the screech of the plane and the shaking walls of the cottage, she had hurried upstairs and lain under the bed, choked by dust and fluff that had accumulated untouched for years.

'That they didn't,' said Ratty.

He hadn't enjoyed an afternoon so much for ages. Once the bloody noise of the enemy plane had died down . . . all the excitement of the fire, the cows leaping about as if the devil himself had got into them, lovely sight of the girls running about waving sticks, then showing the fire engine where to go . . . No wonder his old ticker was pitter-pattering a bit. But then the holy one and the floozie, bless their hearts, had come and given him an arm up the lane. He had privately leaned harder on the holy one than he had on the floozie, was able to smell her sweet sweat among the smoky smell. And here he was, able to pay back Edith's horrible fright with a trick of his own: stop her in her tracks, it would, to see him on the arms of two pretty girls. Though, of course, he'd pay for it later. Last pan out of the window again, no doubt, but worth it.

'Well, we must be going,' said the holy one, so gentle, all smiles.

'Take care, Ratty.' The floozie gave him a kiss on the cheek, bless her heart, must have been reading his thoughts. Ratty had the pleasure of watching his wife's face contort with disbelief.

333

'None of that now,' was all she managed. 'Come along, Ratty . . . your tea's on.'

A lie, of course, showing off to the girls. His tea was never on. Edith handed him a gas mask.

'I'm not putting that thing on, not for anyone,' he chuckled. He winked at the girls, not unnoticed by Edith.

They turned away, waved. Ratty, leaning on his stick, watched till they were out of sight, impervious to his wife's calling. He chuckled to himself. Best afternoon for as long as he could remember, that's what he thought.

When they had left Ratty, Prue and Ag felt in need of a walk before returning to the farmhouse. They took a long way round through fields far from the burnt-out rick, and met Stella coming up the lane. Ag felt a slight shakiness in her limbs – the memory of Nancy's stiff corpse with its burst tongue would not leave her mind. Prue twittered on about having seen a ghost of Barry that turned out to be his friend. Ag was not fully concentrating on the story. But Stella, striding towards them, Ag noticed, was calm as ever: the only one who looked as if the events of the afternoon had cast no traumas.

Stella herself, a yard or so from the others, saw intuition in Ag's eye. Ag never missed a thing.

'Cows all right?' Ag asked.

'They seemed to have settled down. No injuries.'

'Poor old Nancy,' said Prue.

The girls linked arms, marched towards the farm in step. It was something they had never done before, something it would not normally have occurred to them to do. They laughed at their own silliness. They sang. Their relief flowed tangibly between them. Their fierce closeness was apparent to all three, comforting, binding: it had been growing over the months, and the evening of the bomb it was silently acknowledged.

*

334

Joe and his father took several hours to bury the dead cow. Joe dug the deep grave – the ground was hard and dry – with the energy of three men. It was twilight by the time they finished. Walking back up the lane, spades in hand, they heard the first nightingale of the year.

'Don't know what he's celebrating,' said Mr Lawrence, whose gaunt face was grey with fatigue.

Supper was waiting for them in the oven. They quickly ate it in the kitchen, then joined the others to listen to the nine o'clock news. There had been an unusual daytime raid on Exeter: about fifty bombers.

'Lawks,' said Prue, 'they're coming closer.'

She was right. A few days later there were attacks on Bath two nights running. The Nazi destruction of Baedeker towns had begun. A new feeling of unease, which even the hardest physical work could not quite obscure, affected everyone at Hallows Farm.

With one accord, and with great difficulty, Stella and Joe continued to act in public as they always had. They avoided glances, they avoided working together more than usual. Joe continued to share his time in the fields equally with all three girls. The day the cows were taken away in two lorries, he allowed Prue to cry on his shoulder. Ag and he would still spend an occasional evening in his room for 'tutorials'. But the thing that he found hardest to conceal was the extraordinary energy that had come upon him. He worked harder, for longer hours, than he could ever remember. Strangely, he suffered no attacks of asthma, usual in early summer, and never felt tired.

But a profound charge between two people is impossible to conceal completely from a beady eye. To the keen observer, a couple attempting to disguise their state surrender many clues. There's the over-careless tone of voice when addressing the loved one, glances slanting away just not fast enough to escape notice, dozens of small coincidences that result in proximity. Ag was aware of all these things. In one of their rare private moments Stella and Joe agreed Ag must know something, though her own suspicions were also carefully disguised; and they did not care. Indeed, it was a rewarding thought that someone else shared their secret: though they themselves, beyond their certainty, knew little of what that secret constituted.

So few and brief were their moments alone that there was no time to talk, to analyse, to make declarations, to try to explain to each other the mystery of what had happened. All they could do was acknowledge the crystallising of their feelings in broken, inadequate words, marvel at the existence of one another each day – 'waking alert with wonder every morning', as Joe said. They kissed, sometimes, very gently, for fear of conflagration. Strangely, they found themselves possessed of a great calm when it came to physical embrace: as if they knew there was time.

One day in early June, Mr Lawrence set Stella the task of rolling a field of young wheat. It would be a long day, he said, but if she kept at it she might finish by the evening. Mrs Lawrence suggested that, to save time, she would send someone down with a basket of food and a thermos for lunch. Stella, who had become almost as expert at ploughing as Prue, looked forward to the day – hours in the field alone with her thoughts.

Despite the departure of the cows, and no milking, the girls continued to get up at five every morning. It had become a habit, and as the weather grew hotter they were glad to start work in the cool of the early morning. Stella and Prue were usually assigned to some job on the tractors. Mr Lawrence had bought a fine second-hand machine, an International. Ag discovered the knack of harrowing with Noble: she enjoyed her days tramping up and down, hands firmly guiding the ungainly machinery behind the patient horse.

It was still misty when Stella skilfully swung the tractor, trailing the roller, through the gate of the wheat field. The sky was a dull silver, gravid with more light than the human eye could discern, but proving its existence by making the emerald spokes of the young wheat shine. Stella looked up, warily. She no longer trusted clear, silent skies. She turned off the engine to plan her route. The cry of an early peewit came from the adjacent clover field. There was a powerful smell of clover (a single flower would, for the rest of her life, bring back that afternoon of the bombs, she knew), and hawthorn, and dew. Then, as she restarted the engine, these scents were joined by a strong whiff of paraffin.

The job of rolling was easy in comparison to that of ploughing a straight furrow. All the same, it required a certain concentration to make sure not a single green shoot went unpressed. The hours sped, as random thoughts of Joe danced in the landscape: the sky paled to a colourless sheen, and by mid-morning a brilliant sun was warming Stella's bare arms.

Just as she was beginning to feel hungry – love, she had found, had increased rather than diminished her appetite – she saw Joe climbing over the gate, carrying a basket. She was surprised. She had expected one of the girls, or Mrs Lawrence herself, who, trapped in the house for so many hours, had a particular fondness for picnics. With the coming of the warm weather, she often made an excuse to take sandwiches to the girls in the fields, where she would join them for an hour on a rug under a hedge.

Joe waved, began to walk round the edge of the crop to the part of the hedge where Stella aimed to stop.

He helped her down from the tractor. She was stiff, sweating: dungarees were not much less hot than breeches. They sat under a single may tree, in the shadow of its pale crust of flowers. Joe unpacked the basket, spread out egg sandwiches, radishes, young lettuce and strawberries from the kitchen garden, a thermos of strong sweet tea.

'Mother, in all her innocence, said as I was the least busy I should be the one to come. She even apologised!'

Stella laughed. 'What are the others doing?'

'Prue's discovered a natural affinity for the mechanical potato planter. She's roaring up and down West Field, planting at the rate of knots. Any luck, there'll be no more sowing by hand. Your back better?' He put a hand on her shoulder blade for no more than a second. Stella nodded. 'Ag's got a hard job harrowing: lot of stone. But she seems to enjoy it, all the walking. Dad's gone off to fetch a load of clover seed. That's got to be planted among the young corn –'

'– to come up later,' said Stella.

'You're learning. You're not doing a bad job, either, by the looks of it.' He glanced round the field. 'A third done, I should say. You could be finished by seven.'

'What I can't understand,' said Stella, lying back in the long grass, head on her arm, 'is the whole *point* of rolling. Why aren't the shoots damaged?'

'Rolling firms up the earth, giving them more support to grow from. They're so feeble, so malleable, at this stage, they just rise up again soon after the roller's passed.'

'I've noticed that.' Stella yawned, longing to sleep. 'I think I'd rather enjoy learning more about farming.' She screwed up her eyes against the pinpoints of sun that crinkled through the may.

'I never intended to follow the family footsteps. I suppose I shall have to, now. Still, it's not without its interests. I won't mind that much.'

'Yorkshire?'

'Yorkshire.'

'With Janet?'

'*No.*'

'What?' Stella sat up, faced him.

He sucked at a long stem of wiry grass.

'I'm not going to marry Janet. How could I, now? It

would be a travesty. How could I marry Janet now there's you, there's us? *He is no wise man who will quit a certainty for an uncertainty.* Dr Johnson.'

Stella smiled, her mind a turmoil. They were silent for a while. Then Joe took her hand.

'Are you going to marry Philip?'

Deliberately, Stella gave herself no time to think. 'No,' she said. 'Of course not. For the same reasons as you're not going to marry Janet.'

The fluttering shadows, the brilliant haze of the young wheat behind them, the cloudless sky – all trembled, mirage-like, in Stella's eyes. Joe pulled her to him, kissed her, then lowered her head to the security of his chest, arms about her.

'*I know that love is begun by time,*' he said. 'See? I know my *Hamlet* as well as my Johnson.'

Stella laughed, pushing back the tears. 'Ag must be a good teacher.'

'Ag's a very good teacher. An original brain behind all that awkwardness.'

'I love Ag and Prue. And your parents.'

'I do, too.' Joe looked at her, half solemn. '*I love you*: that's the hardest line to say. Must be. For everyone, mustn't it?'

'I only said it politely to Philip – unconvincingly.'

'I hope this isn't unconvincing.' He kissed her hair. 'Stella? Did you hear? I said it to you. I shall go on saying it from this day forth, for the rest of our lives.'

'*Joe.* I must get back – I love you too – on the tractor.'

'Hear that? A peewit. I love you, I love you, I love you: three times. How about that?'

'I heard it this morning. God, I love you too. I keep saying thank you to God. He must be absolutely sure, by now, of my gratitude. How did it happen, Joe? How did it creep up on us?'

'Time. From the safety of mere friendship, just observing. Being near. Liking. Liking more and more. Then, one day, the transformation scene. The magic.'

'You saw first. I just kept on being puzzled by things: not understanding why I was put out if I hadn't seen you for half a day.'

Joe laughed. 'The intimations were all too easy to see. No: they're subtle as the traces of a rat's tail, to use Ratty language. Can so easily be missed by the untuned eye. When, I want to know, my Stella, was the precise moment, for you, that you realised . . . ?'

'I think . . .' Stella hesitated. 'It must have been when you held up the dead lamb, and skinned it.'

'Fastest skinning I've ever done.' Joe laughed again. 'I was showing off, of course.'

'Of course. And when, for you?'

'I was teetering on the edge during *They Can't Black Out the Moon*. When it came to *Falling in Love Again* – well, there was no further hope. Wings irreparably burned. It was like no experience I'd ever known. A kind of rebirth. I'm surprised you didn't notice my peculiar state on the way home. I was terrified of touching so much as the sleeve of your coat. And the funny thing was, of course, what you never knew, was that *you* were falling in love again, too. Only differently from all those false alarms before. *Properly*.'

Again they laughed.

'I only wish,' said Stella, 'we had more time to ourselves, more time to talk. I want to talk to you all day long.'

'We'll just have to wait for lucky chances, like this. Store everything.'

Stella, used by now to the warm smell of Joe's wind-dried cotton shirt, again longed to sleep.

'There's one thing we'll have to talk about, though.'

'I know.'

'What will we do . . . about them?'

'We have a valid reason for changing our minds. A real

reason. The war. If it hadn't been for the war, none of this would have happened.'

'No. True.'

'But there'll be time to talk further, to make our plans.' Joe clasped Stella more tightly. 'I'm terrified of touching you.'

'Me too. There'll be a time for all that.'

'God knows, I . . . But not here, at Hallows. Not the barn, or my bed, or Robert's cottage, or even the woods. Not with you.'

'No.'

'So we'll both wait – magnanimously.' Smiling, they stood up. 'I must go. A man's coming to see about buying all the stuff in the dairy. Christ, to think: if it hadn't been for the bombs we both might have kept our silence.'

'I wonder if that would have been possible? Heavens, I miss the cows. I didn't think I would, but I do already.'

'We'll have a new herd, one day,' said Joe. 'But Jerseys, not Friesians. I've never really liked Friesians.' He picked up the basket, rubbed the back of one hand over her cheek, strode away.

Stella returned to her seat on the tractor. The sun was almost too hot by now. She calculated the vast amount of unrolled field left to finish by evening, started the engine with wild heart, and dreaming eyes, and no doubts that she would have it done by the evening.

Harrowing the stony ground of the hill meadow was a tough job, and Ag liked it. It was a great deal more interesting, working with a horse, than was the endless couching which had been her lot of late. And she knew that soon after she had finished this field it would not be long before she must start thinking about the fruit on the plum trees, a job she looked forward to. If potato planting by hand was the most physically exhausting thing she had ever done, harrowing came a close second. The back was spared, but arms and legs were battered. To keep straight, and to keep continually encouraging Noble – who was inclined to slow to a very slack pace – required intense concentration. This concentration was a merciful antidote to the melancholy cast of her mind. Lately, the odd sense of her lack of obvious attraction, appeal, whatever, had returned to haunt her. While the constant flaunting of Prue's conquests caused Ag little more than an envious smile, the more serious state of Joe and Stella (so plain to a sharp eye, Ag could not believe the Lawrences had not observed it) accentuated her own bereft state.

While Stella rolled the wheat field in a state of high ecstasy, half a mile away Ag plodded behind Noble's bay buttocks, lashed rhythmically by his black tail as flies settled, fled, settled again. Half-way up the hill, the horse suddenly stopped. Ag called encouragement. He did not move. Ag went impatiently to his head. What could she do, stranded in a field a long way from the farm, with a horse that refused to move? She took hold of his bridle, tried to urge him forward. Noble yawned, baring grass-stained teeth. Flies flew from round his eyes. Ag tugged again. Noble tossed his head, but still would not budge.

Despairing, Ag looked at the ground ahead. Perhaps there was something that the horse wanted to avoid. She saw that there was.

Just two yards away, right in their path, was a plover's nest with a sitting hen bird. Ag gave Noble an apologetic pat, kept quite still. The bird shuffled slightly, its feathers glinting, its eye jolted by indecision about whether to flee or stay. Ag took the bridle again, guided the horse away from the nest, which they skirted round in a wide sweep. Pushed into this sensible solution, Noble moved eagerly.

Often, during the rest of the day, Ag glanced back at the plover and saw it still there, sometimes visited by its mate. While ruminating on the wisdom of letting broody birds lie undisturbed, some strange transference of thought wove into words what she saw as a signal: something to do with taking initiative, not letting a lifeless situation decay any further. *Doing something*.

Ag could never be quite sure at what point of that long, hot afternoon of the plover that she made her decision: the decision to take matters into her own hands, write to Desmond. There could be nothing untoward in a friendly letter. If there was no response – well, at least she would know where she was, and could give up the agony of hoping. It must be easier to accept nothing, she thought, than to toy with the endless possibility of something.

That evening, Ag began her letter. She wrote seventeen pages, carried away with her own descriptions of life at Hallows Farm. *Dear Desmond*, it began. *Yours, Agatha*, it ended. She posted it to his college in Cambridge.

Twelve

The fine weather continued. Haymaking began. Mrs
Lawrence had little time to join the others in the
fields. With just six months before the move, every
spare moment was spent with accounts books, calculations,
lists.

One afternoon in late June, she carried the basket of
washed sheets out to the line. It had been hot and sunny in
the morning. Now, the sky was overcast and a strong breeze
was blowing.

She began the job – which she seemed to have been
doing weekly for as long as she could remember – and
which, in fact, she found not without its pleasure. There
was peculiar satisfaction in the whiteness of the coarse cotton, the wholesome smell of the soap which would be
blown away by the wind and replaced with a scent of sun
and earth. How many sheets, she wondered, should she
take to Yorkshire? Should she reduce her linen cupboard,
sell as much of everything as possible? Lately, a dozen such
questions had besieged her mind each day.

There were six sheets on the line, now. In the increasing
breeze they billowed like low sails. Their flapping noise,
softer than canvas above waves, was more like the wings of
a flock of large birds. One of the sheets wrapped itself
round Mrs Lawrence. She felt its wetness through her
apron, her dress. It enveloped her like a ghostly cloak. She
stood there, a moment of sudden and unusual fatigue,

letting it do with her as it liked. Each side of her, companion sheets were now swollen huge with air, tugging at their pegs. Mrs Lawrence dreaded their falling to the ground. She had no energy to rehang them. While they cooed at her, the free sheet still twisted round her, making her suddenly cold. The solid mass of grey sky, she saw, had been blown into a feathering of small cloud, like the breast of a guinea fowl. The dogs were barking in the yard. Mrs Lawrence's misery was so acute that the familiar patch of garden in which she was imprisoned was contorted into a place she no longer recognised. She was aware only of a turmoil of blowing white all round her, agitated cloud above, the nagging of the breeze on her skin. She felt close to drowning.

Mr Lawrence, by chance returning to the farm for a new scythe, came round the corner to see his wife trapped in a sheet, the others blowing angrily on the line. He ran to her. Reaching her, he felt as if he was entering a surreal picture. Her misery reached out to him. He was alarmed by her face.

Quickly, he unwound her, took her icy hands. She leaned against him with so deep a sigh he could feel a shudder right through her thin body.

'I don't want to go, John,' she said.

'I know,' he said. 'None of us wants to go.'

For the first time Mr Lawrence could remember, his wife sobbed – briefly and quietly. He held her for a long time. They stood clasped together, waiting for her to recover, listening to the soughing of the sheets.

With the increased amount of physical labour, even Prue found herself more tired than before, and was forced to cut down her visits to Robert to two evenings a week. This caused her no great sorrow. Her earlier doubts had hardened into a definite *impasse* with Robert – the kind of *impasse* she often came to with a man of scant means.

345

Although her respect for him remained intact – there was something mysterious about him which continued to intrigue her – the affair had withered into an unexciting routine which Prue recognised as a signal to its end. Meantime, Jamie Morton was limbering up as a possible successor – though, as Prue explained to the others, it was only lack of choice that forced her to consider him at all.

Jamie dutifully cycled over to the farm several weeks running to meet Prue in the woods on her afternoon off. On closer acquaintance, Prue discovered that similarities with Barry were few. In fact, the only two things they had in common were the RAF, and heavy smoking. Unlike Barry, he did not like Woodbines: Players were what he preferred. He talked about cigarettes at some length. Sometimes Prue – an accommodating girl in some respects, she had switched to Players to please him – felt she could not bear another conversation about the relative merits of various brands, and stories about how many packets Jamie had smoked on various occasions.

Jamie's alternative line of conversation was hardly more endearing. He would describe to her the nature of his fantasies – such coarse dreams, it turned out, that even Prue was shocked. He did not, however, lay a hand upon her. Although she might have conceded, if the moment had come, Prue felt no great desire to be pummelled by the hefty red hands with their swollen fingers and bitten nails. There was a certain simple charm in his face – Prue still admired his teeth – and she had always fancied the blue of the RAF uniform. But to be quite honest, as she told the others, the weekly appointment to smoke in the woods with Jamie Morton was not the sort of thing that would keep her interest alive for long.

For once in her life, there were two things that preoccupied Prue's thoughts, that early summer, more than men. One was the departure of the sheep and lambs, the other was the invitation to Buckingham Palace.

When she was able to get a word in edgeways, she tried to tell Jamie about the day she had to spend helping Mr Lawrence go through the ewes' wool looking for maggots – he wanted to sell a clean flock. She had found some. The bugs had made red patches of sour raw flesh at the roots of the wool, which had to be treated. The little buggers, Mr Lawrence had said, could get right down into a sheep's bones, drive it mad. Prue had to give two bloody great tablets to each ewe. Persuading it to open its yellow teeth, and swallow the things, was one of the worst jobs she could remember, she said. All the same, she was fond of the sheep, and loved the lambs. When they were finally hustled aboard a convoy of vans, she sobbed her eyes out, she didn't mind admitting. She'd never heard such a noise in her life. The baaing and bleating would haunt her for years.

Jamie conveyed little interest in Prue's stories of the sheep. The invitation to meet their Majesties, though – that was another matter. While Prue described the difficulty she was having in finding bluebell artificial silk, and the picture in her mind of the King and Queen in their crowns on a golden throne, jewel-studded, Jamie puffed faster at his cigarette, inhaled deeply, blew beautiful smoke rings that flew high into the trees before they broke – a man full of wonder and awe.

'Good heavens, Prue,' he said, when her imagination finally ran out one afternoon in the woods, 'that'll be quite something. Not believable, really.' He stubbed the butt of his seventh Players into a patch of virgin moss. 'I've never shagged with a girl who's been to Buckingham Palace. Know that? Don't suppose any of my mates have, either.'

'Don't suppose they have,' said Prue.

Distracted by her thoughts of the Palace, more real to her than the present scene, Prue noticed Jamie had clamped one of his terracotta hands on her knee. She allowed it to stay there, just for a moment, before encouraging him to engage in the whole studied business of lighting the next cigarette.

The weeks of high summer passed with astonishing speed. There were long days of hay-making in hot sun. There was the cultivating, and spreading the sheep and cow dung left in the fields so that it should not sour small patches. To ensure the successful transformation of Hallows Farm into a good arable holding that would attract buyers in the autumn, the jobs seemed never-ending. Prue, to show her gratitude for the privilege of being the chosen one to go to the tea party, worked with extraordinary energy by day – by night, too, there was so much to be done in preparation. A week before the great event, she refused Robert any favours, saying she had to get her beauty sleep, do her finger nails, her toe nails, try out hair styles, choose her hat, generally pull out all stops so as not to let down the honour of the Women's Land Army at her meeting with their Majesties. Robert was understanding about everything except the toe nails.

And suddenly there she was on the platform of the station, a July morning, Mrs Poodle rounding up a herd of other land girls from the district. In their brightly coloured silks and crêpes, with rouged cheeks and waved hair, they jittered about, all shy smiles and nervous giggles.

Joe had paid Prue no compliments on the journey to the station: his silence was unnerving. But when he whispered to her, on the platform, before leaving, that she looked the best by far, Prue's confidence returned.

Glancing about, she could not but immodestly agree with him. But then, she had taken so much trouble: *weeks* of effort and consultation to achieve the final picture. Her dress, though not quite the bluebell she had in mind, was at least a dazzling blue, with a sweetheart neckline copied from her winter red, and a flirty skirt, though, God forbid, nothing that could possibly cause a frown from the King.

Her mum had dyed some old shoes an almost matching blue, and to cover her hay-scratched hands she wore a pair of white cotton gloves which Mrs Lawrence had kindly embroidered with small patches of forget-me-nots.

But the real inspiration was the hair. Having made a hat with a piece of the dress material, Prue had abandoned it at the dress rehearsal the night before and had replaced it with real cornflowers. She had run out into the warm night, frantically gathered cornflowers from tangled beds and long grass, preserved them in water by her bed. At dawn this morning she had, with Ag's help, pinned them randomly among her blonde curls, and prayed very hard that they would not wilt before five o'clock. And indeed the cornflowers were causing something of a stir. The other girls in their stiff and elderly hats admired Prue's great style. While they bobbed up and down practising their curt-sies, at Mrs Poodle's insistence, while waiting for the train, they paid Prue many a generous compliment. All the way to London in the train, warm bristly stuff of the seat prick-ling her thighs through the artificial silk, Prue basked modestly in their admiration. She could not remember a happier day.

Mrs Poodle had had the idea of taking the girls to the Albert Memorial for their picnic lunch. She thought they would enjoy sitting on the steps in the sun, beneath the gaze of the marble sages as well as Prince Albert, and then stroll in Kensington Gardens before returning to the coach that was to take them to the Palace.

Prue, who had not been to London before, was enchanted by the drive from the station. She had not expected to see so many trees, the lushness of Hyde Park, people lying on the grass impervious to the war or the pos-sibility of a raid. She saw only one devastated building: blackened stone, piles of still uncleared rubble, shreds of once private wallpaper exposed to the world. But nothing could detract from her excitement.

349

At the Albert Memorial, she sat on a step a little apart from the others. She wanted to be alone, to take it all in: if only Stella and Ag had been here – but still, she thought she would try to be a good reporter. She opened her paper bag of lunch, unwrapped the sandwiches from their greaseproof paper, then threw them to the sparrows. No chance of eating till she was *there*. Their Majesties would hardly be impressed by smudged lipstick.

The sun shone warmly down on Prue. The cornflowers, she checked, were still perky in her hair. She stood up, impatient – half an hour before they had to reboard the coach. She smoothed the creases from her skirt, wandered round the side of the Memorial. There, the ground had been turned into allotments. Amazed, Prue stood looking down upon a man who was bent over a row of peas supported by twigs. The sight of such country labour in the middle of London reminded her that Stella and Ag, at this very moment, would be working in the fields. She shut her eyes, imagining the afternoon at Hallows Farm, a place by now light years away, a dream . . . But no! This, surely, was the dream: Prue Lumley, land girl, in artificial silk on the steps of the Albert Memorial, about to be presented to the King and Queen.

Prue's imaginings of activities at the farm were not quite accurate. Stella and Joe were supposed to be cutting the clover field: Joe on the new International, Stella on the Fordson, with which she was now familiar. But the old machine, increasingly cantankerous, refused to start. Stella fiddled with the choke, topped it up with paraffin, finally banged the bonnet in exasperation, but to no avail. Eventually, not wishing to waste more time, she was forced to interrupt Joe, needing his help.

He solved the problem at once: dirty plugs. He removed them one by one, held them up, cleaned them on a piece of rag. The simple solution made Stella feel foolish.

'I didn't know about the plugs,' she said. 'I'm not sure I'd have known where to find them.'

'I haven't fallen in love with a mechanic, thank God,' said Joe.

It was hot in the barn. No breeze stirred the broody shadows. There was a smell of chaff and sacking. In the rafters, drowsy pigeons barely cooed. Outside, sun blazed down on the yard. Stella was glad of a time in the shade before facing the heat of the field.

'I've been thinking,' said Joe. 'I'm not going to say a word to Janet until you girls have left, just before we move to Yorkshire. Weighing up everything – it's a difficult decision to make – that would be the kindest thing. Postponing her anguish, perhaps: but I must tell her to her face.'

Stella, leaning up against the warm metal of a mudguard, watched him carefully.

'I think I should do the same. With Philip. Face him, too. Do you think they'll accept our reasons? Vicissitudes of the war?'

'They'll have to. It's the truth. Can't say I look forward to the announcement, though I don't suppose Janet will be altogether surprised. She must have some idea our so-called engagement is a ghastly mistake. Poor girl: she doesn't have much in her life. Sparking plug tester –' he held up the last clean plug – 'little hope of promotion. I presume she's calculated that marrying the wrong person is better than not marrying at all. I'll have to persuade her she's mistaken.'

'Philip, I think,' said Stella, 'will be very shocked. Devastated. He's no idea of my change of heart. He won't believe it. His pride . . .'

'Christ! We're going to be making a bit of a bloody mess,' said Joe, wiping the sweat from his face, 'but I think our plan is the best one. We'll only be postponing the evil day – for them – by a few months. As for us . . . I've been thinking. It wouldn't be easy, your coming with us to

351

Yorkshire as a land girl, my having broken off with Janet. My parents . . .'

'I realise that. I thought I could join my mother driving ambulances in London. In my spare time, go back to the piano. But at the end of the war, there's no reason why I shouldn't come to Yorkshire.'

'There's a small cottage belonging to the farm, up in the dales. Needs complete renovation. I've often imagined . . .' He climbed up into the driving seat, pushed the starter button. The engine growled into life. 'You'd like it there.' He climbed down again, gave Stella a hand. 'Tractor awaits you, my love.'

'Thank you! I'll know next time.'

'Any luck, this time next year, we'll be harvesting Yorkshire fields, and bloody Hitler'll be dead.'

Ag and Mrs Lawrence, at adjacent trees in the orchard, were thinning the near-ripe plums. There were several filled baskets on the ground. Ag enjoyed the job, as she did most jobs involving hedges, trees, fruit. She enjoyed the warmth of the sun on her bare arms. She enjoyed thinking, for the thousandth time, of Desmond reading her letter. It was – she could privately admit to herself – a work of such vivid description that it could hardly fail to give pleasure. And there were still two weeks in which she would carry on hoping for a reply. Beyond that, to presume the worst would be the only sensible thing. At that moment she would have to banish dreams, brace herself for a solitary future. But there were fourteen days before she might have to face that trauma, still a modicum of hope in the summer air. Her optimism among the branches, heavy with warm plums, was not in doubt.

'It was *in*credible. I still can't believe it. The red carpet. Honestly. A deep ruby red. *Acres* of it, all up these great wide stairs, all over this grand entrance hall. I mean, you could've carpeted Lower Pasture, easy, with all that red . . .'

Prue had the full attention of her audience. It was past ten at night, the darkness just light enough to see by, so the windows of the sitting-room were still open, the blackout had not been drawn. Scent from a few surviving tobacco plants came into the room, at odds with the heavy scent of Prue's *Nuits de Paris*, which she had been applying extravagantly to her wrists and neck all day. She was slumped on the sofa, artificial silk crumpled, cornflowers wilting in the curls, blue shoes slung off, dreamy-eyed.

'*So*. We go in, up these stairs, like walking on velvet. There's a huge crowd of us by now, from all over. More than three hundred. Mostly in reds and florals – no blues like this, I'm glad to say.' She patted the weary skirt. 'There's a bit of trouble, you can imagine, getting the counties into alphabetical order. Very smart men in tail coats bossing about, very politely. *Ooh*, and the footmen, just like in *Cinderella* . . . Anyway, at last we're in this great room, the Bow Room, overlooking the gardens. Pillars and so on. There's a band playing. My legs were aching to dance. Then the word sort of went round, despite the music, and suddenly there they were, coming in, *the Royal Family*. Me near them – *me*! King and Queen, two princesses. A path cleared for them. They walked down, smiling this way and that. The whole crowd of us went down in a wobbly curtsy, we were that nervous. Actually, I didn't wobble as much as some. And it was the first of about twenty-nine curtsies I did, I tell you. Every time I saw one of *them* nearby, down I went, just in case. Once, I found myself curtsying to a girl from Derbyshire – she got in my line of vision, didn't half laugh, vulgar bit. Anyway, you could see these gentlemen in charge taking up quite a few of the WLA bigwigs to meet the King and Queen. And some land girls. Not me, actually, though I gave them the nod, several times. *Equerries*, I think they're called. Still, I got very near. Especially to the princesses. They were walking about, almost ordinary. I couldn't believe it. Me, myself, within two feet of Princess Elizabeth in a lovely flowered dress.

'We were urged to help ourselves to tea. Tea! Bloody banquet, more like. These huge great long tables covered in white damask cloths so bright they dazzled your eyes. A thousand cups and saucers, plates and plates of tiny sandwiches. And lashings of chocolate cake: you couldn't taste the powdered egg at all. Perhaps they'd used real. I asked one of the footmen if they had a private supply of hens at the Palace, but he didn't answer, just smiled, too discreet to say. Anyway, best of all were the teapots: enormous great silver things with little silver strainers hanging to their spouts – such a sensible idea, I thought. Truth to tell, I drank my tea – I'll remember every sip of that royal tea – but had no appetite for the sandwiches. Just one bit of the chocolate cake, well, two bits – I thought: can't pass up an opportunity like that. I wanted to bring some back but couldn't think how . . . I took my plate over to the windows – tall as this house – to look out at the garden. Well, blow me down if it wasn't all made over to vegetables, neat beds of vegetables between little paths without a weed. I turned round to say something to anyone who happened to be near, mouth full of chocolate cake, when Princess Margaret, in glorious pink, passed not one foot from me. Her eyes! I tell you, I've never seen such eyes. She smiled at me. At least, I think she did. Course, mouth full of chocolate cake it was a bit awkward – just my luck. By the time I'd cleared my teeth, she was gone. Still, I curtsied, just for safety. Hoped she didn't think me unfriendly, but she caught me on the hop.

'I still can't quite believe it. I tell you, it was a dream. I only know it's true because I got chocolate cake on my gloves. I shall never wash them. Never, ever. For the rest of my life the royal chocolate will stay on my white gloves, proof it happened, proof I, Prue, once went to the Palace . . .'

Stopped only by overwhelming tiredness, further details of Prue's excursion came temporarily to an end that night. But next afternoon, at an assignation in the woods with Jamie Morton, she found no difficulty in retelling the story, refining here and there, guessing at the height of the magnificent ceilings, the yardage of silk curtain, the probable value of Her Majesty's diamond brooch, and her pearls the size of goose eggs.

Jamie was impressed. Prue could see that by the way his cigarette went unusually slowly to his mouth. The inhaling was shallow, the smoke rings careless. He had probably never listened to anyone so long, so quietly, so completely enrapt, reckoned Prue. When she at last finished her story he put one of his wedge-like hands on her shoulder, fixed her with an intensity of eye.

'By golly, Pruey,' he said, 'what a thing. Like I told you, I've never had a girl who's been to Buckingham Palace. Could be my only chance. What do you think?'

In the slipstream of her exhilarated state, generosity of spirit further warmed by her unique experience, Prue was happy to concede. While Flight-Lieutenant Morton prepared to ravish the first girl in his life who had brushed with royalty, Prue lay back on the mossy ground and thought of Buckingham Palace.

The morning came when the threshing machine was stripped of its tarpaulin and introduced to the girls. At first they were bemused by the complicated-looking monster, felt they would never understand the intricacies of so many belts, shaking trays and cunningly placed holes all designed to divide each sheaf into separate pieces. But Mr Lawrence was diligent in his explanations, and managed to leave them with a feeling of admiration for the ingenuities of the machine.

Two middle-aged men from the village came to help with the threshing. The machine took a whole morning to set up on an area of flat ground between two ricks. Work began early one hot afternoon. It turned out to be a job the girls unanimously hated.

The rattling and noisy throbbing of the machine quickly gave them all headaches, exacerbated by the uncomfortable goggles they had to wear to protect their eyes. High on the rick, pitching sheaves required more skill than they had imagined. Frustrated by their own clumsiness, hot, itching all over from chaff and dust that penetrated everything, the few days of hard threshing were an endurance test. But none of them gave up or complained.

Looking back, years later, on those hard days, Ag remembered only a single afternoon with any clarity. She was, as usual, on top of the rick – more skilled by now at cutting the string from sheaves and tossing them on to the man who would drop them into the drum. It was a particularly hot afternoon: the shirts of all three girls were dark with sweat, their bare arms a deep brown. The landscape shimmered in a heat haze, doubly blurred behind the goggles. At some moment, watching her own hands mechanically repeat their mind-dulling actions, Ag remembered that Desmond's time was up. No letter. No reply. Too many weeks for any possible excuse. Only thing to be done. *Forget*. Face a new kind of life.

Tears further confused her vision behind the goggles. But she smiled encouragement at Stella, who was clutching her ribs. She remembered allowing herself the sentimental thought that all hopes of Desmond were being shoved into the thresher, along with the sheaves, and, if she looked down the side of the machine, she would see them pouring out of the hole with the chaff: ground to dust, useless, gone.

By harvest-time, the customary peace at Hallows Farm was disturbed more frequently by passing planes: sometimes a Spitfire, sometimes the dreaded shape of the Luftwaffe monsters. Since the occasion of the incendiary bombs, the old, foolish sense of security in remote country was never quite recaptured. Living in anticipation of the next disaster became part of daily life.

But nothing stopped work on the harvest. It was safely gathered in, for the last time, by the Lawrences.

'There's something very satisfactory,' Ag observed to Prue, 'about seeing the barn filled again. Something very comforting, the annual storing of stocks for the winter.'

Prue giggled at Ag's solemnity. 'What I like the thought of,' she said, 'is all these new beds in here.' She looked round the stacks. 'Hope the new farmer's son and his girl-friend will have a good time.'

The harvest supper took place one warm evening, in the corner of the field where they had lit the bonfire last autumn. Rugs and tablecloths were spread over the stubble. A few sheaves of corn were left standing, leaning against each other in wigwam shapes – they were to be taken to church for the Harvest Festival service next day. Noble was employed to pull the cart that once was used to deliver the churns. It was filled with bowls of food, bottles of cider and beer, hunks of cheese and baskets of plums. Mrs Lawrence had been preparing the feast all day: the harvest supper was the occasion she most enjoyed during the year.

The harvesters gathered at seven – three Lawrences, the two helpers from the village, Robert, Ratty and the girls. It was a warm evening of long shadows. There had been no planes to disturb the peace that day: the quietness felt settled. There were smells of warm earth, and Mrs Lawrence's newly baked bread, unwrapped from its cloth. Poppies wavered in the hedgerow. A few survived in the stubble. The ravenous girls, chewing legs of cold roast chicken in their fingers, could not remember a happier occasion.

Each one had her particular reason. Ag had adapted to

her new life of no hope in Desmond. She had filled her mind with other concerns, made plans for the future, read herself to sleep each night, managing almost completely to obliterate the old yearnings. She had returned to enjoying the present – occasions like this supper – rather than leading a double life with an imaginary future forever there shadowing the actual moment. Her efforts had brought their rewards.

Stella, sitting as far as possible from Joe, cocooned in her ever-increasing certainty of their mutual love, wondered if the others could see the indivisible bond between them. Avoiding his eyes, she drank a whole beaker of cold cider, felt a gold rush through her limbs, and doubted if any girl on earth could be so fortunate.

Prue, corn dolly in her hair in honour of the harvest celebrations, took the opportunity to furnish the assembled audience with more details of her afternoon at the Palace, until they laughingly shouted her down. She didn't care: she didn't mind being teased. She felt lithe, fit, strong, and ravenous. Cutting herself a huge wedge of home-made pie, she longed to shock them all with the secret that made the adrenalin charge through her blood. What would they say if they knew she was servicing two men, concurrently? Robert two nights a week, Jamie Morton two afternoons? And there was no let-up in her work and energy, either. If anything, they seemed to have increased. With secret pride she stroked her bare brown legs – since the 'bare legs for patriotism' campaign in May, Prue had refused to wear stockings. She saw Ratty's eyes on her, and laughed.

'So where's Edith?' she asked him.

Ratty took a long time to finish a mouthful of bread and cheese. 'Coming later,' he said. 'With the tea. Usual custom.'

They sat eating, drinking, laughing for a couple of hours, watching the blue of the sky turn to the indigo of the shadows covering the stubble. Stella began to sing. Her Vera Lynn repertoire, songs that were on the wireless most nights.

> *We'll meet again*
> *Don't know where, don't know when . . .*

Ratty thought he had never heard so sweet a voice. Spurred by a mixture of beer and cider, he ventured to join in. The others did likewise. The chorus roamed from war song to war song, the pure voice leading them, till it was almost dark.

It was Stella – by chance she stood up to relieve a stiff leg – who first saw a figure standing dimly by the cart.

Ratty, facing Stella, stood up too, back to the figure. It was his turn, he reckoned.

'Let's have a hymn now, everyone. What d'you say to "Abide with me" to close the proceedings?' He spoke in his church voice, the one he used to guide rare visiting worshippers to their seats.

Ratty began to conduct with his hands, croaking voice leading them in the familiar words. Stella, watching the figure coming up behind him, saw that it was Edith. She wore a headscarf and a long skirt, an old woman from another age carrying a tin churn by its handle. Ah, thought Stella, she's bringing the tea.

In the speckled darkness, she saw a trembling hand unscrew the lid of the churn, let the lid fall to the ground.

> *When other helpers fail, and comforts flee,*
> *Help of the helpless, O abide with me!*

As the chorus gathered strength, Stella knew in an instinctive flash what was going to happen. In the second that Edith swung back the churn to gain the greatest possible thrust, Stella took a leap towards Ratty. She flung her arms round his knees so that his body was forced to flop over her shoulder. Carrying him in this fireman's hold, she jumped through picnic things and stretched legs, and ran as fast as she could. The confused Ratty's plea to his Lord to abide with him rose in throttled voice from somewhere near Stella's waist.

Thus Ratty was just saved from the gush of scalding tea that Edith flung at her husband. Thrown by the sudden departure of her target, Edith's aim went mercifully awry. The full blast of the liquid fell on to what remained of the food. Prue's bare legs were splashed. She gave a quick squeal of protest, then leapt up to join the general chaos.

In the muddle of semi-darkness, Ag, Mrs Lawrence and Joe found themselves trying to calm an hysterical Edith, who kicked and screamed on the ground. Her feet clanked against the empty churn as she arched her back, pushing off hands. A cluster of cuckoo spit whitened the corners of her mouth. Mr Lawrence shouted that he would telephone for the doctor, and ran off. The others, between them, managed finally to get Edith to her feet, and dragged her to the back of the cart. She sat writhing on the tailboard, a pathetic old figure, legs swinging loosely, stockings wrinkled round the ankles. Between her screams she muttered incoherently: some daft notion about Ratty and the land girls, Prue thought it was. But Edith's accusations were too confused to make sense of her trouble. Prue and Mrs Lawrence climbed into the cart beside her, clinging to her eel body. Ag walked, trying to make sure the old woman would not slip to the ground. Robert led Noble towards the farmhouse. The two men from the village followed, arms full of the picnic stuff. The procession made its way across the stubble lit by a white harvest moon. Edith never stopped screaming, attempting to escape. She was answered by the screech of a passing owl.

360

A harvest she'd never forget, thought Prue. She wondered if the story would make Jamie pause in his smoking.

Stella had landed Ratty back on his feet some fifty yards from the scene of chaos.

'What was all that about, then?' he asked, beer and cider still making merry in his brain. It was the first time he'd been alone with one of the land girls – with a moon and all, too. Not the sort of thing that happened every harvest.

'Edith's been taken ill. Don't worry. The others are looking after her.'

'Is that right?' Ratty sounded unconcerned. He looked up as Joe appeared out of the darkness. 'The wife?' he asked.

'Doctor's coming. Bit over-excited, she is, that's all. She's riding back to the house in the cart.'

'Is that so?' Ratty shook his head, gave a deep sigh. ' 'Course, there've been signs, haven't there? You could tell she was boiling up for something. These past months. Matter of waiting.'

'Stella and I will walk you home,' said Joe, taking the old man's arm.

'Very well.'

Ratty allowed himself to lean on the two of them just hard enough to be polite. But, considering the drama, he moved with sprightly step and head held high.

Much later that night, a heavily sedated Edith was driven away by the doctor and the district nurse. Ratty, asked if he would like to accompany them, said no he bloody wouldn't.

On the October day that the Eighth Army under Montgomery began a big offensive along the coast of El Alamein, at Hallows Farm there was a small celebration to mark the first anniversary of the girls' arrival. Mr Lawrence brought out the ginger wine, and said a few words of appreciation before proposing a toast. He wished them well, however their time might be spent when they left the farm. In particular, he said, he knew the others would want to join him in wishing Stella all the best in her marriage to Philip. In the general flurry of raised glasses and echoed hopes, he saw a look pass between his son and the blushing girl who had caused him some unnerving moments, in the past year, in his own heart. Not allowing himself time to reflect on what he had seen, he knew that, for Joe's sake, it was perhaps a good thing the girls' days were numbered. As for his own feelings: well, the internal unease had run its course, a shameful secret that would go with him to the grave. He could look easily on Stella now, knowing she was firmly committed to another. She had acted as a warning to him – a warning that the most stable of middle-aged men could be taunted by lascivious desire – and he had taken heed. Now, his energies must be concentrated on his wife, so courageous about the move she dreaded. He would support her to the best of his abilities, show his love and gratitude. He raised his glass, last of all, to her.

'And can we drink to Faith, my wife?' he said. 'Because had it not been for her, for her extraordinary insistence, no land girls would have come to Hallows Farm. We would not all be here today.'

It was Faith's turn to blush: a deep, muddy colour suffused her skin. She held up her pink glass, which flashed at her husband's dear face.

Prue, sensing but not understanding the public reaffirmation, was the first to break the tension of the moment. She stood up, jabbing as usual at her bow.

'Well, I'm going to take this opportunity to kiss *everyone*,' she said, 'before I cry. I trust you'll all do the same.'

Thus Prue, in her innocence, afforded Joe and Stella a

bonus chance, in public, to kiss each other quickly on the cheek.

Edith did not return, and Ratty could never remember so enjoyable an autumn. Within days of her departure he had restocked the kitchen with saucepans, and burned a dozen boxes of cut-up paper. For so many years he had longed to live alone. His solitude, won so late, he was now determined to relish to the full. For some weeks, padding about the house, he found it hard to believe Edith was not going to jump out at him in her gas mask or torture him in one of her sadistic, cunning ways. Not till the official letter arrived, confirming her insanity, did he finally realise that the new peace would be permanent. He could listen to Mr Churchill and *ITMA*, undisturbed: take his tea in by the wireless, spill crumbs on the floor, do as he wished in all respects – even smoke his pipe in bed – and never again be chided. As he said to the holy one in the orchard one afternoon – surrounded by baskets of plums, she was, all smiles – never had the autumn days gone by so fast.

It was a feeling shared by all three girls. Their time seemed to be running out with uncanny speed. It was now, more than in the summer when they were so busy in the fields, that they missed the cows, the sheep, Sly. They looked back with nostalgia to their bewildering start as land girls, just over a year ago. They remembered the mysteries of their early days, and laughed, thinking of the mistakes they made: how strange they had found the life which by now was so familiar. The weather they remembered on their arrival returned. The second time round of experiencing farmhouse and land in misted mornings, yellowing afternoons, frosted nights, was no less beguiling than it had been at first.

Once again, with the change of seasons, the pattern of life shifted in the house in the evenings. Instead of going their own ways, everyone gathered by the fire for an hour or so before going to bed. Mr Lawrence forced himself to make lists of farm implements that might be sold in the auction – the farm was to be put up for sale early in the New Year – while he listened to the wireless. Mrs Lawrence continued with her perennial darning, her needle only pausing at news of Montgomery breaking through Rommel's front, or the hideous rumours that the Nazis had been systematically rounding up Jews throughout Europe.

She was never able to quell her anxiety when the telephone rang, particularly after dark. When she heard it ringing in the hall, late one evening in early December, she put down her work with a beating heart and ran into the darkness. A minute later she reappeared.

'It's for you, Stella.'

Stella left the room. Philip, she knew, was in London for two nights – the much postponed trip with his friend. It was his intention to buy the ring. He had rung only a week ago, insistent that he was off to Bond Street in search of an aquamarine. Stella, who thought a Dear John letter was the coward's way out, had decided to stick to her intention of breaking off her engagement face to face. But there had been no opportunity. Guiltily, she hoped he was not telephoning with news of his find.

When Stella had not reappeared after ten minutes, Joe gave up his game of patience, rubbed his face, anxious. His own unease, he observed, was reflected by all those in the room. A long telephone conversation, at Hallows Farm, was far from a normal occurrence.

Stella came back at last. Pale-faced, her eyes swept dryly over each of them. She tossed back her head, spoke with the efficiency of one only just in control.

'That was Philip's mother,' she said. 'She was ringing to tell me Philip's in hospital. He's lost a leg: seems there's little hope of saving his second foot.'

'*Stella*!' said Joe.

Ag jumped up, put an arm round her friend.

'He was on leave in London, staying with his friend in Bermondsey. They had a day in the West End, apparently . . . Bond Street. They were on their way home. There was an air-raid warning: they were on a bus. It seems they couldn't get to a shelter in time.' She paused. 'Would you mind if I took the day off tomorrow, Mr Lawrence? I must go to London. The hospital. See him.'

'I'll take you to the early train, of course,' said Mr Lawrence.

'Sit down, Stella,' said his wife, leaving her own chair.

Joe quietly left the room.

The others did their best: Bournevita, an arm to guide Stella up the stairs, quiet listening faces in the attic, waiting for her to cry, to speak.

Stella thanked them, but said nothing. Before she got into bed she picked up the photograph of Philip that she had kissed with such passion every night, this time last year – and looked at it for a long time. Then she replaced it.

'He expected to be wounded in battle,' she said eventually. 'But to be made useless by a bomb in the street: how will he ever cope with that?'

'Poor, poor Philip,' said Prue, rummaging in her drawer for a black bow which she would wear tomorrow, just as she had for Barry.

The following day was interminable for Joe. Heavy rain, mud, cold. He busied himself sorting out farm machinery in the barn, but flinging heavily rusted iron into various piles was no antidote to his thoughts. Eventually, by late afternoon, dirty light out in the yard, he slumped on to a pile of new straw, tried to slow the thumpings of his heart and think clearly.

Mr Lawrence appeared. He quickly assessed the state of Joe's dejection.

'We're all worried for the poor girl,' he said, 'but Stella's got guts if anyone has. She'll stand by him, legs or no legs.' Joe met his father's eye. 'Look, son, I've got a mass of paperwork still this evening. Would you go to the station, fetch her?'

Joe looked at his watch. 'Tell you what,' he said. 'She might not be up to facing everyone at supper. Might be better if I suggested a sandwich and a stiff whisky at The Bells.'

'Good idea,' said Mr Lawrence.

Stella's train from London was half an hour late. Joe waited in the cold dark of the platform. When finally it steamed in, she was the only passenger to get off. They hugged each other silently, then walked hand in hand to the car park. They sat in the bucket seats of the Wolseley, rich with its smells of old leather and wet dog. There was no moon, dense darkness.

It was Joe who broke the silence. 'I know what you've had to decide,' he said.

He sensed her nod in the dark. 'Joe,' she said, 'you should have seen him.'

'I can imagine. I know what you must do, what *we* must do.'

'I don't know what else . . . I mean, ordinary life has finished for him. Pain, dependency. All the things he hoped for ripped away in a moment. Except me. He was very drugged, of course, but he said the only thing worth living for, now, was me. Us. Marriage. Then he said he'd be the first to understand if I couldn't go through with it, if I wanted my release.' She sighed. 'He was in so many bandages, mummy-like. I looked at his face and I thought: how could I have said to this man, who I don't know at all, or love, that I would marry him? A complete stranger. Just as I was leaving – I was only with him for half an hour, the nurse said he couldn't take any more – he said he'd bought

366

the ring. He said he wouldn't give it to me then, though: that would be tempting fate. But what was I going to do, he said? Somehow he needed to know the answer then. It would be his lifeline, or his death.'

'So?'

'So I said I'd stand by him.'

Joe, one arm round her taut body, moved to kiss away her silent tears. Then he cleared his throat, managed to find a vibrant voice.

'Listen, my love, you must be exhausted. I've said you won't want supper at home, I might take you for a drink at The Bells. Would you like that?'

'I'd rather stay here. Oh, my darling Joe,' she said.

'I love you,' he said. 'There's no new way to say it. I don't know if I can make you believe me, but I shall love you for ever, no matter whom we marry. Remember the certainty of my love. Always.'

'And mine,' she said.

They talked till the cold of dawn. On the journey back to the farm, the wheels of the car split frozen puddles, and early mists rose up from the land.

In their last two weeks at Hallows Farm, jobs began to run out. The girls spent the short dark days helping Mrs Lawrence sort out and pack up things in the house, and Mr Lawrence to do the same outside. Only Prue was grateful for an easing off of physical labour. Busy accommodating and consoling her two men as often as she could before leaving, she was exhausted but radiant. Ag's energies were spent in trying to keep up Mrs Lawrence's spirits. She produced many a reason to persuade her employer that life in Yorkshire could be as rewarding as in Dorset, and was pleased to see the occasional spark of anticipation breaking through the melancholy. Stella's low spirits were understood by everyone: none but Ag saw they were matched, beneath a normal surface, in Joe's heart. To the last, Joe and Stella managed to continue their normal behaviour. To the last, they liked to believe, no one had guessed their secret with its bitter ending.

Mr Lawrence had contemplated for some time how best to manage a swift departure. He was not one for drawn-out, emotional farewells, and to that end he made a plan. He would load the girls' luggage into the boot of the Wolseley while they ate their last breakfast, then make sure they were away fast.

It was a dreary morning, the day of their going: frosty cobwebs the only sparkle in the whitish gloom. The girls wore their coloured travelling suits, the ones that had so alarmed Mr Lawrence on their arrival, he remembered with a smile. Due to the cold, they pulled their WLA great-coats over their shoulders – Prue's had arrived just a week ago. Half-diamonds were sewn on their lapels.

Mr Lawrence hurried them out as soon as they had finished eating, no nonsense. Each girl hugged Mrs Lawrence quickly in the hall. Outside, they stood in a line waiting to see how Joe planned to conduct his farewells. He went up to each in turn, gripped her by the shoulders, kissed her lightly on each cheek. Stella was last. In this, the final part of the act, his behaviour to her could be no different.

Stella sat next to Mr Lawrence in the front of the car. Her natural place, somehow, he thought, after all he had gone through. His private triumph was to be at ease beside her.

Joe stood at the door, his arm round his mother's shoulder. She flapped a hand at some nearby bantams.

'Remember them, Ag?' asked Prue. She giggled. 'You were so bloody snooty just because I didn't know a bantam from a hen.'

'Sorry,' said Ag.

The Wolseley lurched away. Everyone waved.

Mr Lawrence slowed down as they reached Ratty's

cottage. He could see, in the mist, the old man standing at the gate. As they passed Ratty raised his cap, shook his fist in the air, thumb up. He'd meant to come down to the farm last night and say goodbye officially. But he hadn't much fancied a formal parting from the holy one – or the others, for that matter. Besides, with all the things there were to attend to in the cottage, in his new state of freedom, he liked to spend the evenings at home, marvelling at his solitude.

Epilogue

Stella's bed had been drawn up to the window. Propped up on her pillows, she had a good view of the dales outside, a distant farmhouse half-hidden by trees, the church tower. On the day she was supposed to be lunching with Prue and Ag in London, Janice brought her a little poached fish and purée of carrot on a tray. She tried to eat it – the doctor had said she must try to eat to keep up her strength – but she had no appetite. Instead, she watched the cows. Friesians.

Stella had had every intention of joining the others for the annual lunch. Her recent bad attack was over. For the last week she had been feeling better, getting up, pottering round the garden on warm days. The pain had faded. But last night the wretched business had returned, exhausting her. She had taken as many pills as she dared, thought she would be fine by morning. But she wasn't. When she put her legs on the floor, weakness and dizziness overcame her. Back under the sheets, bent in a certain way she had found eased the pain, she tried to will herself to be all right. They would be so disappointed. She was furious with herself. It was such a nuisance, this persistent bad health, this fading of energy and capacity. She hated being old.

An hour later, Stella knew there was no hope of making the journey. She rang the hotel, asked for a message to be taken to the others when they arrived in the restaurant. She hoped they would telephone her before they left.

At about the time Prue would doubtless be ordering a frivolous chocolate pudding, while Ag demanded English brie (she had become so fierce about all things British, in her old age), Stella laid aside her tray. Outside, the cows were halfway up the hill. Lying down, chewing the cud. She could never get used to them, these alien cows. They were very different from the old herd. She didn't know their names, of course. Didn't want to: they were nothing to do with her. Sometimes, in the gloaming, when one of them was lying stretched on its side, she would confuse it with Nancy's corpse after the incendiary bombs. Then it would jump up, but not be Nancy come to life, and Stella would turn her mind to something else.

She lay back, thought she might doze for a while. These days, there was little time to give much thought to the past. She had to conserve her energies for all that had to be organised now: Joe's moving in, the deciding which room should be his, which shed should be converted to a kennel for his dogs – quite a palaver, it would be, establishing everything to his liking.

But on the day of the annual reunion, so annoyingly missed, Stella fell to thinking about the whole spectrum of their lunches in the past: the charting of their lives over the last fifty years. She closed her eyes.

The first lunch was in 1946. Terrible food, but none of them minded, because there was so much news. Prue, in bright emerald, still wearing a matching bow, had hardly been able to contain herself. Even before the arrival of the tinned soup, she had told them about the second Barry she had recently met – Barry Two, as he became known ever after. According to Prue, a rare and wonderful man. Barry Two, at that time, owned a chain of bicycle shops, but had sights on bigger things. He was negotiating to buy a picture house on the outskirts of Leeds. Prue was convinced of his ambition, his potential, his drive. She believed one day he would own a whole chain of cinemas, and she was right. Ten years after the war, Barry Two could claim to be one of the richest men in the north. Today, he was a multimillionaire, and the gold taps, servants and cocktails Prue had dreamed of, as she ploughed, and had described to Stella from the dung heap, had been achieved long ago. Her only disappointment was no children. Still, Barry Two, a 'real ball of fire', but childlike in many ways, took up all Prue's time. She had adjusted to a childless household, bred spoilt poodles, and been happy for years.

Stella's own news, that year, was fascinating to Prue, who had never guessed a thing at the time. Less surprising to Ag, who admitted she had known all along.

She told them that she and Joe had written to each other every week since the departure from Hallows Farm, though they rarely met. When the war was over, they had taken the Wolseley, by now in the last stages of general corrosion, and had driven round the battered French countryside. They had found sun in the Pyrenees, small cafés that still managed to serve delicious coffee, home-made croissants and apricot jam.

Soon after their return, her marriage to Philip took place. She spent her honeymoon in Torquay.

Ag, that first lunch, told them she was at law school. Enjoying it. No, she was still without a boyfriend. The one who kept most in touch with the Lawrences, she and Mrs Lawrence maintained a regular correspondence. She had gone up to Yorkshire to help out for three months. Nothing like Dorset, she said.

They'd all met, of course, at Prue's wedding to Barry Two. Manchester. What Stella remembered best were the silver bells in Prue's hair. Reminded her of reindeer, which was just what Prue had intended, she said, being a winter wedding. Joe and Janet weren't there: Joe had written to Stella to say he couldn't face such a meeting – her and Philip, him and Janet. She agreed, naturally. It would have been difficult.

It was at Prue's wedding Mrs Lawrence made the suggestion that the girls should address her and Mr Lawrence by their Christian names. No such thing had ever happened at the farm, of course. Young girls did not then behave to their employers as they did today, assuming an unrequested intimacy Stella herself deplored. But by 1947, the wedding of Prue and Barry Two, Stella and Philip already married, the girls were grown up. It was appropriate they should now address the Lawrences as the friends they were, always would be. But Stella found it difficult. Faith and John: she had to remind herself, every time she wrote to them. Sometimes, on the rare occasions they met, she slipped back into the Mr and Mrs by mistake.

Stella shifted herself, uncomfortable. There was still an hour to go before she was allowed the next pill. Why hadn't Prue and Ag rung? How long did they intend to linger over their coffee? They must surely be wondering what was the matter, curious to know how she was. Stella shut her eyes again, restless.

Ratty . . . what had happened to Ratty? Oh, yes. Mrs Lawrence – Faith – had written to them soon after VE Day. Stella still had the letter somewhere. Ratty had had a heart attack bell-ringing for victory. He'd rushed to the church soon as he heard the news on the wireless, insisted on ringing, hours on end. They'd had quite a job, Mrs Lawrence said, freeing the rope from his hands. None of them could think of a better way for Ratty to go, she added. Indeed.

Edith? She never came out of the asylum, poor soul. Outlived Ratty by a decade.

The year of the first avocado – 1948? 1949? – she couldn't be quite sure – was a year she would never forget. Ag's turn for good news. She had re-met Desmond. One of those occasions of such chance that Ag found it hard not to believe in fate. She had gone to the wedding of a fellow law student at St Martin-in-the-Fields. Fearful of being late, she arrived much too early. It was raining. She slipped into the

National Portrait Gallery for shelter. Desmond was standing in front of Branwell Brontë's portrait of his sisters. They went for a cup of coffee. He had never received her seventeen-page letter. No wonder. Called up, he was fighting in France. But they made up for lost time, didn't they? Started seeing each other most days. Over the avocado, Ag talked of *certainty*. A few months later came invitations to Ag and Desmond's wedding. Not long after that, Ag began her long and successful career at the Bar.

The telephone rang at last.

'Hello? Ag?'

'It's Prue. I say, what's the matter, old thing?' The northern accent was still there.

'Awfully stupid, I'm so sorry. Can't get out of bed.'

'Rotten luck. Not at all the same without you. We're squashed into a little wooden room – you know, where they put telephones these days. No air. We can hardly breathe. Ag's fanning herself.' Prue giggled. 'Complaining about my *Nuits de Paris*, as usual.'

'Oh dear.'

'We're waiting for Joshua to come and pick up Ag, take her to the station. She says he drives much too fast, a real tearaway. I'm going to slip into Harvey Nichols myself, see if there's anything to wear. Then take the five fifteen back. I'll come and see you soon.'

'Lovely. Was it a good lunch?'

'Usual sort of thing. Chocolate mousse. We missed you. We missed you, Stella. Here, Ag wants to talk to you. Goodbye, darling.'

' 'Bye, Prue. Is that Ag? I'm so sorry – I . . . this wretched business.'

'Rotten luck, Stella. When you're feeling better, why not come and spend a few days with us? You know I can never get Desmond past the front gate, we've got a few farming troubles, the Friesians may have to go, but we'd love to have you. Devon air'd do you a power.'

374

'Probably.'

'Well, take care of yourself. I'll ring you from home.'

'Can't tell you how I wanted to be there.'

'Next year.'

'Next year. Definitely.'

' 'Bye, Stella.'

' 'Bye, Ag.'

Next year. Next year she would be the one with the best news. Joe would have moved in. They might even have legalised their arrangement. Stella smiled to herself, rubbed the finger on which she had worn a wedding ring until Philip died. Once she was free, she had thought it would be impolite to Joe to go on wearing it. Even though he was still unavailable. Ten years ago, was it, Philip's thrombosis? No: eleven in November. Expected, of course. How long after that was it that she sold the Surrey house, came here to Yorkshire? It was such a jumble, thinking back. She must have been here all of seven years. Just seventeen miles from Janet and Joe. Made meetings easier. Mrs Lawrence was put into the old people's home in 1968. For some reason, Stella remembered that very clearly. She died very soon after, before Stella managed to visit her. Ag was with her often, despite the long journeys from Devon. Prue sent boxes of expensive chocolates Mrs Lawrence could not eat. Mr Lawrence? About two years later, he died. In his sleep. Without his wife, he found no reason to live, he kept telling Joe.

Stella stretched for a digestive biscuit on a plate beside her bed. She broke off a small corner, crumbled it, put it to her mouth. Her lips were always dry, such a nuisance. Most of the lunches after the avocado one were taken up with domestic news. Children. Ag had four, two girls, two boys, all very clever. Only to be expected with Ag and Desmond as parents. Stella managed only two: James, very soon after she was married, and darling Euphemia – Effie. Prue was godmother to Effie and Ag's Henry. She was wonderful about not seeming to mind about no children for herself. Always took such an interest.

Then came the grandchildren. Ag had beaten her to it – she had seven. She herself had only four, so far. Must be getting on for tea-time. Dog barking downstairs. Racer barked regularly as clockwork when it was time to be fed. Stella hoped Janice wouldn't keep him waiting too long. She swivelled her eyes to the cluster of photographs above the fireplace. Philip: the photograph she used to keep by her bed in the attic room, hardly faded, considering the years. In his uniform. Another, not long after they were married. Just head and shoulders – laughing. Such a brave man, Philip. Never complained. The children, very young, on their rocking-horse. Effie a beauty, she had to admit, from the start. James, with such a strong look of Joe it was incredible no one had ever noticed, not even Ag and Prue. James's own son, too: little William, the first grandchild. Extraordinary. Even Joe could see it.

No picture of Joe. Well, for the children's sake, really.

Still, Joe always, always near. There when needed. Waiting. Both of them waiting.

Janet, actually, was brave, too, like Philip. She was brave to marry a man whom she knew did not love her. But they made an agreement, and stuck to it. Joe was a conscientious husband: Janet a good wife and mother to the three tall sons. She provided an idyllic childhood for them in the Yorkshire farmhouse. Looked after Mr Lawrence, diligently, in the cottage, once his wife had died.

At forty, Stella remembered, Janet had lost some of her shyness. Stella went and listened to her speaking one day at a Conservative gathering. She was better looking than she used to be, too. Not exactly attractive, but less plain. The *surprise*, though, when she went off, overnight, just after her sixtieth birthday. Stella would never forget Joe's telephone call. '*You're not going to believe this* . . .' And of course she could not, for a time. But it was true. It seemed Janet had been waiting for the children to be married, settled, whatever, before she and this rich butcher, who had loved her for ten years, finally went off to spend their old age together. They'd been conducting a long affair. Joe had never suspected a thing. Just as Janet had never suspected . . . Or had she?

They would never know. They'd been so careful. Tried never to reveal . . . but could not be sure.

Of course, since Janet's departure, it had all been so easy. Wonderful. Joe sold the farm, moved into the cottage in the dales – vacant since Mr Lawrence's death – he had once mentioned at Hallows Farm. They visited each other constantly. God knows why it had taken them so long to realise how much easier it would be if they lived under the same roof.

Stella sighed. Perhaps they shouldn't have wasted so much time. Still, Joe was on his way at last. Nearly here. Cottage almost sold: contract to be signed next week. He should be in by the end of the month. That would be good, good. Stella dozed.

When she woke, it was dusk. Couldn't see the cows. A cup of tea would be coming soon: she always told Janice if she was asleep to leave her, come back later. She pushed herself up on the pillows, pulled her shawl round her shoulders. The evenings were cooler.

At six o'clock precisely, Joe would ring. He rang her every evening, even if he had been visiting her earlier in the day. She wanted to be alert for his call. She wanted to be particularly on the ball in order to try to urge him to get the whole business of the sale of the cottage tied up as soon as possible. Last night he had said he'd do his best, solicitors were always so damn slow with contracts, and surely a few more days made no difference. He didn't want to move his stuff out of the cottage and then find the sale had fallen through: much harder to sell an empty place.

Stella had agreed. She'd said quite right, a few more days made no difference. Essential to get it all finalised before moving in. She didn't want to press him. And so she lied to him, saying of course there was no hurry. Well, not exactly *lied*: just retained part of the truth. First time in her life she had not been completely honest with Joe. She hoped, when he discovered, he would understand. Hoped he would understand she had not wanted to burden him with the probable truth. She had always made light of her illness, been able to quell his worries. Surely that was the best thing.

The final part of their waiting would not be too long, with any luck. God willing, she would be on her feet again by the time he came, full of energy to settle him in. She must remember to get the piano tuned. Married to Philip, there had been little time to play. When he died she had, at last, taught privately for a while. But it was too late. She was out of practice. So she had ceased to give lessons when she came north. Nowadays, she just played to herself, in the evenings. She would say to him when he rang – it was two minutes to six – *Joe, don't worry about the sale* – dealing with solicitors had never been his *forte. Why don't you come as soon as you can?* she would say. On the dot of six, the telephone rang. Firm of purpose, Stella gathered her strength. She must be careful to choose the right words to encourage him to hurry just a little, and yet give no hint of alarm.

'Darling Joe,' she began.